CHILDREN OF THE GODS

S.A. KLOPFENSTEIN

Content

BOOKS BY S.A. KLOPFENSTEIN

<u>THE SHADOW WATCH SAGA</u>

Watcher Origins (prequel tales)

The Shadow Watch

The Rage of Saints

The Darkling Queen

The Well of Shadows

<u>AGE OF FIRE</u>

Children of the Gods

<u>PANTHEON: ROGUE SYSTEM</u>

Den of Thieves

Rogue Assassin

Guild War

To Mom and Dad,
For everything

Author's Note

Children of the Gods exists within a shared story universe sometimes called the Otherverse. My first series, the Shadow Watch Saga, also exists in that universe, and I hope there will be many more related tales that follow.

While there is shared lore and mythology between them, both tales are written to be enjoyed and understood entirely on their own. The Age of Fire series takes place thousands of years before the Shadow Watch Saga, and is set on another world. But if you choose to read both —and I hope you will—there are deeper connections to be found. Some overt. Some subtle. And some warped by such vast passages of time.

I am thrilled to introduce you to the world of Îrithèa, a land ruled by dragonfire, and the mysterious Isle of Faltara, which lies at the edge of it. Here, worlds will collide, and our unlikely heroes will be tested in every imaginable way. Thrown headlong into an adventure that will demand everything. And more.

Welcome to the Age of Fire!

Burn Bright,
S.A. Klopfenstein

CHILDREN OF THE GODS

S.A. KLOPFENSTEIN

UNCHARTED ICY NORTH
SABERCAT TERRITORY
DORNIN SEA
KALENGAL VALLEY
KALENGAL MOUNTAINS
SKARIDA
YERIDA
RIVER'S END
STARHOLM
NARROW PEAKS
EVER SEA
ISLE OF
FALTARA

Age of Fire - Book One

PART FIVE
NIGHTFALL

PART SIX
AGE OF FIRE

PART SEVEN
PATH OF THE GODS

PART EIGHT
INFERNO

PART ONE

RITE OF PASSAGE

Never let us take our duty lightly. We are the Faltari. It is a matter of sacred honor that we should be tested. Prepare yourselves. From whom the gods grant gifts, they demand sacrifice.

—a passage from *The Crossing*

Chapter 1

The Spires

Malik stood at the edge of oblivion, bonespear extending from his arm like a long, menacing claw. He faced the winged jackal without fear.

Sweeping spires of rock jutted into the darkening heavens like fingers of giants, reaching up to blot out the sun.

Malik's chest heaved with labored breaths, blood spilling from a gash in his side.

But he had traded blood for blood.

Eyes wild, the jackal uttered a low growl and circled, gaze never leaving Malik's.

All Malik's childhood, all his training boiled down to this moment. This dance of survival.

He stepped to the side, sending small bits of gravel plummeting to the valley below. The jackal matched the movement, hair bristling along its bony spine.

Malik and the beast faced off on a small ledge, little more than a splinter, jutting from one of the sacred floating mountains at the heart of Malik's island home. A space of twenty feet at most. In this moment, that space was the entire world.

All of Malik's senses were fixed on the beast before him.

The jackal pawed at the ground.

"I fear neither life nor death. I am a descendant of the gods..."

Malik calmed his breaths, pushed back against the terror and focused on the magic pulse at the heart of the world.

Hish.

He reached for the power, drawing the breath of the gods themselves into his spirit.

Malik took a step forward, daring the beast to make its move. He thrust with his spear, and the jackal snarled. Vicious fangs flashed, but it kept its distance, waiting, evaluating.

Blood seeped from a wound in its neck.

Malik had come so close to the killing blow. He could not afford to make another mistake. He drew back his weapon and threw, channeling all the *hish* he could muster. Threads of magic erupted behind the spear with the force of a war bow.

The winged jackal sprang.

The bonespear shot through the air with lightning speed. Ripping through the beast's front shoulder.

Claws lashed out, scraping Malik's calf as he launched upward. Malik soared over the jackal's body and landed behind the attacking beast, then spun.

The jackal's injured shoulder shuddered as it turned on him.

Malik reached for *hish* with the focus of a striking serpent. The magic force collided with the winged jackal as it fought to regain its balance at the edge of the precipice.

With a howl, it fell into the sky.

Malik peered over the edge of the spire. The jackal expanded its primal wings—thick webs of skin lining its chest that flashed outward— and slowed its fall.

Jackals didn't have the power of actual flight. They could only glide. At times, catch strong gales of wind to climb short distances. With its injuries, this jackal would not return to these heights anytime soon, but it would not perish.

And for this, Malik was grateful.

The winged jackal was a sacred beast—one of four on the Isle of Faltara—and their deaths were not a cause for celebration.

But to best one today, of all days, was an honor. Malik had passed the first true test of his Ascension.

It would not be the last.

With deep breaths of relief and exultation, Malik watched as the winged jackal caught a draft and veered toward another mist-cloaked spire a few hundred yards across the expanse of sky. A pair of figures had climbed almost halfway up the massive shard of rock.

Two more of the eighteen young men and women from the Faltari clans making their Ascent this day. Malik hoped the jackal would land far below them.

But not too low either. For the lowest spire was fixed to the mountain at the heart of the valley below, where all their families watched and waited.

Through the mist, Malik could make out faint dots in the valley. Wind rushed through his hair and the forces of the world tugged at his chest like heavy chains, drawing him down.

He pushed back from the edge and rose to his feet. Above him, more spires jutted into the mist, some little more than boulders while others were as large as an entire village. They hovered above the peak of the Mountain of Souls as though caught in some invisible web in the sky.

And today, it was Malik's task to climb them.

An Ascent could be made by several paths, all required climbing at least four of the larger floating shards of rock.

It was the true test of Malik's people. A test that risked everything.

Every year, Faltari youths plummeted to their deaths, just as his Uncle Pender had. Just as—

Above, Malik glimpsed something dark shifting with the mist. Wings, perhaps, but he couldn't be sure. The thought filled him with fear and exhilaration. He was nearing the summit.

A peal of laughter jolted him from his revery.

Malik spun.

A crimson-cloaked figure dropped from further up the spire. The boy drew up at the last moment and landed in a crouch on the ledge, softening his fall with a flourish of *hish*.

The boy's forearm was tattooed with a dark set of bony wings. Dark paint streaked his cheeks, signifying the Dragyr clan.

"And here I thought you might actually make the kill, Jorensein,"

Aram Tulsein said on a derisive laugh. "A damn shame. Thought you might show some spine after your brother's Fall. Some things just run in the bloody family, don't they?"

Malik swallowed the foul things he'd like to say.

A boy shouts back. A man lets words glance off him like wind.

The shamanic mantra came unbidden, drilled into his brain over the past two years. Guiding him. Chastening him.

"I don't blame you for being a coward," Aram went on. "One son is a fluke. But it'd *really* be a bloody embarrassment if our own shaman lost both his sons to the Ascent, wouldn't it?"

Malik shrugged. "I've got climbing to do, Aram." He brushed past the boy, reached for holds on the face of the spire, then, looked up. The ledge Aram had jumped from was his next target.

A dark blur sailed over his head. Aram leapt back up the distance in one *hish*-fueled maneuver, landing on the ledge with ease. Malik loathed the boy's talent. Typical Dragyr, half-convinced he could pull off true flight.

"If that ledge were ten feet higher, he'd be dead."

Malik turned at the familiar voice.

Riese Torendeil clambered over from the other side of the spire, blonde hair pulled back in a series of tight braids, one side shaved to the skin. She flashed a smile and sauntered over to him. Three claws were tattooed on her left wrist, and she wore the dark grey cloak of the Jackal clan.

"I was worried you'd run into trouble on your own," she said, clapping him on the shoulder.

"Convenient you showed up *after* I took care of a jackal," Malik teased back. "But I'm glad you found me again." They'd separated on an earlier spire, and Malik was relieved she was safe.

"Best hope I leave some eggs for you!" Aram shouted down from the ledge, then, he leapt again.

"That bastard'll be lucky if he don't take the never-ending Fall," Riese murmured. "Better him than us, ey?"

Two years ago, Malik would have voiced his agreement, but he knew it wouldn't be proper of a future shaman.

Riese was right, though. Some would die today. Most of them promising young men and women with bright futures.

Just like Derrin.

Malik pushed the thought aside.

Focus.

It might not be worth dying to be the first to reach the summit. But Malik would be damned if he'd be the last.

"Let's climb," he said.

———

Joren Adensein hung back at the edge of the crowd, murmuring prayers his father had taught him since his youth. Prayers Joren had passed down to his daughter, and both his sons.

The prayers of the Faltari shamans.

"Breath of life. Spirit that dwells in my own spirit and that of my ancestors, draw near to my son. Remind Malik of the power that lives in all things. May he remain calm and wise. May all those who Ascend brush against the glory of the gods, whether they rise or fall."

Joren stood on a boulder, and released a thin stretch of blue cloth into the wind and watched it writhe with the currents like a feathered serpent.

The breath of the gods drawing his prayer up into the heavens.

Half the island was gathered in Kalengal Valley at the base of the Spires. All donned the singular colors of their clans. All but Joren, who wore the colors of all four sacred beasts: winged jackal, sabercat, feathered serpent, and dragyr.

Like all shamans. Like Malik would wear, should he survive the ordeal.

A warm presence drew near from behind. Joren could recognize Madri's aura from any distance. His wife's fingers interlaced with his, and her warmth seeped into his spirit, pushing back against the autumn chill.

Together they gazed up into the mists. The floating islands of stone were little more than blurred masses in the haze.

But with his true sight, Joren sensed more: distant spirit resonances of young climbers straining toward the summit, willing their way ever higher, rising to the task before them, as Faltari youth did every year at the solstice.

Madri knew better than to ask for a report, but the same could not always be said for the other parents of the Ascending.

"Please," whispered a young mother, Pelesa of the Saber clan. "Can you sense her?"

Pelesa had stood dutifully at the base of the boulder, anxious for news of her eldest daughter's progress. This was not the first time she'd pestered the shaman.

The Ascent was as much a test for parents as it was a rite for their children. First-time parents were always the worst worriers.

Joren did not avert his gaze from the Spires, but Madri released his hand. Dimly, he sensed his wife comforting the young mother.

He extended his true vision higher into the mists, beyond what his eyes could see. A sudden burst of clarity jolted him.

"Aram Tulsein has reached the summit," he announced.

The anxious silence evaporated at once, and excited voices filled the crowd in a great hum.

The boy's father shouted. "That's my boy! Aha! First Ascendant! Just like his brother!"

How a man like Tul Eriksein became elder of the Dragyr clan, Joren would never understand. But First Ascendant was always met with excitement, no matter who the climber. It brought hope for the others. The valley filled with cheers.

More resonances made their way higher.

"Ulgar Fenrisein has reached the summit," Joren said.

More cheers. It was rare to see a climber from the Feathered Serpents at the front of the pack.

"Leesa Rimadeil."

Over the next several minutes, more sons and daughters of the island reached the summit of the final spire.

"Petyr Bromsein!" Another elder's son.

"Therin Magnasein... Lera Pelesadeil."

The young mother's gasp of relief brought joy to Joren's heart. And then, at last—

"Riese Torendeil... Malik Jorensein."

Joren heaved a sigh, though he kept his focus on the remaining climbers, as was proper. Madri and their daughter Surel both joined him on the boulder, their resonances warm and cautiously hopeful.

As more youths reached the summit, the tension in the valley pressed on Joren's spirit, anxiety quickly crowding out the joy at the successful climbs...

Not a single child had Fallen, but it left little peace for the Faltari gathered in the valley.

For they all knew that the Ascent was the easy part.

Chapter 2

Gate of the Ancients

Malik's fingers ached as he heaved himself over the final ledge to the summit. Standing atop the world, his heart raged but his spirit soared.

For hours, his existence had consisted of nothing but the sharp stone beneath his fingers. Hardly daring to consider anything but the next series of holds and maneuvers to reach the next ledge, attempting to string together a harrowing path up the face of the Spires.

He and Riese had lost time on the third spire, after Malik led the way to an unclimbable section that forced them to backtrack. He worried that his friend regretted climbing with him. Though Riese refused to go on alone, she had taken the lead and kept silent for the remainder of the climb. But now...

"God's breath!" Riese stood upon a small boulder and gazed out beyond the Spires.

Malik scrambled over to her and stepped up.

All at once, the world spread out to eternity. Beyond the spine of mountains that formed the heart of the island. Beyond the glacial walls of ice, towering forests, sweeping green plains, and winding fjords. From here, the Isle of Faltara reached all the way to the Ever Sea, which shimmered at the horizon.

It was the same sea Malik had known from the shore all his life. He'd understood it was vast, but from this height, he was reminded just how magnificent it was. The greatest expanse of water in the world. His island was nothing but a spearhead of rock plunged into the endless waves by the gods. Malik had never felt so small.

A gust of wind swept over him, rushing through shaggy strands of hair, sending shivers down his arms and spine. Malik took one long, focused inhalation, letting it all sink in. The grandeur of the gods.

Malik howled like a wolf.

Riese's voice joined his own.

A chorus of exhilaration. The only experience that came close was the triumph of Malik's first hunt. This was freedom—a world without end, without clans, without tragedies and unwanted shamanic roles—here, at the top of the world.

Well, not quite the top.

The zenith of the final spire was about one hundred yards across, an expanse of rocks splayed out in shards, as though an ancient beast had pounded the surface of the floating mountain with giant mallets. The spire narrowed to a razor's edge, as it made one last gradual ascent to the true peak. A flat stretch about ten yards across.

And there, the Gate of the Ancients rose.

A bony arch of stone wide enough for three men to walk with hands outstretched. A wisp of cloud brushed against the interior of the archway, clouds stretching and vanishing into the center as though drawn into the heart of a whirlpool.

"Well, don't just stand around gawking!"

Malik grinned at the familiar voice. Yuri Alwensein clambered over the peak, chest heaving. He'd taken a different route. The boy was stronger than Malik and Riese put together, but he was also approaching their combined weight, and on an Ascent, even strength could become a weakness if paired with mass. Though Yuri would have found far less trouble with a winged jackal. He'd survived an encounter with a sabercat in the icy north.

Malik and Riese both pulled Yuri into an embrace once he'd moved away from the edge of the spire.

"That's supposed to be the... easy bit?" Yuri asked, glancing back at the precipice and shaking his head.

"Mum said it's all a matter of perspective," said Riese. "Sections of the Ascent challenge everyone in different ways. But hey, I'm glad you caught up with us for the next section."

"Yeah... me too," Yuri said, his raspy words turning to a cough. He stooped over, hands on knees, and took in gaping breaths.

"You know, it's better to stand upright," Riese said. "Gets more..."

"Oh, go to the Abyss, Torendeil!" Yuri waved her off with a paw of a hand, grinning all the while.

The Ascent was a complicated endeavor. The climbers set out at once and might help one another at various stages—the three of them had stuck together on the first spire—but ultimately, each youth was responsible for their own Ascent and took the path that suited their strengths.

But all three of them had found one another for the next stage of their trial, as they had so many other times in their childhood. Before Malik's fate had changed.

Malik took one last glance at the horizon. The sun had drifted behind a mass of clouds but remained high. They were making good time.

When he turned back, a blue-cloaked girl from the clan of the Feathered Serpents was scrambling over the edge.

"We should hurry," Riese said.

Yuri nodded, breaths still heavy.

Riese clapped the large boy on the back with a grin. "You first on the Blade's Edge?"

Yuri huffed and motioned for her to lead.

Riese Torendeil moved lithely on strong and sure limbs as she maneuvered the uneven terrain toward the last challenge on this side of the gate. Malik followed, and Yuri brought up the rear.

Riese paused when she reached the razor-thin span of rock known as the Blade's Edge. It was only about fifteen or twenty feet across, with a gradual rise, but the rock was too narrow to stand with both feet planted. Riese studied the Blade for all of three seconds, and stepped forward, holding her arms out for balance, gingerly twisting her lower body to accommodate each footstep. Soft pulses of *hish* offered added stability.

It was over in moments. Riese turned around and grinned from the other side.

"Oh, come on!" Yuri said.

"Show off," Malik added.

"Just go quick. It's not that bad. Like walking a string of stones across a creek or something."

"Sure," said Yuri, "at the edge of a damn waterfall."

Malik was tempted to take in the height on both sides but caught himself. It was no different than any other maneuver on this climb. One rock to the next.

He drew one long inhalation and slowly released it.

One step. And then another. That's all any journey is, he recited in his mind.

For how much he'd resented his shaman training these past two years, his father's words had provided surprising encouragement during this ordeal.

He focused on the next stretch of rock, and stepped out, planting the ball of his right foot. Malik didn't pause. Once he was sure his foot was set, he shifted his hips slightly and brought his left foot forward.

No rock crumbled or shifted. The Blade was firm beneath his feet. He took another step. Then another.

Riese was right. If not for the height, this was just like walking across stones. Or the trunk of a felled tree. He'd crossed such terrain countless times.

Malik drew on *hish*, using traces of magic to steady his balance.

In the corner of his vision, he glimpsed clouds swelling around the edge of the peak.

"Almost there," Riese said.

Malik's focus narrowed to the next step. Two more. And Riese pulled him to the safety of the true peak.

His heart thundered in his chest as he dared a look down and found himself laughing at the absurdity. It was a four thousand foot drop on either side to the lush valley below.

"Well, shit, Jorensein! Look at that, you didn't die!"

Malik turned to find Aram Tulsein emerging from the Gate of the Ancients, hands on the straps of his rucksack, a cocky grin stretching wide.

Riese and Malik both scowled, until they noticed the lump in Aram's pack. Aram had already found his prize on the other side of the gate.

Malik glanced back at Yuri, who was examining the path across the Blade.

"This is bloody stupid," Yuri muttered as he dropped to the ground and began the slower, but safer route, straddling the Blade with both legs, and shimmying across.

"Oh gods!" Aram groaned. "Let me cross first, if you're going like that."

Yuri huffed. "Go to the Abyss, Tulsein!"

"Oh, I don't think I'm the one who should worry about that." Aram chuckled.

"We were here first," Malik said. "And besides, you got plenty of time."

"That's right." Aram beamed, pulling his rucksack tighter against his shoulders. "First Ascent. First prize. And I'll be the first to the bottom, too."

"We'll see about that!"

Blue-cloaked Ulgar Fenrisein emerged from the gate, as though stepping from the other side of a waterfall. One moment, there was only the expanse of sky behind the stone archway. The next, Ulgar was walking toward them, his pack weighed down by the precious cargo within.

Aram's eyes flashed. Without another word, he sprinted toward the Blade and leapt. Though invisible to the naked eye, Malik sensed the rush of *hish* as the boy powered his superhuman leap over Yuri's head.

"Watch it!" Halfway across the Blade, Yuri hugged the mountain fiercely.

Malik and Riese both drew sharp breaths.

But Aram landed safely on the other side of the Blade, turned and waved. "Have fun sitting around, Ulgar!" And with that, Aram took off, leaping between boulders as he crossed the peak.

Ulgar was tall and built, not quite stocky, but all muscle. A fisherman's son.

He paused at the edge of the Blade, clapping his knee irritably. "Hurry up, Yuri! Come on! Come on!"

Yuri pulled himself forward. "Don't even think about jumping over me."

Ulgar groaned. "I wanna win. I don't have a death wish."

"Come on, Yuri, " Riese said. "You're almost there."

Yuri did not take his eyes off the Blade in front of him, pulling in deep breaths between each maneuver. When he got close enough, Malik and Riese both reached for his hands and pulled him to the safe expanse of the true peak.

"Good work," Malik said.

"Yeah, yeah."

Without a word in parting, Ulgar set off the other way across the Blade.

"Come on," Riese said.

The three of them crossed the strangely flat peak and stopped just outside the archway. Only from this distance could Malik detect what lay within the gate. A thin membrane, almost like water stretched across the entire space. Malik could still see through to the cloudy sky on the other side, though the view was distorted. Darker.

Riese reached out and brushed her hand through the expanse. They all gasped as her fingers vanished from the second knuckle and then reappeared when she withdrew her hand.

She examined her fingers, grinning. All intact. "Incredible!"

"What do you think it is?" Yuri murmured.

Malik knew. With his shaman training, he could sense it. "A concentration of *hish*. My father says the Ancients had a way of harnessing it into something physical."

"Well, you're the future shaman," Yuri said with a shake of his head.

Malik nodded, though as always, something about the statement sent a sinking feeling deep through his gut.

Riese glanced back. A queue had formed at the Blade now as three more climbers began their crossing.

"Okay, enough analysis, boys. Let's go get our eggs."

Riese stepped into the archway. There was a brief moment when her body seemed to linger, like a rippled reflection in water, and then, she was gone.

Malik didn't wait another second. He stepped into the Gate of the Ancients.

———

Joren drew a long breath as his son's spiritual resonance vanished from his sense.

It had been nearly three decades since his Ascent. He had never returned to that lost world beyond the gate, as was custom, even for a shaman.

The Ascent was a once in a lifetime pilgrimage.

Joren released his breath, whispering one last prayer.

No cloths were released this time. This was a prayer only for himself.

For his last living son. As Malik entered the realm that had stolen the life of his brother.

Chapter 3

The Other Side

A dark plain stretched to the horizon, walled on either side by jagged black peaks. Like the stone at the top of the spire, the rocky ground looked like it had been crushed and churned by ancient beasts. For all Malik knew, that was the best explanation.

A shiver ran down his spine, though the air remained still. What unnerved him most was the emptiness he felt in his spirit.

"Should it feel so cold?" Yuri asked.

It was not dark like the night. Though there was nothing resembling true daylight, either. A permanent dusky grey dimness permeated the world, emanating from no visible source that Malik could tell. There was no sun or moon in the sky.

"It's not cold," Malik clarified. "Your senses are trying to sort out the difference between our world and the one our people left behind."

His father had offered few instructions about the world beyond the gate. All his life he'd heard about this place, but always in vague terms, as was custom for all Faltari adults. The Ascent changed them forever, but the experience was sacred and haunting. And now, he understood why.

"We're in the Abyss now," Malik said. "There is no *hish* here."

Yuri shuddered.

"You're sure?" Riese asked.

"Go on and try accessing it," Malik said. "You won't find any power to draw on. Not here."

Riese closed her eyes and focused. Her fair skin looked strangely corpse-like in the perpetual gloaming that haunted this place.

When Riese opened her eyes, she caught Malik's gaze and nodded.

"You're right, but... there's something here," she said.

"I don't feel anything," said Yuri.

Malik felt nothing either, but he nodded at Riese. "Another power rules this world, my father says. Don't try to access it."

"Guys," said Yuri, glancing back at the portal, about one hundred yards behind them. The archway looked just as it had in their own world. The watery center rippled as two more climbers stepped through.

Riese pointed toward a worn path up a rise of dark scree. The silhouette of bony wings flashed against the starless sky, sending shivers down Malik's spine. He had never fought the strange dragyrs that lived in both their world and this.

"Guess we know where we're headed," Riese said.

"Should we split up?" Yuri asked.

Malik shook his head. "There will be eggs for all of us."

"We made it this far," Riese said.

"Well, I'm not gonna fight to be the loner again," Yuri said.

At that, all three of them laughed and began their final Ascent.

The path wended steeply up the foothills of the dark range of mountains. Ancient steps had been formed over the steepest places. Though it was nothing like the climb up the Spires, Malik's breaths grew heavy fast without *hish* to lighten the load, as though stones were being slowly added to his pack as he climbed.

Malik glimpsed more wings in the distant sky, and a ferocious flapping echoed from somewhere above. He wished he hadn't lost his spear in the ordeal with the jackal.

Yuri and Riese drew their spears at the sound of the dragyr, though the creature banked and disappeared from sight. Malik wondered if the creatures had to work harder here as well.

He'd only seen dragyrs from a great distance. He'd been ready to face one at the top of the Spires, but it seemed they'd all retreated to their breeding grounds in the Abyss as the first climbers summited.

Once the dragyr disappeared from sight, the world grew so still, Malik could hear individual stones grinding with their footfalls.

At last, they reached a ledge, which led to a narrow canyon between looming peaks. The ground was still littered with loose scree, but it was easier going on even ground. They'd encountered no other climbers, though Malik knew several of their peers were ahead of them.

The canyon wended through the mountain for another hundred yards before they approached an opening. Malik longed for his connection to the heart of the world. On the island, he might have felt the resonances of the dragyrs, or the other climbers. Here in the Abyss, all he had was his human senses. And his friends.

Bonespears at the ready, Riese and Yuri crept toward the opening, treading as softly as they were able. Malik took slow, deliberate breaths.

The canyon opened into a narrow mountain valley. Lone pillars of stone jutted into the air, the sides strangely smooth. Random blades of rock jutted upward. It was not until Malik spotted the remains of a tower, complete with balcony and arrow slits up one side, that he understood what he was looking at. A dragyr was perched on the balcony railing, long black neck craned. The smaller kin of dragons eyed them as they approached but remained statue-still.

"God's breath," Yuri muttered as they neared the tower.

"This was a damn fortress," Riese said.

"Like they got in the Attican Empire?"

"It was a city," said Malik. The ruins stretched to fill the entire valley, reminding him of the innermost crypts on his own island. An ancient burial chamber that had belonged to the First Ancestors of the island. An underground lake of bones. And this was what they had fled.

His father had warned him not to let his mind linger on the implications of this place. "There will be time after a safe descent."

A sharp cry resounded in the distance. Wings flapped hard somewhere out of sight. A warrior groaned.

Malik steeled himself, hand hovering at the hilt of his dagger—his last remaining weapon—though the skies above them remained clear.

The dragyr on the central tower gazed out over the city, neck rotating. Some sort of sentinel. The creature periodically let out a piercing shriek but remained where it perched. Watching.

Even in the ruins, the remnants of ancient roads were still evident.

The city was set in a grid-like pattern, branching evenly from one main thoroughfare. The main stretch of road was wide open and led to the tower in the heart of the city.

They strode silently, their footfalls muffled, as though sound worked differently in this world.

More cries echoed from somewhere up ahead. Flesh tearing. A weapon scraping against claws or teeth. Someone pitched in a desperate battle. Gravel grinding beneath boots. Moving fast.

Malik motioned the others toward a narrow lane littered with debris. "Here! Quick!"

Riese didn't hesitate, but Yuri stared up the road.

"Come on!"

Malik and Riese both latched on to one of his arms and pulled their friend off the main thoroughfare. Just before they retreated out of sight, Malik glimpsed a boy up near the tower, emerging from another lane at a desperate run.

Sharp cries echoed all across the ruined city.

The three ducked behind a chunk of crumbled building. Wings rushed somewhere overhead. The boy sprinted into view, golden cloak billowing behind him. Malik recognized him as the son of the Saber clan's elder, a boy named Petyr Bromsein.

A dragyr shot after him. Just before he passed out of sight, Petyr stumbled.

And the creature dove.

The boy's cries echoed across the city as the dragyr slashed his back with long claws. The beast failed to latch on to him, though, and shot past. Then, another dragyr shot from the other direction and swooped down for another attack.

Petyr spun, mouth twisted in terror, barely managing to deflect the creature with a manic slash of his bonespear. The creature soared past, banking for another attack.

Malik turned to the others. "We can't leave him."

Riese hesitated.

"That's your father talking," Yuri said. "This is our Ascent, for god's sakes!"

The first creature swooped down, claws slashing Petyr's arm, ripping his shirt to threads.

Malik turned from his friends and drew his dagger. Unlike his spear, it was made of steel. A gift from his brother the year before he died in this place. "You two do what you have to. So must I."

Riese sighed. "Dammit. At least use a weapon fitting the task." She handed him her bonespear and pulled her pale hunting bow from her back.

Yuri moaned. "Maybe I should've gone solo after all."

Malik took one focused breath. Even the air in this world felt different, as though he were drawing less sustenance from it.

A sharp cry echoed.

Riese brushed past him, nocking an arrow. "Now!"

They sprinted from behind their cover.

Riese's arrow struck the attacking creature in the wing. Just before it reached the Saber boy, the dragyr veered, though it remained in flight. The next attacked.

Malik leapt in front of Petyr, and jutted Riese's spear upward. Claws slashed. His spearhead lodged in the creature's leathery chest, wrenching the handle from his grasp. The dragyr swept upward and then dropped.

Yuri's spear pierced it through the throat, and it collapsed onto the ruined street.

Petyr regained his feet in time to meet the second creature. Riese fired off a pair of arrows. One glancing off its spine, the other lodging in its shoulder, where the left wing met its body. It lurched, flapping furiously, and disappeared over a rooftop.

Malik and Yuri sprinted to the fallen dragyr. The dark winged creature was about ten feet in length, skin like a dark lizard. Eyes empty. It didn't move as they neared, and dark blood gushed over the stone.

Yuri removed his spear—still intact—from the dragyr's neck with a splucking sound and turned to the sky. No sign of the second creature.

Riese helped Petyr to his feet.

Malik's spear was snapped in half, the blade lodged deep between two of the fallen dragyr's ribs. It took some wrenching, and some assistance from Yuri, but he managed to free it.

"Sorry," he said to Riese.

She shrugged. "Keep it."

Malik stowed the remnant weapon on his back and turned to Petyr.

The boy's shirt was tattered, right arm dripping blood.

"May I?" Malik asked, gesturing to the wound.

Petyr nodded, and Malik took hold of the boy's wrist, examining the extent of the damage. The wound was deep, but the blood flow seemed to be slowing.

Riese took hold of his arm, and Petyr tensed.

"It's all right," Malik said.

"Just don't move," Riese instructed.

Carefully, she sliced her hunting blade into the boy's sleeve near the shoulder, gripping the shirt, drawing the tough fabric against the bonedagger. Jackal bone was strong, and Riese was always one to tend her tools. The fabric peeled away from his arm in one long cut, and Riese removed it. She grunted as she ripped into the fabric again, and soon handed Malik a thin ribbon over a foot in length. He tied the cloth tight—but not too tight—above the wound. Riese prepared a second piece of sleeve that hadn't already been bloodied, and Malik wrapped the arm as best he could.

Petyr flexed his hand, wincing. "Think I can still climb down the Spires?"

"Just need to get out of this place," Malik said. "Your body will heal, once you can draw *hish* again. Just don't start down too quick."

"Right," Petyr said, rising to his feet. He shifted his pack on his shoulders. Malik could make out the rotund shape of what lay inside.

"Guys," Yuri said, eyes on the bleak sky, "we need to go."

The Saber boy gripped Malik's wrist. "Two streets back from the tower, shaman. Turn left. Go three more streets. Turn right. There's an entrance with six pillars. There's more eggs in there. Just don't look at the faces."

A cry echoed across the dead city.

"Thanks," Malik said. "Er, what faces?"

But Petyr was already hurrying away, staggering across shards of black stone.

Chapter 4

Temple of a Dead World

The resonances of young men and women flowed in and out of Joren's awareness, as they passed through the Gate of the Ancients. Each one a distant flame in his senses, winking out like candles in the wind as they left their world.

Beyond, they were invisible to the shaman's spiritual sight, until the climbers returned from that dead place, and their resonances roared back with the fervor of life. For a moment, their spirits burned even brighter, having tasted true darkness—the absence of the breath of the gods.

Every Faltari adult gathered here had once walked the same path. Out of their living, breathing vibrant island world, and into the bones of a distant past. It was their rite of passage. A pilgrimage to remember where they'd come from, so that they might lead their people into a better future.

Three climbers fell during Joren's Ascent. Two lost in the Abyss itself. One on the climb back down.

The children did not always return in the same order they entered, for many reasons, that need not mean death.

But when Therin Magnasein and Lera Pelesadeil returned before Petyr Bromsein, the boy's mother refused to move from Joren's side.

Madri tried to console her, but Petyr's mother clambered up the boulder and would not leave. She stood beside Joren, waiting for her shaman to deliver her son's fate.

Joren opened his eyes and turned. Her greying blonde hair whipped around her face in a gust of wind.

He clasped her shoulder and smiled. "Your son has returned from the Abyss."

"Oh, thank the gods," she murmured, hand leaping to cover her mouth. Joy and fear coalesced into a sob, and then, relieved laughter.

Joren nodded to her and returned his focus to the Gate of the Ancients.

Two more resonances followed soon after Petyr—Leesa Rimadeil and then a pair of Feathered Serpent youths. They had followed Malik and his companions through the gate. But they returned first.

And all at once, he felt the same fear as Petyr's mother.

He doubted anyone would have guessed it looking at him, but Joren's heart wrung inside, and he fought the urge to clutch his chest.

He did not pray now.

For the only gods that might reside in that dark shell of a world had fallen long ago. And they'd already stolen one son from him.

———

Malik led the way past the pillars Petyr had described, through a crumbling antechamber, and down a series of wide corridors. The halls in this place were vast and lined with stone statues.

Entire walls were engraved with elaborate figures, etched in filigree. Malik was struck by the light in this place. Just as it was outside, this building contained no visible light source—no lanterns or torches—the same dusky light permeated these halls. Despite the convenience, the uncanniness of it left Malik with a creeping sense of dread.

"We need to be quick," Riese said. "There must be some central chamber."

"What is this place?" asked Yuri.

"I think it's a temple," said Malik, his eyes settling on a towering figure on one of the walls. They were shrouded in wispy tendrils of shadow, hovering in the air before what appeared to be a great crowd.

The three fanned out down the main hall, investigating smaller corridors and doorways, picking their way over fallen shards of stone. There were slits high in the towering ceilings, but Malik felt that it did not account for the consistent lighting.

He kept his half-spear out in front of him. It was so quiet, he could hear his companions breathing from halfway down the chamber.

The halls bore no smell that Malik could detect. As the shaman's son, he had journeyed through the musty burial halls beneath the Mountain of Souls. Perhaps this temple was so old, it had lost all sense of life.

Though damaged, the place retained remarkable detail. Walls were carved with a precision beyond the capability of any tools found on the Isle of Faltara. Entire columns formed out of what appeared to be one massive stone, complex patterns etched deep. Figures—human and full-grown dragons, along with other strange beasts he didn't recognize—arrayed in lines and crowds. Ships sailing across skies. Creatures gathered around bursts of light.

This was crafted by an ancient civilization at the peak of its might and power.

The past holds many warnings, his father had taught him, *or temptations, depending on your disposition.*

"Up here," Riese whispered.

Malik retreated back the way he'd come. Riese motioned from the end of the main corridor. Yuri caught up, and they followed her to the end of another hall.

The three of them formed up at a doorway about the height of two men, lined with a pair of dragon statues. Prismatic light poured out from the doorway, brighter than anywhere else in the temple.

They entered a vast circular hall with a dome towering over a dais at the center. Walkways radiated out from the dais with rows of benched seats between. The chamber was nearly the size of a village, several thousand feet across at least, and the peak of the dome must have been two hundred feet high or more. Enormous windows opened up to the grey sky beyond. But that was not the source of the strange multi-colored light that filled the temple.

At the center of the dais, the focal point of the worship chamber was a wide bowl of shimmering stone. It was set high enough that Malik could not see what lay inside from this distance, but he already knew. The bowl bore the same egg-like shape and glowed with a fierce effervescence.

"Holy shit."

Malik and Riese both jumped at Yuri's sharp whisper.

"God's breath!" Riese muttered. "You ass."

The large boy laughed. "Sorry. Just never imagined anything like this when my parents spoke about their Ascents."

Malik glanced around the chamber, but it was still. No wind from the windows, not even the distant cries of dragyrs, elsewhere in the city.

Riese led the way down one of the aisles, and Malik and Yuri followed. Nothing stirred as they made their way across the expansive hall.

Malik marveled at the well-preserved state the room was in. Unlike the outer corridors, there was hardly any damage to the stonework. No cracked pillars or crumbling doorways, not even any dust. Which seemed impossible with open windows to the sky. The dome itself was impeccable, painted in gold and silver. Malik felt as though a procession of worshippers might file into the hall at any moment.

A circle of steps wrapped around the circumference of the shimmering dais. The chamber echoed back the patter of each footfall as they approached. Intricately carved pillars encircled the dais, reaching all the way up to the rim of the dome.

But Malik's gaze was drawn to the bowl, which was even more radiant up close.

The half-shell was formed of tiny colorful tiles of stone like scales, intricately etched with the forms of dragons in flight. It was the most incredible work of art Malik had ever seen. Not that there was much on the Isle of Faltara.

The bowl was roughly the size of a skiff, set upon a platform of marble with stairs leading up to its base.

Malik took the final steps of his Ascent.

His heart pounded against his ribcage. He'd been so focused on the logistics of the climb, he'd hardly let himself picture the prize at the end. Of course, he'd seen the ancient dragon eggs once a year throughout his childhood, as he witnessed the Ascension ceremonies of generations before him. But it was always from a distance.

As his eyes crested the edge of the bowl, he drew a sharp breath. Within, there were dozens of eggs, roughly the size of a child's head. Each shell contained hundreds of tiny scales, like the hide of a sand serpent, and each scale contained gradient shades of blues and greens and purples and reds. The eggs shone with an otherworldly radiance that was brilliant, but never blinding. The only thing Malik could liken it to were the pearls sometimes retrieved from oysters in the tidal pools surrounding the island.

Yuri grinned as he reached for a violet egg. Malik glanced from egg to egg before settling on an emerald one just out of reach. He hefted himself over the lip of the bowl and stretched out his fingers.

The scales were so fine at the surface, the ridges felt like little more than creases of skin, and though cool to the touch, Malik was overwhelmed with a sense of warmth.

It was something spiritual, the way he felt when he drew on the breath of the gods back in his world. Since arriving in the Abyss, he'd not felt it. But within the hallowed shell of this egg, the power of the gods remained. The egg itself weighed only a few pounds, far lighter than any rock of comparable size, though the shell felt as sturdy as the hardest stone.

Yuri had already retreated back to the dais, and Riese stood across the bowl, reaching out for her own dragon egg, a crimson one with nearly black undertones.

Malik pulled the rucksack from his shoulders, wrapped his egg in a shirt he'd brought along, and stowed it inside.

The moment his fingers released it, a chill coursed over him. The absence of *hish* once more. He eased the pack onto his shoulders and stepped back down to the dais.

As he turned around, he found Yuri staring up at one of the pillars surrounding them. Malik had taken little note of them when they arrived. At first glance the pillars had appeared to be more of the same designs as the rest of the temple—smooth stone etched with a lighter colored filigree. But now, there were faces engraved up and down the columns. Men and women, all sleeping or praying, eyes shut.

"What are you doing?" Riese hissed, tugging on Yuri's arm. "Petyr said don't look at them, remember?"

Yuri did not take his gaze away from a woman's face at eye level. Transfixed, he took a step toward the pillar.

Malik couldn't help himself. He followed his friend's gaze. The woman was beautiful. So life-like. Lips full. And her eyes—

They fluttered.

Then, spread wide.

Chapter 5

Don't Look

Malik could not look away from the woman's face. She had been rendered with unfathomable realism. Smooth skin drawn over high cheekbones and a rigid jaw. Full lips pursed as though they'd just released a breath. Radiant eyes formed of intricate milky-colored stone.

The faces had always been on the pillars, Malik realized, an ancient spiritual understanding washing over him. They had just not been ready to see. The woman's eyes had always been open. For this world was not dead at all.

This temple was teeming with vibrant energy. He could feel it now, pressing upon his spirit, washing over him like waves upon the rocky shores of Faltara. Something powerful and wild, entirely unlike the magic he'd known all his life. And yet, not so different from *hish* at all.

And though he knew, dimly, that he ought not to continue looking at the woman, Malik could not bring himself to break his gaze. As though he'd fallen asleep and slipped into the flow of a dream.

The woman's face began to transform, grey stone filling with color. The lighter filigree somehow expanding over her features, brushing over her skin like strokes of paint. Her skin turned pearlescent. A gradient of a thousand hues. Cheeks radiant. Her lips parted. Drew breath. Eyes blinked and shifted, taking in the room. Then, met Malik's gaze.

A smile stretched her lips, and Malik felt warm inside. The face felt familiar, though he couldn't place it, exactly.

Another face shifted above her, and Malik's chest seized as his attention was drawn upward to the engraving of a young man with chiseled features and sad, dark eyes. Also familiar, but this time, Malik knew why.

His brother had never completed his Ascent, because he'd never left this chamber. Derrin Jorensein's stony eyes grew wide, shifting sharply. Malik followed his gaze, and an ache surged deep in his spirit.

In one of the seats beyond the dais, a corpse in late stages of decay was propped up, mouth gaping in an endless scream.

Malik's entire body went numb. He knew it was his brother's body, and beyond it, in seats further back in the room, he spotted more. Dozens.

How had they not seen them when they'd entered?

Or smelled them?

Malik's eyes drifted back to the stone visage of his brother. Their eyes locked. Dark pupils widened over stark white irises, staring straight through him. The pupils shifted. A shadow spread over his eyes and then drifted away from the face entirely.

Tendrils of shifting darkness slithered from his brother's face like spiders reaching out to envelop their prey.

Malik jerked backward. His head thudded against the stone.

"Come on, Malik!"

Riese's voice.

He jolted from his revery. Riese was dragging both him and Yuri away from the pillar. Malik scrambled to his feet, dread shooting through him, suddenly aware of the danger. He reached for Yuri, and the boy looked over, trembling.

Malik and Riese grabbed on to Yuri's arms and pulled, and together, the three staggered off the dais, tumbled down the steps into one of the temple aisles.

Webs of darkness wrapped around the pillars. The faces had vanished from the stone, but a lone, hovering figure clothed in slithering shadow reached toward Malik, its spirit filled with malice.

This was not his brother at all, Malik understood, now that he was free of its bewitching snare. It was one of the dark spirits of lore. A wight.

Riese seized his wrist and pulled, jerking his gaze away.

"Don't look back!"

The three sprinted down the aisle as fast as they could manage. Voices filled the temple behind them.

Dozens. Hundreds. Chanting something in a foreign tongue Malik did not recognize. Impossibly, he could distinguish one distinct timbre among them.

His brother's voice echoed in his skull, the same way he haunted Malik's dreams. Rage. Sorrow. Jealousy. Despair. Resentment. All the twisted emotions associated with his fallen brother surged to the surface of his mind.

Derrin, his father's favorite, the next shaman. The kind, patient, and steadfast one.

And weak!

Malik hated himself for that thought, but it was no less true.

All his elder brother's roles suddenly fell to Malik. The restless boy who, until two years ago, would never have shied away from fights with arrogant pricks like Aram Tulsein. Who was made for adventures like the Ascent in a way his brother never was.

He jolted back to the moment. Pushing against the intruding thoughts.

You're made for this! You can get out of here!

These were not his father's words. They were his own.

This was *his* test.

Not Derrin's.

Not his father's.

They neared the halfway point of the enormous chamber, where a wide aisle ringed the entire hall. They'd followed the same path as before, but Malik knew that was not the shortest way out of this temple.

In the corner of his vision, he saw shadowy figures shooting from the dais. More movements. Bodies stirring across the chamber.

Malik pointed to another aisle as they reached the central ring. "Over there!"

Heart racing, Malik sprinted down the new path through the

worship chamber. Riese was the fastest of the three and reached the door first. She heaved at the stone handle, and it groaned.

Malik joined her and pulled with all his might. The door shifted again but did not open.

A wight shot toward them, a blade of shadow formed in its wispy hand. Yuri huffed to catch them and Malik knew his friend wasn't going to make it.

Malik let go of the door and drew his brother's dagger from his belt. He ran back toward Yuri, blade raised high. Yuri's mouth gaped, confused, but he lumbered past. Malik swept the steel dagger and met the shadow blade.

There was a sharp scraping sound as their weapons met. The wight spun away. Another creature dove, and this time, Malik didn't go for a parry. He drove the dagger straight into the wight's torso. As the tip of the blade met the creature's ethereal form, a chill shot down the hilt.

The wight vanished.

Riese pulled him to his feet. Yuri shoved the door wide enough for them to squeeze through. More wights shot across the vast hall, shrill cries echoing off the high ceilings.

The three hurried out of the main temple and emerged back in the antechamber. Shrieks echoed behind them as they spilled out of the doors and hurried down the stairs onto the ruined street.

Yuri tripped, tumbling down the final steps. Malik and Riese helped him to his feet.

No wights emerged from the temple. They waited, bracing for the ghastly monstrosities to pour out of the stone of the front staircase, but none followed. In the distance, a dragyr soared over the city, its back to them, and passed out of sight.

A burst of laughter broke the silence.

Riese covered her mouth and then giggled again.

Relief flooded over them, and they all laughed. Malik felt at the lump in his pack, suddenly worried his prize might have slipped out during their flight from the temple.

They each had what they'd come for.

"I don't know about you guys," Yuri said. "I always heard that cities were beautiful from the trader's tales. But I think they were full of shit."

Malik grinned.

"Let's get home," Riese said.

They hurried through the ruined streets of the dead city and made for the Gate of the Ancients.

———

Dark clouds poured over the mountains, shrouding the upper spires entirely in muted light, though it was still the middle of the day. Gusts of wind tore across the valley.

Fewer parents asked Joren for news of their children's fates. Most retreated for the cover of the forest at the edge of the valley.

Nearly all climbers had begun their descent. The leader, Aram Tulsein, was already halfway down the penultimate spire. Everyone in the valley knew it. They could spot his crimson cloak even from this distance. Several more resonances were making their way down, somewhere in the clouds.

So far, not a single climber had fallen.

But had any been lost in the Abyss?

It was still too early to tell.

Madri and Surel remained close. Joren could feel the tension in their minds, fear for Malik pressing in like a spiritual weight.

He fought to focus on the resonances of the other climbers. Fought to push back the memories that encroached on his mind.

It was like his family was cursed. First, his younger brother. And then, his eldest son. And now...

There was nothing that could be done.

Madri's hand grasped his as he stood on the boulder, looking up at the Spires. He closed his eyes. His body relaxed. Tension evaporated.

And all at once, relief replaced the fear. A warm and unmistakable awareness swept over his senses. Joren choked back a sob and squeezed his wife's hand.

"They made it!"

"Oh, thank the gods," Madri whispered, a sob catching in her throat.

Surel hugged them both.

Joren opened his eyes, gazing up into the dark clouds sweeping over the Spires.

"Be wise, my son," he whispered. "This is your greatest test."

CHAPTER 6

DESCENT

When they emerged from the Gate of the Ancients, Malik was overwhelmed with sensation. Wind howled across the peak, rushing up from the sky canyons formed between spires below. Icy rain whipped at his face, drenching his cloak in an instant.

There were no other climbers in sight. Back in the Abyss, they'd heard at least two others fighting dragyrs in the ruined city as they fled the temple, so they weren't the last, but Malik had a feeling they were near the back of the pack. Squinting against the wind and rain, they carefully picked their way over to the Blade's Edge.

Malik and Riese followed Yuri's method of straddling the narrow span of rock and shimmying across. The wind stung Malik's face as he crossed the spine of rock, and his slick hands could barely feel their grip they were so cold.

He'd hoped to wait back on this side of the gate to refresh his store of *hish* after the depletion in the Abyss, but with a storm bearing down, they all feared getting stranded if conditions turned worse.

The expanse on either side of the Blade seemed to pull at him, luring him to look out at the expanse of the valley far below. But when he glanced over, the world was entirely shrouded in churning clouds, and the fear dissipated.

Riese pulled him up as he reached the other side of the Blade. They scrambled over boulders to the edge of the upper spire.

This side was lower and more sheltered, and all at once, the wind stilled. Splintered rays of light peered through cracks in the sky. The rain softened to a fine mist.

"Maybe not so bad after all," Yuri said, blowing on his hands.

"Weather is weird up here," said Riese. "It could turn back just as sudden. Whatever you do, keep moving."

"But be safe," Malik cautioned. "Better to be last than dead."

The other two nodded, knowing that no one understood this imperative more than Malik. They peered over the side of the peak. The upper spire was manageable enough to face forward at the outset, but Malik knew it would soon fall away to veritable cliffs in sections.

The dome of clouds surrounding them gave the impression they were alone on an island in the infinite sky. But in reality, they were four spires away from their family, their people. And most of their peers were close.

Still, the Ascent, in the end, was theirs to accomplish.

Riese led the way down, then Malik and Yuri.

The upper section was nothing but rock, and the face of the mountains was much starker than the lower spires, which were strung with more vines and other vegetation. Down climbing proved manageable at first, especially as Malik began fortifying his movements with *hish*, now that his inner source was replenishing. With subtle surges, he pressed his fingers against the face of the mountain, strengthening his holds while simultaneously lightening the load with threads of magic pressing up on his body from below.

Halfway down the first spire, Yuri veered off on his own to avoid a steep decline, choosing the longer path that wrapped around the other side of the spire. Malik fought to keep up with Riese, but she was the better climber, and she'd been honing her skills at down climbing these past two years while he'd been torn between his training and learning the intricacies of inter-clan politics and traditions and spiritual matters with his father.

He lost sight of her when the spire turned to a sheer drop, and he was forced on all fours, leading with his feet. The wind had eased up though, and Malik lost himself in the movement. This foothold, then that crack for his right hand, then this divot in the stone for his left. Another foothold. Each maneuver involved fluid coordination between his mind, body, and spirit. Sharp attention, quick decision-making, precise movements, focused magic—every piece of the process vital. The ground leveled off, and Malik was relieved to see Riese's dark cloak ahead, lingering at a ledge at the base of the spire.

Malik maneuvered his way to her, fingers beginning to feel the strain they'd endured all day on this climb.

"Don't wait for me," he murmured, breaths heavy.

"Needed to plot my moves before the big Leap, anyway."

The peak of the next spire loomed in a shroud of mists across an expanse of at least twenty feet, rising past the height of their ledge. If it had formed any other way, the Ascent would be impossible. All the remaining spires were strung together. But the only way between the uppermost spires was to jump.

Malik's heartbeat quickened as he took in the sky below the precipice. This side had proved an easy target from the opposing peak on the Ascent. The ledge was over ten feet across. A relatively simple jump from the higher point of the opposing spire.

But there was no ledge to target from this side, just the sharp sides of a levitating mountain.

"Use *hish* to slow your fall," Riese said. "That's what my father said."

Malik drew in slow, focused breaths. The mists were thickening again, swirling around the base of the spire, making it harder to see the other side of the chasm, and the rain was picking up.

"The angle looks worse from up here than it really is," Malik said with a nod, more to remind himself than anything. "That's what my father said. Aim. Trust the forces of the world to carry you down."

Riese shook her head. "Well, here goes nothing."

Blonde braids flapping behind her, she sprinted across the ledge, gaining as much speed as possible before the edge. Riese's body shot out from the island of rock, cutting through the mist. She sailed down and down toward the steep face of the second spire, before slowing suddenly, with a precise surge of magic, and grabbing on to a large rock.

Her hands shifted, fingers slipped.

Malik's heart seized in his chest. But Riese only dropped a few more feet before catching herself on another boulder.

Her laughter echoed across the expanse.

Malik breathed out with relief. "Thank the gods!"

"Rock's a bit slick!" she shouted back. "Damn rain."

"You good?" Malik asked.

"Your father was right, slope's not bad over here. Easy enough to stand."

Once you make the jump, and don't slip off the edge of the world, Malik thought.

He drew back, and before his mind had a chance to consider the other possible outcomes, he took off. His boots crunched—three, four, five steps—and then, he leapt.

Malik's stomach lurched. The sharp wind pelted his face, laced with rain. His cloak billowed out behind him, body arced sharply downward as the rock stretched out below.

His vision shifted, and so did his body, as he oriented to the opposing angle of the next floating mountain. Then, all at once, there was Riese, ducking beneath his feet. Malik sailed past her. His stomach jolted with terror.

Even without *hish*, he'd jumped too far.

The rock face rolled beneath his feet. The angle of the mountain opened, and Malik feared he would fly right over into oblivion.

"Use your bloody magic!" Riese's voice echoed somewhere behind him.

And Malik reached for the power behind the world, drawing threads of *hish* into his body in a rush of opposing force, nearly knocking the wind out of him. He drew more, pressing his body downward.

His feet hit first, glancing off the mountain, nearly sending him tumbling. Malik focused with all his spiritual might, drawing more *hish*, pressing his body harder against the face of the spire. And then, he drew up sharply with a final surge of magic.

The tips of his fingers latched on to the edge of a boulder. Pain lanced up his fingers and into his arms, but he didn't let go. His feet found purchase. His vision swam.

Finally, he breathed, clutching the side of the mountain.

"Malik!" Riese's voice echoed from far above where he stood.

He peered into the mists, cursing her grey cloak, but then he glimpsed her golden hair near the top of the spire. Fifty yards above him, at least.

"Gods damn it," he muttered, resisting the urge to pound the mountain itself.

"You okay?" Riese hollered, her voice echoing off the upper spire.

"Y-yeah. I think so."

Malik's fingers ached. He drew in more *hish* and channeled it into his hands. Numbness washed over them. He couldn't even see the ledge he'd jumped from any longer. Malik tried to figure how he'd gone off course. Something about the angles between the two mountains. Or the mists. The entire topmost spire was nothing but a looming shadow, swallowed in thickening clouds.

His eyes settled on Riese, and he calmed his breaths.

The line between life and death is but a thread.

But Malik had landed on the side of life once more. And for that, he must be thankful.

You're made for this, he tried to remind himself.

"I don't think... can go that way!" Riese shouted through the wind. "There's... sort of chasm. You shot over it!"

Shot over a chasm?

Well, that would explain why his perceptions had suddenly felt so wrong. At this angle from below, he couldn't even see it.

"I'll meet you further down!" Malik shouted. "Just stay safe!"

"Oh, I'll be just... shaman! It's you...bloody worried about."

"I'm good! Really. Let's see who makes it first, ey?"

"Oh, it's like that is... I swear to..."

The wind swallowed the rest.

The rain fell harder, but the way this spire was angled, Malik could actually walk for a good distance. Near the base he'd have to down climb and choose between several smaller spires that branched out. Malik moved in a near-crouch, using his hands for balance, trying to conserve his *hish*, and navigated his way down over sharp boulders.

He couldn't shake Riese's words. *It's you I'm worried about.*

Two years ago, he felt certain she never would have said that. And yet....

How had he misjudged that leap so badly? It was a simple enough mistake. But the fact that Riese worried for him like some child drove him suddenly to the edge of rage.

Damn you, Derrin!

He knew Riese could have been much farther by now. She'd stuck close to Malik and Yuri because she feared her friends wouldn't survive without her.

"Be the last down," his father had said the night before. "There's no shame in that. We shamans don't play the clan games."

Tell that to Derrin! Maybe if you'd let him train properly, he would still be here.

Or maybe his brother would have been lost to the Abyss no matter what, and all this was just a raveling in his mind. Triggered by that bloody ghost in the Abyss.

But Malik had survived that dead world. He'd made it this far, and he was determined not to make another costly mistake again.

Storm clouds thickened around him. Rain poured steadily, though the wind had calmed. A faint voice echoed from the mists ahead.

The ground began to even out beneath his boots, and he spotted the thick twists of vines branching out from the base of the floating mountain to form a natural bridge across the sky canyon.

In the midst of the haze, he spotted a cloak. The golden yellow of the Sabers. No, the blue of the Feathered Serpents.

Two cloaks writhed in the wind, out in the expanse between spires.

The wind lashed out with torrents of rainfall. Malik had been sheltered on the other side of the spire, but as he ventured out on to the thick tangle of branches that extended to the next mass of rock, the storm came back with a vengeance.

Malik crossed the remaining distance, picking his way along the web of vines.

As he neared, he spotted two climbers. One clung to the side of a vine as thick as a tree trunk. Another climber latched on to his arms. It wasn't until he was right upon them that he could make out who it was.

Petyr Bromsein on his knees, directing *hish* to keep himself planted as he pulled on the fallen climber's arms, straining to bring him up to safety. The other boy's hand slipped, and he dangled by one arm over a sheer two thousand foot drop into the drowning sky.

CHAPTER 7

CROSSING

Malik grabbed a thin length of vine and supported himself as he scrambled across the natural bridge to the other climbers. Riese had to be close behind him, but the base of this spire branched off to three smaller spires—three different possible descents—and he knew the chances she'd cross on this side were small. This fell to him.

Malik pushed back against his awareness of the precipitous fall on either side of him, the harsh elements waging war all around. His world became nothing but each precise movement. Each section of vine, ensuring each hold was firm before he moved further.

It wasn't until he was feet away that Malik recognized who it was hanging from the edge of the vine bridge by his fingertips: Ulgar Fenrisein. The Feathered Serpent boy had been hot on Aram's heels back at the peak.

"Just bloody pull me up!" Ulgar's voice had gone hoarse, but he'd managed to latch on to the vine with both hands again.

How long was he here before Petyr reached him?

Malik's gut wrenched as he inched closer, now on all fours. Petyr gripped Ulgar's forearms, trying to help him climb up.

"I can't get any leverage like this!" Petyr shifted, letting go of Ulgar with one hand.

Ulgar croaked. "Shit! Don't let go, don't let go!"

Malik crawled closer, the wind whipping so strongly that each movement was a labor. He matched Petyr's stance, wedging his feet firmly into the crease between two massive vines, enhancing the hold with an opposing force of *hish*.

He reached out into the sky, nothing but vines and magic keeping him from plummeting to the valley below.

Malik tried to grab Ulgar, but he was just beyond his grasp. Ulgar groaned as he fought to hold on. Petyr strained, clutching the vines in one hand and Ulgar's left arm with the other.

"I need you to swing up so I can reach," Malik shouted into the howling wind. "Petyr, on my mark, pull back as hard as you can. Ulgar, reach up. Both of you, focus any *hish* you've got left on that one move. I'll take care of the rest."

"I'll try!" Ulgar said.

"Okay, one, two, THREE!"

Petyr heaved back with a scream. Malik could feel the surge of magic beside him. Ulgar groaned as he reached, though it was clear he had drained his *hish* long before. But Petyr had just enough strength to bring Ulgar closer.

Malik stretched out as far as he dared, latched on to Ulgar's free hand, and pulled.

Ulgar grabbed the top of the vine bridge with both hands, and screamed as he dragged himself up, while Petyr and Malik pulled him by the shoulders to safety.

Chest heaving, Ulgar rolled on his back and emitted something between a laugh and a sob.

The wind sent the bridge swinging, and Malik could barely see the spire he'd come from. But away from the edge, the vine's movement was not treacherous.

"Good work," Malik said, patting Petyr on the back. "What happened?"

"I was about to cross," said Petyr, "when I heard a cry. Found Ulgar hanging by his fingers."

"My leg," said Ulgar. "Drained my *hish* trying to heal it enough to make the crossing. Slipped. Used what little was left just to keep holding on."

Malik looked down. Ulgar's pants were tattered and bloody. He pulled the pant leg up, and Malik grimaced. A massive gash. Skin peeled back to the bone. Blood smeared all over, though Ulgar seemed to have staunched the flow before his magic ran out.

"God's breath! You tried to walk on that?"

Ulgar chuckled. "Well, it was easier with my spear. Used it as a sort of crutch after I fell, but that's gone now." He glanced out toward the sky. "Was trying to keep up with that prick, Aram Tulsein."

"He didn't do that..." Malik ventured.

"Nah, jumped too far on the Leap. Used too much *hish* and landed in a chasm in the rock."

Malik shuddered at how close he'd come to a similar injury.

"Don't get me wrong," Ulgar said. "Aram saw it happen. I was right behind him, and he was all too happy to leave me. But nah, this was my own damn fault."

A gust of wind rushed up through the sky canyon, sending the web of vines shaking violently. Malik latched on tight, his stomach twisting as the forces of the world pulled at his body. Thick clouds had completely enveloped the expanse between spires.

"We gotta get off this thing!" Malik shouted.

"Do you think we can make..." Petyr's idea drifted off with the next jarring gust.

Rain pelted at Malik's face and hands, cold as winter seas. He could barely feel his own body, and his fingers felt raw and swollen.

"No way we can cross until this storm passes," Malik said, his voice growing hoarse from so much shouting. "Not with his leg like that. We're twenty yards out at best. Easier to go back."

"Go back?" Petyr asked, incredulous.

"You wanna wait out this squall here or in the shelter of a spire?"

Ulgar nodded. "I'm with you, shaman. Already pushed myself too bloody hard."

Petyr looked back at the looming shadow in the mists ahead, contemplating. Then, he grabbed on to Ulgar's arm, and he and Malik helped the Serpent boy to his feet.

Each step was an ordeal all its own. Rain fell in sheets, biting at Malik's face, drenching his eyes, so he was forced to squint. The vines swayed in the incessant wind.

Malik gripped Ulgar around the back, his shoulder wedged under the tall boy's armpit to help take the weight off his bad leg. Malik steadied their passage as best he could. Ulgar was utterly spent, and more than once, Malik felt Petyr's strength fading too in the fiercer gales.

The descent was the most treacherous part, even without a damn storm.

Malik focused his magic on all three of them, pressing them into the slick ground. It felt like walking on waves, but like waves, there was a rhythm to it. With focus, he recognized the swells of air. They took a few steps, paused, took a few more. Each time, a gust sent the vines swinging, and Malik drew on the power behind the world. The energy of the gods that coursed through all their creation.

The spire was but a mass of shadows in the mists ahead. He could feel his strength waning as he channeled the magic. Slowly, it seeped from his spirit, and he feared he might drain himself too quickly.

But then, his body jolted as he stepped down onto the rocky ledge of the spire at last.

Ulgar staggered forward and collapsed. Malik and Petyr stooped down and helped him scramble to the back of the ledge. They propped him in a seated position against the rock face. It was uncanny how someone so large and strong could seem so frail. Ulgar shivered as he drew his blue cloak around himself.

"You done enough," he said, voice raspy, eyes barely open. "Didn't have to stop. But I'd be dead if you didn't."

Malik nodded.

Petyr glanced back out at the vines, and then, back at Malik. The howling had died down, now that they were no longer in the middle of a wind tunnel.

"Malik saved us both today," Petyr said. "I'd be dead back in the Abyss. Guess I had to return the favor."

"You should go, both of you," Ulgar said. "Think the storm's passing already. I'll ride it out up here till I can heal myself proper."

Petyr and Malik both gazed back the way they'd come. The vines still shifted, but it appeared to be milder now. The long trunks creaked but held firm and steady. It was extraordinary. Out in the chasm, Malik had feared the vines might wrench out of the base of the spire. But here, they felt as fixed as the mountains themselves, anchored firm in the stone.

Malik focused on the resonance of the air. The wind whistled out in the chasm between spires. The mass of vines swayed, but the walls of rock around the ledge created the illusion of a weaker storm. Probably the only reason any of them had ventured out to begin with.

It had been calm here before he left, Malik recalled, but the resonance felt just as violent now as when they were out in the middle.

This ledge was a deceptive harbor from the true ferocity of the storm. Made even easier to believe by the impenetrable mist, and Malik's longing for the safety of the valley below.

In his spirit, Malik knew the conditions were likely worse further out in the chasm. They'd only made it a quarter of the way across, at best.

"I don't think we should leave," Malik said.

Petyr's eyes went wide. "We can't stay here!"

"This ledge is sheltered. I don't think the storm is passing yet."

Petyr huffed. "It's getting dark. You want to be stranded up here all night? What about jackals and the cold? That could kill us just as easy."

If it truly was that late, Petyr was right.

Malik glanced up. It was difficult to tell in the storm. He tried to think back. He would have guessed it was early afternoon when he exited the Abyss. How much time had passed?

Malik retraced his descent thus far. It had taken him all morning to make his initial climb. Most descents went faster, barring hindrances, like jackal attacks and inclement weather. They were about halfway down. It couldn't be dusk yet.

"I don't think it's that late," Malik said. "Let's wait it out a while. You need to recover your strength, anyway."

Petyr cursed softly as he paced the ledge, walking out to the edge of the natural bridge, where the vines drove themselves deep into the base of the spire like the trunks of ancient citadel trees. The Saber boy peered into the mists, his spirit churning with anxious fear.

"Gods damn it," Petyr muttered and strode back.

———

The three boys huddled together, rain drenching their cloaks. Despite the shelter from the wind, the frigid air still cut straight through skin to bone.

Malik managed to scarf down a strip of salted venison. It was so cold, the act of biting into the leathery meat hurt his jaw. Malik could feel his joints stiffening the longer he sat, muscles tightening, body aching. He tried to conserve *hish* for the journey down, but it left him freezing.

Mists thickened, as though a great shroud were being drawn tighter around them. Was it growing darker beyond their nook in the rock? Malik couldn't tell, but he knew it would only get colder. The Ascent always took place at the autumn solstice. Usually the Isle of Faltara remained temperate for a few more weeks, but still, a storm in the mountains this time of year could bring worse conditions than wind and rain.

Of the three of them, Ulgar remained the calmest. Back against the rock face, he sipped water and chewed on venison and nuts, focused all his *hish* on keeping his body warm. Ulgar had accepted his fate.

Petyr began to pace the ledge again, running his hands up and down his arms. The Sabers were hardened by life on the north of the island. They always performed well in the Ascension, and Petyr was an elder's son. He paused and examined the vines and the storm, then resumed his pacing.

The mists remained. The vine bridge groaned softly. The wind was a distant rush beyond their nook at the base of the spire.

Petyr returned and blew warm breath on his hands.

Malik felt Petyr's unease, as his father had taught him over the past two years. *A shaman must understand his people more than any other.*

When Petyr spoke, it was no surprise to Malik. "I c-can't sit around here any l-longer."

Malik nodded.

The Saber boy had been wrestling with the decision since Malik had convinced him to stay. Doubting Malik's wisdom even more than Malik himself did.

"Are y-you c-coming?" Petyr asked, stepping closer to the bridge.

Malik looked over at Ulgar, but the boy was not paying them any mind. He was focused on his own survival, not wasting energy on anything else.

Malik strode over to Ulgar, stooped and met his gaze. Ulgar jolted, as though he'd forgotten he wasn't alone. Malik's insides churned with guilt, but he knew he had to consider his own descent.

"I'm going out to check things on the bridge," Malik said, clasping Ulgar's shoulder. "If it's bad, I'll come back. If I don't return, then the storm is letting up."

Ulgar nodded. "I told you. Don't worry about me. You done all I could ask." The boy closed his eyes and drew traces of *hish* around his limbs like an ethereal blanket.

Malik turned and joined Petyr. "Let's go."

Petyr led the way with determination, and Malik struggled to keep up, not wanting to expend too much *hish* too quickly. His father had taught him to control his magic better than most youths on the island. To let it slowly seep through him.

Malik's body loosened up with the movement. He was exhausted, but his legs were strong, and his balance remained firm. Malik gripped the side of one vine for support and let it guide him forward.

Soon, they passed the spot where Ulgar had slipped. The wind howled somewhere above them. The bridge swayed, but Malik never doubted his stability. Perhaps he'd read the storm's resonance wrong after all.

"You see?" Petyr said, glancing back as they neared a place where several vines converged. "Storm's letting up! I think the mist was worse back there."

Once he'd ensured a firm hold, Malik allowed a glance outward. In the distance, he glimpsed the twisting shadows of the other natural bridges to the other two spires.

Petyr was right. The storm was clearing.

Malik reached the base of the tangle of vines, each as thick as tree trunks. Beneath the knotted growth, Malik suspected there were tiny fragments of floating boulders, as there were between the lower spires. It was the only explanation for how this natural bridge might have formed.

Petyr clambered up and over the tangled vines. The boy grinned from the top. He motioned for Malik to follow, and turned to carry on, disappearing from sight.

Malik lodged his fingers deep into a crease and heaved himself over one vine, then the next. All at once, howling filled his ears, and his body heaved against the vines in front of him.

"Malik!" Petyr's voice was barely audible over the tumult.

The bridge swayed. Wind rushed all around, writhing and clawing like the hands of invisible wights, trying to send him soaring out into oblivion. Malik dug in his fingers and drew *hish* into his body, pressing himself into the vines.

Somewhere in the turbulence, Malik thought he heard Petyr's voice. But it was drowned out by the onslaught of wind.

Malik closed his eyes to the storm and focused. Despite the violent gusts, the vines remained steady. Creaking and groaning and shifting, but strong like the mightiest of trees. Slowly, the swaying eased, until the wind was once more a distant drone above.

Malik climbed farther up the wall, peeking up and over the top of the knot. Petyr was sprawled a few yards ahead of him, clinging to the vines for dear life. He lifted his head and smiled, dark hair drifting in the wind.

Mists engulfed the bridge once more. The wind roared, and Malik could not bring himself to leave the shelter of the tangle of vines. He trembled.

Petyr staggered to his feet, grinning. He gestured toward the spire looming ahead. "Nearly there. I thought I saw—"

A gale ripped through the chasm like a feathered serpent, rushing and writhing, colliding with Petyr's body and sending him reeling.

Malik reached out with *hish*, but it was too late.

The boy didn't even cry out.

He vanished like vapor.

CHAPTER 8

MOVE THROUGH

Raging pain tore at Joren's being, as though the gods themselves were pouring his spirit out over hot coals, then drawing him up and plunging him into an icy sea.

He collapsed to his knees at the edge of the clearing.

Somewhere, hands clutched at his arms. Somewhere, wind howled and rain poured from menacing clouds.

Joren felt nothing except the hollow ache of death, enveloping him, slowly wringing his essence from the inside out.

In one mighty onslaught, three souls were ripped from the Spires at once.

Joren did not know how long he knelt there.

The line between the temporal and the eternal blurred. Moments. Hours. Days. All were one.

A glimpse of the Great Truth of existence that was all too easy to forget during the banalities of village life on the island—even for a shaman. A reminder that all their striving—whether for moments or a lifetime—were drops in the eternal ocean. And they all would soon be drawn back to sea.

When Joren opened his eyes, he could already see the mist beginning to dissipate around the lower spires, and he wondered if his spirit had slipped out of his body for a time. Rare, but not unheard of, for a shaman in such sacred moments.

He found Madri's hand and gripped it, steadying his spirit with the strength of hers. And then, his daughter's, who also knelt beside him, her warm hand on his shoulder.

"Malik?" Madri whispered, her voice trembling.

God's breath! She'd thought that the reason for his collapse, and he'd left his family fearing for gods knew how long.

"No... our son lives."

Joren squeezed his wife's hand, and she clutched her chest with the other, relief washing over her.

The shaman staggered to his feet, and for the first time since the Ascent began, he withdrew his spiritual gaze from the Spires.

Three souls lost.

Three spirits he must tend.

Three families he must guide through mourning.

It had been almost thirty years since his own Ascent, since he'd become a man and taken on the duties of a shaman. Over the years, many of his duties had grown second-nature, even the difficult ones.

But the moment of death was one he never grew accustomed to.

———

Even after the winds truly let up, Malik did not move for what felt like an hour at least. He rode out the last gale in the minimal shelter provided by the tangle of vines, out in the middle of the sky canyon. That little nook was the only reason he hadn't joined Petyr in his Final Descent.

It was only happenstance that the gust that had taken the Saber elder's son had come moments before Malik followed Petyr out into the more exposed section of the bridge.

Malik's spirit ached with a ferocious anguish he'd never known before. Not even after Derrin's death. For that had been a distant thing, before he'd begun the path of the shaman. Before he'd learned to sense the resonance of spirits.

His brother's death had occurred somewhere beyond his reality, while he waited with the others in the valley.

But this...

Malik kept casting out for the boy's resonance. Clinging to the hope that by some chance, some rare interference of the gods, the Saber boy had landed on one of the other bridges. Or been carried to the next spire.

But he knew that Petyr was gone. Snatched up by the spirits of death that had filled that foul storm. It took all the courage Malik had in him to force himself out of his shelter and climb over the wall of vines.

Wisps of mist still hung in the chasm, but the wind was gone. Barely a breeze remained. The sun began to pierce through the veil of clouds, which had turned to shades of white and light grey.

Malik ventured farther along the vines, pressing his feet firmly with threads of *hish*, until he reached the spot where he'd last seen Petyr.

It was so cold. So empty. As though the warmth of the boy's resonance had never been there at all. Malik gazed out into the mists below, where the great green sprawl of Kalengal Valley came into view.

Somewhere down there, a boy's body was shattered and broken. A boy he had saved in the Abyss, only to escort him to his death on this bridge.

Malik never should have come out here. They should have stayed with Ulgar on that ledge. Surely, if he'd tried, he could have convinced Petyr to stay.

The mist dissipated, and the next spire shifted into focus, the true distance becoming clear for the first time. They'd only been twenty yards from the spire. The final stretch was an expanse of thick vines the width of a village path. Easily traversible.

Malik felt the warmth of the sun on his back, but still, he could not bring himself to move.

He hated the weight of bearing the last moments of another.

We all share in this life on the island, his father had taught him. *The unique role of the shaman is to share in death as well.*

But Malik didn't want it.

His father was made for this. He could walk up to a mourning mother, unbothered, but Malik could not bear death on his own, let alone for someone else.

It was not just Petyr's death that tore at his spirit, but his uncle's, his brother's. Every damn youth who'd fallen to their deaths from these Spires.

And for what?

"Oh, thank the gods!"

Malik didn't turn at the voice. It felt like something from a dream.

"Shit, brother, you're nearly across! What are you doing?"

Another voice. Familiar.

A thick calloused hand clasped his shoulder from behind, and he turned.

Yuri Alwensein engulfed him in a hug, his warmth enveloping Malik like a fur blanket. Riese pushed Yuri out of the way and hugged Malik, too.

The fog began to lift from his mind, stirred by confusion.

"How... where?" Cold tears streaked down his cheeks.

He'd assumed Riese was far ahead of him by now. That she'd crossed one of the other bridges. And Yuri... Malik had been so focused on his own plight with Petyr and Ulgar, he hadn't even considered...

"Found a little cave near the base of that chasm," Riese said. "Spotted Yuri coming down from the other side of the spire. He was hollering about a storm, so we holed up."

"Why in the Abyss did you come out here?" Ulgar's voice. Malik turned.

The boy clambered up and over the tangle of vines, shoving a spear over, and Yuri helped him up. Ulgar's leg was still torn up, but it looked better. Once situated upon the broad branch of vine, he used Yuri's bonespear for support.

The bridge barely swayed now. This final section was wide enough for two to walk abreast.

The mist thinned further. Beyond the rim of mountains that encircled their sacred valley, the brilliant colors of dusk bled across the sky.

"Where's Petyr?" Ulgar asked. "Already across?" He looked up and down the next spire for signs of a cloak.

Malik shook his head. "That last gale... he's... gone."

Speaking the words sent tremors through him. Riese kept close, her hand on his shoulder.

"God's breath," Ulgar muttered. "I should've... I was pretty out of it till your friends came along. Healed me up enough to get moving again."

Malik looked to Yuri and Riese.

Riese shrugged. "Shamans aren't the only ones who help people, you know."

"Look," said Yuri, "if it's all the same to you, let's get off this bridge of death. Er—shit... you know what I mean."

Riese patted Malik on the arm. "He's right. Let's go."

———

It was astonishing how quickly they finished the crossing. No violent gusts of wind. No rain or fog. Even Ulgar, staggering on his spear-crutch, made the final stretch look easy.

Petyr had come so close.

Soon, they were on the face of the penultimate spire. It was steep, but pocked with regular ledges where they could pause. They did their best to help Ulgar over the difficult sections.

Far above, the sharp cries of dragyrs echoed from the upper spires. The sky turned to deep greys and swaths of indigo. At the base of the Mountain of Souls, from which the Kalengal Spires rose, Malik saw the crowds gathering to greet the final climbers. Though they were still a fair distance from the bottom.

They reached the final challenge—a sequence of leaps between small, floating boulders, like a disjointed staircase. Malik and Yuri took Ulgar's arms and tried their best to cushion the falls with pulses of *hish*.

Once they reached the base of the last spire, they crossed a man-made bridge of wood and rope, and soon stood safely at the top of the Mountain of Souls. The remaining descent required careful maneuvering near the peak before the angle grew more gradual, and they followed a well-trod path into the forest.

Dusk morphed into a peaceful night as they descended into familiar trees near the base of the mountain.

As he neared the end, Malik focused deeply on the act of drawing in *hish*, strengthening himself as best he could to finish with honor. He was exhausted, but it was his spirit that needed rejuvenation most.

He kept picturing Petyr smiling back at him, that final moment before being torn from the face of the world.

You cannot ignore darkness. The only way to move past is to move through.

All these shamanic mantras instilled in his mind had never felt more like nonsense.

The four kept close, always on the lookout for jackals or other beasts, but the forest was silent, save for the soft crunch of their leather boots on the sodden ground. Walls of trees went on in every direction, and then, all at once, Malik, Riese, Yuri, and Ulgar emerged into the open plains of Kalengal Valley.

They crossed a stream and crested a small hill.

The crowds cheered as they neared. All their people gathered in one place, surrounding them. Hands brushed against Malik's shoulders, patted his back, congratulating him, asking about the color of his dragon egg.

The egg, Malik mused. He'd hardly thought about it since the storm had come.

Malik kept his hands on the straps of his rucksack, wishing he could disappear, fly past them all like the wights in the Abyss, and be alone.

"Malik!"

His mother's warm voice cut through the noise of the crowd. Malik looked up, and she ran to him, arms outstretched, and pulled him into her soft embrace. Something shattered inside him. All the rage and sorrow and fear that he'd been suppressing in order to keep one foot moving in front of the other—all of it burst forth in his mother's arms. His body shuddered. He clutched his mother's cloak tight in his fingers and sobbed against her shoulder.

His sister wrapped her arms around them both. Usually all bright green eyes and mischievous smile, now, Surel's expression showed only relief.

"Gods are good," his mother whispered, pulling him tight. "Gods are good."

Malik looked up to find his father watching the three of them. Tears streaked his cheeks. He released his mother and sister, and his father embraced him.

Malik could not remember an embrace like that from his father before, certainly not in front of their people.

Joren's calming spiritual resonance flooded over him, his hand clasped the side of his head and looked in his eyes with tearful pride.

"You are a man now, my son."

Part Two

The Bloody Company

Better to walk a path of blood and toil knowing the gods guide your way, than to meander through a life of ease. To wander from one's path, that is true suffering.

—Book IV, verse thirteen of *The Paths of Fjuriin*

Chapter 9

Dusk of Battle

A battle could shift tides in an instant—that was the horrific beauty of it in Lady Captain Urla Pelasius's mind.

Life and death stretched along an invisible thread, weaving across the battle plain, through every warrior, every beast, every razor-sharp edge. The difference was a matter of inches and moments.

One moment, Urla's axe was wedged in the crevasse of a Sigan warrior's dark-haired skull. Fire rained down from crimson skies and consumed entire companies of warriors. Smoke rushed into the heavens, and blood gushed from a writhing furor of blades and shields, and the deathblows found between them.

A moment later, horns blared, and cheers swept across the battlefield.

The next warrior Urla faced dropped his weapon and lay prostrate on the blood-soaked ground before her. Her battle axe hovered in the air casting a gruesome shadow over the whimpering man.

The field filled with the clattering of discarded weapons and the pleas of surrender. The Rain of Fire ceased, and the mighty Dragon-mounts of Attica soared over the plains, gargantuan wings blocking the sun before settling on the hills at the edge of the battlefield.

Three fates stretched the bloody plains—the fallen, the defeated, and the victors—threads woven before the war had begun. It was the Fjuriin Path they all trod, whether they believed it or not.

Lady Captain Pelasius had stayed her course, that was all, the gory evidence spread all around her. To her left, Urla had dealt one fate, the man's innards coating the ground in goops of flesh and bone. Now, for the fortunate Sigan heathen kneeling before her, she dealt another.

Urla lowered her axe, though she did not stow it on her back.

The surrender had likely happened several minutes ago. Somewhere behind her, comrades in arms closer to Lord General Raithe had survived, where here they had fallen, crimson cloaks twisted around their mutilated bodies. Somewhere ahead, the battle still raged for a few moments longer.

But Urla felt no regret for anyone she'd slain on this field. It was their path, and it was the price of heathen rebellion finally paid in full.

The prostrate warrior shifted at her feet, and Urla tightened her grip on the leather-wrapped handle of her axe.

"On your face!" she barked.

"P-please, I will not resist. I have family. Please."

How easily warriors could be reduced to pant-pissing cowards. The Sigan man planted his face deeper in the blood and upturned earth, wedged between the bodies of fallen soldiers.

My son lost his father for this? Urla thought bitterly.

She'd been tempted to let her axe fall. She knew plenty of her comrades had done so, but she was Lady Captain now. And besides, the battlefury was already waning, and the ache of buried sorrow seeped back to the surface.

Keivan's death will be avenged by better blood than yours.

The Sigan nobles and high-ranking officers would be tried and executed, replaced with imperial loyalists. The rest of this heathen force would march home in shackles and shame. Nothing to show for their years of independence but a host of orphans and half-starved lowborns.

After a bloody civil war half a century ago, Siga had managed a tumultuous independence, like many nation-states at the outskirts of the empire during the Age of Decline. But under Emperor Athanasius, the tide had finally turned, and a new path lay before the Attican Empire.

Now, Siga would be grafted back into the mighty tree of Attica. A tree that had weathered droughts and storms and was poised to spread the blood-soaked world once more, and bend thousands more soldiers to such a groveling state.

The Sigan man still simpered pathetically at Urla's feet, not daring to look anywhere but the mud.

A series of runners dispersed shackles and chains across the battle-field. Prison carts descended the hills, steel cages rattling, and picked their way amongst the throng. A slow process due to the corpses littering the ground.

Urla knelt on the Sigan warrior's back. He groaned at the weight and the sharp edge of a glowing runemarked greave piercing through his cloak.

"Quit crying, swine," she said, patting his cheek. "You'll live."

A scrawny Attican squire handed Urla a pair of manacles. She seized the Sigan warrior's wrists and shackled them and jerked the man to his feet. He wore only leathern armor, except for a chest plate made of bronze. It was remarkable their little kingdom had lasted as long as it had, in truth.

Urla shoved the man forward, and the rest of her company quickly followed her lead.

Most of the flames had dwindled to smoldering grass across the trodden plains, except for the splintered remains of an Elyan runeship, a quarter-mile to the west. The flying galleon had nearly swayed the battle in the Sigans' favor. Broadsides from the sky were a rare and terrifying thing to behold. Hundreds of Attican warriors had been killed, but the Dragonmounts had done their duty in the end.

Dragonflight could not be matched by any human invention, magic or no. That was what Keivan had always told her.

May you enjoy your rest in the halls of Myrath until I join you, she thought.

Keivan was only days from a different fate. The loss was still fresh, and the full reality of her husband's death had yet to set in. Urla did not think it would until she returned home to her son, alone.

A thick hand clapped her shoulder from behind with a laugh. Urla didn't flinch. She'd seen her comrade approaching in the corner of her vision.

"Final tally, twenty-three, Captain!" Roak said with a chortle.

The sergeant looked like a mossy boulder. All thick muscles and curly dark hair, from his beard to his toes, Urla was loathe to know. There was little privacy in a battle company, even for one of the shield maidens of Attica.

"Roak, if you were counting, you weren't lost in the fury," said Lieutenant Caliphus, shoving his prisoner in the mud. "Bloody shame."

Roak chuckled. "Is it the fury if you just stand there hacking away at the same heathen the whole damn time?"

Caliphus glowered. The officer was her second-in-command, twenty years younger than Urla, and younger than most of the Bloody Company. But unlike most of her soldiers, Caliphus was an academy boy from a decent family. The men liked to razz him over being a soft noble's son, and he fell for it more times than not.

"It was too many kills to count, if you must know," Caliphus countered.

"Hey, I thought you said it didn't matter!"

"Help me out, Lady Captain!" Caliphus said.

Urla smirked and shook her head. "Only kill I ever marked was my very first, twenty-odd years ago."

"Heh, first kill, that's all you marked today too, Lieutenant," Roak laughed.

Caliphus shoved him hard in the shoulder, but he laughed along.

Roak hurried ahead, but Caliphus kept close by Urla's side.

"So... how many was it actually, then?" Urla asked.

"Twenty-two," Caliphus groaned, shoving his prisoner forward. The heathen stumbled over his own feet. "I'd happily make it a tie, however!"

The Sigan warrior shriveled at the words and picked up the pace. He did not trip again.

The dusk of battle was Urla's least favorite hour, when the gruesome throes of fate were exchanged for a strange and raucous amalgamation of screams and frivolity. Of course, she'd had her part in the looting of defeated kingdoms before—shaming and mutilating and enslaving—but over the years, it had grown less appealing.

For years, Urla tried to suppress her displeasure at the post-battle ritual, fearing it was the mother in her, and something deep within felt sure this was weakness festering. Eventually, she could not deny it. If becoming a mother had changed her, then so be it.

Her child would never be left so vulnerable. Still, Urla could not shake the knowledge that her son's fate had been a chance blessing from the All Mother.

How easily Ruan might have been Sigan, born on the other side of a war he had no say in. And when the Attican Empire quashed that rebellion and subjugated its citizens once more, as was their right, it could just as easily have been her own son orphaned or starved or... worse.

So, once her duties were fulfilled on the battlefield, Urla retreated to the outskirts of the war camp while the warriors of the Bloody Company subjugated the Sigan heathens in the name of the empire, and the Dragon Emperor Athanasius himself.

The Sigan capital of Leone was nothing like the great Attican cities of stone, where the history of the empire was etched in every temple and square. Here, everything was made of bamboo rods and thatched together by little more than twine. If the legions felt so inclined, the entire city could be razed by morning—it surely wouldn't be the first time Leone had suffered such a fate. A proper civilized city could be built in its place, but that was not the Attican way.

Yes, they conquered, but vassal states still maintained remnants of their culture. Sure, the Attican conquerors erected temples to the true All Mother and All Father, and over time, monks would bring converts to the Fjuriin Path. But theirs was an empire built on land, not superstition. So long as the Sigans paid proper tribute to the emperor, they could carry on their lives much as they had before. It made the matter of rebellion all the more baffling to Urla. Surely, life in Siga had been worse during their liberation.

But then, she had been raised in the Path, and for that, she thanked the true gods.

Urla walked the edge of the battlefield, where the sounds of spoils were diminished. Clouds hovered overhead, forming a glowing dome over the valley. Most of the pyres had dwindled. The heathen soldiers huddled in prison carts, kept warm by the fires that had incinerated their fallen comrades.

Along the hillsides, the silhouettes of dragons loomed against the cloudy backdrop, wings drawn back like dark sails.

A faint golden luminescence caught Urla's eye near the center of the field, and she ventured over. Several brown-cloaked arcanists shuffled around, picking through splinters of wood, the source of the strange glow.

The remains of the runeship, Urla realized, her curiosity piqued. Now, little more than a heap of splinters. Urla could make out what she thought might be a section of mast jutting out of the wreckage, and a section of taffrail, perhaps, but little else.

She drew closer. The browncloaks hefted a few select pieces of wood into a wagon. For study, Urla presumed. The rest they cast aside into a large pile of charred lumber to be destroyed. The runeship was a terrifying marvel. Urla's armor, like most highborn officers, was rein-forced with runes—they made it possible to survive a single axe blow to the chest, though, rarely two—but to fly an entire ship with magic? That was a sorcery beyond anything in Attica.

Though Urla knew little of magic.

It was a force of the Other, according to the Fjuriin Path, and bore risks far greater than dragons if practiced by the wrong hands. Worlds had fallen from such power.

This runeship was a bad omen. It signified the power of a nation that did not believe in the same restraint towards sorcery.

The Elyans were meddling in Attican affairs, and that was cause for worry. But if the secrets of their magic ships could be unraveled...

The browncloaks shot Urla an aggravated look but carried on about their work. Runes on the salvaged boards continued to glow, despite the decimation of the ship itself. Urla peered into the cart for a closer look. It was as though the boards had been etched with liquid magic, like metal in a forge poured into intricate shapes. The runes themselves came from no language Urla had encountered in all her campaigns, their shape somehow both sharp and fluid.

"I guess I shouldn't be surprised to find you lingering on the battle-field," said a familiar voice. *"Kraal ni Mira."*

Consul General Campos strode toward her from the darkness, his crimson cloak billowing behind him in the soft evening breeze. She saluted him with a raised right fist before answering.

"Soldiers live for spoils," Urla said. "Warriors fight for glory. You taught me that."

Campos had been Lord Captain of her first company, many years ago, and taught her what it meant to be a warrior.

"I did," Campos said with a grin. "But who said there's no glory to be found in spoils?"

Urla shook her head. "Well, I don't see you partaking either."

"I'm a consul."

Urla rolled her eyes. "Well, there you have it."

"But I am sure the men of your Bloody Company are relieved you let them choose their own glory."

Urla smiled. "That would make me a poor bloody mother."

Kraal ni Mira.

The name had come from the moment she proved her mettle in the training camps.

Back as a young officer recruit—far greener than Caliphus. There were few women in the legions, and hardly any female officers, and more than one cocky grunt had tested her. But when one bastard tried to have his way with her after a drunken fest, Urla severed his hand clean off.

The bastard was a fellow noble's heir and took the incident up the chain of command.

Urla denied it. Naturally, it was a worse offense to maim one of her fellow soldiers than what the man had attempted.

"What would you have me do?" Lord Captain Campos had demanded of her before the tribunal. "How else do you explain the blood on your uniform?"

Urla had shrugged. "It's my... time of the month."

And the name was born. The Bloody Mother.

The maimed man was dismissed from duty. The legions had no use for a one-handed soldier, noble or not. Urla, meanwhile, earned her respect and her place among the legions.

From that day forward, there was neither male nor female amongst her comrades, only soldiers. Now, Urla was one of the few lady captains, and her company of a hundred would follow her into the pits of Skrala itself.

"The Bloody Mother." Campos clapped her on the shoulder. "That bastard had it coming, I'll tell you."

She smiled. "You have many times."

"We all liked your fire, we just—"

"Needed an excuse not to send me packing," Urla said.

They laughed. Campos followed her gaze as the arcanists continued their work on the remains of the runeship.

"A marvel, isn't it?" the general mused, surveying the diminishing heap that had once been a ship of terrifying magnificence. "I'm glad there was only one."

"The Flying Armada is a legend, isn't it?" asked Urla.

"If the Elyans can build one ship? Why not a fleet?"

"They might ask the same of our dragons."

"Aye, and we make damn sure we keep that shrouded in mystery, don't we?"

Urla knew he was fishing for information, as usual. Being wed to a Dragonmount, many assumed she knew all the secrets of the order, but her husband had taken oaths long before they'd met, and Urla knew little more than most other members of the legions why there were so few dragons in the world.

Urla shrugged. "Mysteries are mysteries for a reason, sir."

Campos turned to one of the arcanists.

"Will you be able to unravel *this* monstrosity's mysteries, Lord Sorcerer?"

The bald man scowled and set a glowing scrap of wood in the wagon. "I'm not at liberty to say, sir."

Campos chortled. "Good man. Carry on, then!"

He waved the arcanist away and grabbed Urla by the elbow. "Walk with me, will you? I think you're putting them on edge."

"Me?" Urla laughed. "You're the one asking questions."

"Then, permit me the joy of your company, *Kraal ni Mira.*"

Urla nodded. "Of course, sir."

They strode in silence, weaving amongst the pyres dotting the battle-churned landscape.

"Your company fought with honor," Campos said. "Throughout this campaign. You lead them well."

"I learned to follow orders, that's all."

"There were some who feared you'd let grief rule you today."

Urla huffed. If her and her husband's fates had been reversed, she knew he would have received no such doubts.

"I was not one of them, Lady Captain. I knew you'd fulfill your duty, beyond the highest expectations. As you have since the day that bastard lost his bloody hand."

She smiled. "Thank you, sir."

"After this, though..."

"I have no intention of retiring, sir. My path is etched in blood, just like my father's and his before him."

"I hear your son shows promise at the academy. How old is he now?"

"Eighteen. He's already passed the Mountain and the Desert trials. Though he longs for the sky like his father."

"It's a damned shame Keivan's mount was lost with him," Campos said. "Voltari should have been your son's mount, and his heir's after him. Fucking tragedy."

Urla bit her lip. It felt like a betrayal, but that was the news she dreaded sharing with her son the most, even more than the death of his father. Ruan had trained all his life believing he would be Dragon-mount. He'd ridden Voltari on half a hundred occasions, and he possessed rare skill in flight, even without a true dragon bond.

Urla had insisted no word be sent about the dragonfall. She could not bear the thought of anyone else breaking such unspeakable news to him.

General Campos brushed her shoulder, and Urla turned. He'd been a friend of her father's, and after his death, Campos was as close a thing to a father as she had left.

"There may be another way for your son to attempt a Sky trial."

"Only a couple of dragons are hatched each year. I don't know as much as you think about their origins, but I know the chances that my son would be granted one is unfathomable. I have a better chance at becoming Lady General."

Campos smiled down at her. "Some might have said the same about your chances at being captain too. Or even making it out of the training camps. But in my experience, it's always a combination of who you are and who you know. Your son is one of the most promising young novices in the capital, and you are more well-connected than you realize."

"What are you saying, sir?"

"There's someone I'd like you and Ruan to meet when we return to Attica. Assuming, of course, that you're interested."

"You think you can get my family another dragon?"

Campos walked off, calling over his shoulder, "I'll send word after the Victor's March."

CHAPTER 10

VICTOR'S MARCH

The streets of Attica thrummed with the exultation of victory. Crimson banners streamed from every rooftop and balcony, from the *Rue ni Hana* at the outskirts of the city, all the way to the Imperial Square at the base of the palace grounds.

Thousands of soldiers marched along the Attican Way. Trumpets blared and crowds roared as soldiers paused at intervals to pound out a victor's beat on the cobbled stone with their boots and spear shafts. The entire crowd joined together with a furious chant that thundered across the city.

"The streets will flow like rivers," the legions shouted. "No more will our empire fade. Athanasius will take his bounty. Attica! Attica, rise from your grave!"

Urla shouted with the rest. Her company was positioned near the middle of the procession. It was remarkable to look upon the main thoroughfare of the city and consider how much had changed in her lifetime.

Athanasius was the fourth emperor to rule since Urla was born. Many in the world had thought that Attica was in its twilight years in her childhood. A once-mighty nation clinging to a tradition of power more than anything actual. Most of the outer kingdoms ruled and united by Aran the Conqueror in the Golden Age had withdrawn. Great sprawls of land once regions of the greatest empire in the world were grafted in by weak kings at the outer limits of Attica's influence. Peoples once called Attican were known by other names. Old nations were reborn, new ones formed. And Attica dwindled like a wave turning back to sea.

Even internally, Attica was a fractured empire when Urla came into the world. Most of its armies split amongst the three great Dragon Lords, the imperial force was barely larger than the highest lord's standing army. The high lords vied for power in a vicious cycle of war and upheaval and assassinations mixed with famines and plagues and other disasters that heaped on the turbulence. Attica was spread too thin, ruled by too many lords, united by foolish emperors.

Praust the Second had been barely a puppet, so Urla's father had told little Urla after he was assassinated. Emperor Erastlan, a fool. And he died before Urla attended the academy.

But the Good Emperor Vitruvian had done two unexpected things that changed Attica's fate. Two things that forced the high lords to pull their heads out of their own asses long enough to repair some of the fractures.

First, Vitruvian deemed the allotment of dragons be based on a lottery, stripping the Dragon Lords of their greatest source of influence. A dragon was the ultimate path to power for the lesser Attican houses, and for years, the lesser lords had been forced to compete for the chance to join the Dragonmounts. Alliances could change overnight as all tried their best to merit a dragon egg. But as soon as the eggs belonged to the empire, rather than the Dragon Lords, the politics of Attica shifted back into the hands of the emperor.

Second, and most astonishing, Vitruvian refused to name an heir from his own bloodline. Instead, he chose an heir based on merit and character, regardless of the greatness of house.

Athanasius came from the lesser House Octiva, his own domain spanning less than half of a percent of the empire.

House Octiva had no age-old squabbles with the Dragon Lords, and Athanasius was charismatic and cunning. Any who doubted him were quickly won over after he quashed the Rhodan Rebellion, involving the brief secession of one of the oldest and greatest dragon houses Attica had ever known. But Athanasius followed up this victory on the Attican interior with two more on the exterior, reclaiming the lands of Kalkesh and Ytan.

The Fjuriin Path meant something again. For the first time in a century, Attica was growing rather than receding. The Sigan victory on the eastern border was just one more step toward the Path of Eternal Glory.

Urla was filled with sorrow, but buried deep beneath the loss was the knowledge that her husband's dragonfall had been a worthy sacrifice. And with the possibility of another dragon lingering in her mind, Urla could not help but march proudly, bellowing alongside the members of her company.

This was their path.

The legions marched over a series of bridges leading up to the palace, pausing before the great temples of Valyr and Marha—the true All Father and All Mother.

Blood ran down the steps leading up to the pillared entrance of Marha's temple. The life of the greatest Sigan generals spilled as a sacrifice that would be spread upon fields outside the city, blessing the body of the All Mother, where Atticans made their home.

Urla counted herself blessed that her company had been given the honor of the Victor's March. Half the legions remained in Siga, to ensure proper transition of power. A quarter of those soldiers left behind would likely be garrisoned there for two years. Urla knew she had Consul General Campos to thank for her marching orders.

The Imperial Square stretched a half mile in all directions and was formed of brilliant alabaster stone tiles. Each fitted so carefully and maintained so dutifully, that the war chariots leading the procession did not rattle. Chariots were unreasonable on the shattered terrain of the outer kingdoms, but in Attica City, all generals rode them.

In the old wars of the Golden Age, it was said legions of chariots fought in battles on the very plains where crops were now sown to sustain the empire. Chariots circled the square ahead before stopping at the great steps of the pyramidal fortress that was the emperor's palace.

The legions formed up in regiments of five hundred, with a hundred soldiers to each company. The edges of the square were lined with the chariots of the lords of Attica. Urla spotted her husband's banner, a blue tower with a dragon perched at its zenith, and her heart rushed with a longing only a widowed mother could know. The banner rose above her son's chariot. Even from this distance, she recognized his stance, one hand tucked at his side, resting on the hilt of his sword.

Urla's company—all bearing her house's sigil upon their chests—formed up beside her.

For a moment, the square was silent. Ten thousand soldiers stood at attention at the base of the pyramid. A hundred thousand citizens filled the streets surrounding them. And yet, it was as silent as the forests behind Urla's childhood home.

All at once, like an eruption, cheers rumbled across the square.

Every soldier looked upward as the first dragon soared overhead, swooping down from an azure sky. Soldiers pounded their fists on their armored chests, and more dragons followed. Gargantuan wings fanned across the sky. Seven dragons in total, belonging to high lords and the Dragon Emperor Athanasius himself. They swooped down for another pass, while another chorus of "Attica, Rise from your Grave" erupted amongst the troops and carried into the streets.

One by one, the lords perched upon landing pads set into the sides of the pyramid, while Athanasius's pale white dragon drew back its wings and set down upon the vast dais at the top of the stairs, midway up the pyramid's face. He raised a gleaming sword into the air, and the entire city cheered. Soldiers pounded their boots and spear shafts, the sound rising to near-deafening heights. Urla stomped her feet with all her might, a rush of furious patriotism erupting in her heart.

The emperor lowered his sword, and the crowd went silent as their great ruler descended his white dragon.

Urla stole a glance at the western edge of the square, where her son stood at the front of his father's chariot. Dark brown hair reached his shoulders and caught the breeze. Ruan's bronze skin shone, though his face remained expressionless. She wondered what news had already reached him. His father was a lesser lord, so it was not strange his dragon did not fly during the Victor's March.

Ruan glanced her direction, and her heart shuddered. She could not hold back a grimace as his sad eyes glistened, meeting her gaze. There was no searching there.

He already knows.

Her son turned away.

The crowd erupted once more as Emperor Athanasius raised his hands from the dais. Using a runemarked horn, his voice filled the square with what was surely a rousing speech of triumph and glory.

But Urla heard none of it.

CHAPTER 11

INVITATION

The festivities lasted only a day, then most of the imperial troops marched on to the estates of their lord houses, where celebrations would continue.

Keivan's cousins and uncles led companies the same as Urla, and their troops made their livelihoods on Pelasius lands—a two day journey from the capital across the southern plains of Attica Proper. It was not until moments before dinner on the first night, that Urla finally found her son.

In truth, after seeing his face during the Victor's March, she'd needed the time to prepare herself. In all the festivities and marching, there had been little privacy.

Expression stoic as ever, young Ruan greeted Urla with a salute, for they were surrounded by a bustling mass of soldiers and servants unloading gear, setting up camp, ferrying messages.

"Join me for wine before dinner?" Urla asked, motioning toward the enormous tent that had been erected. Two dozen poles of socha and thick furls of Kalkeshi cloth would provide her more space than she'd had in months, though she longed for the vast halls of home.

Ruan hesitated. "Of course, Lady Captain."

So formal. Gods, he was only a boy when we left, Urla thought. *He still addressed me as Mother. Now, he's a man grown. Eighteen.*

Urla gestured to the tent entrance, and he followed her inside.

A flurry of servants engulfed them both. Urla fielded questions from Pisarre, the chief of their family's staff, about dinner and preparations for the larger festivities to be held once they reached the Sapphire Tower of House Pelasius.

As she spoke, Ruan stepped aside and a pair of servants removed the leather fastenings of her steel cuirass and eased the runemarked armor off. Today had demanded only ceremonial garb, so the process was quicker than with battle armor. Urla wore a cream-colored tunic beneath, which was drenched with sweat from riding in the early autumn sun.

Ruan turned his back while the female servants stripped her and dabbed her naked body with damp cloths and perfumes before dressing her in a sleeveless violet gown made of Taikan silk. After a two year garrison at the southern edge of the empire, followed by the campaign in Siga, it was a blessed relief to wear such light attire. But Urla was rarely one for excess, and the process was finished in only a few minutes.

Her son remained in his formal Dawncrest Academy uniform, a tight-fitting crimson tunic beneath black leathern armor, with bronze fastenings, and pauldrons decorated with a small bronze dragon head on each shoulder. A blue sash for his father's house—now, his house—was draped over his chest. And a bronze and leather belt with a gladius sheathed at his hip.

Just like her husband had worn in his own academy days.

So regal. So...

Under normal circumstances, mother and son might have taken their wine at the edge of camp and watched the sunset, but tonight, much as Urla was tired of the walls of tents, it would be improper to speak in public, considering what they must discuss.

Chairs were brought to the center of her tent, wine was poured into bronze chalices, and then, at last, they were alone.

Ruan stood beside his chair, waiting for her to be seated first, but Urla merely gazed at her son, looking him up and down, truly, for the first time in two years.

His dark hair was tied back. Specks of stubble showed on his upper lip. His brown eyes were full of secrets. It was a Fjuriin tenet to remain composed, to master one's passions. To accept fate and remain committed to one's path, but it was necessary to be true amongst a devoted few. This was the role of Attican mothers since the Golden Age, even Lady Captains.

Urla had been her son's confidante once. But now... she could sense the walls he'd erected during his time at the academy.

"There's no need to say I've grown," Ruan said. "I already know full well."

Urla smirked, and Ruan let the crease of a smile slip at the edges of his mouth.

"Ah, there it is," she said, and his smile grew. "Yes, even soldiers are allowed a grin from time to time. Now, are you too old to embrace your mother?"

Ruan hesitated, glancing around.

"You don't have to, if you don't—"

Before Urla could finish, Ruan crossed the space between them and pulled her tight. He was taller than her now. The top of her head only reached the base of his ear, and she was tall for an Attican woman.

Gods, he must have grown half a foot these past two years.

Ruan clutched her back, his fingers trembling. She kissed him on the cheek and pulled back. She'd ordered the servants not to disturb them, but she knew he was on edge about appearances, having just become a proper Fjuriin man.

"When did you hear?" she whispered, taking her seat.

"Cedro, another boy at the academy, he lost his father in the same battle. The messenger talked about a dragonfall. I knew it was Voltari from description alone. I told no one, though."

Urla took a long drink from her chalice, draining the cup. Blessedly, the servants had left a carafe, and she refilled it. The warmth in her stomach dulled the tide of grief that threatened to swell. "I hoped to be the one to break the news."

Ruan sat rigid in his chair. "Truth be told, I'm glad for the time to mourn on my own. Or today's Victor's March might have been far less sweet."

Urla nodded. She'd wanted to be the one to comfort him, but perhaps she'd needed him more than he'd needed her. "Only one dragon fell. Who was this Cedro's father?"

"A low lord from the isles. Lucian Varro. His son is one my bunk-mates at Dawncrest."

Urla cursed. The Varros were barely lords at all. Before the Good Emperor Vitruvian's reign, such a lord would never have bunked with a Pelasius. And she might have still broken the news herself. But then, before Vitruvian, she might never have married a Dragonmount either.

Ruan remained composed, though she noted how he bit the inside of his lower lip in the interim.

"What are you thinking?" she asked.

He sighed. "I've had weeks to consider what this means."

"You're Lord Pelasius now."

"Not just that."

Urla shuddered to mention it. Suddenly fearing it was all wishful thinking. What if Campos was wrong? What if he couldn't do what he said?

But the arrangements were already made, and if there was even the slightest chance Ruan might still become Dragonmount, she had to take it.

"We're dining with the consul general tonight," she said.

Ruan frowned. "Tonight of all nights should be a family dinner. Uncle Adrius has an elaborate feast prepared."

Urla nodded. "Campos is like a father to me, Ruan. He is one of the highest lords in the land."

"He doesn't even have a dragon."

"By choice. He serves on Athanasius's council, just as his father served Vitruvian *and* Erastlan before him. We should be honored to dine with him."

Ruan straightened at her words and nodded, but his voice remained rigid. "Of course, Mother."

"He has an invitation that I think will be of great interest to you."

———

Ruan's eyes went wide, the corners on the verge of tearing up at Campos's words. "You're serious, Consul General? Mother, surely this is a joke."

Urla's stomach churned, fearing the same. They sat at the head of

Campos's table, an honor usually reserved for members of a lord's bloodline, though Campos had no wife or children. A few nieces and nephews had joined them during the meal but left to join their own families as soon as dinner was done. Servants cleaned up the long wooden tables, while the three of them spoke softly.

"No joke, Ruan," Campos said. "I would never trivialize something so sacred as a dragonbond."

"But my father was the first Pelasius to become Dragonmount. The chances of another lottery are abysmally low."

"Your father was one of the first to win a bond under Vitruvian's rule. But there are ways."

"I'll be middle of the line at best for a chance to bond," Ruan said.

"You're right. If you wait until the lottery, you will be middle at best. Each egg will have a chance to be bonded with half a hundred lordlings before it might reach you. Impossible? Who can say? Dragonbonds are a mystery. I've seen two fall to the same house in the same year, by chance. There are many houses, even great ones, who've yet to form a bond. But your blood runs deep, even before the Dragon Lords. There were Pelasius riders during Aron the Conqueror's reign."

"I don't understand."

Urla brushed his shoulder. "Speak plainly, General. For my father's sake."

A handsome servant with fair Valucian skin refilled their glasses. He wore a maroon vest and tight brown breeches and had seen twenty summers at best. Campos pulled him close and whispered something in his ear, then winked and waved the young man away. "Thank you, Baro."

The servant barked an order in Valucian, and the other servants quickly left the room. In the distance, Urla heard the strumming of lyres and the beat of dancing drums. She recognized it as an old melody dating back just after the Crossing, in the lively style of the Old Continent.

Baro stood at the entrance to the tent, arms crossed. Urla thought she had seen him before, though Campos had kept other young men close as long as she'd known him. Clearly, Baro was special to be so trusted.

When it was clear their conversation was private, Campos spoke.

"I've often teased your mother about finding out the origins of dragon eggs."

"It's knowledge entrusted only to the emperor, and the Dragon-mounts," said Ruan.

"You're right, but also to others who've no stake in the matter."

"What do you mean?" Urla asked. "You've always known? You've been pestering me since I married Keivan."

Campos chuckled and shrugged. "Guilty. I was curious about how much is known by families such as yours. Ancient lineage and such. Though, in truth, you'd not have let on to a fool like me, even if you'd known."

Urla fought a smile.

"So, you know where the eggs come from?" Ruan asked.

"I've been entrusted with delivering them for the lottery for the past several years. But this year, our gracious emperor has requested I bring more... assurances. Ruan, I'd like you and your mother to join me in delivering the eggs from their present hiding place. In the process, you'll be one of the first potential mounts to come in contact with this year's selection. And should you so happen to bond with one of them before the lottery, well, what's done would be done, wouldn't it?"

"There's no breaking a bond," Ruan said, eyes alight. "Only death."

"That's right," said Campos.

"When do we set sail?" Urla asked.

"Tonight."

"Before the victory celebrations?" Urla asked.

"It'll be a week of preparations. You'll slip away to mourn your husband's death in private. We'll be back before First Feast."

"Wait, there and back in less than a week," said Ruan. "Where *are* we sailing?"

Campos grinned. "Ah, well, we won't be traveling by ship. At least most of the way."

"What?" said Urla.

"I told you, there was someone I wanted you to meet," said Campos, his grin growing wide and mischievous.

"Out with it, General," Urla said. "Er, with respect."

"Ha! Yes, I enjoy the game a bit too much, I know. But can you fault a man for enjoying himself? Baro, bring in our guest, would you?"

The Valucian man nodded and slipped past the entrance into another part of the tent. He emerged moments later, bowed to the general, and then spoke, "I present Lady Knight Vera Salyr."

An immense woman with dark brown skin strode into the room, bedecked in runemarked armor even finer than Urla's own. Each plate shimmered like polished silver. The shield of her helmet remained closed, but her dark eyes shone. Black hair flowed from behind the helmet in several tight braids.

Despite the thick armor, her movements were silent and lithe, an impossibility made real only through magic.

Ruan's mouth gaped. He glanced from his mother to General Campos to the woman. "A Knight of Caadron?"

Besides the arcanists, the knights were the only other order entrusted with the ways of magic in the empire. This woman was one of the few who walked the Path of the Other.

The Lady Knight stopped in front of them and dipped her head in reverence. "You summoned, Consul General?"

"Take us to the palace," he said.

"Of course," she said, inflection-less.

The Lady Knight drew her broadsword, the long silver blade shimmering with ethereal radiance. An emerald gemstone glowed in the pommel.

Urla had never seen a godblade this close. The gem shone with a ferocious luminescence as the Lady Knight swung the sword in a swift arc, forming a shimmering ring of light. Mist plumed around her, as though she'd just plunged a forged blade in water.

When the mist settled, the ring of light remained, and within it was what Urla could only describe as a window in the air itself. All around was Lord General Campos's tent, but within the ring of light, was an immaculate palatial hall, lined with towering marble pillars, etched with gold filigree.

Urla's breath caught.

"Who are we going to meet?"

Campos shrugged. "We mustn't keep the Dragon Emperor waiting."

Part Three

Festival of Ascension

CHAPTER 12

FATE OF THE FALLEN

The festival began at full dark the day after the Ascension. At the top of a hill near the base of the Mountain of Souls, three pyres illuminated Kalengal Valley in a raging light.

Malik and the other surviving climbers lined up in front of the pyres, while the four Faltari clans looked on.

Three youths had fallen this year, all during the storm. In that way, it was an ordinary Ascent, but somehow, this truth offered Malik no comfort tonight.

His father raised his hands, standing in front of the newly-christened young men and women of Faltara. Fifteen survivors in all.

The valley fell silent.

With *hish* to amplify his voice, Joren addressed the Faltari people, as he did every year.

"Long ago, our ancestors made the most difficult decision anyone can make. To leave the world of their ancestors behind and create a new life. To trust the signs of the gods, even though their destination was uncharted, even though no one before had crossed through this gate."

Joren gestured up at the Spires, shadows hovering behind him.

"Our ancestors did not know what they would find on the other side. But they knew the survival of our people depended on their courageous hearts and adventurous spirits. The world had grown evil, but our people forged a new path and chose a peaceful existence on an unknown island in a strange world.

"It is true ours is no easy life. Faltara is a harsh and breathtaking land. Crops do not come without toil. Winters are long and cruel. We share this island with ancient predators, and at times, we face conflicts within.

"But the gods were wise, and they bestowed wisdom upon our ancestors. The four clans were formed to strike a balance amongst our people. Four chieftains, representing four aspects of the same Faltari heritage. All of you possess your own gifts, as do each of your clans. But each one of us comes to maturity the same way. Ever since the Crossing, it has been so. Each Ascent begins alone, but like the clans themselves, many discover how hard it is to survive without the aid of your kin."

Malik couldn't help but glance over at Aram Tulsein. The tall boy rolled his eyes at the shaman's words. Malik could imagine what the cocky young man was muttering. Aram was the First Ascendant, and he had done it all on his own.

Though, of course, that was untrue. Aram had been trained by members of his clan, like everyone else. But such balanced thinking was beyond someone like him.

"Our survival depends on the sacrifice of us all," Joren went on. "It is a lesson that can cost a life just as easily in the Spires, as anywhere else on the island. We endure nothing alone. We Faltari face all things as one people in the end. That goes for celebration, but also for mourning."

A lump formed in Malik's throat, and his chest ached. For what seemed the thousandth time in a day, he pictured Petyr's smile. There. And then simply... gone.

"Fifteen of you have survived the same dangerous Ascent we all have faced, bringing back relics from a lost world. You've gazed at the bones of our past. Glimpsed the fate of the fallen who've come before. A civilization that choked the very life out of our ancestors. And eventually, out of their own existence. Even the dragons that brought that civilization to its prominence can no longer exist there. And so we journey, once a year. To remember. To face the bitter spirits of our past."

Writhing shadows sifted through Malik's vision. Derrin. The corpses that filled that temple. The faces on the pillars.

"You have endured. You have seen our past. Now, may you lead us into the future, along the path the gods have set before us."

Malik's father paused and held up a cloth of all four clan colors, representing those who'd returned.

Joren released it into the wind, and it writhed through the air, aided by a hint of *hish*, before settling in some child's hands in the midst of the crowd—a special blessing. There was a brief exultation.

Then, Joren produced three black cloths.

"Three of our own did not return to us, a hard and necessary sacrifice, but one we never take lightly. We Faltari are no strangers to death or hardship. We do not fear it. These three Ascended with honor, and they fell, as we all shall fall, one day. May they prepare the way for us in the life to come. Tonight, they feast in the halls of Urshalla, with the gods themselves. Having fought bravely in this life."

Joren released the black cloths into the wind one at a time. Strips of fabric darted across the gathering and fell amongst them. Somewhere in the crowd, other children snatched up each of the cloths and would deliver them solemnly to each mother of the fallen.

The valley fell silent once more.

Crowds parted, forming one aisle. Kin of one of the fallen strode through the crowd, carrying a stretcher made of tribal cloth and bone-white tree limbs. A shrouded body lay upon the first stretcher.

As they neared, Malik recognized Petyr's elder brother, Davar, and his father, Elder Dannsein, head of the Saber clan. They and other family members carried the stretcher, while Petyr's mother walked before them, sprinkling white and purple petals of high mountain ruleas.

The sight sent shivers through him. Two years ago, it had been Malik carrying that stretcher. His mother and sister casting the flowers.

Torches ignited across the crowd, a sea of dancing flames and dimly-lit faces, and a soft chorus of chanting voices ushered up from the crowd.

"Elesa volonai. Menassa elonai..."

"Utlesa sheshonash. Alesa renonash..."

An ancient prayer in a tongue from the fallen world, so Malik's father said. According to Joren, its truest meaning was a reason for contention, but for the people of Faltara, it was a cry for unity and collective sorrow.

The other two fallen climbers were carried to the base of the hill at the center of the gathering. Every man, woman, and child in the valley lifted their voices.

Malik did not join them at first, though he knew the words better than any mantra in his own tongue. He looked out at his people, and then, into the darkness where the shadows of the Spires loomed.

"Elesa volonai. Menassa elonai..."

"Utlesa sheshonash. Alesa renonash..."

The gods move through us. For we are their children.

From them, we were begotten. To them, we shall return.

Malik had sung the words over the fallen every year. Until they were to be sung over the spirit of his brother.

He had not been able to bring himself to sing over Derrin's body and only mouthed the words. He'd intended to do the same now, but then, his gaze settled on Petyr's mother. Tears streaked her cheeks, and she beat her palm against her chest with each line, chanting with all the sincerity in her spirit.

Elder Dannsein kept one hand at his wife's shoulder and began to pound his chest too. And then, their other son joined. Releasing Petyr's spirit from this place. To join the Great Breath of the gods.

The foreign words overwhelmed him with a spiritual sense beyond anything Malik could explain. For the past two years, he had felt so alone in his sorrow. So alone in his despair over a shifted fate and uncertain future. Over the loss of a brother he'd butted heads with but had always loved.

In this throng, surrounded by the voices of his people, all his turmoil drifted into the heavens like their voices.

As the third body was laid to rest at the base of the hill, Malik lifted up his voice to join with his people.

"Elesa volonai. Menassa elonai..."

"Utlesa sheshonash. Alesa renonash..."

The entire song, Malik's father kept his hands raised. As the last line faded, slipping up into the misty night, Joren dropped his hands and turned to the surviving climbers.

His eyes settled on Malik, and he nodded. Malik stepped forward as they had rehearsed. Riese, Yuri, and Ulgar joined him, and they were accompanied by Lera Pelesadeil, who came from Petyr's same clan. The other survivors formed up into two more groups. Five for each fallen climber.

Malik and the others knelt at Petyr's side and bowed their heads. There was no sound but their breaths, and the *shh-shh-ing* of trees in the breeze.

Bodies were not always found. Malik did not know whether these shrouds contained the remains of Petyr at all. That was a matter for Petyr's family, and them alone. From the height he fell, Malik knew Petyr's body would be hardly recognizable. Yet, the stretcher bore a human form wrapped in layers of white cloth, not a pile of crumpled bones.

Derrin had been lost to the Abyss, and yet his stretcher had looked similar. The lie had enraged Malik before, but seeing it now, he understood the words his father had spoken countless times.

Our rituals matter, not because they are the fullness of what's true, but because they point to truth.

Malik raised his head and stood. Each of the five greeted the members of Petyr's family with an embrace. Then, they gathered once more around the stretcher. Malik looked over at his companions. Lera trembled with silent sobs. Riese bit her lip. Yuri remained expressionless. Ulgar nodded to Malik, a lone tear trickling down his sharp features.

Malik nodded to them.

They stooped and lifted the stretcher. It was heavy, but manageable, and together, they strode back up the hill, raised the stretcher above their heads, and heaved Petyr Bromsein's remains into the central pyre.

Flames rushed into the heavens.

Chapter 13

Your Own Way

"You did well today, son."

"You've said that..."

Malik followed his father deeper through the crypt tunnels that weaved beneath the Mountain of Souls. The tunnels were woven with threads of *hish,* which glowed with an icy luminescence. All through the mountain, the magic veins allowed just enough light to navigate without the aid of a torch.

From the front entrance at the center of the valley, the cavern walls were also lined with narrow intermittent shelves, carved straight into the stone. This far down, most remained empty. Further up the tunnels, each box-like shelf contained a clay urn with the ashes of Faltari ancestors, the space decorated with items important to the deceased. The urns themselves told their stories in a series of pictographic inscriptions.

There was no rhyme or reason to the order of the shelves. Shamans chose the location, usually with the intent of separating each deceased person from their bloodlines.

In death, there are no families, no clans, Malik had been taught. *This is the final reminder.*

Faltari families were not laid to rest together as in other corners of the world. For similar reasons, the shamans held no clan identities, which was why Malik had not been marked by a fresh tattoo of jackal claws the night before the Ascent. A shaman's true and ultimate allegiance was only to the gods.

None but the elders and the shamans visited these crypts, except to prepare the internment shelf on the day of burial.

Up the tunnel, Malik could hear the murmurings of Petyr's family. They were the last family in the crypts, and Joren had elected to give them space to mourn.

The crypts glowed brighter the deeper the shamans descended into the heart of the mountain.

"I mean it, son," Joren said, pausing to turn to him. "I'm deeply proud of you."

Malik glanced away. His father's face was painted. Dark wells of ink splotched around his eyes. Slashes of blue graced his cheeks and the shaved sides of his head. It was custom for a shaman, but Malik had always hated looking into those dark wells since he was a child.

Next year, his face would be thus painted as well. And all the years after. Somehow, everything about this realization felt like an immense weight. As though his destiny were closing in around him, pressing down like the mountain above, walls collapsing and crushing him under the pressure.

His father's hand on his shoulder jolted him out of his thoughts.

"Even death is a lesson, Malik."

"Everything's a lesson to you," he murmured. "Nothing more than an excuse to me. To soften the blow from the exact result we should expect for sending our youth up the Spires every year. These deaths are a curse we bring on ourselves."

His father scowled, the whites of his eyes feeling specter-like against the dark rings decorating his face.

Joren sighed. "Come."

They descended further into the mountain. Malik knew where they were going, and the dread creeped in as they neared.

The burial tunnels wended down, growing brighter and brighter before reaching a door made of stone, etched in ancient runes. A language from that dead world, just like the dirge their people sang.

Joren uttered words in the ancient tongue as he pressed his right palm against the stone.

"*Melana esso tanai.*" Joren issued a soft pulse of *hish* as he uttered the spell.

The stone groaned, and Joren pressed firmly with both palms. The door shifted open, grinding against the floor of the chamber.

A flood of brilliant light ushered forth. So bright, it took Malik several moments, even with the aid of *hish*, to adjust his vision.

The floor of the room beyond was blanketed with threads of magic, drawing from the heart of the mountain toward the center of the space, where a coalescence of magic formed in a pool of ethereal mist. Malik could feel the warm presence of spirit resonances all around the chamber of the Spirit Realm.

All the caverns behind were frigid, but here, Malik grew flushed in his cloak. Joren led the way across the chamber, removing his thick shaman's cloak, and then his shirt. His father's back was covered in paint —symbols of the clans, runic incantations, transcriptions from the books of the Ancients.

There was much Malik had yet to learn about all the rites that surrounded the Festival of the Ascension. Next year.

Malik removed his own cloak, and together, father and son stood at the edge of the pool.

"You're right, son," Joren said.

"About what?"

"Of course we ask for this. We choose to send our children up the Spires. We choose to send them to a dead world. What it means to us is also a choice."

"It feels like nothing more than a needless sacrifice. Like the heathens from that dead world slaughtering their children in great wars."

"It is a sacrifice, but it is also a lesson. Because that is the perspective our people chose long ago."

"Even Derrin," Malik said. "Even *his* death was a lesson?"

Joren gestured toward the pool. "Why don't you find out, son?"

Malik crossed his arms, a lump in his chest. He hadn't been here since Derrin died. He knew what his father wanted of him, but he was not sure he could do it.

"He's waited a long time," Joren said. "I haven't pressed you.

Everyone must face loss in their own way. But you're hurting, son. And I think he may offer you some comfort."

"We both know it might not even be him."

"I've visited your brother on two occasions. Whether it is his spirit, or a manifestation of my own... it is no less sacred."

Malik released his clenched fists and took a long breath. His mind was in turmoil. He knew his father was right, and yet, even that truth was shrouded in anger and frustration, and Malik didn't know why.

He drew another long inhalation and slowly released it, attempting to ease the tension in his body as best he could.

Joren patted his shoulder.

And Malik removed his fur-lined boots and stepped into the ethereal pool.

It was wet. Warm. A well fed from deep in the heart of the mountain. But it was more than water.

A rush of light surged through the mist. Magic swirled around him, filled with resonances of ancestral spirits. The subtle vibrations of *hish* that he'd learned to recognize hummed with a soft and steady cadence. Like waves beating the shore or the crackle of fire. Despite the fact that all of them were dead, Malik was struck by the realization that all these spirits were at peace. No anger or bitterness surged in this place.

Striving is the stuff of life, he thought. *What awaits is peace.*

His father had taught him these words when his grandmother passed from the world. He had emphasized them again when Derrin fell.

No one knows what awaits, Malik thought.

But in the warm presence of the resonances surrounding him, the thought drifted away. His body relaxed, and then, all at once. The mists parted around him, forming a space. One resonance drew close.

Malik recognized that vibrant spiritual thrum immediately.

A face appeared from the mist, formed of visible manifestations of the breath of the gods.

Derrin beamed at him, his face a dim reflection of the striking young man he'd been in life.

"I think your Ascent may have been even more exciting than mine, little brother."

Malik tensed at the voice, reminding himself that this might not be

Derrin's resonance at all. Spirits were mysterious, even devious, as he'd seen in the Abyss. But it sounded just like him. Felt just like him.

Malik couldn't hold back a smile. "I'd have taken a boring Ascent, I think."

"Ah, but that wouldn't have made for a good story. You did well, Mal. I'm proud. We all are."

"All?" said Malik.

Derrin's smile widened.

Malik shrugged, knowing he'd get no straight answers from specters.

"You did all you could," Derrin said. "There is never shame in that."

"Even when it's not enough?"

"No amount of striving is ever enough. It takes death to understand the beauty in that."

Malik huffed. "You sound like Father."

"I did train with him for many years."

Malik looked away, suddenly jolted back to the unrest churning inside him.

"I know why you haven't come down here," Derrin said. "I can't say I blame you. I put you in a bit of a... precarious situation. Dying and everything."

Malik couldn't help himself. It was so like Derrin to make a joke, even about his own death. The mists swirled with the mirth of their laughter.

"I know it's been hard on you," said Derrin. "You were never supposed to be shaman. And then, you were. But you showed your mettle today, little brother. The way you helped Petyr in the Abyss. Ulgar on the bridge of vines."

"You could see all that?"

"Resonances," said Derrin.

"You can see us in the Abyss? Even Father can't do that."

"Father is still striving. Much wisdom comes with death. It is no tragedy."

Malik grimaced, shifting his feet and stirring up the mist.

"You don't have to be like me, you know," said Derrin. "Or like Father. You'll find your own way to serve our people."

The words washed over Malik. Mist swirled and slowly evaporated, and he could feel Derrin's resonance slipping away, joining the throng of others in the crypts. Leaving a lingering ache of absence.

Malik didn't move for some time.

His brother had struck at the core of his anger and frustration, and yet, Malik had trained as a shaman for the past two years, and he did not see how his brother could be right.

Malik longed for the Jackal claws etched into his forearms, just like Riese and Yuri. He longed for more than prayers and healings and tending to the dead.

The Ascent had dredged this awareness back to the surface. The thrill of the climb, battles with jackals and dragyrs, fleeing from wights of the Abyss. Even the storm itself, though terrifying, had been exhilarating.

His one and only adventure was done.

And now...

Joren's hand clasped his shoulder. "Petyr's family has finished their burial preparations. I think they would find comfort if you conducted the final rites."

Malik took a long breath, part of him wanting to refuse.

But just as he had during his Ascent, he knew he must be more.

CHAPTER 14

OATHBOUND

The Festival of Ascension always left Joren feeling bitterly torn.
Ceremonies went on for two more days. Once the fallen were interred, the Ascension became a blissful celebration. Every clan gathered the finest from their respective harvests—potatoes and berries, shellfish and pikes, stags and groundlings.

Village bards recounted Ascents of the past with thrilling embellishments. Mead flowed from barrels in abundance, followed by long nights of dancing and contests.

It was a jester's bet around the island guessing how many children would be conceived as a result of the festivities, as well as how many injuries would occur. Mostly from the wild hunts that arose after the consumption of a certain herbal concoction known as *sintash*, which dulled the sense of fear and pain, and sent hunters on one of the most thrilling chases of their lives.

It, like many of the other festivities that accompanied Ascension, was a ritual Joren had always cringed at, but which his own father and grandfather and all the shamans that had come before had insisted was necessary to maintain peace on the Isle of Faltara.

There was plenty of infighting among the clans the rest of the year, but the joy found during the Ascension provided unity. It lowered barriers, formed unbreakable bonds. Dragyr clansmen fought alongside

Serpents for the hides of stags and sometimes even bears. Jackal kin bore children with Sabers. And the Faltari were reminded that they remained one people, despite the year's poor harvests on the western side of the island, despite territorial disputes over hunting grounds, and the inevitable conflicts that incurred over a thief or harlot from one clan or another.

The Ascension was an annual reminder of what they'd left in the world before, and why they'd chosen their secluded life on this island in the first place. In other corners of the world, nations slaughtered one another over such disputes, but here on the Isle of Faltara, they had found another way to exist. When this festival was done, they would leave these mountains, and the outside world would be welcomed for the Festival of the Fading Sun, days of feasting and trading at the port village of Yerida.

There, the Faltari would be unified one last time before a swift autumn turned to a long and cruel winter. As one people, they would welcome foreigners and trade for tools and southern grains.

On occasion, one of their own chose to sail off with some charismatic trader, to see the world. It was common enough, the ritual was given a name—*uhmskara*.

The Wandering.

But within a year or two, the youths almost always returned. The outside world was never as sweet as they imagined. Joren knew this all too well, for he had once gone on a Wandering of his own, after his Ascension.

But that felt like a lifetime ago.

Joren kept close to Madri through the final days of the festival, both of them keeping a keen eye on Surel, who had blossomed into a young woman since the last festival—overnight, it seemed to Joren—and more than one of the village boys had taken a sudden attraction to her.

Since the funeral rites, Joren had seen little of his son, and he kept reminding himself this was normal for a boy just come of age. Surely, no different than any of the other young men and women of the island. But no matter how he tried, he felt a growing distance from Malik. In his spirit. Much like he'd once felt for his own shaman father.

A sense that had been growing steadily since Derrin's death, like a fishing boat trawling peacefully beyond the fjord, until suddenly, you realized the shore had drifted out of sight.

All through the ceremonies, bodies passed Joren like ships on dark seas. Resonances flashing in his spiritual sight. Voices echoing across great distances.

A shaman's role was minimal during the heart of the festival, and at times, Joren's existence felt anchored by little more than exchanges of pleasantries.

Perhaps it was the necessity of a shaman, but for so long, Joren had felt like a soul set adrift amongst his people, tethered to a body that was not his own. And some part of him felt certain it needn't be this way.

There was an inherent separateness unavoidable for his role, sure, but he was also more vital and connected than most others on the island could ever imagine. For Joren shared a spiritual connection with them.

But with that connection came knowledge. Joren, more than any other—even more than the village chieftains—had peered behind the curtains, understood what made his people who they were. And the weight of it pressed upon him.

As the festival whirled around him in bursts of joy and color and song, Joren could not shake a feeling of brokenness and failure. Even his own children felt separate now.

If not for Madri, Joren felt sure he would lose himself to the spirit realms.

Just when he felt like he might slip away, always she would usher him back with some comment. A warm squeeze of the hand, pulling him into a conversation with an old friend of his mother's. Pointing to laugh as a Saber boy's awkward attempt at flirtation sailed right over the head of their oblivious young daughter. Drawing his attention as the sun dipped behind the Spires and fiery colors radiated across the skies.

Each moment warded off the dread of the rites to come at the close of the festival.

————

Horns bellowed across the valley, and Malik waited at the back of the crowd, joy, triumph, and melancholy churning in his spirit.

On the final night of the festival, the Ascendant were paraded once more before the four clans. Torches lit up the mountain valley in myriad colors, burning a special powder reserved only for the sacred dragon ceremonies. Flames of indigo and emerald and magenta cast the sea of faces in a magical light, every color and sound intended to magnify the brilliance of what each climber presented.

Little boys and girls from every clan paraded first, waving banners and twirling ribbons. When they reached the crest of the knoll at the base of the Mountains of Souls, they released the cloths, with a soft rush of *hish*.

Dancers followed. Then, more horns. And then, the Ascendant strode through the crowd to the beat of drums.

For the past several days, their dragon eggs had been stowed in a sacred chest, guarded at all times.

With the festival's many distractions, the entire ordeal in the Spires had begun to feel like a dream for Malik. Until his fingers brushed over the thick ridges of emerald once more. The dragon scales caught the light and flashed like prisms as the climbers made their way through the crowd.

The clan elders greeted each Ascendant as they crested the hill. Flames from a single towering pyre shot into the skies behind them, dancing and crackling, while drumbeats thundered and echoed off the walls of the secluded valley.

Aram Tulsein reached the elders first and held his dark blue egg aloft, eliciting cheers across the valley. Then, he took his place standing before the pyre, facing the clans.

"Get ready, son," Joren murmured.

They were to bring up the rear of the procession.

In his hands, Malik sensed a soft resonance emanating from within the shell of hollow stone, and he could not suppress a swell of sadness. He had not accessed his true sight since he'd returned from his Ascent— ever since he'd begun shaman training, the spiritual awareness felt overwhelming in such crowds. Reaching for it now, the weight of this final ceremony pressed on his spirit.

Dormant for centuries, Malik knew without doubt there was life inside this egg. Even in the Abyss, he'd sensed the dragon's spirit.

Riese and Yuri marched ahead of him, walking with the other Ascendant of the Jackal clan.

Joren nodded to him.

Malik held a deep breath, released, and set out in front of the crowd, his dragon egg held at chest level. He'd spent the afternoon scrubbing and polishing the emerald scales. Up close, they contained more colors, and the shell refracted the torchlight with breathtaking brilliance. Malik felt the gaze of the crowd as though it were something physical. He held his head high and forced himself to focus only on the joy in his spirit. His mother and sister stood near the front of the crowd, beaming with smiles as he passed, and he found himself smiling in spite of himself.

As he summited the hill, horns blared one last time, and the valley went silent. Malik bowed a greeting to each elder, and then lastly, he bowed to his father.

Malik held his egg above his head and the final chorus of cheers resounded across the valley.

Joren, dressed in the colors of all four clans, held up his hands, and the people quietened.

"The life we share on this island is beautiful," Joren began. It was a similar speech every year. "But this life has not come without sacrifice. It is a truth the world over that you can never fully appreciate something until it is gone. It is this truth that lies at the heart of the Ascension ceremony. To remember where we came from. To recall what was left behind, and the life we formed anew. And perhaps most importantly, to remember what we forsake to maintain this peaceful existence.

"The outside world is not so different from that dead world we left behind. Beyond our shores, empires rise and fall. Nations slaughter one another over arbitrary borders. Dragon riders destroy ships and armies, entire villages. In the days to come, we will welcome emissaries from many shores. It is important we do not forget that this world is not ours alone. But tonight marks the way in which we are different. We do not live this life of peace by accident. It is a choice. To forsake the darkness and embrace the light. Our Ascendant have again faced that darkness, and they have returned braver and wiser for it. They have tested themselves. Now, let their sacrifice be complete."

Malik's gut twisted as Aram Tulsein stepped forward one last time. Malik had never seen a living dragon. There were few on the island who had, but he had heard tales of the riders of the Attican Empire. He could imagine one of the dragyrs he'd faced during his Ascent, and picture them five or ten times that size. Even the thought filled him with terror and awe. But he could not deny that part of him longed to see it. That wished this last rite of passage didn't have to be performed. Malik could feel a similar turmoil in the spirits of most of his fellow Ascendant.

But Aram stepped forward without hesitation. He held his dark blue egg aloft and spoke the words they'd all heard every year, all their lives.

"I do not long for an easy life. I choose a sacred path. I am Faltari. A child of the Flame. And may the world be brighter for our burning."

Aram turned to the raging pyre behind the Ascendant and hurled his dragon egg into the flames.

The blaze engulfed the egg. For several seconds, nothing happened. Aram stood before the pyre, studying the flames with his hands slack at his sides. Then, a surge of dark blue shot into the air.

Horns blared across the valley, and the Faltari cheered at the destruction of the dragon—the most powerful weapon in the world.

Aram turned to the villagers and recited the final words.

"I have seen the destruction of the worlds of old. And I turn from it. I am a Watcher at the edge of the world. A descendant of the gods. May I burn rather than betray the secrets of my people."

From the flames a surge of *hish* burst forth. It was not visible, but Malik could sense the magic, as Aram was bound to his oath.

Aram looked down at the tattoos on his wrist. The wings of the sacred Dragyr glowed with a fiery light, and his Ascension was complete.

He pumped his fist, grinning.

Malik's heart ached. He gripped his egg tighter, the resonance within suddenly overwhelming, as though it were reaching for him. Pleading.

Ulgar stepped forward and continued the ritual. One by one, the Ascendant completed their sacrifice. Plumes of purples and reds and oranges exploded from the flames as the eggs were destroyed. Oaths seared themselves into the skin of each young Faltari woman and man.

Yuri stepped forward and completed the deed and recited the oath.

And then, Riese.

Malik sensed her hesitation as she stepped up to the pyre. Her ability to hold fierce tenacity and ambition alongside compassion had always impressed Malik. Riese did not even visibly pause, but as she stepped toward the flames, Malik felt the hitch in her spirit. A lone tear trickled down her cheek.

But she, too, cast her egg into the flames.

Now, it was Malik's turn, and for a moment, he allowed his mind to entertain a scenario.

According to Faltari legend, not long after the Crossing, one young shaman named Rayne Seversein had refused the oaths, had stolen a batch of eggs, and left the island seeking power and fame. Some claimed he went on to found the Attican Empire, after a fraught journey across this new world.

Malik had no idea if this was history or legend. How had Rayne managed the incantations to hatch the eggs if no one else knew about dragons?

But it didn't matter. Suddenly, Malik understood why the man might have been so compelled. In his mind, he imagined himself fleeing, journeying the breadth of the world in search of the proper spells, perhaps finding some old hag with ancient tomes from the dead world, hatching the egg, tending to the dragon as it grew from a hatchling to a beast capable of snatching stags up in a dive, to a fire-breathing behemoth capable of destroying entire armies. He pictured himself returning to Faltara on dragonback and running off with a following of other descendants of the gods.

Malik the warrior. The leader. The world shaker.

His vision shrouded in flames, and he was jolted back to reality, to the egg in his hands, which he knew he must destroy.

He closed his eyes, then, met his father's gaze. Joren nodded at him, eyes dark holes of black paint, hair braided with the tiny bones of all four of the sacred beasts of Faltara.

Malik shuddered at the thoughts that had nearly overtaken him. He stepped forward, reminded, as he knew was intended, that power and glory was a temptation they all must overcome. Malik ignored the resonance in the shell between his hands and approached the pyre.

Searing heat pressed against his face, making his eyes water. He drew back, suppressing the screams in his mind, and hurled the egg into the flames.

CHAPTER 15

TRAPPED

The Ascension celebrations continued late into the night. As the dragon pyre burned down to embers, the people of Faltara danced and drank and feasted. The pain of the sacrifice still lingered in Malik's spirit, despite the joy surrounding him.

Not pain over what happened to his dragon egg so much as the cost of bringing the eggs here. Petyr and his brother and uncle, and all the other Faltari youths who had died over the years.

"Come on!" Yuri shouted, pulling him into a circle of dancers. Malik's hand was suddenly pressed into the palm of a Feathered Serpent girl two years his junior. "Have fun like the old days, Malik!"

The girl's fingers were slender and warm, and her smile shone bright in the colored torchlight. Her cheeks turned red, but she held his gaze and smiled. Long blonde braids were tied behind her head with blue ribbons.

The dancing circle shifted directions, and the girl tugged him along after her.

Yuri clasped his other hand, stumbling, because his gaze was so fixed on the Saber girl behind him. A fellow Ascendant he'd been flirting with all night. The dance shifted again, and they broke out into partners.

Malik had never been a great dancer. After a couple foolhardy moves, his partner pulled him close and whispered, "Just follow my lead, shaman. Okay?"

Not shaman's son, Malik thought.

The girl shifted, soft hands pressing against his own, her movements turning his hips, and his feet followed. The two of them broke apart, and she twirled, the feathers of her blue dress flashing in resplendent colors, and then, she was back. And Malik felt warm all over.

Have fun like the old days!

He knew Yuri was right. Three years ago, they'd danced till sunrise. Malik's moves had been no better, but he hadn't cared. It had been fun, and that was all that mattered. That night, Malik had kissed a girl for the first time—a spritely Saber girl—and Yuri had found out the hard way that Riese was not into him. Or any other boy.

Yuri was howling with laughter nearby. Malik guessed he'd had half a dozen ales by now, and even for a husky young man, Malik expected his friend would be collapsed at the edge of the ring any minute.

Riese danced with a young Dragyr woman who'd Ascended last year. She had dark hair and icy blue eyes.

The Feathered Serpent girl guided Malik through the remainder of the song, then, the music picked up, and everyone began alternating partners, locking arms briefly and twirling, then, carrying on around the circle. Malik always had a hard time keeping up with the transitions of these types of dances. Everyone seemed to know when to pause or twirl or spin their partner or change partners, and he found himself freezing up.

He exchanged a couple awkward dances before partnering with Riese. She winked at him.

"She's cute," said Riese, pulling him toward her. She shifted their arms over his head and slid them back out again, ending with a clap, before drawing close again.

Malik shrugged, fighting a blush. "Yours too."

Riese glanced away, and Malik sensed a shift in her spirit, though she remained smiling.

They stepped back, then pressed together, and Riese whispered in his ear. "Enjoy yourself, shaman. After the past two years, you deserve it."

Partners shifted again, and the Feathered Serpent girl was back.

At last the music slowed, and the girl drew closer. Malik could feel the warmth of her presence and her resonance was even stronger.

The top of her head barely reached his chin, despite Malik's altogether average height. Her full cheeks were ruddy, blonde braids damp at her temples, and her chest heaved from the exertion. She smiled up at him.

"You dance alright," she said, still leading the slow dance. "But I think you're a better climber."

Malik blushed. "I don't know about that."

"It was brave what you did, Malik," she insisted, as though she'd watched it.

"Er, thanks, uh..." Malik realized he'd never asked her name.

"Syrese," she said. "We met at the festival three years ago."

"Oh, right," said Malik, not remembering. "I, er, thought you looked familiar."

"You were distracted that night," she said with a wink. "And I was still a kid, then. I didn't expect you to remember me."

Sometimes Malik hated how small the island was.

Syrese pulled close, then pushed away and spun left, then right, and he followed her movements, before settling in together again.

"Well, you're no kid now," he said, instantly wishing he would have thought of something better.

"Thanks," Syrese whispered, pressing close again. Her cheek nestled into his chest. "I think you're brave, risking your life that way. After the past two... well, no one would have blamed you if you'd just looked out for yourself. My mum says that's the mark of a good shaman."

Malik drew back a little.

"What?" she asked.

The others danced around them, but Malik had stopped.

"Sorry, it's just..."

"You can't ignore the darkness, right?" she recited. "We move through it together." Syrese interlaced her fingers with his.

Malik pulled back, creating space between them.

"What's wrong?" Her bottom lip quivered.

"I don't want to talk about the Ascent, Syrese."

"Is it me?"

"Er, what?"

"I might not be some wild huntress like Riese Torendeil, but..."

Malik rolled his eyes. "It's not that, and besides, Riese—"

Syrese's hands were at her hips. "Then what? I'm not pretty enough for you?"

"No," Malik said, bewildered. "You're very cute, I just—"

"Cute? I'm *not* a bloody child, shaman!"

"I literally just—"

"Just too young for a brand new Ascendant, am I?"

"God's breath," Malik said. "You're very pretty, is what I meant."

A tear streamed down the girl's cheek, and then, as though catching herself, her face contorted, lips pursing. Syrese stepped forward and shoved him in the chest.

Malik stumbled back, nearly tripping over a dancing couple. "Look, maybe, we should just..."

"You have no idea how lucky you almost were, shaman!"

With that, she stormed away, leaving Malik alone, couples twirling around him. Nearby, Yuri shook his head, laughing.

Malik hurried from the dance circle, weaved his way amidst the torch-lined lanes, past tents spilling dreamsmoke, past a group of laughing old men gathered drunkenly round a small barrel of imported *szaka.*

He reached the edge of the festival and kept going, until the grass grew long, and Malik was wading through it thigh-high. He reached the top of a hill and took a seat beneath a broad-limbed socha tree. From here, the Spires loomed at the edge of the valley. He could see the entire festival to his right, and to his left, the vast rim of mountains that formed the spine of the island.

Nothing could match the view from the top of the Spires, but this was one of his favorite places on the island, looking out on the whole valley.

Red leaves were just beginning to fall, and as he sat, a few drifted out over the valley, slipping from the fingers of the long and twisting limbs. Malik turned from the festivities and gazed up at the stars, swirls of light brushing across the indigo sky like dyes.

Women remained a mystery to him. Malik could only sit and marvel at how quickly his encounter with Syrese had turned from flirting to floundering. How suddenly he'd felt like the girl was suffocating him, pulling him into the maelstrom of a writhing past and an inevitable future.

"That went well."

Malik turned to find Riese cresting the hill toward him. The shaved side of her head was painted with the claw marks of the Jackal clan, and her face had been dusted with a cosmetic that made her pale skin shimmer. She shook her head and chuckled as she neared.

"I believe I told you to enjoy yourself."

Malik shrugged. "Who says I'm not?"

"Heh, fair enough," said Riese. "Can I sit? Or are you enjoying yourself by yourself?"

"You could phrase that better."

Riese grinned. "If I wanted to..."

He rolled his eyes.

"Okay, fine," she said. "Would you rather be alone, Malik?"

"No, you can—"

But Riese was already plopping down in the grass beside him. "Wanna talk about it?"

"Syrese?" Malik said with a laugh. "No."

"And the reason for you running away from a cute girl who was definitely into you?"

"Cute, that was the whole problem. Thanks for that, by the way."

"Huh?"

"Never mind. What about *your* dancing partner?" Malik asked.

Riese shrugged. "Oh, Lysa's just fine."

Malik had noticed them pair off last year as well, and he knew he ought to inquire further, but he didn't really want to talk about dancing and partners any more.

Riese turned to him, holding his gaze. "You're still one of my best friends, Malik. Even now that you're shaman. I hope you know that."

"I do."

"Yuri feels the same way, even though he'd just make it some joke. We've missed you."

"I'm not a hunter anymore," said Malik. "Not even part of the clan any—"

"Things change. That's life. Doesn't mean they can't change together."

Malik nodded. Words only meant so much. The reality was that Malik would serve all the clans. He wasn't a Jackal anymore. Riese would be a hunter for the clan, like Malik had planned to be. Yuri would plow fields and tend crops on Jackal lands. And sure, Malik would be around. He'd preside over their weddings, bless their children, tend their fallen kin, but he would be set apart. His father had no real friends besides his mother.

And why couldn't Derrin have just bloody stayed alive?

They sat in silence for several minutes. But with friends like Riese, it was comfortable.

"I've hardly slept all week," Riese said eventually. He looked over. Here alone, she'd quit smiling, quit putting on a front. She looked exhausted.

"Really?" Malik asked. "The climb? The wights?"

"Yeah..." she said. "Must be..."

Riese never finished her thought, and the silence stretched again.

"I haven't slept much either," Malik said. "It's not just Petyr. I mean, I'm sorry he died. But I didn't know him that well, and deep down, I know there's nothing more I could have done."

"Then... what is it?" Riese asked.

"It's... everything. Becoming shaman, my brother, my father, this damn island."

Riese chuckled. "You ran away from Syrese because of your father and the island?"

Malik sighed. "I feel trapped. Like I'm still up there in that storm huddled against the wind, waiting for everything to let up, but it won't. This is my life now. Funerals and ceremonies and tending spirits. And... it's not me, Riese. You know it's not."

Riese scooted closer. Then, punched him in the shoulder.

"Ow! What was that for?"

"You think I don't know what all that feels like? To have to pretend to be something I'm not?"

"That wasn't—"

"Of course it wasn't what you meant. Because you didn't even think about that. My parents don't know who I really am. They think Lysa is just a friend from another clan. And even if they did know, it wouldn't matter. Do you know what they were doing while you were off tending spirits?"

Malik shook his head, a sinking feeling in his gut.

"Introducing me to my match," Riese said.

"Oh... er, who is it?"

"Vinder Perinsein. Ascended last year."

"I know him. They didn't ask for your input?"

"Sure, they did. What was I supposed to say, Malik? Vinder's a fine hunter. A good man. And I'm meant to carry on the damn bloodline. Bear kids, preserve the ways of the island."

Malik looked into her eyes and shook his head. "I'm sorry, Riese. I didn't..."

Riese laid her head on his shoulder and sighed. "You're not the only one who feels trapped, Malik. I knew this was coming, and I just... couldn't say anything. Not to my father. And maybe I don't know what I want, okay? Me and Lysa had fun, but it's never been anything outside the festivals.... I wish I didn't have to figure it out already. We just bloody came of age. And ever since we got back... I don't know..."

"Yeah..."

"When I was up on top of the Spires, looking out at the world beyond, all I could think was how I wished I could sail away from this place. And when I cast my egg into the fire... I felt like I was throwing away that chance for good."

Malik glanced away from her, feeling ashamed at his self-absorption the past few days. The past two years. "I've felt the same way."

"I know," said Riese.

"Is that why you came up here?"

"I came to be with my friend," Riese said, her head still on his shoulder. Malik wrapped his arm around her, and they sat like that for a long time. The music began to quieten in the valley below.

For a moment, Malik envisioned them running away on *uhmskara* just like his father. Sailing to Beirus or Valgland, maybe even Attica. Seeing for themselves why their ancestors had chosen to remain on the island while all the other peoples who passed through the Gate of the Ancients during the Crossing had sailed off and formed new civilizations, new nations, and forgot about where they'd come from.

And why shouldn't they go on a Wandering?

Malik's father was healthy and still had plenty of time to serve their people. Surel wouldn't Ascend for several more years.

Maybe the island would need him one day, but not now.

A cold wind rose up from the valley below, and both of them shivered, neither wearing their fur winter cloaks. It had been a warm evening, but autumn could be deceptive, especially in the Kalengal peaks.

Malik glanced at Riese. She was not watching the festival but gazing up at the Spires.

Tomorrow, they would venture out of the valley to the coastal village of Yerida, for the Festival of the Fading Sun. And after that, both their futures would unfold as their parents intended.

Unless...

"We should go back, shouldn't we?" Riese said.

Malik nodded, though he didn't want to. Silently, they strode down the hill back to the encampment. Most of their people had turned in or were gathered around dwindling fires.

"You know," said Riese, "usually I'm glad to leave by the end of the festival. Tired of the cold nights and the threat of jackals. Excited to see the traders and feel the warm air again. But right now, I wish we had more time."

Again, that hitch in her spirit. Something she wanted to say. Something she was—

"Malik, there you are!"

He turned to find Surel bounding toward him, her dark grey dress fluttering behind her. Her lips formed a strange grin.

"Father's been looking for you for hours!" she said, giggling. "He's *not* happy, and when he hears you were running off with Riese Torendeil when you had duties to attend—"

"What duties?" said Malik.

Chapter 16

Truths Unspeakable

Malik and his father walked to the edge of the Faltari encampment and ascended the hill where the dragon pyre had long since dwindled.

Together, they hauled a pair of engraved wooden chests in a small wagon. The chests were covered in ancient runes and contained urns for gathering ashes of the dragon eggs, just as Malik's people would gather the cremated remains of one of their island kin. But for the dragons, it was a ritual that belonged to the shamans alone.

The valley had gone silent. No tents were erected within at least one hundred yards, and Joren and Malik were alone. They retrieved long metal rods and began shifting the smoldering remnants of logs away from the center of the pyre.

Malik was glad for the effort. His cloak was thin, and his skin pricked with shivers. Even the coals were barely warm any longer.

"I'm sorry it's so late, Father," Malik murmured.

Joren shook his head. They worked together to move a particularly large log. "The ritual is always late, but I must remind you, you have duties that surpass any other matter now. Whether it be a festival, or something personal."

"Father?"

"You were with Riese, were you not?" Joren's face was solemn.

Malik rolled his eyes. "She's a friend, nothing more."

"Yes, I know," Joren said. "Like a sister. I expect you've always been closer to Riese than your own sister. And I know you'd never speak of it, out of respect for your friend's privacy, but as shaman, we sense much about our people, like when someone's words and actions do not match the timbre of their spirit."

"Yeah?"

"All of us must sort through such things to some extent. Learning to navigate the treacherous shores of duty and family and one's desires. It always requires balance and often sacrifice. Certainly, I had to learn this when I was your age."

Malik's father had never spoken of his journey to the outside world, but Malik knew that was what he was hinting at.

"For Riese, I think it's a little different."

Joren patted him on the shoulder and smiled. "Yes, I believe you're right. And for you?"

Malik heaved at one more large cinder and moved it aside. He could feel only slight warmth through his leather boots.

Surely, his father sensed something had been off with him since his Ascent. Since his brother's death, truly. Was he acknowledging it? Speaking against the thoughts Malik entertained?

"What do you want from me, Father?"

Joren sighed. "I want you to find your way."

"Why did you run away after your Ascent? Why did you come back? Why don't you ever talk about it?"

Joren traded his pick for a wooden shovel. "Bring an urn, would you?"

Malik sighed and stepped out of the ashes, shifting the latch and opening the first runemarked chest. It was empty. He opened the second and found the urns. Each one had been fashioned to look just like each of the dragon eggs retrieved during the Ascent. The clay makers from the Feathered Serpents were especially adept with dyes. At the top was Aram Tulsein's dark blue urn. Malik retrieved it and, with a twist at the center, the clay egg opened. It was remarkable how similar the urns were in size and weight to the original eggs they replicated.

Joren scooped a small shovelful of ash, and Malik closed up the egg and set it in the empty chest.

So the process went for several more eggs. Removing the urns from one chest, placing a small scoop of ash within, and replacing the urns in the other chest. When the time came for Malik's own emerald urn, he felt only a dim sense of melancholy.

Neither he nor his father spoke as they performed the rites. Tomorrow, each climber would inter their egg in the crypts beneath the Mountain of Souls, and they would journey back down the passes to Yerida.

Malik set his own clay egg in the second chest and reached for another urn.

When he turned, his father had stopped digging. Joren stooped in the ash and motioned Malik over. At first, he thought his father had struck a rock at the base of the pyre. Joren brushed at the stone with a bare hand, exposing the soft ridges of dark blue scales.

It was Aram Tulsein's egg.

Joren pointed to another spot beneath a pair of crossed cinders, and Malik stooped, heart racing. He brushed away the ash, revealing crimson scales.

Riese's egg.

The scales were shimmering with a light they'd not possessed before. A faint inner glow.

He looked to his father.

"Th-the eggs... they don't truly burn?"

Joren hesitated. "Most of them are destroyed. Most of these eggs could never have been hatched, left dormant for too long perhaps. But there are always one or two that survive the flames. It is how dragon eggs have always been tested, I expect. Tomorrow we will take the urns to the crypts, as we always do."

Malik drew a long breath. His chest tightened, as though the air had suddenly grown thin.

"You asked why I left the island," Joren murmured. "I left because I learned an unspeakable truth. One I could never share until this moment. Until it became yours to bear as well."

"What truth?" Malik demanded.

Joren picked up Aram's egg and set it in front of the chests upon the fading grass. Malik did the same with Riese's egg. Joren shifted away an ember with a grunt at the heat, then stooped and retrieved one more egg.

"A third survivor," Joren said. "That is especially rare."

A golden one. Malik recognized it from the ceremony. Petyr Bromsein's egg, cast into the pyre by his father. It had survived not only the flames, but the fall from the Spires as well, and now, a soft luminescence permeated its scales. Joren set it with the others, then picked up the urn that looked like Petyr's egg.

"I left because I learned the true reason for the Ascent," Joren said. "The reason we send our youths to the Abyss. Yes, it is about confronting our past, how we came to be set apart from the rest of the world. But we shamans know the full truth. The eggs are not all destroyed. Some survive, with the possibility of being bonded and hatched."

Joren began to fill the urn that looked like Petyr's egg and set it with the others. Joren handed Riese's urn to Malik and took up Aram's for himself.

Malik looked down, his gut wrenching. Riese's dragon lived. With the potential to be bonded. And tomorrow morning, she would lay her urn to rest just like the others, an inexplicable turmoil gnawing at her spirit as it had tonight.

Joren placed the three surviving eggs into a rough-hewn sack.

"What is done with the eggs that survive, Father?"

There was a tremor in Malik's voice. Anger, confusion, and even more resentment. Before he voiced the question, he already knew the answer.

The life his people had always known, their isolation, their piety and peace and superior simplicity compared with all the rest of the world, and...

All of it is bullshit, Malik thought bitterly.

CHAPTER 17

DUTY

Yerida, the lone seaport of Faltara was located at the end of a narrow fjord on the southwestern side of the island. Joren suspected it had been built there, centuries ago, for its defensibility.

The sheer cliff faces that lined the entrance to the fjord made the passing slow and vulnerable for an invading ship to navigate. There were other possible landing points on the island, but sea dragons and icebergs made the northern passage too treacherous. To reach any other Faltari settlements required anchoring far out from the dangerous shoals that lined the majority of the southern coastline, then marching across unfamiliar mountains filled with jackals and sabers and frigid conditions most civilized soldiers had never experienced.

All that risk, for what? Joren mused. Only a few people in the world knew what treasures resided on this island. *But centuries ago? Why did the ancestors establish settlements with defense in mind if they fought no wars?*

Perhaps it was a different story. Or perhaps it was merely care and foresight on behalf of their ancestors.

It had not been clear to Joren until his Wandering years, just how mythologized the history of Faltara had become. Until he learned that all peoples the world over—whether Attican or Taikan, Chardonian or

Valgish, even the mysterious Elyan trader he'd encountered in the great free city of Beirus—all of them spoke of Crossings many millennia ago.

Some spoke of migrations from the north, which might correlate to the gate at the top of the Spires. But others spoke of incredible journeys across treacherous seas from a distant continent. Some spoke of Crossings from worlds that did not match the mighty fallen empire found in the world of the Abyss at all.

Perhaps there were many Gates of the Ancients. Perhaps there was only this one, and the time since the actual event was so much greater than they were taught on the Isle of Faltara, that the tale of the true Crossing had been convoluted by all the peoples of the world. Perhaps there was some truth to the Faltari version of the Crossing.

Or perhaps, there was no truth at all.

It was not until Joren spent time amongst the Fjuriin monks on the tiny Isle of Parduum that he first heard the Attican version of the settlement of Faltara itself.

A persecuted Valgish clan had fled north from a corrupt king, during the Attican Golden Age.

What was truth?

Truth lies not in tales but in duty and honor. Truth lies in what we do each day.

Joren's father had taught him this, just as Joren had taught Derrin, and now Malik. And one day, Joren hoped, Malik would teach it to his own son or daughter.

What Joren had come to understand during his Wandering was that there were questions he might never find the answer to. When he was younger, he did not know if he could live with that.

But there were worse things to live with. He'd learned that too.

Joren envisioned the battlefield in Taika, one of many revolutions that had occurred there. Severed limbs and skulls bursting with brain and blood. But it was not the images—every living beast was made of similar stuff on the inside, and it was nothing unnatural to see—no, it was the screams that haunted him.

Anytime Joren questioned the history he was taught or wondered if it mattered whether the Faltari had always lived here, or whether they'd come from Valgland or somewhere else, he needed only to take himself back to the screams of battle. To the young men barely come of age wailing for mothers, screaming, shrieking, writhing, desperate for the agony to end.

And it had been Joren's duty to heal, to prolong that wailing life for as long as possible. To determine if there was hope, or to make the decision to end that fading life.

Only Madri knew what he'd endured in his spirit during *uhmskara*, and even she knew only a part. The deepest truth was known only by the gods, and Joren supposed this was always so.

The life they preserved on the island was good in a way most people in the world could never know. The stories didn't matter. The sacrifice was necessary.

Malik would come to understand one day.

The journey down from Kalengal Valley took two days, following the long and winding Soul Road. Joren saw little of his son during that time. As shaman, Joren led the way, the three surviving dragon eggs stowed safely amongst his shaman's chests, sealed by locks as well as runic incantations, no different than all the other sacred supplies loaded in his alkine-drawn wagon.

There were many rituals performed during the Festival of the Ascension, rituals performed only once each year, which required tinctures and urns, sacrifices and herbs, incense and ceremonial garb and inks and ward stones and scrolls and bones of sacred beasts and more. Shamans always hauled wagons of ceremonial supplies up to Kalengal Valley. No one knew what horrible treasure was added to the lot for the journey back.

Joren guided his wooly alkine down one last stretch of road, before coming to the edge of a wall of rock, and the world of mountain passes opened up to the glacial valley of Yerida, at the foot of the fjord.

Shouts erupted behind him. A dozen vessels were already anchored offshore, the glorious white cloth of sails catching the bright afternoon sun and beaming. Skiffs ferried goods to the docks. The sacred Festival of Ascension was over.

Now, it was time for the Festival of the Fading Sun.

The last rite before winter set in.

————

Riese shook Malik's shoulder and pointed. Yuri howled as they rounded the last bend of the Soul Road outside Yerida.

"God's breath!" Yuri murmured. "Look at all the bloody foreigners! It'll be a grand festival this year! I wonder if there's any lemons. Gods, I hope they brought lemons!"

Riese grinned. "You don't want fruit. You want those Chardonian tarts!"

Yuri patted his stomach. "Earned it, I did! I'm Ascendant now!" This elicited a giggle from Yuri's festival dance partner, Elda Laradeil, who walked the road beside him, arms linked at the elbow. They'd been matched at the end of the festival, and had been flirting nonstop ever since.

"That's not all we earned," Elda said, nudging him.

Riese rolled her eyes.

"Don't tell me there's nothing *you've* got your heart set on," Yuri said.

"Well...I would love an Attican spear," said Riese.

"Ha! There's only half a dozen on all Faltara."

Riese huffed. "I'm bloody Ascendant and one of the best hunters on the island. A spear of Kirithian steel would make the hunt far easier."

"How dare you suggest our spears are inferior," said Yuri with a laugh.

"What does a shaman look forward to at the trading?" asked Riese.

Malik gazed out at the ships. Many Faltari had ridden ahead of the caravan to welcome the foreigners. Already, in the square, Malik could make out carts and market stands arrayed with colorful cloths. In the past, he'd always been excited for the bards and the ales and the foreign knives, the delicious smell of breads that could only be baked with foreign flour and yeast. But this year, he didn't care about any of that. His focus was on the flags flying from the anchored ships.

Malik managed to push back the thoughts, and said, "My father speaks only of herbs, so I guess I'm excited for that too."

He winked at Yuri.

"For dreamsmoke, of course," Malik added, and the boy howled with laughter.

Yuri grabbed Elda's hand and spun her around, and Malik envied their joy. The ease with which his friend leapt right in to this new life ahead of him. Yuri was thrilled to take a wife, to settle down and farm the foothills of the southern Jackal lands surrounding River's End. He'd survived the Ascent, and now, his adult life was coming together.

Malik felt guilty for how much he resented that. How much he wished he could find that same joy for himself.

Riese's match, Vinder had joined them a few times during the journey down the Soul Road, and she feigned happiness each time he came near. They'd gone hunting together before nightfall the previous evening, and Yuri and Elda went dancing. And Malik was left to sort through his thoughts.

Today, Vinder was sent to secure the village of Yerida, before the foreign traders were allowed to ferry ashore.

Yuri bounded down the path, hollering for Riese and Malik to join him and Elda for a mead after supper.

Finally, for the first time in two days, Malik and Riese were alone.

They paused on the ridge overlooking the bay, letting the procession pass them and meander down the foothills to the village below. Children paused nearby, gesticulating towards the ships with uncontainable enthusiasm.

"Quite the sight," said Riese, gazing out at the sails. "I've always thought so."

Malik nodded. Every time he saw Riese, he pictured her egg in the ashes, still glowing, felt her inner turmoil as she threw it in the fire. Now, he couldn't take his eyes away from the crimson sails in the harbor bearing the white dragon of Attica.

"What if we left?" Malik whispered.

"What?" Riese said, jolting.

"What if we left Faltara? Hop aboard with one of the traders at the end of the festival and go on a Wandering?"

Riese drew back and investigated his face. "Don't mess with me, Malik Jorensein."

"I'm not," said Malik. "I'm serious."

Riese gazed out at the shimmering sails, and a smile curled her lips.

Part Four

The Fading Sun

All nations speak of a Lost World. A World Before. And a Crossing in some distant past. Could it be that our paths are so entwined now, as then? Perhaps, we've all lost our way.

—from the *Meditations of Edamus*
a heretical Fjuriin philosopher

**usually attributed to the late Golden Age*

CHAPTER 18

NEUTRAL GROUND

The cold sea air stung Urla Pelasius's face as their ship, *Teranus*, navigated the narrow fjord leading to the Faltari village port of Yerida.

The passage was wide enough for two vessels to maneuver. Sheer walls of rock shot up on either side of the channel. The captain of their ship claimed the sea floor descended at a similar angle, plunging near straight down into the depths of icy water, both sides of the channel meeting somewhere hundreds of feet below.

This knowledge did not ease Urla's mind as the captain brought their Attican vessel within a dozen feet of the cliff face while passing a Taikan vessel at a similar distance, with that ship brushing just as close against the opposing wall.

Urla braced herself, gripping the taffrail with warrior's strength, waiting for the inevitable crunch of wooden hull against unforgiving stone, or else the splintering of hull against hull, should the Taikan ship draw too close.

But a few moments later, they had the channel to themselves again.

"Ha!" cried Captain Sentius, grinning at her. "It does me good to see a warrior of great renown in such distress."

Urla glowered. "I don't trust the sea. Never will."

"Never trust the sea," said the captain. "That's wisdom. Trust the seaman!"

"Both are equally dangerous, in my experience."

"Aye, that we are! Ha!"

Urla was relieved she hadn't offended him. Clearly, the Attican captain was a fine navigator, but in her mind, the sea would never be anything but a cruel and flighty wench. It would take all it could, and then take more, ultimately leaving daughters to be raised by uncles, mentored by their father's old friends.

Consul General Campos, on the other hand, was unperturbed by the precarious passage. He stood at the prow of the ship with Ruan and three other youths from the Fjuriin academies, one other boy, and two girls. All recently come of age. Like Ruan, they were sons and daughters of Attican lord houses, though none belonged to noteworthy families.

"Not all of them will manage a bond on this journey," Campos had explained to Urla, before they'd traveled through the godblade portal, from the palace to the northernmost port in the empire and set sail for Faltara. "But our empire is at the cusp of greatness for the first time in generations. The Dragon Lords still hold sway, and our wise emperor must balance the scales. Attica needs Dragonmounts loyal, first and foremost, to the empire, not to the traditions of their lord houses."

Of course, Emperor Athanasius had not been so straightforward when he'd blessed the company that would make the journey to Faltara for the Festival of the Fading Sun. But Urla had sensed that they were carefully chosen, either by Campos, or perhaps, the emperor himself. Two from each of the major Attican noble academies.

The ship reached a bend in the fjord, and the narrow cliff walls opened up to a small inland bay, set into a glacial valley. In the distance, a towering range of mountains loomed, nearby foothills rising into stark peaks that dominated the inland horizon. The first dusting of snow clung to the precipices of the tallest ones. There would be no snow in Attica—even the mountains—for another two months at least, and the lowlands would only see snow once or twice, most winters.

The walls of the fjord eased to green slopes, though it would be a toil to climb, except near the center of the bay where the snowpines and thick undergrowth were stripped away to make room for a quaint village. Even the buildings were rugged, longhouses built primarily at one level, crudely carved out of timber. A fort wall of bone-white logs encircled the village, each trunk carved to a sharp spike at the top. Urla could only imagine what beasts must roam such a wild place.

She marveled at how people could choose such a harsh land to inhabit, but the warrior in her admired the savagery. It reminded her of their own barbaric rituals in the academies and legion training camps. The greatest test of a soldier's mettle, save for battle itself, was to throw them in the heart of the wilds, and let them prove their valor.

Though, these exercises typically lasted a week, at most.

Here, it was life. Crude and harsh, by choice.

A dozen ships had already laid anchor in the bay, all forced close together.

Urla spotted a Chardonian banner—a forest green field with three silver lances jutting from a lone tower—and tensed.

The Chardonians had long been sworn enemies of the empire. Most Atticans prayed for the day they would invade the bastards.

"This is neutral ground," said Captain Sentius. "Don't worry."

Urla kept her thoughts to herself. *There's no such thing as neutral ground, and if this is the source of our dragon eggs, then it is treacherous ground, indeed.*

Campos gesticulated widely as all the youths, including her son, marveled at the strange civilization here at the northern edge of the world.

A tall soldier with wavy blond hair approached her. Lord Captain Adrius Rykus, father of the female representative from Ruan's school, a dark-haired girl with piercing green eyes. Urla had pieced together the man was of Valucian descent, one of the hero traitors who'd ensured Attican victory. He'd married an Attican spy during the Valucian Uprising and together, they had helped quash the rebellion. The wife had not joined them on the journey, but Urla guessed their daughter, Ava, took after her mother. She looked more Attican than her father, save for the green eyes.

Rykus strode to where Urla stood. Except for meals, Urla had kept to herself during the short voyage, and her privacy had been blessedly respected until now.

The first-blood Attican lord stood straight and offered her a salute of equals, pounding a fist to his chest.

Urla stood tall and reciprocated. Technically, their station was equal, though part of her resented this truth. It would not have been so in her father's generation. No Valucian would have become captain, no matter who he married.

Sailors scrambled across the decks of *Teranus* to ready the longboats. Most of the crew had been operating oars below, the only way to navigate the fjord with the necessary precision. Sentius deftly maneuvered around an anchored vessel, barking orders, which were echoed below by one of his mates.

"Makes you wonder, doesn't it? This journey?" Rykus asked.

Urla nodded, waiting for him to answer his own question.

"Has the lottery always been rigged?"

"The allocation of dragons has been rigged for ages," said Urla. "Long before Good Emperor Vitruvian introduced the lottery."

"Well noted," said Rykus. "I shan't complain about my daughter's being chosen as part of the leveling of power."

Ava Rykus was intelligent, that had been clear at once, but Urla had to confess she was surprised the girl had been chosen, considering her... condition. Though Urla supposed two good legs weren't strictly necessary on dragonback.

Urla shrugged. "Don't get your hopes up, Captain. It's the law of the land that few children will ever bond."

Just like a first-blood lord to feel special at the first hint of attention shown by the emperor.

Rykus shot her an unabashed grin. "Let alone twice in succeeding generations, right?"

Urla's stomach tightened, though she let the tension slip before it rose to her face. She loathed verbal sparring. Put her in a ring with a pair of spears—or better yet, a war axe—and see how Rykus would fare.

Longboats ferried goods from other vessels. Their ship drifted among them, slowly making their way to the far end of the bay. It was a vulnerable position, one Urla guessed was mandated for the sake of peace. The Attican vessel could easily be trapped here should something go awry.

"I'm sorry about your lord husband's death," Rykus said. "He flew magnificently."

"You saw him?"

"My company fought in the battle. His fall shook the troops. The death of a rider is one thing, but a dragonfall against a barbaric foe like Siga? Many of the troops feared it was a bad omen."

"Not you?"

"We won the battle, didn't we? And the rebellion was crushed soon after. No, Lady Captain, I've fought on both sides of Dragonmounts. A single dragonfall never turns the tide. One is a tragedy. It takes two or three to turn a battle when dragons fight for only one side. The heathen Valucians had dragons too. Long ago, you may recall."

"Not since the First Age," said Urla. "And it's not properly Fjuriin to recount such times. It was not Valucia's path."

"I recount them only as Attican. As one of the blood-traitors. It was right for the ancient Valucian mounts to fall. And certainly, I am honored to see Attica reclaim its rightful place over our soil. Only now, do the isles feel like home."

"Certainly, my mistake."

"You're right, of course, Lady Captain. I should have been clearer. Though my visage might betray me, my line traces back to the Golden Age when Attican blood was far more widespread. Tainted blood, yes. But we kept the Fjuriin ways. All the more reason it would be a glorious honor for my own daughter to become a Dragonmount of Attica."

Urla met his gaze. The curious man glanced over at his daughter proudly. Supporting herself on a sleek black cane, Ava was chatting with Ruan and the girl from Bastion Academy.

"She must be brilliant," said Urla, "to be admitted to a Fjuriin academy as a second-blood."

"Very," said Rykus. "Ava has her mother's wits. Though my daughter tells me *your* son is top of the class."

"Does she?"

"They're friends," said Rykus. "Our children. Did you know that? Sorry, I know it's a sensitive matter after war and tragedy, but my wife and I could hardly contain our excitement when Ava informed us that she had befriended the son of a Dragonmount. I was thrilled to tell her that I fought beneath the shadow of that dragon's wings. Er, sorry."

Urla shook her head, remaining composed. "No need. You honor my husband with your words. Thank you. And your wife, she's..."

"Home. She's been ill for... a long time now."

"I'm sorry to hear that."

"We don't choose our path. We merely make the most of it. How's that for properly Fjuriin?"

Urla smiled at the man. It took great skill and charisma to rise to become captain as a first-blood, she couldn't deny him that.

A tall guardswoman approached Rykus. "Sir, the cargo is ready for your approval."

"Cargo?" asked Urla.

"Kirithian steel, trademark of my house," said Rykus.

The runemarked weapons were well-liked among the troops.

"You brought goods on a mission like this?" Urla asked.

"That's our whole damn facade, isn't it?" the young woman countered.

"You'll excuse Deven," said Rykus. "Captain of my personal guard. And full of the sort of fire a lady captain like you can surely appreciate."

Urla nodded without response. Deven fought off a blush.

"Anyway, I must go, but it was a pleasure, Lady Captain."

"Yes, of course."

Rykus and his guardswoman disappeared below deck for a short while, and Urla welcomed the moment of peace as they eased into a cove near the northern edge of the harbor.

The ship soon came to a stop, and Campos led the youths to the quarterdeck, where their parents and a retinue of Campos house guards gathered.

Urla moved closer to her son as Campos began a series of instructions for all coming ashore. Ruan stood beside Ava, and so Rykus, too, remained near.

The children whispered back and forth. Urla couldn't determine whether the two shared an attraction or were only friends, as Rykus suggested. Before Urla left for war, she would have known.

Two years, she mused. *When I left, he wouldn't look a pretty girl in the eyes, let alone hold an animated conversation.*

Ava *was* pretty, Urla had to admit, save for the unsettling eyes. She had light brown skin and properly dark and wavy Attican hair. But those bright green eyes stood out like a wart on her face.

A pity, Urla thought. *If the girl'd taken dark eyes and her mother's name, she might have had hope of forming a greater house.*

Urla had seen enough to know the girl stood little chance at actually gaining a dragon on this venture.

"What do you mean?" asked Lady Thenius, the Bastion girl's mother.

"No weapons?" Rykus chimed in, flabbergasted.

Urla was jolted from her thoughts, as General Campos handed off his sword belt to his manservant, Baro. He withdrew two more daggers from another belt wrapped tight on his chest and traded his Attican sigils for a plain cloak the color of everwinter needles.

"No weapons of war," said Campos. "The policy is strictly enforced by the local magistrates, er, chieftains. Don't fret, Rykus, an exception is made for goods of trade, though the Faltari are interested only in short spears for hunting, no lances. Daggers are welcome, but no swords. All goods will pass through tribal inspections."

"This isn't about trade, I assure you, General. This is about bloody sense. Never once have I gone into a heathen market unarmed."

"This is a market unlike any other," said Campos.

"You expect me to go to a foreign shore teeming with barbaric Valgs and Chardonians, with no weapons of any sort? With my only daughter?"

Rykus was red in the face, and Urla was embarrassed for him. He was not the only person in the company who was upset, but he was the only one voicing it.

Campos smiled. "Yes, if you want your daughter to have any chance at a bond, that's precisely what I expect, Captain Rykus. But if you'd prefer to stay aboard..."

Ava flushed but said nothing.

Rykus crossed his arms. He'd already traded his seafaring clothes for armor to go ashore. "Well, you might have warned us sooner, Lord Consul. Only to save time, of course."

Campos drew closer to the man and patted him on the shoulder. "Ah, I don't worry about your time in the least. I care only about the emperor's time, and the time of the select youths he ordered me to bring here. I don't need you to escort your daughter. Your accompaniment is a privilege, not a right."

Rykus and his guardswoman hastened below deck to change attire, along with the Bastion boy's father and several personal guards.

It was a familiar high officer's power move to save such information for the last moment, and Urla was surprised a captain like Rykus had been so easily riled.

Typical first-blood lapse in restraint.

Urla handed her own weapons to her servant, Pisarre. But she fixed her attention on the instructions Campos was passing along to her son and the other youths.

"Faltara is neutral ground. This is the only time each year that trade is permitted and foreigners are allowed on these shores. I needn't have to remind you how important it is that we maintain cordial relations, considering the nature of our voyage. If a Chardonian bastard tries to provoke you, walk away. If a Valgish hothead bears a hidden weapon, you walk away and report it to a Faltari chieftain. And if a Beirusian courtesan invites you for a Journey Amongst the Stars, well, best hope your parents aren't watching and your purse is full, because she's not asking to go for an evening stroll. Ha!"

The youths all laughed in spite of themselves.

Urla smirked at her son's flushed cheeks. Perhaps he was not quite the grown man he portrayed.

Surely by now, he'd...

Then, she caught his glance at Ava.

Mother's intuition hasn't entirely lapsed since you've been to war.

"All right, it's time to go ashore!" Campos announced.

CHAPTER 19

DAUGHTER OF VALUCIA

Halfway to the docks, Ava Lucila Rykus nudged Ruan's shoulder, and pointed at the sky as a prismatic shimmer flashed above their skiff. She held her breath as two slender creatures emerged from low-hanging clouds. Feathers of many vibrant shades caught the light of the evening sun and the creatures twirled through the air.

"Feathered serpents!" Ruan said.

"I've only ever heard tales." Ava marveled as the graceful creatures rode currents of wind. Thin membranes expanded from their sides like tiny sails. A fin of feathers on their spine guided their path in perfect synchronicity, as though the creatures were performing an ancient choreography across the heavens.

The feathered serpents dove toward their ship, and even the rowers stopped to watch as the pair plunged into the bay, submerging for a second, maybe two, before shooting out from the water. Feathers plumed, catching a firm breeze that rushed from the depths of the fjord, and they soared back into the sky.

"Marvelous!" General Campos shouted. "A mating dance."

The serpents writhed in tandem, catching an upward draft that sent them spiraling up and up, until they disappeared into another cloud.

The general pointed to the cliff back the way they'd come. "They've a roost back there, I'd guarantee it."

"Surely they don't mate this late in the year?" Ava's father asked.

Ruan was blushing again, and Ava held back a smile.

"Ah," said Campos. "The ways of the great creatures of the north are curious, indeed. Feathered serpent eggs gestate for the entire winter. The creatures hibernate for much of the year, and the warm season is desperately short, so they must perform their duties most... vigorously to ensure fertilization before the snow and ice sets in. Of course, this is nothing like the gestation of a dragon egg, eh?"

Her father nodded. Ava could tell he did not particularly care for the general, but he was honor-bound to hide it as best he could. His outburst over the armor was an uncharacteristic lapse, though perhaps it had been intentional. For all her father's faults, he did few things carelessly.

"I think it's brilliant," said Ava, eyes still on the clouds. "All must adapt to survive, right?"

"Take what is and mold it how we may," said Campos. "Spoken like one on the Fjuriin Path, if ever I've heard it."

Ava raised a brow as her father glanced her way.

"Spoken like a teacher's pet, more like," Ruan murmured so only she could hear.

"Adapt and survive, comrade," she said, shooting him a wink.

He rolled his eyes, but the corner of his lip turned with a smirk, and Ava nudged him in the ribs.

Ruan didn't seem to mind.

Ava wondered whether the boy ever suspected why she'd initially befriended him. Whether he cared.

Ruan was a brilliant boy who just needed a little guidance in the social dynamics of the academy, while Ava needed access beyond her station. Never could she have gained an audience with the consul general during his guest lecture term last year without a connection like Ruan, that was damn certain. Just a second-blood girl from the Old Empire, Ava could never have afforded to be timid or unsure the way Ruan was when they arrived at Dawncrest.

But Ruan had grown much since then, she had to give him that. He took in the village and spoke with the other students with confidence, shoulders back, head high. And Ava... she was on the Isle of Faltara, the best-kept secret in the world, with one of the emperor's closest advisors. *Gods, I even bowed before the emperor himself!*

Her time at the academy had not been pleasant in any sense of the word, but all of it had prepared her for what was to come.

Campos's personal guards maneuvered their longboat to the Faltari docks and tethered it to begin unloading. The guards disembarked first, led by the Knight of Caadron, Vera Salyr.

Her father disembarked, and his captain of the guard, Deven, helped Ava from the boat. Her right leg ached as she rose. She'd remained far too stationary on that damn ship.

A pair of fur-cloaked natives greeted Campos at the end of the docks, then ushered them to follow, pointing to a wooden shack at the edge of the teeming square outside the walled village.

"Every visitor will be checked for illicit materials," Campos announced to the group.

"Gods, are we entering the palace pyramid?" asked Lady Thenius.

"It is standard procedure for this particular festival, and all will honor it or return to the ship."

Thenius rolled her eyes, adjusting her casual cream-colored gown. Far plainer, Ava was sure, than anything the lady was used to wearing.

It amused her, for all that Attican nobles valued temperance, how easily flustered they could be, if they believed their honor had been maligned.

"I think Thenius *needs* a good frisk down," Ava muttered, and Ruan chuckled beside her.

Her father brushed her shoulder from behind, and she paused near the end of the dock, letting Ruan and his warrior mother walk on ahead.

Lady Captain Pelasius also looked uncomfortable in her plain-woven dress, though this was more from her build than anything else. Thenius struck Ava as a woman who didn't know what to do when not wearing fine silks and being ferried around on a litter. Urla, on the other hand, looked like she ought to wear armor at all times—tall, broad-shouldered, strong. Ruan's mother surveyed the village as though a threat might emerge at any instant, hand hovering near the sash at her waist, where a blade would normally be worn.

When Ruan and his mother reached the shack, Ava's father turned to her, eyes narrowing.

"Be careful around them," he said.

"I wouldn't be here if not for Ruan," Ava murmured. "I know what I'm doing. I saw you getting on just fine with the lady captain."

"Just be careful. Few are more petulant than love-struck youths. What can be given, can be taken away. And *that* would ruin all we've worked for."

Ava glowered up at her father. "You think I don't know that?"

Rykus's jaw tensed. "All of us must sacrifice for the sake of this family."

"I got us here, didn't I? Trust me."

Rykus smiled and patted her cheek, his fingers lingered under her chin, and he looked deep into her eyes. "You've done well, darling. But don't let it go to your head."

Ava nodded and followed the others before her father could say anything more.

———

Men and women were sent through different examination stations within the Faltari shack, where they were undressed to their smallclothes and checked for weapons and other contraband. The Faltari women were gentle with Ava, letting her support herself with her cane the entire time, and being especially courteous with the leathern brace that extended from knee to hip on her right leg.

The entire process amused her. It was so much more modest than in Attica. The Valgish ancestry that was said to run in Faltari blood, Ava supposed.

The thick dress she'd been instructed to wear covered her shoulders, which, considering the cold, she'd thought was just practical. But something about the way the Faltari women handled the inspection was so sterile.

Perhaps it was not modesty at all, but something about her foreignness. The women barely met her gaze, which was *very* much not Fjuriin.

Ava found it fascinating. There was so much to learn about the world.

When they emerged from the checkpoint, a pair of Faltari men approached, one as young as she, and one about her father's age.

Campos drew his hands together and bowed, an extraordinary act of respect from someone of his station. Quickly, the rest of the Attican entourage followed suit, though Ava noted the disgust in Lady Thenius's expression.

The two Faltari men, father and son it appeared, were the epitome of barbarians. Long hair reached their shoulders, braided with tiny bones and colorful feathers—serpent feathers, Ava guessed with excitement. Their cloaks were formed crudely from the hides of multiple beasts. More crude than the guards who'd greeted them, and yet, Campos paid only these two the honor of an Attican Dragon Lord.

"It is good to see you, my friend," Campos said to the elder Faltari man, holding his gaze briefly.

Campos motioned to the others. "May I present Joren Adensein, Shaman of Faltara, and this must be your son, yes? The second born?"

The man nodded, and Ava wondered what was act and what was truth in this performative interaction.

"Yes," said Joren, "this is Malik, also Shaman of Faltara."

Campos bowed to the boy. "Ah, you've come of age, then. Congratulations on your Ascension!"

The young shaman dipped his head in respect but said nothing. Ava watched the boy carefully. Malik's eyes were bright like her own, hair a light brown and crudely cut. Dark rings of cosmetic were painted around his eyes, just like his father's, and dark streaks of the same paint traced the side of his face. His jawline was narrow and chiseled. Without the paint, she suspected he was handsome. Not in a Fjuriin way, but perhaps more like her own Valucian heritage.

The father was tall and slender, but the young shaman was shorter and well-built. A young man who might have given some of the Dawn-crest boys a run for their money in the academy athletic games. A glance at his muscular forearms suggested he probably handled a spear well too. Malik took in each of the foreigners, one by one, and when his gaze met Ava's, he paused, examining her carefully.

An inexplicable paranoia swept over her. Fear that the Faltari boy could see right through all her guises to her true soul. Like her mind was a secret scroll being unraveled, though she could not explain how or why. She forced herself to smile and nod, and Malik's gaze passed on.

"You brought a larger retinue this year," the elder shaman noted, a hint of suspicion in his voice.

"The Festival of the Fading Sun is an experience unlike any other," Campos said. "There are more ships in your harbor than I've seen before as well. It was a year of good harvests across the southern world. Attica is no different."

Joren nodded. "Yes, well, trade is good, but this is a sacred land, and we do not wish it to be disturbed beyond what is required."

Ava detected hidden messages in their words, though she could not say what they were.

"We come in peace, as always," Campos said. "You know as well as I, how much we value the sanctity of this place."

Joren nodded, but the younger shaman hitched. Ava doubted anyone caught it, but she had been trained to notice the subtlest shifts in human expression.

Malik was angry about something.

"We should speak further in private," said Joren.

Campos nodded. "Of course. I'll meet up with the rest of you during the ceremony tonight. Lady Captain, I would be honored if you would serve as my guard."

A couple of the parents grumbled at this, but Ava's attention remained fixed on the young shaman.

Malik caught her watching him, and she glanced away and hurried after the others to explore the market.

CHAPTER 20

LONG LOST

Joren led the way through the village lanes. The crowds were thick with foreigners, along with the entire population of Faltara. No one missed the Festival of the Fading Sun any more than they would the Ascension. Though less sacred, the Fading Sun was the livelier extension of the celebrations. The streets of Yerida were bustling like no other time.

Joren and Campos made small talk as they walked. The general was accompanied by a tall and impressive Attican shield maiden. Urla Pelasius said little, though her eyes were watchful, and her spirit betrayed her suppressed inner turmoil.

A timbre of loss and hope, Joren recognized.

Malik, too, had been hiding something since Joren had shown him the truth of the Ascension, and unlike the shield maiden, his son was more practiced in putting up walls against his father's shamanic sense. Whatever Malik hadn't understood immediately, he'd certainly figured out over the past hour. And Joren, of all people, understood how that knowledge weighed on one's spirit.

As they neared the northern edge of the village, Campos spoke at a whisper. "I apologize for the increased guard this year, old friend. Season of war in the empire, you know."

"I was told you secured a victory in Siga," said Joren, images of his own time at war rising up anew.

"It's always a season of war in the empire," Campos said with a laugh. When no one else joined him, he offered an addendum. "There is some unease regarding an Elyan runeship that fought in the final battle, outside the Sigan capital."

"Leone," said Joren.

"You know it? Ah, yes, I forget you sailed the world for a time. Forgive me."

Joren sensed a tension in his son at the mention of his Wandering. He patted Malik on the shoulder.

"You've heard of the runeships of Elya, then?" Campos asked.

"Only trader's tales," said Joren. "Were any of your mounts harmed?"

Campos glanced at the shield maiden, grimaced, then resumed. "We lost one dragon and her rider. Not from the runeship. Just a damn lucky shot from a restored wing-render bow."

Joren was familiar with the wing-renders, enormous crossbows fixed to parapets that fired bolts of iron with razor tips the size of skulls, enhanced with rune magic for farther and faster flight. They dated back to the ancient wars of the empire, and most were destroyed during the Golden Age.

"No kingdom in their right mind would fight Attica without a few wing-renders up their sleeves," Campos continued. "But a runeship... that is the first I've heard on this side of the Ever Sea in a decade. And the first to be used in battle. Of course, the Elyan ambassadors claim it was stolen, and we've no proof, but..."

"So, it wasn't piloted by—"

"The Elyans?" Campos finished. "Gods, no. Bloody mercenaries is all."

"What does it mean, then?" asked Malik, suddenly jumping into the conversation.

Campos raised a brow and grinned. "What do *you* know about the Elyans out here in the wilds, boy?"

Malik shrugged. "They ignored the warnings of the World Before, just like Attica."

Campos straightened up at this. "That so?"

"Excuse my son, he means no offense," Joren said.

"None taken, my friend," Campos retorted. "We all have different tales, don't we? Where we came from. Why we left. What it means. It is an interesting thought, all of us coming from some distant shore, long lost. All sharing some distant common ancestry. Even the Elyans, I suppose."

"You fear them," said Malik.

"Son..."

"No, he's right," said Campos.

"They pose a threat to your power, if only one of these runeships causes such fear."

Campos shrugged. "We all fear what we don't understand, don't we? The runeships are real. And they might serve a mighty weapon for an empire that thinks nothing of magic. Thinks it should be taught and shared widely."

"Why shouldn't it?" asked Malik.

Joren kept his thoughts to himself. It was not like his son to be so forward.

On the island, every person practiced magic. Of course, that was because they were blessed by the gods, and they were good stewards of their gods-given gifts. But Joren had seen the might of kingdoms and empires, and he shuddered to think of an empire founded on such power. Few had the restraint of the Faltari.

Campos smiled. "Young man, you said we Atticans never learned our lesson from the World Before. I'll forgive this as a slip of ignorance, but I would contend that you are wrong in this assessment. Very wrong, in fact. We Atticans learned the lesson that power in the wrong hands, or even in too many hands, leads to chaos and destruction. Power must be tended carefully. I daresay you Faltari believe something similar when it's all said and done. Thus, our accord, yes?"

Malik quietened at the general's admonition.

"Again, I apologize," said Joren, shooting Malik a stern look.

Campos waved him off. "I welcome the challenge. The earnestness of the young is a strength. It is good to question. Good to defend your reason. But like magic, like dragons, and yes, maybe even like runeships, that earnestness must also be harnessed and contained. Wielded with precision and restraint. That's where real strength lies. But I suppose some of us must unleash some destruction before we can learn."

Campos patted Malik on the shoulder. "And *that* is why I fear Elya, young man. Why we all should. Our dragons decimated that lone runeship with little trouble. But should those heathens decide to meddle in our corner of the world, well... we might learn the full lesson of the World Before too late."

They stood at the edge of the village now, outside the temple. It was ornate for a longhouse and the tallest building in Yerida, as was true in every Faltari village. The steps were made of runemarked stones leading to a portico supported by intricately carved pillars of socha wood.

Joren led the way through the vast foyer, where dozens of small shrines were erected, where any Faltari villager was welcome at any hour to weave prayer cloths or meditate. Incense smoke hung thick in the air, an aroma that had always felt like coming home to Joren. No matter what turmoil might reside outside this hall, or even in his own spirit, it drifted away with a few focused inhalations of that musty scent.

The tall interior walls of the temple were etched with mantras, both in runes and in the Common Tongue. Along one side of the chamber, life-size graven visages of the All Mother and All Father were set in nooks. The rear wall was lined with fine-woven tapestries depicting each of the sacred beasts of Faltara.

They proceeded through an arched entrance and entered the back hall, which stretched past several smaller chambers where healing rites were performed. Past the inner temple, where sacred texts were made available to the people, though few could actually read them.

Near the end of the hall, Joren paused outside a runemarked door, much like the one in the sacred crypts at the base of the Spires. Joren pressed his palm against it, spoke the ancient words, and reached for *hish*, threads of magic connecting his spirit briefly with the power sealing the door. Recognizing his resonance, the magic untethered, thick iron mechanisms released at the edges of the door, and they entered the inner shaman's sanctum.

There were no windows here. The walls were lined with shelves, mostly filled with ancient scrolls: Faltari histories and lineages, runic spells, sacred rituals, prayers, mantras, incantations, and recipes for tinctures. All the knowledge the shamans of Faltara had accrued regarding spiritual matters over the generations.

There was a small desk and a couple of wooden chairs where Joren had spent countless hours in study. Behind the desk, there was a graven chest etched in runes.

Malik, Campos, and the shield maiden followed him inside. Joren sealed the door behind them and activated the locking spell with a surge of *hish*.

"The way you Faltari work runes," Campos said. "With no channel. I've seen it half a dozen times, and every time, I remain impressed."

"Channel?" asked Malik.

Before Joren could explain, Campos continued.

"In Attica, few practice magic, young shaman. Only an Arcanist of Peroia may learn runework. They train at a sacred and mysterious school to learn the use of sorcerous instruments, called channels, that allow them to harness the forces of the Other."

"The Other?" Malik asked, brow furled. Every question his son spoke was laced with suspicion. Joren was tempted to shut down the conversation, but he feared that might only further Malik's agitation.

"Here, we call it the breath of the gods," Joren clarified. "*Hish*, because that is the sound of an intake of breath. Malik, would you help me with the chest?"

His son nodded and took the leathern handle on one end, while Joren seized the other. The small chest was not terribly heavy, but it was good for Malik to be involved rather than an observer during this exchange.

Whatever Malik's fate after the Festival of the Fading Sun, it was important that he understand it all.

They set the chest upon the desk, and once the seals were disabled, Joren opened it, as every shaman had done for generations. Urla Pelasius drew a sharp breath at the sight of the three dragon eggs. Both she and Campos drew closer. Malik stood behind.

"Remarkable," Urla murmured.

"Outside the residents of this island, you are one of only a handful of living people privy to this experience," Campos said. "Few people see a dragon egg in their lifetime, let alone the land of their origins."

Malik fought back a smirk, but it was not lost on Joren.

No, son, they don't know everything.

All Faltari were oathbound, even those who left the island. From the village of Yerida, the Spires looked like nothing but mountain peaks, until you reached the valley itself. Atticans knew little more than that the Faltari Ascension festival occurred high in the mountains. And when they returned, the shamans brought a fresh supply of dragon eggs for their heathen lottery.

"Three this year," Campos said. It was the best haul in some time. The man leaned over the chest. The crimson egg shimmered at the seams between stone-like scales, as though brimming with the potential of life. The general inspected it, picking the egg up gingerly with his hands. It shone brighter than the other two.

"Why is this one different?" asked Urla.

Campos glanced at Joren with raised brow. "Shaman? Don't think I've ever seen one of your eggs bonded before the exchange."

"Bonded?" Malik asked.

Joren cursed. It was Riese's egg. "Potential to bond," Joren clarified.

"You'd have seen this yourself had we waited till the lottery," said Campos to the shield maiden. "When an egg encounters a potential bond, it makes it known by glowing brighter. This egg was handled by a potential Dragonmount."

"Dragonmount?" Malik asked, turning to his father, anger barely held back.

Joren nodded. "It is rare, but not the first time this has happened for an Ascendant."

"First that I've seen," Campos restated.

"Yes, well, you're rather new to the post, aren't you?" Joren said with a condescending smile.

All eggs that survived the trial of flame glowed for a time. But they normally dimmed by the time they were delivered to the imperial consul.

"Just as the potential for sorcery extends far and wide, so, too, does the potential for bonding," said Joren.

"Which is why we ensure both fall into the *right* hands," said Campos, grinning at Malik, despite the boy's suspicion.

"The bond will fade," Joren said, "with distance. Don't worry, there are many Atticans who could potentially bond with this dragon."

"That is the entire principle behind the lottery. Why your son is here to begin with," Campos said to Urla. "A chance at forming such a link before the true lottery."

The woman nodded but remained silent.

Campos handed the egg to her while he retrieved a large rucksack. Carefully, he took the egg, wrapping it in a thick cloth, and stowed it within. The general proceeded to handle each egg the same way, until all three were secured within. He slung the pack over his shoulders with ease, looking like he was hauling supplies, as he had when he'd entered.

"Well, shamans, it's always a pleasure," said Campos. "We'll see you around the festival."

Just like that, the exchange was over, and Joren and Malik were alone for the first time since they'd unearthed the eggs at the pyre.

The door shut, and Joren sealed the runes again. When he turned, Malik was shaking his head.

"She'll never know, will she?" Malik muttered.

"Riese believes her dragon egg was consumed in flames, just like all the others. So no, she will never know. And it is important she does not."

"She could be a Dragonmount?" Malik demanded.

"Potentially."

"She deserves—"

"You've *just* come of age, son! You know nothing of what Riese or anyone else needs or deserves."

"And you do?"

"Do you understand what just happened? What has gone on for generations?"

"Let's see. We lie to our people. We sacrifice our own lives every damn year to get these eggs, so the Attican Empire can rule the world. Yes, I think I understand just—"

"No," said Joren, his voice flaring, grateful for the runic wards in this room. "You are so full of your own thoughts, you haven't even considered *why* we do this. Our entire livelihood depends on this. Don't you see? The safety and sanctity of Faltara, of our people, depends on this agreement. Have you any idea what would happen if the world discovered what's on this island?"

Malik threw up his hands in fury. "You believe that's worth lying to our people? Sacrificing our own children?"

"Yes!"

"Worth Uncle Pender's life? Derrin's?"

Joren pounded the table. "Yes, I believe it's worth our lives! Our tradition! Yes! Gods damn it!"

The words hung in the air, all Joren's guilt and frustration and bitterness rising up all at once.

Malik stared at him, fire in his eyes. Rage, confusion, bitterness. And Joren didn't blame him.

"I don't know who we are anymore," Malik said.

The words pierced like claws into Joren's heart, digging and wrenching, but there was nothing he could do.

"You haven't seen what I've seen," Joren murmured.

His son's next words seemed inevitable. "Well, maybe I should."

Chapter 21

Worlds Collide

Riese let her bonespear fly with a surge of *hish*. It shot through the air and struck the tusked boar in the chest mid-stride with a resounding thud.

Without even a squeal, the beast collapsed on its side.

Cheers resounded around her. Half a dozen Faltari youths paused to congratulate her on the first kill of the contest, before bounding off through the trees, whooping and hollering, keeping tabs on the other contestants.

Yuri remained. He wasn't much of a hunter and had mostly come along for support. He clapped Riese on the back.

"Ha! Imperial soldier, my ass!" Yuri shot a pointed grin at Riese's hunting companion, an Attican woman named Deven.

It was custom for the Faltari to pair off with foreigners for the games. Deven jogged past the boar and retrieved her own spear, which had sailed over its head.

The woman was tall and strong. Dark hair and sun-specked pale skin suggested she was likely of mixed Attican race. Deven stooped to inspect the kill as Riese joined her.

Already, its breaths had stilled, and Riese thanked the Mother for the quick kill. She had learned long ago the agony brought about by a poor shot. Her first stag, she missed the vitals and was forced to slit its throat while it squirmed to get free. It had been a slow, gruesome death. She made sure not to make a mistake like that again.

Deven shook her head. "No shit! Perfect shot, and on the run, no less. I'm impressed."

"Not bad for a bloody heathen, ey?" Yuri jabbed.

"Yuri, god's breath, leave it alone," Riese said.

"Nah," said Deven, flashing a smile. "Not bad at all."

Riese smiled. "Thanks."

"And I'm captain of the House Rykus guard," Deven said. "Not some imperial frontline grunt, I'll have you know." She shot Yuri a smirk.

"So... never seen any action, ey?"

"Oh, I earned my rank, don't you fret, heathen boy. There's a world of difference between a boar hunt and real action."

Yuri shrugged. "What about a sabercat?"

Deven guffawed. "Are those real?"

Yuri drew up his sleeve to reveal the long scars on his forearm. "Reckon they must be."

The woman shook her head and laughed. "Probably getting closer to a battle."

Deven was perhaps in her mid-twenties. Skin weathered from hardship, much like most Faltari hunters. Some might have found the woman's firm jaw and chiseled forearms off-putting, but Riese thought her nice to look at, and she had a remarkably pleasant demeanor for a foreign guard.

Riese felt a twinge of guilt. A lingering anxiety had nagged at her spirit since the minute Malik suggested they might leave. The idea of seeing the world held an undeniable appeal, but gods knew, they'd have to befriend some foreigners to make that happen. So, she might as well start now.

"You see, Riese thinks all that matters is stealth and accuracy," Yuri went on. "But I bet in battle it really comes down to brute—"

Riese shoved Yuri hard enough he nearly lost his balance.

"Hey!"

"Give it a rest, Yuri. She's too nice to tell you you're a dumbass."

Yuri scowled. "Well, lucky for me I have you, then."

Riese patted him on the back. "That's right. I'm here to save you from yourself. And if you compare you're half-grown saber encounter to a bloody war one more time, I swear I'll tell Elda about—"

"You wouldn't!"

Riese shrugged. "Try me."

"That was told to you in confidence."

Deven grinned. "Who's Elda?"

"Oh, mind your own heathen business." Yuri crossed his arms, but said no more.

Riese stooped down beside her kill. She pulled a bonedagger from her belt and prepared to gut the beast, but Deven stopped her.

"Here." The woman handed her a shimmering steel hunting blade.

"Damn," said Yuri. "How'd you smuggle that?"

Deven shrugged. "I'm not exactly trying to hide it, am I? It's for trade."

Yuri shrugged but peered closer.

Riese turned the blade over, light flashing on the silver edges. She brushed her calloused finger sideways against the edge. "Bloody sharp."

"Kirithian blade," Deven said. "Runemarked steel beneath the hilt for added strength and durability."

"Are you sure about gutting with it? I'd hate to dull the blade before you try to sell it."

"That's what the runes are for. Go on. My master's orders."

"Your master?"

"I'm supposed to show these off so Lord Rykus can make his trades. Don't worry, only a couple were allowed through your... customs."

Riese proceeded to gut the boar, the blade slicing easily through the abdomen. The sternum was more work, but less than Riese had ever experienced. Steam wafted from the beast's insides as she drove her hands in and pulled out the boar's innards.

When she was finished, she wiped the blade off on her pant leg. It was remarkably clean as she handed it back.

"Clever runes," she said.

Deven smiled and stowed it back in her pack. "You just Ascended, I gathered."

Riese nodded.

"And betrothed too," said Yuri.

"Well, well..." Deven winked at her. "Tell your father he ought to consider a Rykus blade for a gift, for either occasion."

There was another cry farther off, and more cheering.

"Second kill," said Yuri.

"Well, we best not let them catch up," said Riese, hefting the emptied carcass over her shoulder.

———

Everything about this strange festival at the edge of the world was magnificent in Ava's eyes. It reminded her of the free city of Beirus, but without the enormous crowds and the influence of the eastern missionaries.

Beirus was the only place on the continent of Îrithèa where the Empyreal Church of Elya had found a foothold. Where the power known as the Other was hailed as god itself, rather than a gift of the gods.

The only place in the western continent where magic was practiced openly, and where there had been any chance at finding someone who might heal Ava's injuries sustained during the Valucian Uprising when she was but a child.

The healing was incomplete, and required a sacrifice Ava would bear on her conscience the rest of her life. If it had been a true healer of the Elyan orders—or maybe even a shaman from this very island— perhaps it might have turned out different.

Now, her injuries had settled, and she limped around on one bad leg rather than two. Without that botched healing, she would likely have had no chance at entering Dawncrest Academy. Certainly not at becoming Dragonmount. But if not for that healing, perhaps...

Ava pushed the thoughts from her mind.

If not for the foul memories, she'd thought Beirus a beautiful place.

But the Isle of Faltara elicited a different freedom, even from that of Beirus. Ava felt like she could breathe here, in a way she'd only ever felt back on Eòreth, her family's island. She'd spent most of her youth in the sprawl of Attica City. The academy, too, was stifling, even if it was at the edge of the city. All walls and towers and training grounds.

But here at the edge of the world, she felt at ease, like she did in the hills of her island home. Ava wished she could hold on to this feeling, though she knew wishes were as fleeting as a summer breeze.

Already summer seemed long past. This northern air cut straight through her woolen clothes and skin and chilled her bones.

The other Attican youths, including Ruan, had joined the locals in a hunting contest along with a host of other foreigners. Even Deven had gone.

Ava's father was busy chatting with merchants about long term trade agreements and foreign gossip, and Ava wandered the markets alone.

People from across the lands perused foreign trinkets and delicacies, but Ava hung near the outskirts, watching, taking it all in. She was used to lingering at the edges of things. People always hurried about, even friends like Ruan, forgetting she moved slower. Apologizing—always the damn apologizing—and then, the cycle would repeat all over again.

It wasn't that Ava didn't mind being overlooked. But she'd learned to take what was given to her and make it a strength. Ava Lucila Rykus had learned to watch people with the precision of a gods-damned falcon. Learned to read them, predict them. Bend them, when necessary. She'd built her own strength. But that did not mean it wasn't lonely.

The markets of Yerida began in the outer square at the waterfront, and then, spread through the village itself and beyond the southern walls across a field dotted with crude barns and pens. A dirt path lined with vendor stalls led out to an open meadow filled with colorful tents.

Unlike the meadows in Attica or Valucia, the grass only reached halfway up her ankle-high leather boots, but the blades contained the deepest shades of green Ava had ever seen, perhaps amplified by the stark black rocks that jutted out from the hillsides all around the meadow.

Beyond the stalls and the meadow and the columns of snowpine, a wending path traced its way up the foothills. It disappeared into the passes of the swiftly rising peaks of the island, where the Faltari came back from their Ascension ceremonies.

Ava wondered if this was where all dragon eggs came from, or if there were more secret lands such as this.

"Curious place, isn't it?"

Ruan's voice.

Ava turned, shifting her weight on her cane. Her hip ached more in the cold, but she never complained.

"Hunt's over?" she asked.

Ruan shrugged. "Thought you might appreciate some company."

"You're thoughtful," she said, smiling. "And yes, this place is quite curious, but I think it's lovely, in a primitive way."

"Sounds like Campos has finished with his meeting."

Straight to the point. Ava liked that about Ruan.

"They were at the temple," Ruan added.

"Did they get our cargo already?"

"I don't know."

Ava spotted Campos and Urla Pelasius near the edge of the meadow, speaking with traders from Ytan. The stall bore thick sacks of rice and small displays of herbs.

"I suppose we could ask your mother, couldn't we?" Ava teased, knowing Ruan was equal parts embarrassed and proud that his mother had been chosen to join Campos as his guard.

The others were jealous. Ava's father feigned offense in front of the others, though Ava knew he hadn't expected any such honor as a first-blood. Even before his little outburst.

It was all chance. Whose house's lands happened to be where, and which kingdoms happened to secede from the empire over the past century. Rykus blood was as ancient as any great house. They'd been dragon lords once, in the First Age, her father claimed.

"My mother is too good at tending secrets," Ruan said.

"Maybe you just need to be a more trustworthy son."

Ava shot him a wink.

The festival stretched into the evening, but to Malik, it felt like eternity until nightfall.

Hundreds of people milled around him, and Riese was nowhere to be seen since she'd returned from the hunting games. In truth, he was annoyed with her for playing at all. But it wasn't her fault. She had no idea the truth Malik had just uncovered.

Malik found Yuri and Elda within the village, but Yuri was infatuated with his new match and carried a mug of ale with him at all times, and Malik was tired of nothing being serious to his friend. All Yuri wanted to talk about was Riese's hunt, and some runemarked hunting dagger. Or else, gossiping with Elda, predicting more Faltari matches that were sure to come over the next couple of days.

In the past, Yuri's lightness had felt like a counter to Malik's headiness. Tonight, it only caused aggravation. But Malik couldn't fault Yuri or his bride-to-be for that.

It was what all Faltari did at the festival. All except his father, Malik supposed, and now, him. Cursed to bear weights no one even knew about. It seemed everywhere he turned, there was one of the Attican youths or their parents, or some of the other tall and muscular Attican guards who'd joined them.

The foreigners laughed, bandied stories, drank, and formed impromptu dance circles in the streets as bards struck up lively tunes. People were happy and content, and their minds swarmed around Malik like a raging torrent of frivolity.

All Malik's existence seemed to form a nexus around this moment, and he couldn't even hear himself think.

He was shaman now, and he had a duty to be seen and to be friendly. To offer blessings to Faltari families as they enjoyed their last nights of inter-clan unity before the traders left, and they hauled their supplies back to their respective villages and the impending gloom of winter settled on the island and sealed off their lands from the world once more.

The sun descended over the walls of the fjord, and the crowds gathered in the meadow in the fading light. Malik's father and the chieftains of the four clans gathered at the crest of a small knoll, overlooking the crowd.

Malik probably should have been with them, but he'd avoided his father, and his father had not come hunting for him tonight.

He stood at the back of the crowd, barely listening as Joren told the tale of the Crossing. How their ancestors had fled a land on the brink of destruction. How some had not learned the lessons and had gone on to form empires and fight wars over land and power, just as had been done in the World Before.

It was the same ritual his father performed every year, but Malik never realized how intentionally vague the tale was. Joren did not speak of the gate located on this island. He spoke of their people arriving first on "these shores" and proceeded from there.

Faltari would apply their own meaning, and the others would do the same. Joren spoke blessings on the foreigners gathered, praying they would see the sanctity and peace of this sacred land, and remember.

"Look around this meadow. Here, there are gathered emissaries from every corner of the world, all coexisting in peace, for a day. It is not too late to learn."

Did we learn anything at all? Malik wondered.

When his father had finished his speech, the chieftains thanked the traders for another successful festival. And then, a troupe of minstrels from Beirus struck up a song, and people began to dance.

Food vendors mingled with the crowds, selling roasted meat and vegetables on skewers of wood from Chardonia, bowls of rice noodles from Ytan, legs of grouse from Attica, and more.

At last, Malik spotted Riese near the edge of the crowd with her family. He worked his way through the teeming masses.

"Malik!" cried Riese's mother, Toren. "Good to see you, young shaman. My, it's hard to believe you're both Ascended now. And god's breath, Riese and Yuri both getting matched."

Vinder Perinsein turned from his conversation with Riese's father, Ulrik, and nodded to Malik.

"Vinder, you know Malik, I trust," said Toren.

The young man nodded with respect, placing an arm around Riese's shoulder. "Of course, shaman. May the breath of the gods remain upon you."

"And you," said Malik.

Toren laughed. "Riese and Malik have been friends since they were in babe's wraps! But Malik, when are *you* going to be matched? Even shamans have to carry on their lineage. I seem to recall you dancing with a pretty girl during the Ascension ceremonies. Where has she gone off to?"

Malik was growing tired of the pleasantries. He felt he'd been exchanging them for months, one festival after the other.

"I've been learning the shaman ways, ma'am. Little time for courting, I'm afraid."

"Oh, yes, quite understandable... we're most grateful for your service to our people. Where would we be without men like you and your father? Certainly don't mean to make light of it."

"No, of course, ma'am. Er, do you mind if I borrow Riese for a moment?"

Riese was scowling. "Can't it wait until later, Malik? I'll find you after—"

"It'll only be a moment, I promise."

"It's no problem," Toren said. "You two hardly see each other anymore, and with Malik being shaman now, and you being matched, Riese... well, after the festival, you might not see one another for some time."

Ulrik laughed. "We'll be with you all winter, dear. And besides, I've been wanting to challenge your new match to a round of spears."

"The way Riese hunted today, I reckon I don't stand a chance," said Vinder.

Riese nodded. "Okay." She glanced up at Vinder. "It'll just be a moment."

The young man shrugged. Malik could sense his irritation, but Vinder ventured off with Riese's father, both men laughing as they went.

Riese seized Malik by the wrist and dragged him away from the crowd. She said nothing until they'd withdrawn within the walled fort encompassing the village.

"I told you I wanted time with my family tonight, Malik."

"This is important."

Malik led the way deeper into the village. A few youths were huddled in corners, drinking mead, and a young couple was pressed against the wall of a longhouse, lost in their passion.

"If we're leaving, Malik, I want to spend my final moments with my family before—"

"Just trust me, okay?"

Malik stopped near the great socha tree at the center of the inner village square and lowered his voice. There was no going back now.

"It's about your egg."

Chapter 22

Bloody Southerner

Ava watched General Campos with curiosity as he mingled amongst the festival-goers, chatting with a Faltari chieftain, then, with Urla and Ruan. The young shaman came by alone and exchanged brief words with the general, though Malik kept glancing toward a girl across the meadow who never looked his way.

Curious, Ava thought.

Ava had seen the two slip away for a time and was tempted to follow. The girl exuded irritation, though she went willingly, none-theless. Ava was tempted to follow, but knew she wouldn't be able to keep up.

That feeling she'd had when she met Malik lingered. It must have been some form of shaman's power, brushing up against her own.

The shaman moved on, vanishing into the crowd, and now, Campos spoke with Lady Thenius. Next, an Ytani trader.

The general had a friendly exchange with a Chardonian swindler, and if that wasn't a sign of the strange magic permeating this festival, Ava didn't know what was. The pleasantries were surely an act—the hostility between Atticans and Chardonians stretched back centuries—but both Campos and the swindler played their parts for a full five minute conversation, nodding and laughing at the other's jokes and jibes.

All around, strange peoples intermingled and feasted and drank and danced. There was beauty in it. At its root, this possibility was the same that drove her own family's ambitions, she supposed.

Lady Thenius's daughter, Iriana, came by to speak with Ava for a few moments, only out of courtesy, for she swiftly moved on, flirting with Marcus, the boy from Bastion Academy, as well as a reserved Valgish boat hand who'd taken a liking to her. Iriana was playing the two of them, whether for the pleasure of the game or some other reason, Ava couldn't quite deduce.

Evening stretched into night. Radiant swaths of stars brushed across an inky sky, and Ava remained at the edge of things, watching and listening, trying to get a read on the true essence of this island. It held secrets she longed to understand. She could feel power here that did not exist elsewhere. Perhaps it was the free-flowing relationship the Faltari maintained with magic. Or perhaps it was more. Something native to the land itself. But the Other held so many mysteries they were only beginning to unravel, and mostly in secret societies, or else, across the world.

Mum would've been able to sense it, she thought, then swiftly suppressed the swell of emotions that threatened to rise at the thought of her mother. It was an uncharacteristic lapse on her part.

Ava spotted the elder shaman across the crowd. Joren exuded power and strength, but there was anxiety there too, especially when near his son. She hadn't noticed the two together since the evening festivities began. Malik was nowhere to be seen now.

Her own father spent much time sharing mead with the merchants, especially the Faltari.

"Do they know?"

Ava turned. She hadn't felt the intruding presence, but she recovered quickly, smiling at the young shaman as Malik took a place beside her.

"Know what?" Ava asked.

"I sensed what you were the moment you stepped off that ship," Malik said. "Thought Atticans had strict rules about accessing magic."

Ava bristled at being found out so easily. She shrugged. "Your gifts must be great, indeed, shaman. None of my schoolmasters know my affinities."

"You take tests, don't you?"

"The Arcania tests all academy students, but they assume the test-takers are hoping to follow the Path of the Other. I failed by intent."

"Attican magic is focused on material things."

"Alchemy and artifices, yes."

"But you focus all your *hish* on minds."

"Focus my... what?"

"The breath of the gods, what you call the Other. That breath flows freely here. It's invigorating for you, that's easy to tell. I'm sure you're better at hiding it back home."

Ava flashed a smile. She liked this shaman. "You notice much. I'm Ava, by the way. Ava Lucila Rykus."

"Malik Jorensein," he said.

"Yes, I caught that when we arrived."

"Why do you hide your gifts?"

She shrugged. "The thought of sitting at desks, studying runespells and crafting channelers all day... it bores me."

Predictably, the shaman glanced at her cane but said nothing.

"I suppose," said Malik, "nothing can compare with the lure of being a Dragonmount, can it?"

Ava pursed her lips and held his gaze. His blue eyes danced in the torchlight at the edge of the field.

"You want something," Ava said.

Malik hesitated.

"Why were you speaking with Campos?" she continued.

"Merely exchanging pleasantries," said Malik, though a flit of the eyes gave him away.

"Yes, shaman's duties, I'm sure. Yet, you've been gone for much of the celebration. Something tells me you've been distracted. Something to do with that blonde huntress you ran off with earlier?"

Malik blanched.

"Yes," said Ava. "I don't know what I'm talking about. Just a foreigner with a faint affinity for sorcery, reading too much into things. If that were true, you'd walk away. But even though you like to be the one with the upper hand when it comes to sensing such things, I think whatever you want is too important. So what is it, and what's your offer?"

"My offer?"

"This is a trading festival, isn't it?"

Malik huffed, glancing away, then looked her straight in the eyes. "When your ship leaves tomorrow morning, I want to be on it. Me and my friend, Riese. The blonde huntress. Is that possible?"

"Possible after Campos already dismissed you? Extremely difficult."

"You have a gift of persuasion."

Ava raised a brow. "Perhaps. So what's the offer?"

"I'll teach you to wield your magic like a Faltari."

"And in exchange, you want me to use my gifts on the general?"

Malik glanced around for a moment. He lowered his voice. "I am forbidden from using my gifts to manipulate my own desires."

"But I'm a bloody southerner with no such scruples, is that it?" Ava's eyes grew wide, then she smirked. "All right, have it your way, but the first lesson starts right now."

———

Ava and Malik wandered from the crowd separately. The shaman stopped to speak with village elders and a young Faltari couple.

Ava paused once she reached the other side of the festival, where colored canopies and strings of small Beirusian paper lanterns were stretched between poles of wood.

Ruan spotted her and hurried over, nearly spilling his ample mug of ale. "Where are you off to?"

"Wherever the winds take me. Did you find anything of use?"

"The exchange has already been made," said Ruan. "We'll sail at first light."

The eggs won't travel by sea, surely, Ava thought. *But the general hasn't been back to the ship. And the Lady Knight could never have smuggled a godblade ashore. Or could she?*

"We need to be the first to see them, Ruan."

"She said you'd say that."

"Your mother?"

"She's wary of your low-blood ambition."

"Your mother is friends with an advisor to the emperor. You're son of a Dragonmount. Some of us weren't born with such connections."

She impressed a hint of guilt with her magic.

Ruan Pelasius straightened, frowning. "I didn't say I agreed with her."

"Maybe neither of us will bond, but we could at least have the greatest chance."

Ruan nodded. "I overheard Campos say he'll be sleeping back on the ship."

"Then, we should too. Perhaps we could ride back with him."

"Only he and the Lady Knight will be permitted on the ship tonight."

Shit, Ava thought.

"Maybe we could be first to the ship in the morning?" Ruan ventured.

No, that will be too late. Everything hinges on being first contact with the eggs.

"Tomorrow, it is. Thank you, Ruan. You're a good friend. Go back and enjoy the festival."

"Are you sure you don't want company?"

"You know me," Ava said. "I like my privacy."

Ruan nodded. "We'll get our eggs, Ava. I'm sure of it."

He returned to the festivities, and Ava hobbled away from the tents and into the copse of snowpine that encroached on the village.

CHAPTER 23

THE FJURIIN PATH

Malik's mind was a stormcloud of emotions, but he could not let himself dwell long on it. His path was laid before him.

He watched the dark-haired Attican girl approach from the thick cover of trees and foliage, fumbling through the uneven ground, leading with her cane, grimacing only when she half-stumbled over a rock or root in the darkness. Her mind was steady, focused, controlled. He'd sensed that the moment he saw her, and it impressed him how well she held herself despite the constant pain she suppressed.

Ava Rykus was on a mission. Malik could give her something that would help her fulfill her task, and she could do the same for him and Riese.

When Ava reached him, she paused and studied him, the warmth of *hish* brushed past him.

"Why my ship?" she asked. "You could go with any trader."

"I think you know why."

"The cargo, of course." Riese emerged from behind a boulder and walked toward them.

Ava took a step back, raising her cane instinctively, almost like a weapon.

Riese held up her hands non-threateningly as she neared. "There's no one else out here. I scouted. Malik says you can help us."

"With matters of cargo?" Ava asked, lowering the cane. "I don't have any say about that. But I may be able to get you onboard our vessel. You have an... attachment to our goods, do you?"

"I've just Ascended," said Riese. "And mine is one of the few that survived. And it seems that I'm... bonded."

Ava's eyes lit up at this. "Really?"

"I don't know how it all works," Riese said.

"Does it happen often? A Faltari bond?"

"I don't know," Malik said. Like so many things, it was shrouded by a past of lies.

"And you want to be Dragonmount," Ava said.

Riese offered a tentative nod.

"You would have to become an Attican citizen," Ava went on. "It would take the advocacy of a great noble."

"Is it possible?" Riese asked. There was fire in her eyes and a pained desperation in her voice. The fear of losing her egg again.

"Perhaps," Ava said.

"Campos wants control over the riders chosen, right?" Malik asked. "That's why you're here before your lottery."

"And you want me to give up my chance for you?"

"There are three eggs," said Malik. "Enough for you and your friend too."

"You want to fight for Attica?" Ava asked, turning to Riese.

"I... I don't know. I just found out what I am."

"Well, all mounts fight for Attica, don't they? So, you'd better dig down and find out what you want before I think about bothering the consul general with something like this."

Riese drew a long breath. "Look, I don't know how any of this plays out. I don't know if I can be a mount, or if I could ever convince Campos or anyone else to advocate for me... all I know is that I have a path set before me, and if I don't follow where it leads, I'll never forgive myself. I have to try."

Malik watched Ava as she listened to Riese bear her soul. There was a tell in the Attican girl's spirit. Something subtle, but unmistakable. Something about Riese's experience that was shared.

"Okay," Ava said. "But first, the exchange."

Malik nodded and stepped toward her. "You have skill with magic, but it's unfocused."

"What do you mean?"

"You treat *hish*—er, the Other—like it is something threatening, a flame that can only be held at arm's length."

"That's a good metaphor," Ava said. "We're raised with that belief."

"Our words shape our world," Malik said. "They determine what is possible. If you believe magic is a threatening force that could destroy you, you will approach it only a certain way. Yes, it is powerful. Yes, it could destroy you. But only if you don't know how to handle it. You can pass your hand straight through a flame if you do it with precision and speed. The breath of the gods is little different."

Ava focused, and Malik sensed the pulse of *hish*.

"But it *is* something outside us, isn't it? Even the Elyans believe that. Clearly, it's stronger in some places than others. I've felt that since we arrived."

Malik nodded.

"It is out there," Malik said, gesturing at the sky, only barely visible through the pine branches. "And it is also here." He pressed his hand against the right side of his chest, where Faltari believed the spirit resides. "There are traces everywhere, like vapor in the air. We draw it in and out like the air we breathe, into our own spirit."

"We are the channel," Ava realized.

"With practice, some can be," Malik said. "You've been trying to wield a torch when you have the ability to breathe fire."

Riese rolled her eyes, but Ava marveled once again at his words.

"You can sense the power around you, yes?" Malik asked, stepping closer.

Ava straightened, supporting herself on her dragonhead cane. She closed her eyes like Faltari children did before they learned to see the forces of both physical and spiritual worlds with the same eyes. For they were not separate as these southern barbarians believed. All reality was intertwined.

Eyes open, Malik saw the currents threading through the world, emanating from the ground, shifting on the breeze, swirling across the sky, pulsing in his spirit as he focused his true sight on the breath of the gods.

Threads of magic circulated near Ava, drawing close, though most slipped past her. She was unpracticed, but when she opened her eyes, they flashed with wonder.

"I feel like I've been breathing underwater through a reed all my life, and I've just come up and taken my first full breath."

"That's not a bad metaphor, yourself," Malik said. "But you're still far from a full breath. Even my father, the most powerful sorcerer on the island, must take care not to draw too much *hish* into his spirit."

"Incredible." Ava sighed, eyes still closed, drawing more in.

"We have practices and rituals for honing this skill," Malik said. "Learning to hold *hish* for later use. Perhaps I can show you more on your ship."

Ava shook her head. "There's a Knight of Caadron aboard. I haven't dared use magic around her. But here, all you Faltari are using it, so her senses are surely muddied."

"We are children of the gods," Malik said. "Blessed with the awareness of their greatest gift."

"Alright," said Riese, butting back in. "Now, it's your turn, Lady Attica. How are we getting on your ship?"

———

Urla Pelasius stuck close to Campos throughout the evening, slowly sipping a flagon of Attican wine as the evening waned.

Campos kept his satchel close, his servant standing watch over it and several other goods they'd brought ashore. No one paid the satchel any mind. Not even the shamans.

It was clever, Urla thought, to hide the most valuable possession in the world right here in the open.

"If you want them to believe you've nothing to hide, hide nothing," Campos had said when she protested the risk of such a brazen act.

But most traders carried their own satchels of possessions, all of which had been thoroughly searched upon their arrival. What could anyone suspect?

Soon, Urla's attention drifted to Ruan, especially when he was near Ava Rykus. Urla was relieved when the girl ventured off.

"She's using you to get close to Campos," Urla had told her son.

"Are we not using Campos the same way? Does that mean you're not his friend?"

"Don't be foolish. He was your grandfather's best friend."

But her son's words lingered in her mind.

It was true. She'd taken a liking to Campos as a young girl, when her father still lived and ruled House Vestra, and she was not yet a Pelasius. Vestra was a middling house. Campos had been a powerful ally, and she'd recognized the value in endearing herself to him. Campos was without wife or child, and an outcast in the capital, as Urla was an outcast in most Attican circles.

Clearly, Ava was an outcast amongst her own peers.

And Ruan...

Well, he had long lacked the most valued Fjuriin traits: charisma and cunning. Even after his time at the academy, he remained quiet and pensive. Ruan was different than the consul general in countless ways, but he was still a lonesome man in need of someone to care for.

Yes, Urla recognized the similarities between herself and Ava just fine, and that was precisely what unnerved her about the girl.

By now, most had reached the point in their festivities where talk of the world and politics and rumors had dwindled to bawdy tales. It would turn serious again soon enough, she knew.

Ruan sauntered over, laughing with the girl from Bastion Academy. Iriana Thenius was high-blood like Ruan. Dark-haired, bronze-skinned, and brown-eyed like a proper Attican girl.

She giggled at a whispered joke, taking a long swig of wine as they neared. Iriana was the sort of girl Ruan would have been sheepish to speak with two years ago.

"What do you think, Consul General?" Iriana asked, turning to Campos and flashing a pursed-lipped smile. "Are we entering an age of peace or war?"

Urla sighed. It was turning serious again.

"What do you say?" Campos asked, smiling.

"Well, there's always a lull between campaigns," Iriana ventured.

"You're not wrong, though how much of that lull is within our control? The Sigan conquest was not planned. It was a retaliation over disputed land. Our wise emperor simply made the best use of the moment. If I can say anything about Athanasius with certainty, it is that he is always calculated."

"Exactly!" said Iriana, grinning at Ruan. "In just a few decades, we've reclaimed Taika, Ytan, Valucia, Kalkesh, and now, Siga. No one else would dare rise up. Not for years. And surely, we must revel in our conquests for a little while."

Campos raised a brow. Urla glanced around, but their present company had dwindled to members of their own party. The din was loud enough, it was doubtful any passersby heard Iriana. Still, it left Urla on edge. It would not do to disturb the harmony of this festival.

Campos shrugged and kept his voice low. "What are your thoughts, young Pelasius?"

Ruan straightened. "It's the same thing every Attican is speculating. With Siga, we've retaken all the lands most commonly regarded as true Attica. The Good Emperor Vitruvian ended his reign with years of prosperity. Will his protege choose the same?"

"Clearly, Lady Thenius believes this to be the case."

"Or at least a longer stretch of peace than we've seen yet under Athanasius's rule," said Iriana, nudging Ruan in the shoulder. "Our victory is fresh and in everyone's minds. The Valgs are no threat. The Chardonians are surely pissing their pants. I've seen how they look at us when they think we're not watching at this bloody festival. Attica is properly feared again."

"But you don't think so, Ruan?" Campos asked.

Ruan paused, weighing his words, or at least pretending to, in true Fjuriin fashion. "I believe Iriana is right that we are feared. And right that our neighbors would be fools to wage war with Attica so fresh off a victory. But I do not believe our Dragon Emperor will settle for an Age of Prosperity. Not yet."

"Why is that?" Campos smiled.

"The continent remains divided. All Atticans long for another Golden Age, and what emperor wouldn't want to usher in such an age? No, I think we are on the verge of an Age of Fire. And the first real act of Attican conquest is coming soon."

Urla watched the fire in her son's eyes. How he longed to be a hero in such an age, as all soldiers did. To fight for honor and glory and lift their great nation to heights not known in centuries.

And if he were Dragonmount...

Campos smiled. "Ah, you two have had much to drink. You want an answer, and that, I do not have. But I expect there is truth in both your words. Prosperity or conquest? That is the great question of history, and the answers are always intertwined. There can be no peace without conquest but reach too far and you risk unraveling all that has been won, and the peace and prosperity of victory is lost. History is full of many lessons of such overreach. But the present path forward is unclear and the answer not ours to determine. We may only choose how we hold ourselves, in times of peace *or* war. The Fjuriin Path, no?"

Both youths smiled in reverence.

"Very wise, Consul," Iriana said, her hand resting on Ruan's shoulder. Ruan glanced around, and Urla knew he was searching for Ava Rykus.

Perhaps he's playing her as well, Urla realized with bemusement.

But Ava was nowhere to be seen.

"Well, my friends," said Campos. "I believe it is time for this sage to retire for the evening. Festivals are wasted on old men like me. Enjoy yourselves. But be sure to return to the ship at first light. Good night."

CHAPTER 24

THE SHRINE

Malik's nerves were on edge as he and Riese slipped amongst the trees beyond the wharf. They hid near the path—barely more than a game trail—that wound through the woods on the outskirts of Yerida village.

The docks, of course, were located just outside the village gates. The vast dirt-trodden square, where Malik and his father had greeted the Attican party, bridged the space between the village and the forest. On most nights, gates on both ends of the village would be shut at sundown to keep out predators, but during the festival, the gates remained open, monitored by Faltari hunters.

A pair of longboats, lit by lanterns, made their way toward anchored ships, ferrying leftover cargo from the day's trade under the moonlit night. Some exchanges occurred between nations, but most of the actual trading was made with Faltara and was finished before the evening's celebrations began. Likely, these ferrymen were lowly servants doing the work while their masters feasted and enjoyed themselves. Or else, they belonged to the pleasure barges of Beirus, escorting traders and the occasional Faltari.

Malik had noted more than a couple traders slipping away with a painted woman, though of course, their garb remained modest on Faltari shores. He'd heard bawdy tales from a few boys a couple years his senior.

Dragyrs were especially known for sending their newly come-of-age sons to the barges during the Festival of the Fading Sun. A taste of *uhmskara*, they claimed.

I bet Aram Tulsein is one of them, Malik thought, as he watched a man and woman pass through the gates, making their way toward the docks.

Even a shaman's son couldn't help but be curious about the ways of the beautiful women of foreign lands. He sensed the practice was wrong. Yet, it was not forbidden, even among the Faltari.

From a few of his mother's comments over the years, Malik was certain his father had spent an evening with a courtesan during his Wandering, before they were matched. But every tale was always left vague, even from his mother.

"What are you thinking about?" Riese asked.

Malik felt his cheeks flush. "Just, er, wondering about the world beyond. You?"

They'd both been quiet for some time.

"I was thinking of my family," she said. "I won't even be able to say goodbye."

In truth, Malik had given his family little thought. He was angry and curious and restless, but not sorry about his decision. "We'll be back in a year or two."

"Maybe *you* will. If I actually were to be a Dragonmount... I might never return."

Malik nodded, chastened by his self-absorption yet again.

"What do *you* want?" he whispered.

"You're a damn shaman, Malik. You know more than anyone that's not how we've been taught to make these kinds of decisions."

"No. We're taught to protect family and clan. More than anything else in the world. We're taught lies. About the Ascent. About what happens to the eggs. Who knows what else?"

"It's that simple for you?"

Of course it wasn't. Malik had never been more torn in his life, but the words he spoke were filled with a conviction he was trying to instill in himself as much as Riese. "We have to figure the truth out for ourselves. We have to find what *we* believe. I think that's what *uhmskara* has always been about."

"Another of our wise traditions," said Riese with a huff of laughter. "I just wonder... maybe that's exactly what Rayne Seversein thought too."

Malik grimaced. "Maybe he was right to leave. Maybe he wasn't a traitor like we were always taught. Maybe Rayne is just one more in a long history of lies."

"Maybe."

"So, what is it you want, Riese? Because I can sense you're not as torn about leaving as you'd like me to think."

Riese put on the air of an affront but settled into a smirk. "I've always wanted to test myself. But ever since I first touched that egg, I've felt a restlessness I can't explain. Like I've been dying for something all my life, and now I finally know what it was. Something... shifted when I touched that egg. And when I thought I destroyed it, I felt like a part of me died too."

"The blood runs in your veins."

They both spun to find Ava Rykus behind them. Malik had been so focused on the gates and their conversation, he hadn't sensed her resonance approach.

"I feel that, too," said Ava. "I think I've always felt it. I just didn't always know what it was. I'm meant to be Dragonmount. I'm going to be Dragonmount. And if what you say is true, I think you will be too. My father says the lottery is less about the dragons and more about the rider. You've already shown the potential. But quiet now. Here comes the general."

Ava pointed to the gates with her black cane, where Consul General Campos emerged from the village, accompanied by a manservant carrying a large rucksack. They were followed by several other men and women, members of the general's personal guard, if Malik had to guess. All of them carried packs and trunks. The Attican goods of trade from the day. He wondered which one was the Knight of Caadron that Ava had mentioned.

"Come along but hang back a ways," Ava instructed. "He should see you but not feel threatened."

Malik and Riese nodded.

The girl made her way toward the center of the square, right leg hitching only slightly as she walked.

Malik and Riese followed, emerging from the path and pausing at a wooden bench near the edge of the square.

They were too far to make out words, but Campos was shaking his head at Ava, who offered calm responses.

"What if he refuses?" Riese asked.

"He won't," said Malik.

"How could you know that? He refused you once already."

Malik focused his senses on the man's spirit. No, he could not make out words, but he could gather the timbre of Campos's resonance.

"He's a politician," Malik said. "His actions are a show that don't match his spirit. He was open to the idea when I spoke to him, but we couldn't speak plainly in the middle of the festival. I think maybe he was testing us. Seeing if we'd give up that easy."

Malik had got the same sense from the man at the exchange, the minute he realized there were three eggs this year, not one or two. Else, Malik never would have approached Ava with this proposition at all. Campos was wary of eggs falling into the wrong noble's hands, even among his own party. And he held a deep fascination with the Faltari.

"You sensed that when you approached him the first time?"

Malik shrugged. "Perhaps. I was planting the seed. And I think this girl will make it grow."

Riese punched him in the shoulder. "And you didn't say anything?"

"I'm no master," Malik said. "I didn't want to... you know... get your hopes up."

Riese snorted. "If you were worried about that you never would have told me the truth about the egg."

"Look."

Malik and Riese both watched as Campos spoke with his retinue of plain-clothed guards, and then, the men and women marched across the square, made their way to the docks, and began loading things onto multiple longboats. Only Campos, Ava, and the manservant remained.

Slowly, the three meandered across the square, strolling past Malik and Riese, before pausing a short distance away, at the edge of the square. Campos turned, met their gazes, and smiled.

"Well, hurry along, will you?" the general said. "We must speak quickly."

Malik and Riese rose from the bench and strode over. The general

led the way to the narrow path near the edge of the docks, which
wended swiftly through the woodlands outside the village. They paused
at the entrance. Malik glanced back at the Attican guards, noting one
powerful-looking woman with brown skin, who did not help load goods,
and watched Campos and the others carefully.

"She's a knight," said Campos.

"Of Caadron?" asked Malik excitedly.

Campos shrugged. "On this shore, she is only a servant, isn't she?"

"Does she have her..." Riese began, then thought better of it.

Campos smiled. "Malik tells me that you, young Riese, wish for the
opportunity to embrace your destiny. If what he says about your connection is true, this may be a possibility. Come, I've instructed my guards to
allow us some time before I must depart. But, of course, such sensitive
matters can't be handled in the open air of the village square, now, can
they?"

Malik nodded, realizing they were playing parts out here in the
open. "Would you like to see our Unity Shrine, Lord General? It's just
up this path."

"Lead the way, shaman."

It was only a few minute's walk from the docks. Over a small hill,
across a stream that spilled into the fjord, and partway up the steep
foothills that surrounded the village. Timber had been cleared from a
shelf in the hillside long ago, leaving a flat expanse the breadth of a longhouse. The place was dotted with wooden poles carved with runes and
other ancient symbols. The largest poles contained the heads of the
sacred beasts, looming over them with sharp features and watchful eyes.

Campos gazed up briefly at the majestic totems, then knelt as his
servant removed the pack from his shoulders and set it at the general's
feet.

The servant stood back, arms crossed. The man was built like a
warrior, thick shoulders and thighs evident despite his loose-fitting pants
and woolen tunic.

Malik, Riese, and Ava gathered around Campos as the general
untethered the leather fastenings of the rucksack. Riese and Ava both
drew a sharp breath as he removed the first egg.

Chapter 25

Bound

The egg was the size of a human child's head, somehow small in Campos's large hands. Thick, hard-ridged scales shimmered in gradient shades of red and black with a distinct crimson glow emanating from its core.

The sight sucked all the breath out of Ava's lungs. All her life, she had anticipated this moment. To see a real dragon egg with her very eyes. A pang coursed through her, knowing this egg would never be hers.

"It shines even brighter now," said Campos, glancing from the egg to Malik. "You weren't lying, shaman. There is fierce potential—even a longing—for this bond. Of course, nothing is final at this stage, but..."

Campos extended the egg to Riese, who hesitated. The Faltari girl had the build of a warrior, muscles rippling down her shoulders and arms like mighty rivers of sinew and bone. A strength Ava envied, no matter the pride she took in her own mental and spiritual abilities. Riese had the look of a Dragonmount, yet still, she hesitated.

Riese held out her hands, then, withdrew. Her fingers trembled.

"It is daunting to face one's fate," said Campos. "There is no going back from a bond, once it is fully formed."

"When is it final?" Riese murmured.

"When the bonding rites have been completed, which, of course, cannot be accomplished until we reach Attica. You could walk away now, and this egg would bond with another rider. But if this were an Attican lottery, such potential for a bond would never be denied."

"I don't even know what it means to be Dragonmount," Riese said.

Campos chuckled. "Nor do I, my dear. They are a mystery to all outside their ranks. The guardians of the world."

"But I'm not Attican."

"You've never thought of yourself as such," said Campos. "But these lands are under Attican control and protection, whether you've known it or not. Your people have served the Dragon Emperors for ages. The influence of the Dragon Lords has proved problematic over the years, and the emperor has chosen me to find riders who will serve the empire, not the interests of one gods-damned lord house. Two riders were chosen before we even reached these shores, and I've a third egg. So it would seem our fates have entwined."

"You don't know me," said Riese.

Campos nodded and gazed at the glowing egg. "I know who you are, Riese. And I am Fjuriin. I know a path when it's before me. Do you?"

Riese hesitated.

"My father taught me something," Campos continued, "and I've always conducted myself with that teaching in mind. The world is a ruinous place for those who run from who they really are. Always stay true to your path."

You speak the truth, Consul, Ava thought.

"But time is not in your favor," Campos added. "You must choose, Riese. Will you follow your path or flee from it?"

Riese took one long breath and released it, then she took the egg between her hands. Instantly, the glow surged, expanding from the core of the egg to cover its entirety.

"I believe that dragonling approves your decision. Now, two more."

Campos reached into his satchel and removed a dark blue egg. Ava's heart pounded, the pang raging in her gut as the egg glowed with an icy luminescence.

"Well, well," he said, extending the egg to her.

Blood rushed in Ava's body. Energy surged in her mind, swept her back to her childhood—before the Fall of Valucia, and the toll the war took on her own young body—when Ava would race through waves of long grass with her parents. Soaring down hilly meadows, weaving amongst copses of elm trees and towering oaks. Running till her entire body was flushed and her lungs full and gasping, and all the world thrummed with the immediacy and fervor of life as it was meant to be.

Her fingers grasped that egg, and her spirit soared just the same.

All at once, Ava felt the rush of the wind washing over her. Magic surged through her, the radiance of the Other filling her within and without, and she recognized her unity with that power behind the world.

The Other.

The shaman's lesson appeared all the more obvious as she recognized that unity and separateness between her own self and the resonance radiating from the egg in her hands.

They were both separate and one, and Ava would never let anything come between them.

She looked up, and Campos was smiling.

"Yet another fierce potential," he said. "And now, the third."

Surprised, Ava glanced at Malik, who drew back, waving his hands dismissively. "Sorry, General, but I'm afraid I have no bond."

"No, of course not, son."

"He's talking about me."

Ava glanced up at the feminine voice.

Iriana Thenius stepped from the path behind them. The girl had come alone, following the same path the four of them had taken.

Three eggs. Ava and Iriana were always his choice, and now, the third was given to a foreigner.

He never intended for Ruan to bond, she realized.

Iriana joined them, a thin smile on her full lips. The young woman was a more typical Attican noble. Tall and athletic and beautiful. Ancient blood, if from a middling house. But did she have the mettle of a warrior of crimson skies?

Ava had doubts about the Bastion student.

"It is not my choice, Iriana," Campos said.

It was talk. Whatever might be said of Campos, it was clear he knew exactly what he was doing. Ava hadn't needed to manipulate him about Malik and Riese. She suspected he'd planned this the moment he discovered the third egg already with the potential to bond.

"Our choices are only part of this game," Campos said, clapping

Iriana on the shoulder and drawing her over. He reached inside the satchel and withdrew the final dragon egg, a gorgeous golden one that seemed to be coated in an effervescent sheen. Ava couldn't determine whether or not this was a glow, or the nature of the dragon egg itself.

But as Iriana took the egg in her hands, it shone perceptibly brighter. *Poor Ruan,* Ava thought.

Sure, she'd used him to get here. But it didn't mean she felt good about it. She kept telling herself she'd make it right, someday, when everything came together. Yet, she hadn't invited Ruan to join this little charade any more than Campos had.

Because you didn't want him to get hurt, she reminded herself. Tried to convince herself. *No, because you didn't trust him. Even after all he's done. Despite his goodness and his knowledge about the true ways of the world. You feared he would choose duty. Just like you.*

Iriana's cheeks flushed as her mind made contact with the spirit within that sacred shell. She closed her eyes, and Campos smiled.

Ava seethed inwardly for Ruan's sake.

But perhaps this was for the best. Iriana's presence already complicated things plenty.

As for the Faltari... she'd see if she'd chosen the right path soon enough.

The clearing was cast in darkness as the moon slipped behind a large cloud.

"We should get going," said Campos. "You've all made contact. So long as you remain near the eggs, another will be unable to form a bond, and the lottery will go as we please, so long as no one knows how it was accomplished, it will appear a random selection. But for now, the eggs must remain in my possession, until this game is complete. Baro?"

"Of course, master," the manservant said. He turned to Iriana and set the satchel upon the ground in front of her. She reached down, hesitated only a moment, then set the egg inside.

As she rose, there was a meaty crunch as Baro seized the girl's head between his hands and wrenched.

Iriana slumped to the ground in a heap.

Campos cried out, horrified.

Malik and Riese both staggered back. Fear and shock overwhelming them.

Ava leapt into action.

This was the moment she'd waited for, trained for, spent all her life pandering to the fucking Atticans for.

And she would not fail.

Campos lunged at Baro, rage, terror, and confusion distorting his face.

He did not even glance at Ava. She pressed the secret lever located in the head of her cane.

The Faltari hadn't taken it from her while they'd checked her.

Oh, the poor, poor cripple. Be gentle.

Grimacing at the quick motion, Ava whipped the concealed weapon around, a razor-sharp Kirithian blade the length of her hand jutting from the end of her cane.

With a perfectly executed flourish, she swept it across Campos's throat. His skin spread like the peel of a fruit against her runemarked blade. Her father's gift to the Atticans would be their gods-damned demise.

Campos dropped to his knees, clutching his throat, blood gurgling over trembling fingers. Desperate intakes of breath mixed with a gruesome croaking sound.

Though it was her first kill, the gore had no effect on Ava. She had seen more horrors in her first years of life than most academy girls would see in a lifetime.

There was a crunch and thud behind her.

Ava spun.

Baro's body slumped against the back of a tree, unmoving.

For a moment, she didn't understand. Neither Malik nor Riese had brought weapons, she'd watched them both too carefully.

Magic...

Ava's insides knotted as she faced Malik and Riese. The shaman's spirit pressed against her own. With horror, she realized she could not move, though she felt no pain.

Malik's face contorted with rage and fear.

"What have you done?" he demanded.

Riese took the cane from Ava's frozen grasp. She hurried over to investigate Baro's body.

A Valucian servant earning his way into the good graces of one of the most powerful men in the empire. Serving Campos however he required. Biding his time, for this moment.

Riese checked the manservant's pulse and shook her head, returning to Malik's side.

It was a good death, Ava thought. *A Path of Flames.*

But her mission was not complete.

"Malik, Riese, I need you to listen to me. I mean you no harm, I promise. And neither did Baro."

Malik shook his head, huffing with uncontrolled laughter as he surveyed the carnage. The general twitched on the ground, unconscious as he neared death.

"Oh, well, that's comforting." There was no tremble in Riese's hands as she held the cane-blade up to Ava's throat.

Ava felt the release of the shaman's magic, but she did not dare move.

"Give me one good reason not to slit your throat," Riese said.

"I'll give you three," Ava said, glancing down at the dragon eggs on the ground.

Malik knelt at the general's side, tore a long strip of cloth from his tunic and wrapped it around the man's bleeding throat, whispering words in a language Ava did not recognize. Her blade had struck true. The general would be dead any moment. She was sure of it.

Campos remained still.

Malik stood and faced her. "Where are the others?"

"Others?" she asked.

"You weren't sent here alone," Riese said. "Who sent you?"

Ava took a calculated breath, looking both the Faltari youths in the eyes. "Whatever bargain your ancestors may have struck, Attica represents the exact opposite of this place. You've been forced to serve the empire. We all have. But the time has finally come to—"

Riese struck Ava's shoulder with the broadside of the cane, sending piercing pain shooting down her spine and into her leg. Ava dropped to the ground, body drawing inward.

"Answer the question," Riese said.

Ava bit the inside of her lip, and forced herself to ignore the pain, as she had so many times in her life. The ground trembled beneath her feet. "Don't you hear what's happening?"

They all went quiet.

From this distance, it was difficult to distinguish from the din of the festival. But the sounds of the night had changed. Laughter and singing drowned out by raised voices from the waterfront.

The commotion spread, growing louder.

And then, the sky filled with flames.

PART FIVE

NIGHTFALL

The Path of Flames is not chosen lightly. But it is no less a gift of the gods. How else should the world be made to see?

—Book IX, verse twenty-seven of *The Paths of Fjuriin*

Chapter 26

Up in Flames

Bursts of fire exploded across the night sky from the direction of the harbor.

At once, the serenity of this quaint island festival vanished. The crowds descended into madness all around, and Urla's battle instinct took over.

She sprinted from the fields on the far side of the village, weaving between frantic bodies, heading toward the flames.

Urla had to find Campos. And Ruan. Where the bloody Abyss had her son gone? He'd been right there only minutes ago.

But she'd let her guard down. Lulled by the magic of the night, Campos's assurances, and the strange beauty of so many disparate cultures gathered in one place. Pulled in conversation with Thenius and Rykus, recounting tales of battles with her fellow captain and sharing capital gossip with Thenius who'd become far more amiable after a few hits of Faltari dreamsmoke earlier in the night.

Gods damn me to the pits of Skrala, I should have watched Ruan more carefully.

She hadn't wanted to be *that* mother. Her son was a man grown. A potential Dragonmount. And she was a Lady Captain of the imperial legions, ordered to mingle with the other parents and act fascinated by the ritual, and she'd fallen into the role even more than expected. Not realizing just how much she'd longed for a night of frivolity after the Sigan campaign, after the dragonfall.

Dark plumes filled the sky on the other side of Yerida as she raced through the village lanes. Only two things could trigger such an explosion, and there were no Dragonmounts here.

Her lungs kept a steady rhythm as she lumbered forward, the cadence of a body built for war, honed over a lifetime of training.

Most of the crowd ran in the opposite direction, and Urla found herself pressed against a raging torrent of frantic villagers and traders. Most of whom, Urla knew, had seen nothing of battles. She'd never seen a firebomb used anywhere but the battlefield.

Urla leapt over a toppled vendor cart and shouldered her way between a pair of shrieking Ytani traders. She longed for the comfort of her war axe in her hands. Her body responded with the focus and precision of the battlefield. Eyes noting every movement, every space to maneuver, every possible threat.

A scream. Somewhere to her right. Different than the others.

Urla turned.

The attacking creature appeared in the lane ahead as though it had formed from the air itself.

Sharp wings protruded from a naked humanoid torso with a span of at least ten feet. Its skin was dark as pitch. The thing leapt into the air, fiery eyes scanning the crowd, before settling on Urla.

It flapped hard toward her, shooting over ducking heads with remarkable speed.

The crowd parted around her, and Urla leapt to the side, narrowly missing the slashing attack of long black talons. She rolled on the hard ground of the village lane, eyes fixed on her attacker.

Urla had never encountered such a creature before. It seemed to be a gruesome cross between dragyr and man. Urla sprang back to her feet. The creature landed in the middle of the street where she'd stood a moment ago and transformed in an instant back into a fully clothed man. Hair was dark brown, skin fair and smooth as ivory.

Valucian!

The crowd thinned around him, save for a Chardonian woman.

Urla backed toward a toppled cart, eying a long rod that held the tattered remnants of a vendor's curtain.

Without fear, the Chardonian woman came abreast of the shapeshifting creature.

What in the Abyss was it?

But Urla knew who it served. Such dark magic was possible in only one heathen land.

The Valucian man nodded to his Chardonian companion and both creatures morphed, taking on hideous dark-winged forms, faces distorting, eyes turning feral, teeth flashing long and white and menacing. They leapt into the air and shot forward.

Urla ducked their attack, this time letting her momentum take her toward the cart. She rolled on the hard-packed dirt and seized the splinter of the curtain rod, ripping it out of looped fastenings, and whipped it around to face her attackers.

The first creature soared out of reach. Urla ducked the other's swooping attack and drove straight up with her splintered weapon.

It did not pierce easily. Urla thrust with all her strength, forcing the dull wood through thick leathery skin. The rod wrenched from Urla's grasp with a sick squelching sound, and the creature tumbled onto the ground.

Urla raced over, seizing the weapon. The creature morphed back into the form of the Chardonian woman. Sheer black hair and sandy skin. Face trembling with fury and frailty. Urla drove the rod deeper into her chest, timber scraping as it slid between her ribs. The woman's eyes and mouth gaped, blood seeping from all orifices.

The impact of the second monster ripped Urla away from the kill, talons tearing into her shoulder, sending her reeling.

Urla fell back on to the road. Her skull crunched against something hard. Wooden. *The cart!*

She shook her head to ward off the swirl of haze filling her vision. The creature pinned her to the ground, talons boring into her chest.

She might not have worn weapons, but she'd had the sense to wear a leathern chest piece beneath her gown, at least.

Urla's fingers searched the ground, latched on to something hard, and she whipped it around. The piece of pottery shattered over the creature's skull. Its head jerked back, but it did not let go, talons digging through her armor, piercing her chest. Its face was hideous up close, mouth blood red, though its breath was strangely sweet.

Talons gripped Urla around the throat.

"Where's the boy?" it asked, voice thick and gravelly.

"Wh-wh—"

"Your son!" it snarled.

"If I knew, I'd never—ah!"

The creature's talons slashed her face. It shoved her head against the ground sending waves of pain shooting down her spine. Urla cursed herself for getting pinned.

The creature traced one talon up her cheek and pressed into the soft tissue beneath her eye. She shrieked.

"Where is he?"

"Do your worst, you bast—ah!"

The pain was among the worst Urla had felt in her life. Her vision went dark.

Blood gushed over her face with a horrific squelch. Pain leached through her skull. She thrashed, but the creature was stronger than any warrior she'd faced on the battlefield. Supernaturally strong.

"Tell me where—"

Its voice cut off with a croaking howl of pain. Talons ripped out of Urla's body, and the creature's weight was gone.

Urla flailed around, vision dark on one side, a blur on the other. There was another shriek. The scrape of weapon on bone that Urla knew all too well. Her fingers grasped another piece of pottery.

She scrambled up, forced herself to her knees, and brandished the pottery.

"I'm no threat, Lady Captain."

Urla recognized that calm voice. All other sounds were distant. Screams. Flames. Mayhem.

She wiped blood from her face, and her vision focused. The elder Faltari shaman.

He'd saved her life, she realized. Her mind whirled. Pain lanced through her skull like a thousand needles pressing from all sides. She slumped back, and the pottery slipped from her grasp and shattered on the ground.

"The creatures..." she murmured. Her voice was a gurgle. She spat blood.

"Both dead," Joren said, kneeling beside her in the darkness.

"My eyes," she murmured.

Warmth swept over Urla's body. She'd felt healing power before, but this was more powerful than any arcanist. Pain dulled in her thighs and torso. And then, her face. Her head pounded, but she could see more clearly again. The glow of flames filled the smoky sky. To her right lay the body of the female creature, back in her human form.

The shaman stood before her, but she could not see him entirely until she turned her head.

"You're lucky. That beast would've taken the eye next, I expect. I believe you'll see fine once the swelling goes down. This will have to do for now."

"Thank you, shaman."

"We must go," Joren said. "Where's the consul general?"

"Campos returned to the ship for the night." Urla eased up to a sitting position with the shaman's help, then got to her feet. She forced herself to focus, ignoring the throbbing in her temples.

Joren pulled the length of a bonespear from the male creature's chest and drew a short axe from his belt and handed it to her.

Clarity swept over her at the hilt of a weapon in her fingers.

"Hurry," said the shaman.

Urla grabbed Joren's wrist. "They're not just here for the eggs. They wanted my son."

CHAPTER 27

HUNTED

Screams echoed from the village, but the trees were too thick for Malik to see anything beyond the plumes of flame and smoke.

"Who's here?" Malik demanded.

Riese held the Attican girl's cane-blade to her throat.

Ava remained curled up on the ground, but she did not flinch at the threat.

"The force of change," Ava said.

"Quit playing bloody games."

Ava's green eyes flashed. "Don't speak to me of games, shaman. You have been playing games with the empire for years, while nations fall and cities burn, and while *my* people pay the—"

"Pah!" said Riese. "You're a damn Attican noble. What have you got to complain about?"

"I am Valucian. A daughter of Flame and the Stone Spirits, no matter what the Atticans forced us to forsake. We have remained. You've no idea what I've suffered. No idea how many *thousands* have suffered beyond these shores, because of what your people provide the empire. Now, we will have our freedom, and you have a choice to make."

Ava glanced at the sky, grimacing. Riese did not take her eyes away from the girl, but Malik dared a glance at the dark heavens.

The moon emerged from behind a dark shadow. Strange glowing lights filled the sky, like golden stars in strange patterns.

They formed a familiar shape. And they drifted overhead, toward the harbor.

Malik gasped, struck by what Campos had discussed with his father about the Attican war.

Those lights belonged to one of the Elyan runeships, like the one that had fought in the battle at Siga, that Campos had described. Winged shadows darted from the sides of the floating vessel, flapping hard toward the flames and the screams.

Riese lowered the cane, but she kept her gaze fixed on Ava.

"Do you know what my people could do with dragons?" Ava asked, slowly easing herself to her knees and then her feet. "With a Flying Armada and Rebelmounts and the wrath of the Stone Spirits? We could rule our own lands again, just like you do here. You could be part of it, Riese."

"What?"

"The empire is not the only way to be Dragonmount. I know why you hesitated to accept your egg. You question fighting for the empire. I know you do."

"Riese, we need to—"

"And you, shaman," said Ava. He could feel the warmth of *hish*, her magic brushing up against his spirit. "I may not be well-trained in magic, but I know minds. I sensed your turmoil over the truth of those eggs. The truth of what role your people have played in the state of the world."

"Enough," said Malik.

"That's why I led you out here. You don't have to—"

Ava's words cut off as Riese swung the cane around for a second time. The ebony wood cracked against the girl's head. Ava crumpled to the ground and went still.

Malik gaped.

Riese shrugged. "Our island is under attack. We don't have time for some self-righteous speech from a bloody mind witch. You deal with the general. I'll deal with her."

Malik glanced over at the manservant impaled upon the tree. Only now did he realize his hands were shaking. The reality of what they'd done finally ringing true in his spirit. He and Riese both, attacking the man with magic in an instinctive burst. Using magic to kill, it went against everything he'd been taught.

"That bastard murdered an innocent girl," Riese said. "He deserved it."

Was that true? Malik had no idea what to believe.

He glanced down at Iriana Thenius's body, head drawn back at an impossible angle. Dead the instant Campos's servant released his hold.

Malik didn't know whether the dead girl had been good or evil. He had no idea about the outside world. About Attica or Valucia or the Elyans across the sea, but he knew he ought to heal when he could.

Malik knelt beside General Campos. The tall man was unconscious. But Malik had managed a healing spell, while Ava had been distracted, which had at least staunched the bleeding. Malik's knees drenched, and he shuddered, realizing how much blood the general had spilled on the ground around him.

Focusing his senses, Malik drew *hish* and channeled that mighty energy into Campos's spirit.

Two souls—even though one was unconscious—could manage a stronger healing. The skin of the general's throat began to close over, threads of magic weaving with tissue like strands of cloth, as Malik aided Campos's body in the natural force of healing that was always there.

Riese lifted Ava over her shoulder as though she were a stag from a successful hunt. She set the girl down behind the jagged pillars of the clan shrines, somewhere beyond his vision.

By the time Riese returned, Malik had done what he could for the general. Campos's chest lifted with weak intakes of breath.

"Will he live?" Riese asked.

"I don't know."

"Should he?"

Malik sighed. "I don't know. What about Ava?"

"Not going anywhere anytime soon." Riese took the general's satchel with the eggs safely inside. "They're here for these. We should move them before—"

Riese was about to go back toward the pillars, when a voice came from behind them.

"What in the Abyss happened here?"

They turned to find an Attican boy gaping at Campos's bloody form in horror.

———

Urla and Joren encountered only one more shapeshifter, which they dispatched easily enough, working together. Urla was impressed with the shaman's skill with a spear. He struck with the precision of a trained lancer. If anyone ought to have been given pause at the gruesome demands of combat, she would have guessed it would be a shaman from a remote and peaceful island. But when the shapeshifter morphed back to its human form, Joren did not hesitate.

He launched his spear masterfully, impaling the man through the chest. A better shot than many Attican warriors might have managed.

Joren wrenched the bonespear from the creature's chest, and they continued on, down one last lane, and through the gates to the wide village square at the edge of the waterfront.

Urla's heart shuddered at the sight of the Attican vessel. Flames lashed at the sky from each mast, tattered bits of sail floating down to the water like fiery bits of parchment.

The deck was already half-submerged in the harbor.

Shadows streaked overhead, and the looming form of the mysterious runeship drifted out over the village behind them. Only now, in the openness of the square, did Urla realize there were flames on the other end of the village too.

Unintelligible shouts filled the night. Echoing across the island. From the sky, from the village proper, from the longboats out in the harbor where Attican guards were desperately trying to save their ship with buckets drawn from the sea.

Urla scanned the square, searching for signs of Ruan or the general. Traders frantically loaded goods onto longboats. Many had abandoned their goods entirely and were making for their ships to flee before the invaders came for their vessel next.

Joren gazed back at the flames and shook his head. "Decoys," he muttered.

Urla spotted Captain Rykus near the edge of the square. Lady Thenius was in hysterics, beside him, standing over a body on the ground. The Knight of Caadron stood a short distance away, eyes on the sky, her glowing godblade in her hands.

Urla and Joren hurried to them. Relief swept over her as she realized the body did not belong to her son, but to Marcus Tindarius, the boy from Bastion Academy.

"What happened?" Urla demanded.

Rykus answered, his voice like ice. "Half a dozen of those monstrosities bore down on us. We all would be dead if not for the Lady Knight."

Vera Salyr wore no armor, and she was drenched, head to foot. She glanced at Urla, before returning her gaze to the sky.

"Where are the others?" Urla demanded.

The Lady Knight gestured toward a small path at the edge of the woods. "Campos took the Rykus girl up there before the attack, along with the younger shaman and a Faltari girl."

"Riese?" The shaman cursed.

"Iriana was meant to meet them there," the Lady Knight finished.

"And my son?" Urla demanded, unable to mask the desperation in her voice. "Was Ruan with them?"

Vera Salyr shook her head. "I've not seen your son since the attack."

Urla's heart wrenched in her chest. Images flashed. Her son sinking beneath the surface of the flaming sea. Or snatched into the heavens by one of those vile creatures.

Prayers came unbidden to Marha the Mother. *Please, please, not my son as well.*

Joren placed a hand on her shoulder, warmth coursing from his spirit, calming her mind.

"Ava," Urla said. "Ruan would not have gone far from her. Not after all this."

"They're searching for the riders," the shaman said.

"Then, we must find them first," said Rykus. "We know where to look."

"We don't want to draw all these creatures along with us," cautioned the Lady Knight.

Two winged monsters emerged from the clouds and soared over the flaming Attican ship.

Urla's fingers closed tight around the handle of the axe the shaman had given her. "What are those things?" she whispered. "I've never seen anything like them."

"Whatever they are, they're well-trained," said the Lady Knight. "Look at their formation."

Two more creatures joined them, circling the water. All four flew as one mechanism. Banking on dark wings, flapping in unison, as though they shared one mind.

"They bleed like any other creature," said Urla.

"Yes, and they'll happily sacrifice their blood to get what they've come for," said the knight. "They've been watching us ever since they killed Marcus."

"We have to find Iriana," Lady Thenius whimpered. "We have to go. Now." She began to move toward the forest path, but Rykus held her back.

"What if we go one by one?" Rykus asked.

"No," said Urla. "We must all go at once. Split in separate directions."

"And who will go the right way?" Thenius demanded. "You?"

"Not me," said Urla. "The shaman."

Chapter 28

Son of Attica

Ruan Pelasius stood at the edge of the clearing. He'd come from the track in the woods they'd taken to get to the shrines. Malik recognized him from the arrival of the Attican party. The shield maiden's son.

Screams of terror echoed up from the harbor. The Attican boy's eyes were wide with fear, rage, confusion. His spirit was a maelstrom.

Who was ally? Who was foe? Where was the girl he loved? All of it swirled in Malik's mind.

Malik extended his hands before him, as he rose from Campos's unconscious form. "I've done what I can for your general, but he needs proper care."

Ruan took in the gruesome scene. Campos lying in a pool of blood. Baro in the tree. The dead Attican girl, neck twisted.

"What happened?" Ruan asked, voice tremulous. An unnerving sound coming from someone so tall and powerful.

"Campos's servant," Malik said, pointing to the impaled man. "He was a traitor. And we made him pay for it."

"Y-you did this?" Ruan's eyes narrowed at Malik.

Malik did not look away. He would not be shamed for it, any more than he would for killing a jackal threatening one of his kin. He nodded.

"Baro killed Iriana," said Riese. "Just before the explosion. He came up behind her and just... snapped her neck like it was a twig. We did what we had to do. If we'd hesitated for even a moment, your general would be dead."

"Why was Iriana out here?" Ruan asked. "Why were any of you?"

Malik sensed fear and jealousy in the boy's spirit and thought it best not to aggravate it. "Iriana was hiding in the woods, following us."

"She was after the eggs." Ruan's eyes traveled to the satchel in Riese's arms. "And Ava... was she..."

Malik was unsure what the boy had seen. Did Ruan know that Ava had been with them? The boy's spirit wavered like a flame in the wind, though his face held a practiced lack of expression.

"She was here..." Malik said. "Ava did this to Campos."

Ruan's face tensed. "That's not possible. She would never..."

But Malik sensed the boy knew it was very much possible.

Riese picked up the dark cane from the ground and extended the handle to him. The concealed blade still jutted out from the tip.

Ruan drew in a long breath, inspecting the weapon.

"She fled," Malik said. "Ava is gone. We don't know where."

Ruan hesitated, glancing around, taking in the bloody carnage. "You just let her go?"

"It was either chase her down or try to save your general," Riese insisted.

"Campos has lost a lot of blood," said Malik. "We need to get him back to your ship."

The lies came so easily, Malik and Riese both playing off one another, making it up as they went along, subtly bending the truth of what happened to their own end, like children weaving lies about where they'd gone during a festival.

Ruan turned and stared back toward the harbor. "Our ship is... gone."

Shadows shot overhead. Malik was grateful that they had no torches to give away their location. Riese held exactly what the attackers wanted.

"We have to go," said Malik. He and Riese each took one of the general's shoulders. "Take his legs."

Ruan snapped back to reality and did as he was told.

They inched their way down the track. It was slow going. Campos was a large soldier, and with the man unconscious, it was all dead weight. Ruan led the way, facing forward, holding one of the general's legs cradled in each hand, still clutching the cane-blade awkwardly.

The chaos in the village grew louder as they neared the harbor. Shouts. Screeches. The splinter of rending timber. The roar of flames.

Malik braced himself, longing for his bonespear. Anticipating an attack from above any moment. Expecting Ruan to change his mind, see through the lies, and lunge at him with Ava's secret weapon.

They pressed on. Riese kept the eggs safely slung over her shoulders.

Anger and pain raged in Ruan's spirit, though he said nothing. Lies and deceit always led to pain. Malik knew that well enough.

They reached the bottom of the hillside, leading down to the village. One smaller knoll lay between them and the harbor. Flames illuminated the sky ahead in a fearsome glow, and the forest was cast in long, menacing shadows.

Ruan stopped at the bottom of the hill and gazed up the path.

"What are you doing?" Riese demanded.

Ruan dropped the general's legs and held the cane-blade in front of him like a sword. A man appeared at the top of the hill and barreled toward them, clutching a bonespear in front of him.

Malik knew the resonance anywhere.

"Ruan, that's my—"

Joren waved his arms. "Get down! All of you!"

A pair of shadows streaked overhead, diving through the trees with a *craack!*

Malik grabbed Riese's hand and jerked her to the ground, as a hideous black creature lashed out with long talons. Riese cried out in pain, but the creature lurched back into the sky and vanished.

"Help!" Ruan cried.

Malik jumped back up to find the second creature on top of the Attican boy. A spear jutted from its back.

It had fallen on top of Ruan. In an instant, the monstrous black wings shifted back into human flesh.

The creature twitched, and Malik's father snatched up the cane-blade and drove it through the back of the man's neck, up into his skull. He went still.

"Holy shit!" Riese said, chest heaving. "Shaman, you just—"

"Get this thing off me!" Ruan groaned.

"God's breath," Malik said, unable to believe what his peace-loving father had just done. Blood gushed from the Chardonian man's wounds. Brown skin streaked with crimson.

"Help me, son," Joren said, patting Malik on the shoulder, jolting him back to the present.

Together, the three of them heaved the corpse off of Ruan, and the boy sat up, gasping for breath as though he'd just emerged from the depths of the sea.

Joren scanned the woods behind them, then, back to the sky, but the other creature was gone. "We have to get the general out of here. Ruan and Riese, you too."

"Me?" said Riese.

Joren nodded. "You are Dragonmount now, it seems, and these rebels seek you and what you carry."

Joren leveled a fierce gaze at Malik.

"I'm sorry, Father... I—"

"Apologies are nothing but wind. You brought this fate to her. Now, you must follow the bloody path you chose."

Joren pulled the bonespear from the Chardonian man's back with a squelch of flesh and handed it to Malik. His father took the cane-blade for himself.

"The Knight of Caadron," said Joren, "she is your way off this island. Riese, Ruan, you two must carry the general. My son and I will fight these beasts off as best we can. There will be more as soon as we reach the square. Now, come!"

Chapter 29

Godblade

Urla had never fought alongside a Knight of Caadron before, but it was more remarkable than anything she had ever beheld.

Vera Salyr's glowing godblade was sharper than any forged steel, its shimmering edge tearing through wing and bone, even the shapeshifters' weapons. The Lady Knight's movements were fluid as a river, lithe as one of the emperor's ceremonial dancers. Forms perfectly executed.

The first wave of aerial attacks were strung out. Two or three creatures soared after each Attican as they made their diversion for the shaman.

Urla had traded Joren's short axe for the spear of a fallen shapeshifter. She took on one beast, managing a blow to the creature's shoulder, which sent it careening down the dock. It morphed back into its human form and charged her with a saber, injured arm loose at its side. Urla attacked, narrowly missing a fatal error when the shapeshifter slashed with a stealth blade protruding from the bracer on its injured arm.

She staggered back, parrying a saber blow with the end of her spear. The greater reach of her weapon won out in the end.

When Urla looked up from her kill, two more beasts were already slain, and the Lady Knight was braced for the next wave. Shadows streaked from the deck of the runeship overhead.

"Two more coming our way," the knight shouted.

Urla spun around, whipping the lance in her hands, and thrust the end up, then slashed it hard, shredding the webbed skin of the creature's wing. An Attican guard leapt in to finish it off, bludgeoning the beast with a length of lumber.

The knight needed no help with the other creature. Salyr barked orders to ready a long boat, even though their ship was sinking in flames and most of the other ships were already fleeing the harbor. The Attican guards did not question her.

Hopefully the ruse will draw enough attention if it appears we are defending the boats.

Another trio of beasts descended on them from the harbor, wings roaring as they flapped and dove. Urla adjusted her grip on the spear and braced for impact.

At the last moment, the creatures shifted.

All three shot past the docks and soared over the square.

Urla spun. Her chest convulsed.

The shaman and his son emerged from the forest path, brandishing weapons. Ruan and Riese followed, carrying the limp form of General Campos.

Cries echoed across the water as Urla sprinted from the docks.

———

Malik thrust with the bonespear, but the hideous creature shifted at the last moment, and before he realized what was happening, his weapon wrenched from his grasp. His body lurched from the ground. Pain lanced through his shoulder.

The world hurtled end over end.

Ships, the village walls, flames, all swirled in his vision.

More pain.

The world went black.

———

Joren's spirit raged as Malik vanished somewhere in the trees at the edge of the square.

Riese dropped Campos and let loose a terrifying surge of *hish* that sent the next beast off course.

Joren slashed with the cane weapon, splitting the creature's neck with the razorsharp blade jutting out of the end.

Runemarked Kirithian steel. He'd never wielded such a blade from so strange a weapon before, but it was no less effective.

Joren spun to find Ruan shooting into the air, talons latched on to his shoulders.

The boy screamed.

Riese released a massive burst of magic.

Joren reached for the same threads and pushed with all the strength in his spirit.

The shapeshifter lost its grip on the boy, and Ruan dropped.

Joren reached out with *hish* to slow his fall, but another creature flashed in his vision. Reaching for Riese. Joren sent the creature hurtling across the square with a surge of power.

Ruan collapsed upon the hard-packed ground. He did not move.

Riese gasped for breath beside Joren, as though she'd just hefted the trunk of a tree. His strength was also fading. It had been a decade or more since he'd drawn so much power in so short a span. Even longer since he'd seen such combat.

He could not afford to draw much more *hish*. Utterly spent, Riese dropped to her knees, the satchel of eggs still on her shoulders.

Joren's spirit searched for his son's resonance. But his gaze remained on the battle at hand.

One creature was dead.

The other two regrouped, both unharmed.

Joren focused his vision on the beasts as they turned back toward him.

———

Urla watched helpless, halfway across the square, as her son crumpled on the hard-packed ground.

The creatures arced in the air for another attack.

In the corner of her vision, Captain Rykus sprinted from the village gates, a bonespear in hand.

Riese struggled to her feet, searching for something she could use for a weapon. Her movements were slow and languid. Ruan did not get up, and Campos lay unconscious close by.

Another wave of creatures descended. Urla sprinted toward them, but knew she'd never make it.

The shaman brandished the splintered remains of a crude weapon.

The shapeshifters dove at the shaman.

And Urla let her spear fly.

———

Malik's vision swam. His back shuddered in waves of pain, temples throbbing as he pulled himself to his feet. A hand helped steady him.

"Now, we're even, shaman."

"Ulgar?"

The Feathered Serpent boy knelt beside him in the woods at the edge of the square. "Malik, what in the Abyss is happening? What are those—"

Malik seized his wrist. "My father! There's no time!"

Ulgar braced Malik with his shoulder, and together, they scrambled through the foliage and back into the square.

The waterfront was a swirl of violence. Screams of fear and death filled the night.

Malik and Ulgar staggered forward. Ulgar held a bonespear, but Malik's weapon had been lost in the attack that had landed him in the woods.

Dark wings flashed overhead. One of the shapeshifters hit the ground, tumbling, then, went still, a lance protruding from its chest.

Ulgar leapt in as the creature struggled to its feet, driving his own spear through the beast's neck.

Blood spurted, and the monster transformed into its human form.

"God's breath!" Ulgar roared, pulling back his weapon from the gaping wound.

Malik wrenched the other spear from the creature's chest. His vision swam.

Magic surged through his body. And one of his father's shamanic mantras came to him.

Without the mind, the body fades.

Malik focused all the *hish* his spirit could muster, channeling the healing energy into his mind.

The world slowed, sharpened.

The glowing mass of the runeship blotted out the moon, casting the square in twisting shadows. A horn bellowed across the sky.

Fifty yards ahead, his father leapt into the air, meeting one of the creatures in an incredible twisting aerial attack. For a moment, his father looked to be flying. The creature wasn't ready for the attack either. It attempted to shift directions midair, but Joren's weapon drove into its side, sending them reeling.

Another monster descended, straight at Riese.

Malik leapt into action, movements guided by pure instinct and will. He sprinted forward, vision fixed on the attacking creature. He sent his spear flying with a surge of *hish*.

His aim was true. The felled beast collided with Riese, both of them tumbling on the ground.

An Attican man hurried to help. Together, Joren and the man shoved the body aside, and pulled Riese free.

The Attican man wrenched the bonespear from the creature's chest, turned. Horror filled Malik's gut as he realized the man was Ava's father.

Malik shouted. "Father, no, he's a traitor!"

But it was too late.

Captain Rykus whipped the butt end of the bonespear around, clubbing his father over the back of the head.

Joren slumped over.

Malik screamed, and sprinted as fast as his limbs would go. Twenty yards. Ten. A creature dove at him, and he leapt to the side, dodging the attack, as Ulgar leapt in to make the kill.

He looked up. Ten yards might as well have been ten miles.

Rykus picked up an unconscious Riese and, beyond all possibility, shot into the sky with a surge of magic, taking Riese, and all three dragon eggs with him.

Rykus disappeared over the deck of the runeship as it lifted higher into the sky.

"Holy shit!" Ulgar shouted. "He just flew with no bloody wings!"

Malik crossed the remaining distance and knelt at his father's side, the warmth of Joren's spirit still radiating.

The ship disappeared into the thickening clouds. The remaining creatures shot into the sky after it.

Holding his father's head, Malik unleashed an incoherent torrent of curses.

The eggs were gone.

Riese was gone.

Malik had failed.

The Lady Knight reached them, magic blade glowing. She swung the sword in an arc that cut straight through the fabric of the world.

A window seemed to open in the air itself. Malik could see through the hazy opening to an immaculate hall, painted pillars and tapestries and oil lamps flickering. Red-cloaked Attican guards in runemarked armor rushed down a staircase and across a vast hall. Toward the opening in the air.

Urla Pelasius thundered past Malik and leapt through the sorcerous window, bearing Ruan's unconscious form in her arms.

Ulgar pulled Malik to his feet, yelling in his ear, voice tremulous.

"Shaman!" Ulgar pointed to the knight.

The Lady Knight met his gaze, her spirit filled with pain and urgency. "Campos!"

Malik and Ulgar hefted the general between them, his body even heavier than before. They inched the unconscious man through the portal, laying Campos on a pristine tile floor beside Ruan and his mother.

Green-cloaked servants came rushing to help. Soldiers shot past, weapons flashing in the light.

Malik felt as though everything was happening in the haze of a dream.

"Shaman, back through! I can't hold it much longer."

The Lady Knight's voice was strained. She held her shining godblade above her head, one foot in this immaculate hall, one back in the village square.

In the corner of his eye, Malik spotted a man in elegant black robes, descending a staircase.

No, it's a throne.

The golden seat was framed by dark stone dragon wings which cast sharp shadows across the hall. The regal man was flanked by a retinue of guards.

Ulgar gaped. "Is that the Dragon Emp—"

Malik grabbed his wrist and pulled him back to their own world.

A surge of magic pulsed behind them.

When Malik turned back, the portal was gone.

CHAPTER 30

REBEL BASTARDS

The imperial healers assured Urla that both Ruan and Campos would live, and that she should rest, but she would be damned if she let anyone else tend to her son. She'd already lost Keivan, his dragon, and now, her son's best chance at becoming Dragonmount.

Rykus would pay for what he'd done. Through the night, she turned things over in her mind, trying to understand what was happening. First, the runeship in Siga. Now, another at the edge of the world, manned by shapeshifting monstrosities, whose human forms were either Valucian or Chardonian.

The former, a fraught kingdom who'd seemingly bent the knee, the other, long seen as the next battleground for Attica.

And the runeship...

All her youth, Urla had heard tales of the mysterious threat from across the sea, how Elya was growing in power, how they might one day meddle in affairs in the continent of Îrithèa. These fears may have lessened as Attica regained prominence in the world, but always the rumors of Elya lingered—their heathen politics and reckless use of magic, their conquests and unquenchable lust for power, and of course, their pagan Empyreal Church whose false teachings spread across the eastern world like a disease.

How did a Valucian blood-traitor and his daughter fit into all this?

Valucia had been grafted back into the empire years ago, and Rykus himself had played a pivotal part in the peaceful transfer of power. Betrayed his own kin to aid Good Emperor Vitruvian and had become a minor Attican lord as reward. Rykus's company had fought alongside Urla's own in the Sigan conquest.

Through it all, it seemed, he had been biding his time.

The eggs were gone, along with the Faltari girl, Riese. And they'd tried to take Ruan with them.

If not for Joren...

Across the imperial bedchamber, Campos lay unconscious, while healers changed bandages at his throat, applied medicinal salves and tried to force down a tincture. Through it all, he did not waken.

Ruan's head and neck were covered in bruises, a mottled purple and grey tapestry, hints of yellowing flesh beginning to seep in, which worried Urla all the more.

The healers claimed it looked worse than it actually was, but Urla knew they were only guessing. They could not see inside her son's body with true clarity, even with their runemarked instruments. It was all gods-damned guessing and hoping. And Ruan still hadn't moved, except for the steady rhythm of his breathing.

Hauntingly peaceful coming from such a damaged face.

It had happened so fast. Had Ruan landed on his head? Broken something in his neck? Her mind's eye filled with memories of her own days at Dawncrest during her Sea trials.

She was seventeen, and they were performing an exercise that involved traversing between two ships in games mimicking maritime combat. They swung on ropes from deck to deck. Traversed across moving oars, deflecting blows from instructors. A boy ahead of her on the course lost his footing and slipped between oars into the water.

So sudden. No sharp crack or sickening thud.

Their teachers pulled him from the water in only a few seconds. But the boy didn't wake for three days. When he did, he couldn't move. Couldn't even speak.

After months of attempted healings and medicines, the boy's parents had done the only thing an honorable Attican family could do.

Urla gripped her son's hand and shuddered at the thought of being forced to make such a decision.

Ruan's face was peaceful, bits of stubble darkening his upper lip. He looked so much like Keivan when they'd first met. Strong chiseled jaw. Slight curl to his dark hair. His chest rose and fell. Eyelids shifted but never opened.

He's just sleeping...

How much longer could she tell herself that?

Across the room, Campos's breathing came in fits and waves. When they first arrived, the general had thrashed in pain, and the healers had given him a tincture that knocked him out cold while they mended the skin of his neck with needle and thread, then used a runemarked instrument to repair what the young shaman had neglected beneath the skin in the haste and demands of the moment.

Thank the Mother for the shamans, Urla thought, willing herself to hold on to hope. To be grateful that both her son and her mentor were alive yet.

"Gods damn those rebel bastards."

Urla jolted at the voice.

She turned from her son to find the Lady Knight, Vera Salyr, striding across the regal bedchamber toward her.

If the emperor were wed, this room might belong to one of his own children, Urla thought.

Ruan and Campos were being tended by the emperor's personal healers. Surely, that was a blessing. She could practically hear her mother reminding her of this. And yet, Marha the Mother had not spared her either.

The Lady Knight stopped and watched Campos for several moments. His face distorted with pain, even in sleep.

"Has he..."

"He's drugged," said Urla. "Woke in pain during the surgery. But the healers say he's got a fighting chance."

"That's all the general would ask for," said the knight.

Urla nodded, a slight smile at the edge of her lips. She'd not seen the woman before this damned excursion, but it was clear the knight knew Campos well. Perhaps another of his apprentices.

Salyr crossed the room and stood beside Urla.

"Your son lives," the knight said. "The Mother watches over you."

Urla had nothing to say. Everyone said such things until hope faded, then they said things like, "The Father must've needed more brave warriors."

Such sayings were wind.

"What's happened back on the island?" Urla asked after a silence.

"We found the Thenius girl's body near the Faltari shrines, as Malik described. As well as the general's traitor servant. No sign of Ava Rykus."

"Her father flew," Urla said.

"Without wings," the knight finished. "Unlike the rest of those morphing beasts. I've never seen anything like it, but it's Elyan witchery, no doubt. And if Rykus has dabbled in dark magic from across the sea, why not the daughter? Ava was hiding magic ability, the shaman says."

"She's escaped, then."

"We believe so. According to Malik, Ava fled into the woods, and he and the Faltari girl let her go, so they could help the general. Ava was the one who tried to kill Campos. The servant, Baro, was responsible for Iriana Thenius."

Urla squeezed her son's hand again. "Rebel bastards."

"You can say... that again," murmured a raspy male voice.

"General Campos!" Urla and Salyr cried in unison.

Urla was flooded with relief.

The Lady Knight hurried to Campos's side, helped him sit up, propping him with pillows. His neck was covered in bloodied bandages, but he could hold up his head enough to meet Urla's gaze with barely open eyes. Campos attempted to smile, grimaced and groaned, then slumped back against the pillows. His hand drifted to his throat, felt at the bandages engulfing his neck.

"Baro..." he murmured.

"Dead, sir," the knight said. "The work of the Faltari girl. She and that young shaman saved your life. She paid for it too. They took her."

"Took... Riese?" he asked. Each word was a struggle.

Salyr nodded.

"Fucking... Valucians," said Campos. "Where's... the emperor? He..."

"He knows everything we know, sir."

"Good...good..." Campos closed his eyes and sighed. His voice was barely a whisper, yet still, commanding. "Right under our damn noses. If this goes beyond Rykus…"

"No Valucian is permitted in the palace for the time being," the knight said. "The emperor sent two Knights of Caadron to Valucia to investigate the extent of this treason."

Campos's head lolled on his pillow. For a moment, Urla thought he'd lost consciousness. Then, he spoke. "I feel like I've gone… to Skrala and back… It's shit…. if you want to know."

Urla and Salyr smiled, then the general's face twisted in pain. He raised a hand toward his bandages, but didn't quite reach them. His hand fell to his chest. "I'll be… fine."

"I'll get the healers. You probably need another tincture," the knight said, rising to her feet and disappearing into the corridor beyond.

Urla glanced from her son to Campos, fury rising up in her spirit. How she wished she could have been there with them. Rykus had made sure that didn't happen, keeping her distracted with the other nobles.

"Lady Captain," Campos said, his voice raspier. His eyes creased open. Bloodshot and hideous.

"You should sleep, sir," Urla whispered, drawing close.

His fingers clasped hers, skin cold and clammy. And weak. Campos's grip had never felt so slight.

"The island," Campos murmured. "The eggs."

"Rykus stole them, sir."

"Not those ones." His fingers tightened around her wrist. "More. Many more… the bastards will be back."

"They must know we'll be ready for them, sir. They wouldn't—"

"No, damn it! Listen, girl!"

Suddenly, General Campos sounded like her father's best friend, the stern voice of her youth, toughening her up, preparing her for the academies and the trials and her first appointment in the legions. That *no-bullshit* voice that had made her what she was, after her father died.

"Vitruvian…" Campos whispered. "He feared dragons… all the emperors have… even Athanasius… that's why there's so few… but that time is done… you have to tell him…"

A shudder of fear wracked Urla's body, a chill settling over the room, stifling her breathing like she'd stepped from a warm hearth into the winter snow.

"You can tell him," she insisted. "The emperor will be here any moment. He wants your counsel more than ever, sir!"

Campos's grip slackened. "No... you—"

He coughed, and Urla froze. Blood bubbled up from between his lips, dribbled down his chin.

"Help!" she shouted. "I need a healer!"

Urla scrambled for the door, but Campos brushed her hand.

"No..."

More blood oozed from his mouth. Trickles of crimson from his eyes and ears. His neck began to swell, bulging around the edges of his bandages.

He chuckled, blood gurgling.

"Lord General!"

Campos gripped her hand. His fingers trembled, and his face had settled into a strange serenity. For a moment, Urla feared he was gone.

Then, Campos's bloodshot eyes fixed on hers.

"We all hoped for... another Golden Age... what we need is an Age of Fire. Make him see, girl! Make the emperor see!"

Campos slumped back and his body spasmed, limbs shuddering. A long breath.

And he went still.

Healers poured into the room, felt Campos's pulse. Shouts. Sorcerous instruments glowing.

But Urla knew they were too late.

"I don't understand," said the Lady Knight, staring in shock. "He was just..." A tear streaked down her cheek.

Urla did not cry.

She looked from Campos to her unconscious son. All at once, the anger and sadness faded. She had an order to carry out.

Urla stood and left the room.

Salyr called after her, and when Urla ignored her, the knight hurried after, out into the towering halls of the lower palace.

"Lady Captain!"

The knight seized her wrist.

"I need an audience with the emperor," said Urla. "There is no time to waste."

Chapter 31

Dragonbound

Riese Torendeil woke in darkness. Her bowels churned as though her stomach were an angry sea, pitching and diving within her belly. The ground shifted beneath her, nearly made her lose her balance before something tightened at her wrists.

A loud groan. Voices nearby. The creaking of wood, and the flapping of cloth in the wind.

"Wh-where..."

Her voice croaked, throat dry as sand.

She sensed the warm rush of *hish*. More than she'd ever felt in any one place, except near the Spires, where the Mountain of Souls was a blazing presence.

Magic radiated all around her.

Aches shot down her spine into stiff limbs as she struggled to sit up. Chains clinked with her movements. Cold pressure on her wrists. Something hung around her neck, heavy and steeped in magic. Though it felt different, somehow. Her spirit felt different here.

Hazy images of the attack on Faltara seeped into her mind. Pillars of flame. Dark winged creatures. The Attican girl's neck cocked at an impossible angle. The twisted, dying expression of the man she killed.

Magic is a blessing of the gods. It must never be used to harm another person.

She could hear Joren's words resounding in her mind, as he'd taught her and the other children of the Jackal clan how to access the powers behind the world as children. She had sworn an oath to use the breath of the gods only for good, and last night, she and Malik had broken that oath.

That bastard killed a girl in cold blood. We had to protect the general.

And save yourself, another voice in her mind seemed to counter.

Riese could not piece together where she was, why the room seemed to be shifting, why she had no memory of how she'd gotten here.

And her dragon!

What had happened to her egg? There was a hollow aching in her spirit at the loss of it.

A shift of cloth. Not outside. Very near.

Someone was coming.

Instinctively, Riese reached for *hish* and realized what felt wrong about this place. Despite the magic surging all around her, she could not draw it into her spirit. It passed through her like water through fingers. Icy fear tore through her bones.

"No need to be frightened, Riese Torendeil," a woman said. Faintly familiar. "Your bindings are only a precaution."

Riese remained still, but tense.

Footsteps neared. Resounding with hollow clunks on wooden boards.

"Who are you? Where—"

Cold fingers brushed her temples and removed her blindfold. Slowly, her eyes adjusted. There were no torches or lamps, but hints of golden light peeked through slats in the walls. Riese was chained on some sort of medic's table, though she'd at least been given the courtesy of a blanket, draped over her legs.

The whole world shuddered with a resounding boom. Violent light flashed. The room shuddered again. Cries echoed from somewhere beyond.

"We're in a storm," Riese said.

"Yes," said the woman. Her face was shrouded in shadows.

"We're at sea?"

"Close."

A light ignited from a device in the woman's hand. A lantern, except there was no flame. Within the glass case, a runemarked ball of metal glowed. The woman set the lantern on a hook and drew closer.

Riese's vision settled on the tall woman standing over her, recognition dawning. Sun-specked skin. Angular jawline. Piercing dark eyes. Still wearing the crimson cloak of the Attican guard she'd worn during the hunting games. Except now... her hair shone. Silver, not dark brown the way it appeared when Riese had met her during the hunt.

"You..."

The walls groaned, shifting. The woman reached out, gripping Riese's shoulder to steady her. "Deven lé Nir. Nice to properly—"

"Don't touch me."

The woman smiled. Her wavy silver hair hung loose to her shoulders. "Very well, if you'd rather heave each time this vessel shifts, that is your right."

"Vessel... the runeship," Riese realized aloud, picturing the shadow of it looming over the village. God's breath, so much of what she knew about the world had changed in one night.

"Yes," Deven said, "and we're at the edge of a storm. I'd tell you to hang on, but..."

Riese glared at her, and Deven stepped back, holding on to a support beam a few feet away.

"How long?"

"We've been traveling for a day and a half. You were beaten up. Unconscious when Rykus found you. We let your body heal for a night before applying the collar."

"Is that why I can't draw *hish*?"

"A precautionary measure, that's all."

"You... serve House Rykus."

Deven nodded.

"We didn't meet by accident on that hunt, then, I take it."

"No, indeed. Many of us were sent to infiltrate your people during the festival. To gauge whether you were a threat."

"I killed one of yours."

Deven cocked a brow. "Impressive. Well, we all make mistakes."

Riese's unease showed.

"You are not sure where you stand," Deven said. "I get it. Rest assured, we would not have brought you here if we weren't sure of our decision."

"Then, you know more than me."

"Most definitely."

"You're one of them, aren't you? One of those..."

"Morphs?" asked Deven. "That's what we're called. Metamorphi. Shapeshifters trained in the ways of the Other."

"Is that silver hair real or just another guise."

"Am I Elyan, you mean?" Deven shrugged. "Yes, the hair is—"

The world spun sideways, and Riese flopped hard on the table, bindings straining against her arms.

Deven grinned.

"Don't say anything," Riese muttered.

"We're nearly out of the storm, so it should steady soon."

"What do you want with me?"

Deven peered at her. "That depends."

"On what?"

"On you, of course." Another voice, deep and gravelly.

A broad-shouldered man stepped into the runelantern light. Riese had seen him at the festival. Ava's father, and Deven's lord.

"So, you're the one we must thank," Captain Rykus said.

Riese glowered at him, longing for *hish*.

"For the eggs, that is."

"Yeah, I brought them right into the hands of murderous traitors."

Captain Rykus smiled. "Traitors? That's a matter of perspective, isn't it? For years, my people thought me a traitor, and Attica thought me a saint. Now, this is suddenly reversed. But I'm the same man I've always been."

"Why am I here? Why not kill me like the Attican girl?"

"Thenius?" Rykus asked. "She's dead, then."

"The general's manservant snapped her neck like gods-damned kindling. So yeah."

Rykus barely blinked. "The Thenius house is as old-blood Attican as they come. If we'd let her go, she'd have become a Dragonmount of Attica, utterly loyal to the empire. But you, well..."

He turned to Deven. The woman shrugged. "There's potential."

Riese huffed. "That so?"

"What does it feel like? After the bond?" Captain Rykus asked.

"Wouldn't you like to know."

"A lot of loyalty to the Attican Empire, have you?"

"Say what you want, the Attican Empire never set fire to my village."

Rykus nodded. "Carefully placed fires."

"That servant murdered a young woman. Your daughter tried to kill the consul general."

"Judging by the way he looked when we left, I expect Ava succeeded in killing Campos. And yes, we attacked the Attican bastards and destroyed their ship. We set fires at the edge of the village to sow enough chaos to accomplish our true mission. But our war is with Attica, not Faltara. And so you live, Riese Dragonbound. Your kinsmen do as well. My rebels were given explicit instructions."

"Even those monsters?" Riese shot a look over at Deven, who had stepped back, allowing her master to take over.

"They defended against the enemy. Bravely. But we lost several of our own. Some by your people's hands. Even so, we did not kill a single Faltari."

"Well, I guess I just have to take your word for it, don't I?"

Captain Rykus shifted back, crossing his arms over his chest. "The remainder of our conversation will be dictated by what follows, Riese."

"What do you want with me?"

"You are bound to one of the eggs we carry. For my people, Dragon-mount blood is a sacred and rare thing."

"Unless it is Attican Dragonmount blood."

"You've grown up on an island at the edge of civilization. One that has been spared the hardships endured by the rest of the world, because your elders have secretly supplied the most powerful nation in the world with its source of power. You've no idea the true history of the world. You've no scope of the cruelties my people have endured at the hands of the Attican Empire."

"Well," said Riese, "enlighten me, then."

Rykus studied her. "Shortly after the Crossing—before the Golden Age of Attica, before we were occupied and enslaved, our culture stolen —Valucia was the first Flameholm in Îrithèa. Home of Dragons."

Riese wondered how this tale might fit with her own myths of the

Crossing. The traitor who fled Faltara, taking dragons to the rest of the world.

Did Rayne Seversein take them to Valucia?

"That was before the Curse," Rykus said. "Before the Atticans turned our blessing against us. Dragons soared in the sky. The Stone Spirits blessed our lands. And Valucia was a mighty kingdom. We did not seek to rule the world. Rarely did flames rain from our skies. That was over a thousand years ago, according to our histories. A thousand years since honor meant something in Îrithèa, and dragons brought peace instead of war. A thousand years, but we have not forgotten. And now, that same blood runs in your veins. And in my daughter's veins."

Riese tensed at the mention of Ava. What had become of her after Riese left her bound and unconscious behind the shrines?

"She is Dragonbound," Rykus said. "Just as you are, yes?"

Riese nodded.

"What happened after?"

"She's not... here?" Riese ventured. "We lost her in the forest. I assumed she must have—"

Rykus shook his head. "The storm is letting up now. We should be able to see it."

He crossed the room to the far wall and proceeded to unlatch the shutters of multiple small square windows. Daylight poured into the chamber.

Deven held up a key. "The collar will remain. But if you cooperate, I will release you from the table."

Riese nodded, and the woman unlocked her chains. Riese shifted, so her legs dangled off the side. Her body ached, and she longed for the strength of *hish.*

Deven helped her rise, and they crossed to the window. Her hands remained shackled, the collar hanging heavy from her neck. Deven held tight to the chains as they neared the captain.

"You must make a decision, Riese Dragonbound," Rykus said. "But before you decide who is ally and who is foe, you should be given the entire truth."

Rykus pointed out the window. "Come see the true nature of Dragonmounts under Attican rule."

Riese stepped up and looked out.

They soared high above an endless expanse of sea. Blue skies shone at the horizon at one side, but menacing clouds plumed at the other, like pillars of billowing darkness, looming over what looked to be a small island dotted with villages and rolling hills of pasture and farmland. Or what remained of them. The ground was fiery, black earth flickering with red and orange.

"That is the Isle of Eòreth, the sovereign lands of my house," Rykus said.

"Those aren't clouds," Riese realized, a churning in her gut that sent her vision spinning. "It's smoke."

The entire island was on fire.

CHAPTER 32

DEN OF WOLVES

When Urla was a young girl, she never could have envisioned herself seated in the High Council chamber of the Dragon Palace alongside the greatest of the Attican lords. She was a high noblewoman only through marriage, privy to knowledge about the origins of Attican dragons only because of her connection to Campos.

Yet, here she was in a vast pillared council chamber. The ornately painted dome rose fifty feet above a room-spanning map depicting the region of the Crescent Sea. Emperor Athanasius sat upon a high-backed ivory chair carved in the shape of pluming dragon wings. A gargantuan skull was fixed on the wall at his back so that the jaws of an ancient dragon faced every other man and woman in the room. Like all ruling bodies in Attica, the council largely consisted of men.

Urla was one of four women among twenty-three dragon lords gathered around the table. And she was the only one whose house was not currently in possession of a dragon.

Everything was a maelstrom of activity after the news of Campos's death. Within hours, the council was gathered, and the emperor had insisted Urla join the meeting.

"You're about to enter a den of wolves," Athanasius told her before they entered. "Cornered wolves. Rykus poses a threat to our very source of power. I will need your good sense in there."

"Lord, I am honored, but—"

"Do you wish to serve Attica?" Athanasius asked.

"I live to serve, Lord."

"Campos's estimation of you was well-founded. And that's good, because secrets are unraveling. The balance of power is tipping. And dragon lords respond to threats in one of two ways. Either they hunker down in their towers or they lash out in fear, and rarely at the correct target. We are at risk of losing all we have gained these past three decades. We must convince them to resist both those inclinations."

As the lords and ladies took their seats, the chamber filled with anxious murmurings.

Most of them had seen many more years than the emperor. Athanasius was not much older than thirty summers. It was strange to think that the man who ruled the world had been a child when Urla saw her first battle. But she understood how easy it was to mistake age for wisdom. She'd seen this enough times in the legions.

Urla wore her imperial uniform, befitting a Lady Captain of the legions. She was the least decorated person present. All the other council members were dressed in fine silken gowns and pristine ceremonial robes.

When all were seated, the emperor stood.

"The Isle of Eòreth has been brought low. Thanks to the swift action of Houses Regata and Marius, we sent our message to the other Valucian lords before Rykus could return. What follows will require action from all of us in the coming days. This is an historic moment, and we must meet it with all that the gods require."

"The Valucian lords are in an uproar," said Tersius of House Regata.

Regata hailed from the Isle of Theleset, a close neighbor of Valucia, though with Attican loyalties that had historically never wavered. Regata looked like he hadn't slept in days. He spoke carefully, but his trepidation was not lost on anyone in the room. "There were uprisings in the streets, Lord."

"Peasants," said Athanasius. "The Valucian lords have expressed passionate loyalty to the empire."

"Outwardly, yes," said Rodrick Marius.

"Speak your minds," Athanasius said.

Regata hesitated. "I... fear we may have sent the wrong message, Lord."

"Everything we have striven to create is at risk of unraveling," Athanasius said. "A full-blown Valucian rebellion could set us back a decade or more. A warning had to be made."

"I'd say it was received..." Regata said, shaking his head. "I just pray it does not incite further unrest. Rykus was a blood-traitor. As are most of their lords. But if his loyalties were a ruse, then what of the other Valucians?"

Athanasius nodded. "We share the same fear. Hence, the warning. If they want to play at rebellion, they must know the cost. It would seem they have forgotten what a few dragons can do."

"My Lord, there were hundreds lost on Eòreth," said Marius. "Women, children. There are some calling it a war crime."

"Who?" the emperor demanded.

Regata simpered. "Murmurings."

"It was an act of retaliation for treason," Athanasius said evenly. "Rykus attacked unarmed Atticans. Two lords are dead, along with two noble youths just come of age. Murdered in cold blood."

Regata was not the only noble on edge, but he was the most vocal. The three ancient Dragon Lords said little, all watching how Athanasius handled the council.

This is a test in their eyes. Urla suspected the ancient lords would gladly lose Valucia, and plenty of other lesser regions of Attica, if it led to their return to prominence. Fifty years ago, this would have been a council of four.

Athanasius spoke again, quietly now. "Valucia has been a point of contention for many centuries. And their people have suffered the consequences for the decisions of countless foolish lords. For the past decade, they have prospered. Their lives are far better now. Their keeps are stronger, their cities rebuilt from war-torn shambles. Regata, your island has known the effects of both scenarios all too well."

"We've reaped the benefits of peace, Lord," said Regata. "And we have taken the brunt of the carnage in times of Valucian rebellion. They are a stubborn people, and I fear what we've done to Rykus's kingdom, small though it may be, could rally their rebellious spirits once more."

"Do you know why Ava Rykus was chosen to contend for a dragon before the lottery?" Athanasius asked.

No one in the room seemed surprised by the word *chosen*, and Urla realized for the first time, that the lords and ladies present had been in on the decision to rig this lottery.

Regata shook his head.

Urla noted the way the ancient Dragon Lords shifted.

"Valucia has a long history of dragon riders," Athanasius said. "Old as Attica itself. A proud history. But there has not been a Valucian Dragonmount in three hundred years. After years of peace, I intended to rectify that proud history and bind Valucian loyalties even closer."

The irony of the intent was not lost on anyone.

"I believe it was the right plan, but the wrong lord," Athanasius said.

"You still intend to give Valucia a dragon?" Lord Cassian asked.

All eyes fixed on the emperor, along with several raised brows.

"We need to show the other Valucian lords that nothing has changed," said Athanasius. "This is a matter of Rykus, not Valucia. Regata, you know their lords better than any in this room. I'd like you to choose the Valucian house best suited to serve on this council."

Urla barely held back a smirk at the way the man puffed up at the honor. "I'll choose wisely, Lord."

Athanasius nodded. "I have full confidence. Now, to the next matter. General Campos has overseen the acquisition and distribution of dragons on the Isle of Faltara for several years. Fortunately, before he died he had a successor in mind."

Urla glanced around the room. Campos's station as a dragon-less lord had been pivotal to his role. Everyone in this room possessed a dragon. Except her.

Urla's chest tightened as the emperor's gaze fell to her. She thought she was here to inform the council about what she'd seen on the island, not...

"M-me?" she stammered.

"Campos has spoken highly of you throughout your service," Athanasius said. "And as you are no longer the wife of a Dragonmount, your loyalties are well-suited to the needs of the realm. And of this council."

"Lord, surely there is..."

Athanasius smiled. "It has already been put to a vote."

Several of the lords, and all of the female council members nodded their heads to her.

"Campos was a good man," said Lord Marius. "We'd be fools not to select his first choice of successor."

"First choice..." Urla muttered, still unable to wrap her mind around what was happening.

"We have little time to waste," said the emperor. "The situation on Faltara is dire."

Urla was overwhelmed. Campos had been dead less than a day. Her son still lay unconscious a few rooms away. Not to mention, what this would mean for her son's chance at reclaiming a dragon.

But since the day she'd come of age, Urla had put the empire first, before any other role.

It was unfathomable to consider refusing the recommendation of her superior officer, or her duty to the empire.

She stood and bowed to Athanasius. "I would be honored, Lord Emperor."

Athanasius nodded. "Our future depends upon the Isle of Faltara, and the secrets that reside there. Consul Pelasius, tell the council every-thing you know."

———

After the council, Urla sat at her son's side, a churning mix of emotions in her gut.

Was this what Campos planned all along? Did he ever intend for my son to bond with one of those eggs?

She wished Keivan were here, though she knew what he would say.

It doesn't matter. Our duty is to Attica. Before house. Before family. Before glory. Even before dragons.

Ruan moaned, eyelids shifting as they do in dreams. His fingers twitched at the tips, a gentle fluttering that made her spirit surge.

"I'm right here, son," Urla whispered. "I'll make this right, I promise you."

Ruan did not waken.

"It's good for you to speak to him."

Urla jerked her head at the voice to find Athanasius entering the chamber. He was followed by two Knights of Caadron, one of them Vera Salyr, the other a tall Attican man. They flanked the entrance, hands on the hilts of their godblades. Even sheathed, the emerald glow tinted the lamplight that flickered off the walls.

Standing to attention, Urla crossed her right fist over her heart as Athanasius drew up beside her.

"That's what the healers told me when Emperor Vitruvian lay in such a state," Athanasius said. "They encouraged me to read to him when I visited."

The emperor's short, dark curls wove around the slender golden crown on his head. Up close, Urla could make out the individual branches and barbs of thorns. Though the crown still bore the emblem of the flaming dragon at the front, the band hearkened back to the rose crest of Athanasius's house—Octiva.

The emperor dipped his head to her and gestured to her chair.

"Please, sit, Lady Consul. It's good your son knows you're by his side. His soul can sense everything in the room, the healers say."

Urla had forgotten that Athanasius's predecessor had also slipped into a coma from an unexpected injury. She tried not to let her mind linger on the fact that Vitruvian never woke again. It was the sudden tragedy that had thrust Athanasius into power as a young man.

"Thank you, Lord." Urla sat and took hold of Ruan's hand once more.

"The world changes all at once. Or else not at all," Athanasius said, standing beside her. Even at a whisper, the young man's voice was strong and comforting. "My mentor taught me that. One moment, you're just another middling young lord at the academy. The next, you're shadowing the most powerful man in the world."

"It is the greatest honor of my life to serve you in this new capacity, Lord."

Athanasius smiled. "Ah, but you didn't let me finish. For a time, you're serving beside a man you admire more than any other. Then, in an instant, you are stumbling alone in a dark world that demands your entire body and soul. And you dare not show fear or weakness, else you risk destroying the world built by greater men."

"I'm not so sure about that, Lord. You've done more for a greater Attica than Vitruvian himself."

Athanasius raised his hands and shook his head. "I've done my best to build upon my mentor's foundation. His legacy is set firm. He brought the ancient Dragon Lords to heel, spread out power, united the lords. My own legacy is still being written. You saw the way the ancient lords were looking at me in there."

Urla nodded.

"This is the great test of the new Attica my predecessor envisioned, led by lesser and younger houses. What follows will determine everything."

Athanasius's gaze drifted to Ruan, then met her own, his dark brown eyes piercing her spirit, as though asking, *Will you have the strength to put duty before all else? Even your own son, if it comes to it? As your husband did?*

"My mission lies on Faltara. I trust the work of your healers while I'm away."

"Even they have their limits. My mentor is testament to this."

"A sparring injury," Urla recalled.

Athanasius nodded. "Not so different from your son. A fluke injury that struck the right place at the wrong time. I insisted we try every avenue of healing available. Even those beyond traditional Attican measures. But Vitruvian had written into his will against such experimental sorcery. To this day, I wonder if I should have defied that, somehow. If the empire would have been better served if I had."

"The empire has thrived under your leadership, Lord."

"What I'm saying is that your son need not share the same fate."

"Lord?"

"The Faltari shamans know magic, beyond that of our orders. Take your son. He was chosen to go to Faltara for good reason. And I, for one, would still see him become Dragonmount. Gods know, we'll need brave men such as he in the days ahead."

"But if I am consul..."

"There are ways around it. You are a widow now. You could take up your father's crest again. Or marry into another house."

The thought of remarrying was unthinkable at the moment, but Urla's heart surged nonetheless, and she swore her son gripped her hand back.

"We will need more riders than ever before if this is to be an Age of Fire."

The emperor left, and the male knight followed after, but Vera Salyr lingered, waiting for her.

Urla crossed the room and saluted her.

The Lady Knight returned the gesture, but remained where she stood, blocking the door.

"What is it?" Urla asked.

"Lady Captain, er, Lady Consul..."

"Urla is fine," she said. "You're a Knight of Caadron, for Marha's sake."

"Of course, Urla," said Salyr. "I am sworn to the emperor, but I have served General Campos for the past several years. I have joined him on journeys to Faltara, and other nations as well. As the new consul, it would be my honor to serve you on this coming mission, and whatever may follow."

"Lady Knight, I would be—"

In a flourish, the knight drew her glowing runemarked blade. In the same movement, she dropped to one knee and extended the flat edge of the blade between her hands and dipped her head to Urla.

She touched the knight's cheek so that she looked up at her. Her deep brown eyes were close to tears.

"You are my lord's chosen successor," the knight said. "A servant of the True Mother, the First Swordmaiden. By Marha's Blade, my blood is yours, whatever fates may divide."

Urla took the godblade from the woman's grasp, the soft pulse of magic thrumming even before her fingers brushed the cool surface.

She extended the hilt to Salyr, and the knight took it proudly.

"Welcome to the Bloody Company."

Chapter 33

Secrets

The clamor of angry voices echoed off the walls of Yerida's mead hall. Malik and his father sat together with the four Faltari clan chieftains around a ceremonial fire at the center of the room. Flickering light danced around the hall, and smoke drifted through an opening in the roof.

After the attack, all attention had first been focused on the safety of their people and ensuring that the last of the foreigners left the island swiftly and peacefully. The injured were tended to, the fires at the edge of the village were extinguished. Then, witnesses were gathered and questioned, some by one chieftain, some before the tribunal.

During the inquisition process, Malik relayed the details of his and Riese's planned *uhmskara*, and the fallout of that decision.

The bonding, the Thenius girl's murder, the attack of the shapeshifters and the runeship, the abduction of Riese and the eggs. All of it.

Joren had insisted he hold nothing back, and Malik had complied as best he could.

The Faltari elders understood the true meaning behind the Ascent ritual, but the rest of their people did not. How were they to explain the attack and the company of Attican soldiers that had been stationed on the island in its aftermath?

"What do I tell my clansmen?" demanded Tul Eriksein, father of Aram Tulsein, and chieftain of the Dragyr clan.

All the elders looked from one another to Joren, barely sparing a glance at Malik during the proceedings, except during his questioning.

Joren sat back in his carved socha chair and motioned for the Dragyr elder to continue.

"They want to know the reason for this attack," Tul went on. "Why a flying ship and a band of shapeshifting monsters broke the peace of countless festivals."

"Several of the Sabers are calling to close the borders," said Brom Dannsein, Petyr's father.

"A lot of good that would do if these rebels come back on a bloody flying ship!" said Lysa Anadeil of the Jackal clan, Malik's own mother's clan. His clan, until Derrin fell.

Lysa was the eldest chieftain in the room, the only one accompanied by a successor, a younger woman with red hair, who supported Lysa by the arm each time she stood to speak. Like Malik, the successor only listened, learning the ways of the tribunal under crisis.

"I'm not saying it's an actual bloody solution," Brom said. "But it is from my kin's perspective."

"I don't think the empire would allow it, anyway," Joren said.

"Perhaps it's worth the declaration. Close our borders to all but the empire just to make a show of action while we figure out the real solution."

"There is only one solution," said Olma Marudeil of the Feathered Serpent clan. "There has only ever been one solution. My clan's elders have known this for many years. Need I remind you that we rejected this entire charade from the beginning?"

Tul Eriksein rolled his eyes. "Serpents always have to inject their self-righteousness into every—"

"We never should have got in bed with the Atticans," Olma continued, ignoring the jibe.

"This is pointless talk," said Lysa. "What's done was done long ago."

"It is never too late to correct a grievous error," Olma said. "We should have destroyed the gate when our people first made the Crossing. We should have destroyed it when the Attican emperor unraveled our secret centuries ago. And we should still do it now. It is, and always will be, a curse!"

Silence fell over the room. All eyes settled on Joren. Malik's father had said little during the deliberation. Angry as Malik remained about the secrets his father had harbored, he understood the wisdom of his tactics now.

The first part of prudent speech is silence, his father had taught him.

"Whether an act of our ancestors was right or wrong is not the point." Joren enunciated each word slowly, deliberately. "This is the reality we inherited. They made their choice, and we must make ours in the world we are in right now. A world in which secrets have been kept, for the good of our people.

"However we may feel, our peace and livelihood has long depended on imperial protection. But now, it is not just our fate that rests on our decisions. Indeed, the livelihood of all Îrithèa may very well depend on it. The gravity of this matter for the rest of the world must not be lost either."

"Why should we care?" Tul demanded.

Joren leveled a fierce gaze on the man. "These eggs have bought us peace at the edge of the world, but they have also brought stability elsewhere. Across Attica and all Îrithèa. A balanced distribution of power."

Olma shook her head. "After everything you've witnessed in your life, and you still sound just like your father, Joren. It's a bloody shame."

Malik watched his father carefully, wishing he knew what the chieftain spoke of. There was so much about his father that he didn't know.

His uncle's death. His father's *uhmskara*. How his father had learned to fight better than an Attican soldier.

"I've seen what the empire does, Olma," Joren said. "But I have also seen much of the outside world too."

"And no one else has learned anything from the outside world, is that it?"

Joren glanced away.

"What happens in the empire and beyond is not our concern," Tul said.

"We are Faltari," said Olma. "Our task was not to hide. *May the world be brighter for our burning.* Our ancestors lost sight of that calling, and now, we reap the consequences."

"You wish to argue over the texts, right now? What do you think the empire will do to *this* island, Olma, if we were to do what you say? To destroy the gate would be an act of rebellion. Assuming we even could."

"You *know* we could!" Olma shouted. The flames surged at the center of the room, a flash of magic accentuating her point.

No one dared speak.

"So you admit it, then?" Olma said, calming herself. "This life we lead—it truly is a lie. We are just as beholden to the empire as any other nation in this world. All this talk of freedom, being chosen, our gifts from the gods. It's all babble."

Joren shook his head. "After everything that's happened, Olma, *you're* the one who pretends the world to be as simple as your dreams."

Olma smirked. "My mother taught me to let my voice be heard, and I reckon I've done so. Whatever may come, the time for secrets is over."

The woman met the gaze of each person in the room, most glanced away, saying nothing. Her blue eyes were like stars in the winter sky, and they seemed to cut straight through to Malik's soul when she met his gaze. Igniting a fire in his spirit the same way her words had.

There came a knock outside the door, and for the first time, Malik realized that the clans had quietened outside the meeting hall.

Joren crossed the room, and Malik tensed as he saw Aram Tulsein whisper something, then leave.

Joren returned to the circle. "General Campos has fallen. Now, his successor wishes to address the tribunal. We will adjourn for dinner and return to make our final decision."

———

"Look, I know you can't say anything," said Yuri, between bites of a hastily prepared porridge. "But it just makes no sense. Why would they take Riese, of all people?"

"I don't bloody know," said Malik. Yuri's betrothed had remained close to her parents after the attack, and every time Malik wasn't being questioned or sitting in on tribunal meetings, Yuri leapt at the chance to jabber to someone.

"But you were there! When she was taken."

"I told you, we were trying to save Campos. We followed that traitor girl, Ava, into the woods, and found the consul in a pool of blood."

"And now, he's dead," said Yuri. "God's breath. That girl with the cane. I didn't see that one coming."

Malik just shook his head, wishing his friend would take a damn hint. His heart was sick with worry for Riese. But Olma's words haunted him too.

So many secrets...

The Faltari gathered in the field outside the village, where people from all over the world had been peacefully celebrating another successful festival only two days ago.

There were few smiles now, and no music. Children huddled close to their parents. Joren was off visiting with their kinsmen, calming fears, and Malik's mother was performing a similar role for scared mothers and their children.

Malik probably should have been doing the same, but he couldn't bring himself to. So, he'd taken his dinner with his sister, who largely ignored him and chatted with a couple of her childish friends about boys from other clans.

But Surel kept glancing over and smirked at Malik as Yuri went on and on. She never took anything seriously, even an attack on their damn village.

Normally, Yuri was the same way, but Riese's abduction seemed to have shaken him. And Malik couldn't blame him. He wished he could talk to Yuri about what he knew. He wished he could talk to anyone.

In one night, all the lies about the Ascent had shattered, and no one outside the council knew. And Malik was dying inside.

"What I wanna know is how the damn Elyans fit into all this..." Yuri was saying.

"And what do you know about the Elyans?" Surel asked, winking at Malik as she left her friends' conversation and egged Yuri on.

"What does anyone know about them?" Yuri asked, glad for the attention. "They come from across the Ever Sea. Even the Atticans hardly know anything about them. Except it's a land of free magic. Shit, maybe it's not that different from here?"

"Well, listen to you!" Aram Tulsein plopped down beside Yuri. "You talk to one drunk trader, and you think you understand the world, don't you?"

"Yeah?" said Yuri. "And what do *you* know?"

Aram huffed. "Seeing as I'm fit to succeed my father as Dragyr chieftain one day, I'd guess a fair bit more than you. Just like I know why they *actually* flew off with your friend."

Malik glared at Aram. "Leave Riese out of this."

"What?" said Aram. "I just thought Yuri deserves to know that you're lying to his face."

"I'm honoring the will of the council."

"I'm not talking about the council, I'm talking about you."

"Lying?" Yuri demanded.

"Yuri, just ignore—"

"Malik didn't follow the consul into the woods," Aram said. "He and Riese went there *with* Campos. And that cripple girl. Supposedly, they were going to go on *uhmskara*. Oh, wait, you didn't know that?"

"What?" Yuri asked, pain written across his face. "You were... leaving?"

"Yuri, I'm sorry we didn't tell you," Malik said. "It all happened so quick."

Aram stood. "Not even smart enough to lie. You're pathetic, shaman. You know what I think? I think there's more you're not saying. Even in that council. My father thinks you're a damn liar and a traitor. Maybe even the reason all this—"

"Go to the fucking Abyss, Tulsein!" Malik shouted.

A girl gasped nearby, and her mother shot Malik a harsh look.

Surel and her friends were grinning, wide eyed.

Yuri stood back, glowering.

But Malik didn't care. He stood, glaring across the table at Aram, fists clenched.

"Easy there, shaman." A hand clasped his shoulder from behind.

Malik spun to find Ulgar Fenrisein. He shrugged the boy's hand away, but Ulgar held tight.

"Ignore Tulsein," Ulgar said. "He's just jealous that you're sitting on the council to begin with. He's been bitching and moaning about it all day."

"For god's sake," said Aram. "The shaman saves your life, and now you're his bloody dog?"

"Least I en't delusional about my standing," said Ulgar with a shrug. "Fit to succeed your father, my ass. You're second born. You'll never sit on that council."

Aram rolled his eyes. "Whatever. Lie all you want, both of you. But the Dragyrs see right through it." With that, he sauntered away.

Yuri got up from his seat.

"Wait!" said Malik.

"You gonna tell me what's really going on with Riese?" Yuri asked.

Malik sighed. "You know the council is confidential."

"Well, then, I guess we don't have anything to talk about, seeing as you didn't even trust me enough to tell me you were gonna leave the damn island."

"Yuri, come on, I didn't—"

But the boy stormed off.

His sister raised a brow. "Well, that was smooth."

"Enough, Surel!" Malik shouted.

"What's going on?" their mother demanded, marching over from a conversation with some of the Jackal mothers.

It was only then that Malik realized just how many people had taken notice of the altercation at his table. Dozens of his people were watching him from nearby tables. Their new shaman shouting and cursing. At a time when all Faltari were on edge.

"Nothing is going on," said Malik, grabbing his still-full bowl of porridge.

His mother brushed his shoulder. "Son, stay and eat."

"I'm not hungry."

"Maybe it's from all that foot in your mouth," said Surel.

"God's breath!" Malik muttered and hurried away, weaving between tables and around cookfires as fast as he could, brushing off questions from some of the other kinsmen gathered.

He spotted his father watching him from the other end of the field. But Malik hurried on. He needed to be alone. To think.

He nearly made it out of the gathering, when Riese's father, Ulrik, emerged from a tent near the village gates.

"Malik!" Ulrik motioned him over, a worried look etching deep crevices across his weathered face.

Malik cursed to himself but joined the man. Fear and lack of sleep made him look like he'd just emerged from a days-long hunt.

"Is it true?" he asked.

"I'm sorry?"

"That you and Riese were with the Atticans when the consul general was attacked."

Gods damn you, Aram.

Malik nodded.

"What was she doing?"

Malik didn't know what to say. Of course, he couldn't speak of the eggs—that the man's daughter was Dragonbound. That all the Ascent was a bloody lie.

But he couldn't just run off, could he? Malik had gotten Riese into this, and her father had been like an uncle to him all his childhood.

"Please, Malik," Ulrik whispered. "I'm trying to piece this together, but it doesn't make sense. Riese was with us the whole evening, enjoying herself. And then you came by, and she ran off to meet the Atticans and got caught up in this whole bloody mess... Why?"

The man clutched his forearm, fingers trembling. Malik clasped the man's shoulder, knowing he had to give him something. Riese's father deserved that much.

"We were seeking passage away from the island, sir. We were going to go on a Wandering."

The man's face twisted in a pained grimace. "Leave? But why? Riese was just matched. She seemed so happy."

Malik sensed the deeper turmoil in his spirit that no words could convey. Fear of losing his daughter. Fear of failing her. Driving her away. Despair over what he might have done differently.

But it was Malik who had acted wrongly. He'd gotten his best friend caught up in a bloody rebellion.

"It was my idea. I convinced her to go."

Ulrik covered his mouth and shook his head, pain emanating from his spirit. His words were muffled. "I just don't—"

"I'm sorry I can't say more right now. But your daughter loves you very much. I know that for damn sure. She'll find a way back, I know she will. Riese is the toughest person I've ever known."

Filled with rage and regret, Malik slipped past the grieving man and entered the village, weaving down the narrow lanes between longhouses. He paused near the outer wall, a sob catching in his throat.

Every time he thought of Riese, he felt sick. Was she a hostage? Something else? They'd had no problem killing the Attican girl. Why did they take Riese alive?

Not only that, but they'd tried to take Ruan Pelasius as well. Whose mother was the new Attican consul.

Riese's father was right about that much. None of this made sense.

The autumn dusk fell quickly on the village, and Malik knew he didn't have much time before the council reconvened. He hurried to the temple.

Still carrying his bowl of uneaten porridge, he ascended the steps and entered the main hall. The vast chamber was lit with candles and smelled of woody incense. A handful of villagers burned prayer cloths before the statues of the All Mother and All Father. Nameless, for no human name could ever be worthy of them.

Were the gods even real? Or was that just one more secret his father had kept all these years?

Malik hurried into the narrow hallway beyond. Which led to rooms for private rituals and divinations and healings.

The temples in each of the clan villages had always felt like home to Malik, but nothing felt right anymore. Like an earth tremor was destroying everything he knew about the world, piece by piece. Debris pressing in on him, choking the breath from his lungs.

He nearly jumped when a figure emerged from the darkness at the other end of the hall, but was quickly relieved to find it was just Ulgar.

The Serpent boy offered Malik a querulous brow, glancing at the door to the inner sanctum.

Malik glanced back down the hall. They were alone.

Swiftly, he pressed his palm to the wood, whispered the words of entry, and opened the runemarked door, ushering Ulgar to follow.

The room was quiet within, lit only by a single runemarked lantern.

"You're sure no one followed you?" Malik asked.

Ulgar nodded. "Don't think I draw much suspicion in my own village."

That was why Malik had sought his help in the first place. And because Malik had a sense about him ever since the storm on the Spires. A sense confirmed when Ulgar had saved his life during the attack.

Ulgar was a good man. Someone he knew he could trust. Much like Riese.

Gods, I wish she was here.

A soft muffled sound emitted from the desk across the chamber. The Sacred Hall always buzzed with *hish* from all the runework that secured the room from listening ears, but that magic resonance was even stronger now.

Malik and Ulgar crossed the room. A lone chair was set in the corner between shelves of sacred documents.

Ulgar checked the bindings fixing their prisoner to the chair.

"You learn anything from her this morning?" Ulgar asked.

"That's why we're here," Malik said. "I need a second opinion before I decide what to do with her."

"And... I'm the obvious choice to help you... not the high shaman of our people?"

Malik grimaced. "I wish it were that simple. But no, I can't tell my father. Not yet."

Ulgar pulled back the hood, and Malik untied the strip of cloth from Ava Rykus's mouth.

Malik felt the pulse of *hish* as Ava pressed his mind with silent questions, assurances, and attempted manipulations.

Ava was not as untrained as she'd seemed during the festival, but Malik was more than strong enough to protect himself against her. She was like a child who could swim, but she was no pearl diver.

"Enough," Malik said, warding away her magic with a pulse of *hish*. "No magic. No bullshit. Tell Ulgar exactly what you told me this morning."

CHAPTER 34

PRISONER

Ava Lucila Rykus had woken in darkness, her body jostling. Hands gripping her arms and legs. Carrying her through the forest.

While the village had scrambled to deal with the aftermath of the rebel attack, the shaman had enlisted the help of a boy named Ulgar to help in hauling Ava from the shrines to the village temple.

No easy task in the darkness. But Ava was weak when she woke, hands bound, and she did not resist them.

Somewhere between the Faltari shrines and the outer walls of the village, they'd stopped.

There were other people in the woods near the village walls, but there was plenty else going on. The air was filled with cries of children and frantic villagers within the walls, and Ava's hood was drawn, and it was the middle of the night yet.

They crawled through a tight nook between an old socha trunk and a large boulder, then dropped down a small hole in a space behind another tree, and they were out of the forest, venturing down a tunnel leading to this inner sanctum within the temple. Malik had used a significant amount of magic to direct attention elsewhere when they neared that secret entrance.

Even now, Ava could sense the guilt gnawing at Malik's gut, the intrusive magic clearly against the moral code of these shamans. As was harboring a murderer in the inner sanctum of their temple, Ava expected.

She'd never held such reservations about magic, at least none that had not been forced upon her by the academy or the demands of secrecy. But it told her much about the shaman. The boy, Ulgar, she had less of a read on.

He struck her as a simple man, and he smelled faintly of fish. Not a brute, but the sort of boy who let others do the deliberating.

So, why had the shaman brought Ulgar now?

Ava groaned as she craned her neck to face them. She'd spent nearly two days tied to a chair, and her whole body was stiff. Her head throbbed from when Riese had knocked her unconscious. And her bad hip was like a constant fire lapping up her right side.

A small sacrifice, she'd told herself over and over.

The shaman had at least let her remove the brace from her leg. Worn too long, it cut off circulation. Now, it flopped against the side of the bookshelf in this inner temple chamber.

Ava peered up at Malik, then her gaze drifted to the porridge in his hands.

"You going to eat that in front of me?"

"Er, no." Malik set the bowl before her.

He'd only brought a flagon of water when he'd visited her this morning, and she was the hungriest she'd felt since the academy trials that had sent her out to survive in the woods for three days with only a spear. Her hip made it difficult to hunt game, and she'd subsisted mostly on nuts and berries.

Ava glanced at the bowl of porridge with longing, but she couldn't resist another jab. The shaman always reacted.

"So... do I lap it up like a dog, then?" She leaned her face forward, arms straining against the ropes fixing her hands to the back of the chair. She stretched her neck toward the bowl.

Malik blanched. "What do you think?" he asked Ulgar.

"Eh, her legs are still bound." Ulgar moved behind the chair and untied Ava's hands.

She grunted as she stretched her aching fingers and rubbed the raw lines formed by the ropes on her wrists. "You're both noble gentlemen," she said.

Malik glared as Ava extended a soft flare of magic at them both.

"No more warnings," he said. "If I sense any manipulation, we turn you over to the consul."

"Consul?" Ava asked. "Surely not Campos, the way I left him. That must mean..."

"Enough," Malik said.

"You brought it up, not me." She flashed a full-lipped smile. "I don't suppose it would help to remind you my actions were entirely—"

Malik sent a flash of magic her way, pressing into her mind.

"Sorry," she said. "You've no idea what it takes to survive an Attican upbringing. Valucians all thought we were traitors. Atticans thought us saints, but they still looked down on us as lesser lords. It required a lot to make my way here."

"And look at you now," Ulgar said.

Ava smirked. "Yes, still caught somewhere between traitor and saint, aren't I?"

These two had no idea what she'd been through. What her family had sacrificed. What her people had endured.

But you can't blame them for that, Ava reminded herself.

The shaman was a good man, and at the very least, he questioned what should be done with her. Ava had to build on that.

"Tell Ulgar what you told me," Malik said again.

He was growing frustrated. Ava took that, and Ulgar's return, as good signs.

She took up the bowl and scooped the goopy porridge into her mouth with her fingers. It was cold, and lacked any seasoning, but her body relished the sustenance.

"Your friend is safe," Ava said. "Your people are safe, at least as far as the rebellion is concerned. I can't speak for the empire."

"Safe? Tell that to all our kin," said Ulgar, crossing his thick arms and stepping closer so he towered over her.

Ava had seen enough academy boys try to overcompensate for their insecurities to ignore the intimidation. "Were any of your villagers killed in the attack?"

Ulgar hesitated. "I don't believe so."

Ava scooped another bite of porridge. "I'm relieved to hear it. Our enemy is Attica, not Faltara. But if a new consul is here, I fear the island won't be safe much longer. The shaman fears this too, I think."

Malik dipped his chin.

"If our island is unsafe, it's because of what you've done," Ulgar said. "No one has been killed here in cold blood like that in ages."

"We did what we did because of what *your* people have done for ages. Without dragons, what power would Attica have? Your people did that."

Ulgar stepped back, then shrugged. "I expect you know more about all that than me. I'm just a lowly island boy from the edge of the world."

Ava smiled. "Perhaps."

"What is it your people want?" Ulgar asked.

"Freedom," said Ava. "Something you value here on the island, I'm told." She glanced at Malik, who seemed to be striving to maintain an indifferent demeanor.

He was not so worried earlier, Ava thought.

"And the Elyans?" Ulgar asked. "How do they fit?"

"Freedom is a value we all share. They lent our cause the use of one of their runeships. We are not the first."

"And what about those creatures? Where'd they come from?"

Ava shrugged. "They're not creatures, but I'll say no more. I don't know if I can trust you."

"Seems to me, you're the one who needs to prove themselves."

"Does it seem that way to you?"

Malik shifted. He was so jittery.

"Why were you left behind?" Ulgar demanded. "Your father didn't so much as look back. I saw him go. And you don't seem too concerned about it, either."

"The mission always comes first," Ava said.

"Or he left you here for a reason," said Malik, finally interjecting.

Ava nodded, pleased with how the conversation had gone.

"Because he's coming back," Malik said.

"You seem to know as much as I do."

"Quit playing games," Malik said, straightening, jaw tensing.

Ava sighed and leaned back from the desk. "You're cute when you're frustrated, shaman."

"I mean it," he said. "No more bullshit."

Ava pounded the empty bowl on the table. "That is the one thing I have never done. My family is ready to *die* to free Valucia from Attican tyranny. And if you think that your own island is exempt from their cruelty, you're the one bullshitting yourself. Your island is the home for the dragons that fuel the empire, and the secret's out. You're all going to have to decide which side to take."

The two young men glanced at one another. Brows furrowed, hard lines etched into their faces. Even without her magic, Ava could sense the tension in them. It was all she could do to not try to probe further.

"How many eggs are there really?" Ava asked. "Every year more of them are allotted to Attican lords. And according to my father, dragons can't reproduce in this world."

"This world?" said Ulgar.

Malik shot a glare at the boy, and Ava grinned.

"Maybe your father doesn't know what he's talking about," Malik said.

"There is always that possibility... but I'd wager that dozens of eggs have passed from this place. Maybe hundreds. And I think there are more. Far more. And if something isn't done, the empire will seize them all. Maybe they'll hide them someplace else. Maybe they'll hatch them all. And *that* would be the end of the world as we know it. An Age of Fire."

Silence hung over the room. Ulgar shifted, glancing at the door.

Malik sighed. "So what?" said Malik. "We should give them to your rebels instead?"

"You seriously think we'd tell you where they are?" asked Ulgar.

"Oh, that's not why I'm here," said Ava.

"I don't think you're here for any reason," said Ulgar, but she could sense the doubt in his voice.

"We'll find out soon enough." Ava sat back in her chair. "You're right, the rebellion will return. And the empire is going to try to seize as many eggs as they can. And they won't care who dies in their wake, that much I promise you. Not Valucians. Not Faltari. No one will be safe."

Ava drew a long breath, letting the tension build. "I'm here to warn you. It's time for your people to leave this island. For good."

CHAPTER 35

THE EYRIE

Watch your step," said Deven lè Nir.

The floor of the runeship shifted beneath them, and Riese held tight to a rail as they ascended narrow steps to the main deck. She was no longer bound, though the runemarked collar remained.

Riese could not shake the images seared into her mind. The entire Isle of Eòreth smoldering like the coals of a cookfire. It wasn't the Rykus estate that haunted her, but the villages outside, the charred skeletal remains of incinerated huts. Roofs caved in or consumed. Walls collapsed. They'd been too high and distant to see the bodies. But her imagination ran wild.

"They had no warning," Rykus had said. "Women and children who'd no part in what happened on Faltara. This is the swift wrath of the empire your people have empowered, Riese Torendeil."

To think she had entertained joining their legion of dragon riders. To wreak carnage in the same way on other unsuspecting innocents. Her ancestors had been right about the nature of the Dragonmounts.

And yet, they'd also made this possible, content to look the other way as they delivered Attica the keys to their power. Hours later, her stomach still churned at the images in her mind.

Rykus's words rang over and over in her head as they sailed away from Eòreth, quickly lost back in the darkness of the storm.

Now, Riese and Deven emerged on deck. Clouds enveloped them in all directions, but the sky was calm. A golden glow hung over the deck of the ship, reminding Riese of her village illuminated on a snowy night, the light of hearths and candles magnified by the weather.

Only here, the light came from *hish*-infused runes. And something else, too.

Tiny flashes of golden light darted all around the flying ship, buzzing loudly as they whisked from sails to rigging to the sides of the vessel. One brushed past Riese's face, and she barely resisted the instinct to swat it away like a pesky deer fly. It drew up at once and hovered near Captain Rykus's shoulder. He stood at the foredeck, beside a woman with fiery hair who manned the helm.

The woman was slender, dressed in form-fitting navy trousers and a long officer's coat that nearly reached her knees.

The dark-winged creature was the size of a handspan. Small horns protruded from an ugly head, and its skin was covered in fiery veins. Dark eyes examined Riese up and down, then the creature turned to Rykus and spoke.

"Lord Rykus, Sky Captain Verina, we are nearing our destination." Its voice was raspy and guttural, befitting the fearsome face, though Riese had expected a higher pitch based on its size.

"Very good, Lir'ghe," Rykus said.

The creature scowled, eyes darting to the Sky Captain and then to Riese.

"Lord, should not this prisoner stay out of sight?"

"She is no prisoner, Lir'ghe."

"Aren't I?" Riese chuckled, hand drifting to the runemarked collar around her neck. She glanced at Deven, who stood beside her, hand hovering instinctively at the hilt of a saber.

The Morph shrugged. "You're still a sorceress."

"And a Dragonmount," Rykus added.

Lir'ghe buzzed softly, arms crossed over its tiny humanoid chest, remaining close to the Sky Captain's shoulder. Verina held tight to the helm, subtly adjusting numerous levers on a panel beside the wheel as they sailed across the skies. Lir'ghe whispered something sharply to the Sky Captain. She shrugged and focused on the task before her.

"Well, since my opinion is not being heard," the creature murmured, "I return to work now."

Without another word, it darted away.

"Moody fellow," Riese said.

"Small vicious creatures usually are," Rykus said. "Your dragon will be worse as a hatchling."

My dragon, Riese thought.

It was such a bizarre thing to say so casually. But that bond was a part of her now. Over the past several hours, she longed to feel the dragon's spirit again. She could sense it was nearby. Despite the destruction she'd witnessed, she still longed to see her own dragon hatch. To meet it. To complete the bond.

But there was much left to determine, even if she was sympathetic to Rykus's cause. There was so much she did not understand.

Riese marveled as the fiery creatures flitted from place to place on the ship, rune to rune. The winds shifted, jostling the entire vessel. Riese grabbed on to the railing to steady herself.

The Sky Captain hollered an order as she adjusted several rune-marked levers. Sails shifted, and the ship groaned as it turned in the misty skies.

"God's breath! Are those creatures flying this thing?"

"Of course," the Sky Captain said.

"What are they?"

"Kroqala," said Rykus. "Demon faeries from the Lost World."

"From before the Crossing?" Riese asked.

"Well, she's a sharp one, at any rate," said the Sky Captain, with little enthusiasm.

Rykus nodded, though he made no further answer.

"We're close," said Verina, gripping the helm. "Best hang tight. The winds are always stronger up close."

"Up close to what?" Riese asked.

Rykus winked but did not answer.

"Come," Deven said, pointing to the bow of the ship. They crossed quickly, and Riese held tight to the railing, peering over the side. Her stomach roiled. All she saw was swirling mists, but she knew they must be hundreds, maybe thousands of feet above the sea. One slip, and...

No Dragonmount would fear such a height, she thought, steeling herself. *This ship is safer than most places on the Spires.*

"So, are you going to tell me where we're going, or you going to keep playing this game?" Riese said, shifting her gaze ahead into the gloom.

"Where do you think a rebel would go between missions?" Deven asked with a wry smile.

"Well, I thought we were heading back to your master's island before it was destroyed."

Deven grimaced. "We never used his own kingdom as a rebel outpost for just that reason. But we heard word of an attack, and Rykus had to be certain."

"How did you hear so quickly?" asked Riese.

Deven shrugged. "There are many things that can be done with the proper rune work. We were fortunate the Dragonmounts had already left. No doubt planning their next moves. Everything will converge on Faltara. But first, we must confer with the others."

"What others?"

Deven pointed toward the darkness ahead. Riese peered into the thick clouds, mists dampening her hair, chilling her skin. Wind rushed over the deck, sails roaring as the Kroqala and some of the rebel soldiers adjusted their position once more.

Ahead, amidst the billowing darkness, shapes appeared. A mass of rock jutted before of them.

"We're lower than I thought," Riese said.

"Oh, we're thousands of feet above the ocean right now."

"You mean, that's not a mountain?"

"It's a mountain, all right. But it's nowhere near land."

"What?"

The ship veered to the right, and more looming masses of stone appeared in the night, lights glowing at the peaks. There were five total, that Riese could see.

"It is known as the Eyrie," Deven said. "A long lost secret of Valucia."

The ship slowed, gliding between two of the floating mountains.

Riese drew a long cold breath, her entire body shivering now. Wind pressed against her body, and she held tight to the rail, her knowledge of the world unraveling once more.

There are more Spires?

The Sky Captain barked an order as the runeship drew up close to one of the levitating peaks, adjusting furiously as they slowed. From the mists, a short wooden dock jutted out from the top of the mound of rock, and the vessel came to a stop.

Soldiers transformed, clothes vanishing, dark wings shooting out from their backs.

The Morphs flew from the deck and fixed ropes to large metal hooks, tethering the ship to the skydock. In the mists, it was difficult to make out just how large the spire was, but Riese could not see the other side.

The crew began to disembark across a plank with rails on both sides, anchored firmly with ropes on both the ship and the dock.

From the darkness ahead rose a lone building made of stone, weathered and crumbling, older than anything Riese had ever seen. Except in the Abyss.

"Shall we?" Deven grinned.

Half the crew had disembarked. Riese struggled to find words.

"I... what is this?"

"You're trying to act confused," said Deven.

Rykus joined them at the plank. "We're all still learning to trust one another," he said. "So, I don't begrudge you. But understand, we're risking much bringing you here."

"That was *your* choice. Not mine."

Rykus made his way across the plank and turned back from the safety of the dock. "You're going to have to take a side, Riese. All your people will."

"Might as well make an informed decision, right?" Deven said.

Riese hesitated. "And if I choose wrong? Am I really supposed to believe you'll let me live after I've seen your hideout?"

"Well, certainly not with your dragon. But you could never find this place. I promise you."

Riese crossed her arms.

Deven softened her gaze and brushed Riese's shoulder. This time, Riese didn't flinch. "If you choose to forsake your dragon and your destiny, I will take you back to Faltara myself. But if you truly believe we're as heartless as the Atticans your people have served for so long, well, you're dead either way, I expect."

Riese followed the woman across the board of wood, sky plummeting on either side. Her vision swam, and she had to focus on placing each foot in the center of the board. A few more steps, and Riese stood on solid ground.

The lone structure on the spire was unassuming, barely larger than the mead hall back in River's End. A few flying Morphs soared over the entrance wall, and then, the ten foot wooden doors groaned open, and Captain Rykus led the way through, Deven and Riese following quickly after.

They entered a hall about fifty feet across, circular in shape, entirely flat but for a staircase on one side. The room contained no tapestries, no murals, no statues, just walls made of crude rectangular stones that looked to have been taken from these very Spires. All contained the same brown tint as the ground outside.

One of the Morphs entered behind them in human form, holding a small wooden chest, and Riese felt a burst of warmth in her spirit. Deven took the chest from the man.

"Are those..." Riese began.

Deven nodded. "All three eggs from the festival. Yours among them. Though I expect you've already felt it."

Captain Rykus approached, placed a hand on the runemarked chest. It flashed at his touch, and he uttered words in a strange tongue. Carefully, he opened the top and withdrew the resplendent crimson egg that had been burned in Riese's memory.

Riese had felt a deep longing even knowing the egg was near, but at the sight of it, that longing blazed in her spirit. The warm resonance reached for hers, filling her with hope. With light.

Rykus smiled. "A breathtaking marvel, isn't it?" He turned the egg over in his hands, scales shimmering in the low lantern light. He drew closer, and the radiance in Riese's spirit flared even stronger. The feeling consumed her awareness. Being so close to the egg. To the soul tethered to her own, even if it had not yet come into the world.

He held it out to her. "You are bound to this dragon, Riese Torendeil. But it is not yours and will never be yours unless it hatches, and that requires sacred knowledge and ancient rites. The window is short. If you and this egg were to be separated for long, the bond would fade, and the spirit of the dragon within would seek another to release it from dormancy."

"Speak plainly, Captain Rykus."

"You've seen a taste of one path you nearly took. The fate of a Dragonmount of Attica, sent to burn innocents. Should you forsake this bond and return home, you would choose a second path. You might feel depressed at the absence, but the memory of the bond would fade, and you would only be tormented by the question of what might have been. But there is a third path. Would you like to see it?"

She spared a glance at Deven, still holding the chest. The young woman smiled.

Riese took the egg from Rykus's hands. The dragon's resonance pressed against her spirit, a near tangible urging, assuring her that she must continue on this path. She had to know. Both of them did.

"Show me," she said.

Rykus closed the chest, took it from Deven, then crossed the room, making for the staircase, which descended below the hall.

It was wide enough for several people to walk abreast and wound downward out of sight. Riese followed Rykus, and Deven came after.

They wanted something from her, but Riese was growing to trust them. Or at least, she didn't fear them. This rebellion needed her. And she needed to know more.

The staircase wound down for what must have been several hundred steps, walls lining the entire staircase. Wind rushed upward, growing stronger as they went. All at once, the inner wall faded, opening into a massive lower hall, two or three times the size of the one above. They descended from the top of the second chamber, which was much taller than the other. The room glowed with an incandescent light emanating from the floor.

As they neared the bottom, Riese realized she could see through the floor, like looking through foggy glass. The pulse of *hish* was furious here. She could not draw it in with the collar on, but she could feel the power rushing just as powerfully as the wind.

"We're near the base of the mountain," Rykus said, grinning at the bottom of the stairs.

A small walkway formed a rim around the expanse. Riese gazed up to find a domed cavern filled with menacing spears of stone in the ceiling. She looked closer at the floor and realized the wind was rushing from the floor itself. It was not glass. The floor was open, and those were clouds. Mists surging beneath them.

The wind and *hish* filled Riese's senses with a near-overwhelming charge of energy. The egg in her hands pulsed, urging her onward.

Captain Rykus moved to the edge of the walkway and peered into the expanse. Riese inched closer, trying to make sense of the strange glowing coloration. Near the rim, the skies were dark, but the colors shifted as they neared the center of the expanse. Lighter shades of blue and white clouds.

It was different from the passage Riese had experienced, but she knew this feeling. It was unfathomable, and yet, she knew exactly what this expanse was. She'd seen that strange film before, peering through to a different sky.

"So, this isn't your first time," Deven said, standing beside her.

"No... well, not like this... but... how do you..."

"How do you cross?" Rykus asked. "You fly."

With a surge of *hish*, Rykus levitated from the ground. Only a few inches, but it was no less jolting. Awe-inspiring. Marvelous.

Rykus drifted out over the expanse, still holding the chest.

Deven's body shifted, dark wings shooting from the breadth of her shoulders, skin turning leathery and dark like a dragyr's. Last night, the transformations had been terrifying, but Riese found herself fascinated now. Deven grew over a foot in height. Her face turned fearsome, but still retained a familiar shape. The woman grinned and reached out a leathery hand.

Riese cradled her dragon egg in the crook of her arm, tight against her chest, and clasped Deven's fingers with her other hand. Fear and excitement flooded her.

But from the egg, she felt a sense of calm. The way her father's presence had comforted her as a child.

This was the right path.

"Ready?" Deven asked.

Riese took in a long breath and nodded.

Magic rushed over her entire body, pulling, lifting, as Deven flapped her wings. And Riese also rose from the ground.

"God's breath!"

"Oh, you haven't seen anything yet!"

With a rush of her wings, they soared over the expanse with a burst of speed that made Riese's stomach sink.

They plunged downward.

Through a second Gate of the Ancients.

PART SEVEN

PATH OF THE GODS

From death to new life, we crossed. Filled with strength from the Father, courage from the Mother, we stepped into an unknown future.

—a passage from *The Crossing*

Chapter 36

The Other Side

"There is no time to waste," Consul Pelasius said, addressing the Faltari council.

Joren's stomach twisted into knots as he listened. He could sense the sincerity in the Lady Consul's spirit.

"The rebels *will* return," Urla continued. "This arrangement has benefitted both our nations for many years, but it is time for the nature of our arrangement to evolve. These dragon eggs pose a grave danger. Both for Faltara, and all the empire."

Joren feared what must be done, and he was not the only one.

"Even Campos did not know the true source," said Olma of the Feathered Serpents. "Why should we think a few backwater rebels will be able to find it?"

Urla Pelasius remained calm. "Are you willing to gamble all these innocent lives on that hope, madam?"

Silence hung over the room, and it spoke louder than any voice yet.

"How many people live on this island?" Consul Pelasius asked.

"Roughly six hundred," said Joren. "Across the four clans."

Olma crossed her arms over her chest.

"Most of our people do not know the true nature of our... alliance," explained Brom Dannsein of the Saber clan. "They believe the eggs are destroyed each year after the Ascension. What reason could we give them for leading an Attican company to our sacred valley?"

The chieftains nodded. Joren grabbed his beard to prevent himself from shaking his head. *What would an imperial soldier care about what we hold sacred?*

Whether Urla thought it or not, she responded judiciously. "We all do what we must to protect those we love. I am sure our ancestors had good reason for conducting matters the way we have until now. But, as my father used to say, when the world shifts, you may go with it, or be destroyed by it, but you cannot fight such a force."

Again, silence filled the chamber.

"My hope is that your people will see no more destruction than what has already been meted out by this party of rebels. I know the choice before you is difficult. The attack took a toll on my own family. Stole the life of my mentor. I do not wish your kin a similar fate."

"If our ancestors were able to keep the alliance a secret, then I believe we can find a way to keep this matter a secret as well," said Tul Eriksein. "It's clear those bastards are coming back. It's a matter of how soon."

"Days at best," answered the consul.

"No force could come so swiftly," Olma said with disbelief.

"With the right passage, great distances may be crossed in an instant."

"You think they've got one of your godblades?" Olma demanded.

Eyes drifted to the towering Lady Knight standing directly behind the consul. It was no secret any longer that the woman's sorcerous blade formed some sort of portal. There had been too many witnesses during the doomed attempt to save Campos.

"There is much we do not know," said Pelasius. "But we must be prepared. A company of Dragonmounts are heading this way as we speak. They are too large to come by godblade. It is a long flight, but they will be here tomorrow. And it is my duty to prepare the way. We must know Rykus's true target."

The air seemed to grow heavy in Joren's lungs. The world had changed all at once, on his watch. And no matter how he worked scenarios in his mind, he did not know how he could prevent the inevitable.

"No outsider has ever been brought to our sacred valley," Joren said. "That is the whole of the matter. It would unravel our way of life."

"It would unravel our lies, is what you mean."

Everyone in the room turned, and Joren's heart wrung out inside his chest.

It was his son who'd spoken.

Malik stepped up to the ceremonial fire at the center of the room. His face remained impressively calm. This was not an outburst. It was a calculated defiance. Malik looked out at everyone gathered in the room. The four chieftains, Lysa's successor in-training, Urla Pelasius, and the Knight of Caadron.

Malik's gaze settled on Olma last.

"Elder Marudeil, earlier you said that the time for secrets is over. And I agree. Our people deserve to know the truth. All of it."

"What?" said Dannsein. "You can't be serious!"

"Sit down, boy," Tul Eriksein said.

But Joren dismissed him. "My son is a member of this council, a shaman who serves our people. Let him finish."

Malik barely masked his surprise, but he continued. "Our way of life has been preserved by lies. Perhaps this was wisdom in the past, when all we knew was peace. But our island was attacked. Visitors were killed because of the secrets this council has kept."

"God's breath," Tul said. "You were going to run away from our people just last night!"

Malik nodded. "Yes, I was. And I convinced my best friend to go with me. Now, Riese is gone. Taken by the rebels that attacked our peaceful festival. I accept my responsibility for that, no matter my intentions. I call on this council to do the same. Our entire livelihood is in danger. The dragons we have long forsaken are coming here. No matter what happens, our people deserve to know why. And they deserve to choose what they do after."

"What they do?" asked Olma tentatively.

"Son, what are you talking about?" Joren asked.

"War is at our doorstep," said Malik. "While these rebels run free, Faltara is not safe. I propose we offer our people the choice. To stay. Or flee the island until this rebellion is over."

"Leave the island?" Tul demanded. "Enough of this madness, boy!"

Murmurs filled the chamber. All council members glanced from Malik to Joren to the Lady Consul.

"I meant what I said before," said Urla. "We do not wish any further harm to come to the Faltari. If this is your decision, Attica will honor it."

Joren nodded to her and joined his son.

There were times in his life—so many bloody times—when the path was unclear. When Joren had felt torn about his responsibilities to his people. But all at once, that responsibility came into focus.

"I believe my son is right," Joren said.

There was a moment of silence.

Then, the room erupted in a clamor of protests, and assents, and deliberations.

This had always been the way of the council.

———

Riese emerged from the portal on solid ground, though she nearly lost her balance, the shift from flying downward to walking right side up was so jarring.

She stood at the edge of a steep hillside, looking down upon a lush green valley, illuminated in a strange purple light. Dark skies radiated with stars, far brighter than on Faltara. Thick bands of them spanned the horizon like rivers of light.

Deven stood beside her, already back in her silver-haired human form.

Rykus stood ahead of them, pointing down the hill. "Welcome to Flameholm!"

An overgrown castle with thin spires was nestled against the opposing hillside, surrounded by the strangest copse of trees Riese had ever seen. Narrow white trunks topped with leaves of blue and violet. There were plenty of Faltari trees that turned gold or red in autumn, but this place left no indication of autumn whatsoever. It was warm, almost too warm with her cloak on. Bubbling brooks flowed from the rolling hills, collecting in a small lake near the castle. Flowers bloomed all around the valley.

Riese felt a surge in her spirit and shifted her gaze upward.

A pair of dragons twirled across the sky, as though dancing. Riders were mounted on their backs, holding tight as their dragons spun through the air with lightning speed and remarkable grace.

The egg in her hands was radiating brighter than before, and Riese's spirit filled with joy.

"The bond is powerful, isn't it?" Rykus said.

Riese could not take her gaze from the dragons. One an icy blue, the other an emerald green. Their scales shimmered across the sky. Her spirit swelled in her chest.

"It sees what you see. Feels what you feel."

Riese had heard such things from bards that came to the Festival of the Fading Sun each year. But she never could have imagined a feeling like this. She felt as though she'd been only a portion of herself all her life, and now, she was becoming whole.

"Even before they hatch," Riese said. "It's incredible!"

Rykus nodded. "That sense grows stronger the longer you're together. It can become overwhelming at times, particularly in moments of heightened emotion, especially once the bond is completed at the hatching."

"How do you know so much?"

The man smiled and gestured at the sky. "Well, clearly, the Dragonmounts are not the only dragons in the world. I told you, Valucians have a long and complicated history. Now, come, we don't have time to gawk at dragon flight, no matter how right we might be in doing so."

Rykus strode down the hillside, still holding the chest containing the other two eggs. Riese followed him on foot, while Deven flew ahead on her Morph wings.

They were a couple of miles from the castle, and the journey took the better part of an hour, if Riese had to guess. As they descended and crossed the valley, Riese spotted more winged creatures in flight, much smaller than the dragons. As they neared, she realized they were more of the Morphs. Half a dozen were practicing mid-flight sparring maneuvers, the clang of clashing blades echoing across the valley.

Above it all, the dragons continued to soar.

"Where did they come from?" Riese asked.

"Those dragons are the best kept secret in Valucia. The eggs were hidden since the ancient days. Hatched during the Uprising in hopes they might produce an army, but sadly, just like Attican dragons, they are infertile."

"Why?"

Rykus smiled. "That is a question every Dragonmount in Îrithèa has asked countless times. No one knows. Dragons are not native to our world, and I suspect the reason is connected to that."

Riese pictured the Gate of the Ancients at the peak of the Spires. That ruined world haunted by dark spirits.

The secret resided with her people. It always had.

"At any rate, the Uprising was already lost before these two grew large enough to fight. And the secret of their existence has remained. But we never lost hope in forming a company of Rebelmounts. It is the only true hope for freedom in Valucia. Or in all Îrithèa. A power to rival the imperial Dragonmounts. But we don't just need dragons, we need riders, Riese."

"I'm not even Valucian," Riese said.

Rykus shrugged. "Neither is Deven. Nor many others who risked their lives for these eggs we carry. And that, I believe, will be our strength in this rebellion."

"What do you mean?"

"The old rebellions were about Valucia. And they failed. The Sigan revolt was about Siga. Same with Taika in years past. And on and on the cycle goes. A few hornets attacking a bear can do little, but a whole hive, well..."

"Who else have you recruited?"

Rykus smiled. "That is where our conversation ends. Until you decide your own role in what is to—"

Half a dozen Morphs flew toward them at a blinding speed, Deven at the front, coming from the direction of the castle.

Once standing on solid ground, they transformed into human forms, and Deven rushed forward.

"What's wrong?" Rykus demanded.

"The Atticans, sir," Deven said. "Dragonmounts have attacked Chardonia."

CHAPTER 37

CHILDREN OF THE GODS

The people of Faltara gathered in the fields outside the village of Yerida one last time.

Joren's heart was a boulder in his chest as he made his way to the front of the assembly.

Failure lies only in choosing the wrong path.

For so many years, even after he returned from *uhmskara*, Joren had questioned his role among the Faltari. But he convinced himself it was his responsibility to lead, to follow in the tradition that had been handed down to him from greater and wiser ancestors.

Perhaps this was true and perhaps not. Maybe the lies had served his people in the past, but anything short of the truth would be their undoing now.

War had come to their tiny corner of the world.

For days, his son had not been able to look at him, just as Joren had been unable to look his own father in the eye when he found out the truth. But when Joren announced his intentions to the council, he felt the quickening in his son's spirit.

Joren ascended the hill alone. None of the chieftains, not even Olma, joined him for the task. He turned to face the people he'd served all his adult life.

Madri and Surel stood near the front.

He was about to begin when Malik pushed through the crowd. Joren's spirit leapt as his son approached.

Malik wore his shaman's attire, the same as Joren. His cloak formed of the hides of all four sacred beasts. His hair braided with bones and feathers, face painted with black markings.

With his son at his side, Joren addressed their people.

For the first time in centuries, the Faltari would know the truth. About the Ascent. The eggs. The empire. All of it.

———

There was confusion. Outrage. But most of all, there was fear.

Joren did his best to assuage them at the outset, but he knew there was only one way to convey the severity of this circumstance and ensure that all chieftains were not blamed.

"It is the sworn duty of the shaman to care for the good of our people. Above his own self. Above the interests of the chieftains or any individual clan. Certainly above any tradition of the past. Considering all that has happened, I fear I have failed you all in this sacred duty. Our island, our way of life is no longer safe. And I hold myself responsible. Secrets have kept us safe for many generations, but in my own generation, they have become our undoing."

The valley had grown silent as the crypts beneath the Mountain of Souls.

"Before any of this," Joren said, "before the attack, my son spoke against the lies our ancestors harbored. But I did not have the courage to heed that caution. You all deserved to know the nature of the Ascent, the reason our children—even my own eldest son—were lost. You deserve to know precisely why our island is unsafe now.

"As a boy, my father taught me that there are certain breaches of trust that are irreparable. And I've come to know that to be true. I will help lead those who wish to leave the island, while the empire does what they must. But that will be my last act as your shaman."

An eruption of murmurs spread across the valley, including the chieftains. None had known Joren's fullest intentions for this speech. Not even Malik.

Olma stood and raised her hands for quiet. She strode up the hill to join him, and the murmurs died.

"And who will tend our spirits when this is done?" she asked.

Joren could feel the tension in his son's resonance, but there was nothing for it.

"I believe Malik will make an excellent shaman, should he so decide. But I fear much is about to change. Maybe the very structure of how the Faltari are governed. Perhaps this ought to have happened long ago. For now, we must ensure there is, indeed, a future for our people, before we concern ourselves with building it. War is coming to our island. We set sail for Valgland tomorrow."

———

The village of Yerida did not quieten until the fullness of night had descended upon the island.

Urla established a garrison in the crude square outside the village. Where days ago, vendors from many lands had set up their carts, now, it was home to the soldiers of the Bloody Company.

Prior to the council's decision, Urla had come with only Vera Salyr and a few trusted soldiers. But now that the shaman had prepared the way, the Lady Knight used her godblade to bring Urla's entire company through to the Isle of Faltara.

It took half a dozen passages over the course of several hours. By the final journey, Salyr looked like a soldier come from a days-long stint on the battlefront.

Urla clasped the woman's shoulder. "You should rest, Lady Knight."

Salyr's face was flushed, hair drenched in sweat. But she shook her head. "I swore to remain at your side, Lady Consul. And I intend to do so."

Urla knew the woman still blamed herself for what had happened to Campos. Had she remained at his side that night, things might have turned out very different. It was a gnawing feeling they both shared.

"The passage takes a mighty toll," Urla said. "Even a fool could tell that. And I will need you at your strongest tomorrow, when we march to these Spires. I've got plenty of guards to look after me tonight."

Salyr looked crestfallen.

"That *is* an order," Urla said. "Rest."

The knight saluted her. "Yes, Lady Consul."

Urla watched the knight go. It was strange to be in a position to give orders to a Knight of Caadron. Of course, she'd been a captain in the legions for years, and a lesser officer for years before that. Urla was no stranger to giving orders, but most of those orders were simply passed down through a long line of command. They were rarely her own.

Now, her orders came direct from the emperor himself. A top secret mission depended on her and the Bloody Company, and the fate of Attica's most powerful resource was at stake.

"Lady Captain."

Urla turned to find her young lieutenant, Caliphus, saluting her.

"Er, sorry, I mean, Lady Consul."

"It's alright, Lieutenant. The title still sounds strange to me as well. At ease," she said, and the man relaxed, hand on the hilt of his sword.

"All our squadrons have made camp, Consul. I've ordered double guard duty along the perimeter of the camp, and stationed patrols in the village, as well as the Faltari encampment in the fields beyond."

"Good," said Urla. "Send Roak and a scouting party further down the fjord as well." She pointed out over the water, where the cliffs dominated the horizon. "Another up by those shrines on the mountainside. And we'll need a patrol to scout ahead along this Soul Road. Check for any other path from the village as well."

"Of course, Consul. Anything else?"

"We march at first light. Make sure all duties are shared. Shifts kept short. I expect tomorrow will be a long day."

"I'll see it done," Caliphus said. "Excuse me if I overstep, but many of the troops are wondering about the nature of this mission. What is in these mountains?"

"The future of the empire, Lieutenant. You'll be briefed with more information when the time is right. You know the drill."

"Yes, Lady," Caliphus said. "A strange place for a rebel target. A strange place, period."

"Aye, Lieutenant. And these are strange times. They will demand our all. Our emperor is counting on us."

The young academy man stood tall and saluted once more. "I'm proud to serve at your side again. And I must say, they couldn't have chosen a better consul."

"Caliphus, flattery is *not* part of your duty."

He smirked. "Of course."

"What about my son?" Finally, she asked the question that had been nagging her for hours.

"He's been brought to your tent, Captain. Along with a pair of imperial healers."

"Is he awake?"

"It did not appear so."

"That will be all, Lieutenant."

Caliphus marched off, and Urla began to walk the camp as she had done so many times before. Weapons were cleaned, blades sharpened. Cookfires were tended, and rations packed. All for a top secret mission in the mountains at the edge of the world, against an unknown enemy.

Even Urla did not know what they might face. How far did this rebellion reach? Athanasius seemed to believe it remained a fledgling operation, but if more Valucian lords were involved. Or Elya, gods forbid...

The Chardonians, at least, would not think of supporting Rykus. By now, the first dragons had surely struck, along with an elite force that had required all the other Knights of Caadron, save for those tasked with negotiating with the Valucian lords.

So much at once.

Urgent energy permeated the camp, even through small acts of preparation, despite the vague orders. It was the sort of mission any imperial company dreamed of.

They're among the finest soldiers in the empire, she thought.

But it felt different now, as consul. After the events of the attack. Urla felt separate from the men and women of the Bloody Company in a way she'd never felt before.

As Urla passed among the troops, her soldiers saluted, eyes drifting to the new uniform she wore. Gold pauldrons with crimson frills, the imperial white dragon sigil emblazoned upon her black leathern chest plate. The uniform of a high-ranking officer. Few made verbal acknowledgment, though they all nodded and smiled proudly as she passed.

Whatever this mission was, it came from the emperor, who had chosen their own captain to replace Consul General Campos. And they carried themselves with a shared pride.

For Urla, it was mixed. Not only because of the tragedies clouding her mind. But the finality of this separation. Whatever happened, she expected this would be her last hurrah with the Bloody Company.

Urla reached the gates of the village, crude doors made of split logs. The Attican guards ushered her through.

A few Faltari villagers scurried about, but for the most part, the place was silent. Most of the Faltari were camped in the fields beyond the village.

Urla stopped outside the pillared entrance to the village temple. The shaman's wife sat on the top step, smoking a long, narrow pipe. The woman eyed Urla carefully.

"Madri, is it?" Urla asked. They'd met briefly during the festival, before the world turned on its end.

The shaman's wife looked pensive, perturbed even. Brow furrowed and jaw tight. "It's the middle of the night. Hasn't your empire done enough today?"

It was a feeling she expected most Faltari shared, though none yet had given voice to the sentiment.

Urla dipped her chin. "I know this has taken a fierce toll, madam, but it is my prayer that none of your people will come to harm. It is why we've acted so—"

"Oh, we've already come to plenty of harm," Madri said. "More than you could ever know."

"I'm sorry for that, from one mother to another."

Madri shrugged. "Your son was here at the festival. Where is he now? Hiding back at your capital?"

Urla grimaced. "No, madam. My boy is here. Ruan... has not woken since the attack. Since that Valucian traitor tried to take him along with the Faltari girl they abducted. If not for your husband, my son would be lost the same as Riese Torendeil."

The woman's face softened at the remark. There was a bond among mothers that transcended even the gravest differences. "Your healers..."

"They say there's nothing that can be done. That's why I've come tonight, in truth. I know it is much to ask after all that's happened, madam, but—"

"Call me Madri," she said, with a wave of her hand. "And I'm sorry to hear about your son. Much as I wish you weren't here at all. Much as I wish none of this had happened. My husband is tending to our people at the moment. Many prayers are being burnt tonight, as you might imagine."

The notion was odd to Urla. In Attica, prayers were given to priests, who would offer sacrifices to usher the blessings of the Heavenly Mother and Father.

"I heard Joren is stepping down as shaman," Urla said.

"We'll see what comes to pass," said Madri. "Anyway, not until after all this is over, and until then, Joren will continue his duties."

Urla could sense there was tension over the matter. "Well, if he's busy, I'll come back later. If you wouldn't mind letting him know I—"

"Stay, he's nearly done."

"Are you... sure?"

"It's rude in Faltara to question the sincerity of an invitation, you know." Madri gestured to the steps, a slight smirk teasing at the edge of her lips. "Sit."

Urla did, awkward though it might be. It was not lost on her how the Faltari viewed this campaign. They might not be friends of Valucian rebels, but there was little love for Attica here, least of all after what had transpired, and the revelations that had come to light. Everywhere she'd seen, these people looked angry, confused, distraught. Their entire way of life had been upended.

"I do not relish the thought of leaving," Madri said after a silence.

"Must you leave?"

"All of us? No, I'm sure a few will stay. Me? It would be seen as an act of dissension if I were to remain while my husband led our people away."

"You don't believe they should go?"

"I don't believe we should lead your kind straight to our most sacred place. But it seems it's been desecrated for a long time, so what does it matter? What's sacred is already lost."

Urla didn't respond. The next silence stretched longer.

The door burst open, and the young shaman emerged. When Malik met Urla's gaze, he glared and turned to his mother.

"What's she want?"

"To see your father," said Madri.

"I'm sure it can wait until—"

"It's about her injured son, Malik."

The boy hesitated. "Oh."

"Don't jump to insinuations until you know all the information. You've already been living at the edge of your spear too much in the past day."

Urla watched the exchange carefully. The whole family seemed to be *at the edge of their spears*. The son harbored bitterness toward Urla too, that was plain to see.

But the mention of Ruan triggered something in the boy she could not quite place her finger on. She decided to offer a little more.

"Malik, you helped Ruan get Campos to safety. I owe you a debt of gratitude."

Malik grimaced, seeming to be torn between anger and something else. Remorse? Sympathy?

The boy dipped his head. "It was my duty, Lady Consul, that is all. And it accomplished nothing, it seems."

"I'm not so sure about that. You risked your life to save my friend and mentor. It is not nothing."

"How is your son?"

Urla told him.

Malik pondered this for a moment. "I'll fetch my father."

"I'd hate to pull him from his duties."

Malik shrugged. "The last of the Faltari left a short while ago. He asked to be left alone."

Madri scowled. "I'll be the one to fetch him, then."

———

Joren knelt in the secluded prayer hall near the back of the temple.

The walls were covered with runes, much like the Hall of the Ancients, a vast cavern beneath the crypts and the Well of Souls. There, walls were etched in runes and pictographs, the first source of the tales of the Crossing.

At the end of the prayer hall, a carefully transcribed copy of their most sacred document, *The Crossing of Worlds*, was laid out on a pedestal, before the engraved mural of the All Mother and All Father, both pointing the way toward a stone archway in the Dying World.

The mural was a magnificent work etched into the walls, painted with dyes harvested from various kinds of shellfish. It was older than this temple. Hundreds of years old, according to tradition, though it had been restored and repainted many times over the generations.

A dim voice in the back of Joren's mind had always wondered what the original looked like, how it compared to the depiction he'd knelt before all his life.

The gods ushering them through, guiding them, choosing their people to start over in a new land. In the days when gods still roamed the Dying World as ancient souls.

A prayer cloth burned on embers in the hearth, and Joren read a passage from *The Crossing* for what must have been the hundredth time:

From darkness, we followed a guiding light. Across plains of obsidian stone. Across wine dark seas. Across worlds themselves.

From death to new life, we crossed. Filled with strength from the Father, courage from the Mother, we stepped into an unknown future. A destiny that would transcend generations.

We were chosen to be a people set apart. Children of the gods. Let us become that guiding light. Sons and daughters of the Flame.

And may the world be brighter for our burning.

Shivers ran down Joren's spine. It was a passage that had haunted him all his life. It contained so many unspoken questions. Why had his people come to this place? How had they come?

It was a passage that seemed to contradict the Crossing described in Faltari history, which required no crossing of seas. Shamans had proposed that this referred to other explorations, the expansion from Faltara to the other corners of this new world. Perhaps they had ventured from here and returned.

Yet, no other nation in Îrithèa believed the Crossing originated from Faltara.

In his youth, the sacred passage had instilled doubt about all his people believed—their version of the Crossing, their set apartness, their very way of life.

And yet, that final part about burning to make the world brighter, as children of the gods. That had always lingered in Joren's mind. The nagging question it demanded.

Have you *lived up to this, Joren? Have your people?*

Footsteps resounded behind him. But Joren didn't move. He knew those steps. Slow, methodical, with a bit of a shuffle across the uneven stones of the hall.

Madri's hand brushed his shoulder from behind, and she knelt beside him. Her hand found his, and her warm spirit washed over him. He did not deserve her, that much he knew.

"That damn passage will be the death of us all," she said, chuckling.

Joren did not know what to say. His wife had always been the better communicator of the two of them. Joren could tend to mourning families and address their entire people, and the words flowed as though coming from the gods themselves. But put him before an angry wife, and he drew inward.

Madri always seemed to know what to say, to understand the things he bottled up.

"I don't begrudge your decision to step down as shaman," Madri said, releasing his hand. "I'm hurt that you did not live up to that damned passage with *me*. I understand why all this has remained a secret from our people for so long. But from me?"

"Madri, I—"

"That's silly. Yes, I know. And bloody selfish."

"It's not," said Joren.

Madri drew closer to him, wrapped her arms around his shoulder, and looked over the sacred parchment. "Children of the gods. Do you believe it's true?"

Joren shrugged. "Who could say after all this time? Most shamans of the past would say yes. Though not all. Few in all this world wield magic as our people do, and in that way perhaps we are special. But magic is not unique to us by any stretch of the imagination. I struggle to believe that we're truly uniquely blessed. We've simply held to a tradition and close bloodlines... For a time, I thought it was bullshit."

"And now?" Madri whispered.

He sensed she was agonizing over this, too. Perhaps many of their people were.

"Now... perhaps it is better understood as a metaphor for our people.

A calling. A bar to reach for. That's what I believe this passage is truly about."

"May the world be brighter for our burning... makes you wonder if we were ever meant to remain on Faltara, doesn't it? Hiding from the sufferings of the rest of the world to hold tight to our traditions. If the Flame's a metaphor, I fear we've been nothing but smoke."

Joren looked his wife in the eyes. A tear streaked the left side of her face. He reached up and brushed it away, and she pressed her face against his hand. He pulled her into an embrace, both of them trembling.

"I thought you didn't want to leave," he said into her wavy hair.

Madri pulled back to look at him. "All your life, you've been a man of conviction. I'm not angry about leaving. I'm angry it took this tragedy for you to do the right thing."

Joren nodded, her words piercing deeper than any blade ever could.

"This is the right path, my shaman. My love. And I will follow you to Valgland. I'd follow you to the edge of the world, if it came to it. Even into death."

Joren clutched her tight, tears streaming, body shuddering with silent sobs.

Gods, he loved this woman.

They held each other for some time. Eventually, Madri pulled back.

"There's more I wish to say, but there's a mother outside whose son needs tending."

Chapter 38

Healing Rites

Malik was angry with his mother for sending him with Consul Pelasius. Hadn't they sacrificed enough for the empire? *Let them heal their own sons!*

But Madri had insisted, and his mother was not a woman to be argued with when she set her mind to something she believed to be right.

"When the gods bring a problem to your door, you do not run," she'd said.

Malik knew she was also jabbing at his attempted *uhmskara*. The unspoken mistake that hung over every interaction between them since the attack. He had almost left his family and his people for a far-off land without a word, and he felt guilty each time he looked at her.

What might have been different had he and Riese remained celebrating with the rest of their people? Malik had been impulsive, cowardly. Reckless.

He knew that now.

His father said Malik was right for being disturbed by the truth, but he could hear what his mother would say to that.

You do not run...

And yet that was what their entire people were preparing to do. Was that what she was upset about?

Malik had watched the quiet tension between his parents all evening. She did not believe he or Joren to be right.

Should Malik have told her the whole of it? Why he was sure they must run this time?

Urla Pelasius did not speak a word to Malik as they crossed the Attican encampment, and for once, Malik resented the stillness.

What if he was wrong? What if Ava was full of shit, and only manipulating his hope that Riese might be safe with the rebels?

He was relieved when they reached Consul Pelasius's tent. A soldier pulled back the flap, and Urla ushered Malik inside.

The tent was vast, nearly as large as his family's log home in River's End, and remarkably luxurious. Multiple rooms were partitioned with large flaps of ornate cloth. A pattern of diamond stitching crisscrossed the dark material in gold thread, looking like mountains stacked atop one another by their peaks.

The smell of death filled the entire tent, though there was no sign of Ruan in the main chamber.

A healer emerged from behind one of the flaps to greet them. She was a young woman with bronze skin and frizzy hair, dressed in forest green robes. She dipped her head to Urla but made no acknowledgment of Malik.

"Your son lies at peace, Consul," the healer said.

"He isn't..." Malik began, nearly overwhelmed by the stench.

The healer shook her head. "Ruan yet lives, shaman."

"Prepare a stretcher," Urla ordered. "We're taking him into the village."

The girl's face contorted, and she shot a glare at Malik.

"Are you certain, Consul? I've seen many dark effects from sorcerous healings. Many a lordling has fled desperately to the Free City in hopes of a magic touch. Most regret this in the end. Witches are swindlers, and their arts always have a price. Are you prepared to pay it?"

"This isn't a Beirusian witch," Urla said. "The emperor knows the risks, or he wouldn't have suggested this course of action."

"Pardon, Lady, but I expect the emperor knows little of witchery, and even less of healing, gods save him."

Urla patted the girl's shoulder. "I appreciate your concern for my son. But my mind is made up."

The healer nodded, then ushered them into the chamber.

Ruan lay upon a mat at the end of the room, head propped on a feather pillow. The skin of his face was drawn loose over his cheekbones, as though he'd aged fifty years in a day. His pallor had turned a deathly porridge-grey. But what disturbed Malik most was how faint the boy's spirit resonated. Distant, as though half-departed from the world already.

It pained Malik to see anyone in such a state. At once, his anger dissipated, replaced with sympathy. He wished it were easier to see the Attican boy as an enemy, but in his heart, he knew it was never so simple. The boy had been brave during the attack. And he had paid a greater price than any Faltari. Death seemed a fearsome hand clenching its fingers around them all.

"I'm sorry, Lady Consul," Malik murmured.

Urla knelt at her son's side, while soldiers prepared a stretcher. Her lip trembled. It was so strange to see a woman like her—fierce, formidable, devoted to the empire—brought to tears like any mother in such circumstances.

Malik almost reiterated what the imperial healer had said, for it was true that there was little hope for Ruan Pelasius. But Malik did not have the heart to speak it.

"I know there is only a prayer that my son will wake," Urla said. "And an even smaller chance that he will thrive if he does. But that chance is all I have left. Do you understand?"

Malik nodded. "It is good you've brought him to us. His wounds are deeper than flesh and bone. But my father is the greatest spiritual healer on the island. We should hurry."

———

One look at the boy and Malik's entire family began scrambling about the healing room to prepare for surgery.

First, a tincture of edelgrass and noxium root to numb the pain.

Malik's family often assisted with healings. Malik had endured fitful screams as bones were set, changed sheets drenched in sweat from villagers tossing and turning in fever dreams. Few times had this room been so utterly still.

His mother bit her lip as she fixed leather bands to Ruan's arms and legs, fixing him to the surgical table. Malik wondered if the bindings would be needed. Ruan hadn't moved an inch during the entire transfer from the consul's tent. The boy was so distant from this world, it seemed the slightest nudge might send him over the brink into death.

Surel gathered cloths in silence, and if that wasn't a testament to the direness of the situation, Malik didn't know what was.

Joren held instruments over a torch to sterilize them. Several long needles and a slender spike with a flat head on one end, like a nail.

Urla watched with remarkable calm, clutching her son's limp hand.

Malik stoked the fire in the hearth, then he and Surel draped thick leaves of fireweed on a rod above the flames. One leaf ignited, and he had to douse it. The leaves were on the verge of being too dry for the ritual, and if they burned hot, the effect would not last.

"A little more water," Madri instructed, handing Malik a basin to dip the leaves in before adding them to the rod.

Smoke began to permeate the room.

"What is that?" Urla asked.

"There is swelling in Ruan's skull," Joren said, fetching a tiny iron hammer and a spiral-crank needle from a drawer of healing elements in the corner of the room. "The pressure will have to be relieved, or I fear he will not wake again. The process is terrifying, but the smoke will help dull the senses and draw *hish* in to strengthen his spirit."

"You don't use channelers?" she asked.

Joren took hold of her hand and looked into her eyes. "You brought him to me, Lady. You must decide if you will trust my methods."

Consul Pelasius nodded.

"I can promise nothing," Joren said. "But I performed this procedure once before on a soldier bludgeoned to near-death by a war hammer. This is the only way I know to help him."

"Of course. Do whatever you must."

"We will have to drill a hole in his skull. Too far and he will die. Too little and he will die."

Malik and Surel draped a long cloth over the boy's body. It was unnerving how still he was.

"Even with the tincture and dreamsmoke, he may wake during the operation," said Joren. "And he will be in the worst pain of his life. An unsteady hand could mean..."

"I will hold him still," Urla insisted.

Joren shook his head. "The spiritual toll will be great, and you are untrained. It would be better if you remained out in—"

Urla brushed off his comforting hand. "Shaman, I've fought in dozens of battles in my life. I've lost comrades in my arms. A few weeks ago, I lost a husband. I will *not* leave my son."

"Very well. Malik, you hold his feet. Madri, tend the smoke. Surel?"

Malik's sister was frightened, biting her lip as she fought not to show it.

"I need you to pass instruments the moment I ask, do you hear?"

Surel nodded and stood straight, suddenly seeming much older than the annoying adolescent girl she was.

Malik stood at the side of the table and took hold of Ruan's knees and chest. He could feel the swell of *hish* all around the room as the smoke heightened his senses.

It would make the healing more powerful, but it would also make the pain...

"Surel, razor."

Joren began to trim away hair from the back of the boy's skull.

Urla stood beside Malik, holding either side of her son's head with immense warrior's hands.

"Drill."

Surel handed the spiral-crank to him, and Malik leaned over the boy, pressing down, head growing light from the smoke.

The only sound was the soft scraping of bone as his father cranked the drill.

"Hold steady!" Joren said.

Now, the soft ping of the hammer and spike. A faint crunch.

Ruan's body twitched.

"Oh Marha," Urla said. "I think he's—"

"Hold steady!"

Joren tapped again.

The boy groaned.

Crunch, crunch, then a squelching sound.

Ruan spasmed.

And then screams erupted.

———

Malik's parents claimed it all lasted but a few moments before Ruan Pelasius fell back into unconsciousness, but the look of the boy's face twisted in agony, eyes wide and bloodshot, was seared into Malik's mind.

He slumped in a chair in the corner of the room, while his parents finished the ritual. The dreamsmoke drifted out an open window, and the intensity of the operation began to dissipate. But Malik could still hear those screams in his mind, feel the way the boy had writhed beneath his grasp.

Surel had left the room the minute the operation was complete.

Now, Ruan slept peacefully, chest rising and falling with steady breaths.

Urla Pelasius had been unfazed by her son's screams throughout the procedure, but she slumped beside her boy now, body shaking with heavy breaths while Joren completed the final healing rites, carefully drawing rune spells on the boy's skull and neck, whispering the words over and over as he wrote them in the boy's blood.

First, attend the body, then the spirit. That was the only way with such a wound.

Malik leaned forward, elbows on his knees, head propped in his hands, nearly as spent as he'd been from his entire Ascent.

His mother handed Joren tinctures and salves and then came the bandages.

The operation had affected Malik more than all the other healings he'd assisted with. Even worse than the time a hunter had died on his father's table. He was not sure why.

Madri removed the fireweed leaves, and now, only traces of smoke hung in the rafters of the chamber. His mother whispered in his father's ear, then prepared a prayer cloth and burned it in a clay bowl beside the bed.

Then, she joined Malik, taking a seat in the other chair, and met his gaze.

"You look like you could use some air, son."

"I'm fine, Mum. Most of the smoke has worn off."

"I think your father could use one of the rune books to complete the healing."

Malik shot to attention in spite of himself. "In the Sacred Hall? Sure, I'll get them right away."

He cursed to himself. He'd nearly forgotten about Ava Rykus. He'd managed to keep her presence a secret until now. His father had been so pre-occupied, the one time he'd needed into the room today—to fetch one of the clan ledgers—he'd gladly let Malik get it for him. And the room was warded by many spells.

"Why don't I come with you?" his mother said.

Malik tensed. "Er, no, it's fine, I can—"

"I could use some air, too."

Only shamans were able to open the Sacred Hall, but there was no good reason for his mother not to come with him. His father had taken her there countless times before. But if she saw...

"Come." Madri took his hand and led the way out.

The moment they exited and breathed clear air, Malik's spirit lightened further.

"The spiritual toll is worse healing outsiders," his mother said. "Bloody Atticans think their aversion to magic keeps them safe. Perhaps it does. But their spirits are weaker, and ours were forced to compensate for the boy's weakness tonight."

"Makes sense," Malik said, trying to feign casual conversation. His heart thundered in his chest as they neared the Sacred Hall. "Guess I've never been part of a foreign healing."

"Your father learned that on the battlefront. During his *uhmskara*, he fought in the Taikan Rebellion."

His father was such a kind, non-violent man, it was difficult to picture him anywhere near a battlefield. That is, until Malik had seen him fight off those creatures during the attack. He'd fought with skill beyond what could be explained by hunting experience.

"Yet another secret, then," Malik muttered.

Madri nodded. "He is a complicated man with a complicated role. One he never wanted to be his."

"Never wanted? But he was the eldest. It was always meant to be his role."

His mother smiled and shrugged. "There is much you do not know. Much you have assumed. The problem with men is you keep everything pent up inside and think it a strength."

Malik's mother took his chin in her hand and turned his face to look directly in her eyes. "You are brave, son. You are strong. And the past few days, you have shown yourself to even be wise. At times."

She winked, and Malik laughed.

"But you hide much inside. From our family, yes. But also from your friends. Don't think I haven't noticed the way you kept Yuri and Riese at arm's length these past two years. Thinking they could never understand what you're dealing with."

Malik nodded. "Riese and I worked things out... before all this. But Yuri... I don't know. I've made a lot of mistakes."

"Oh yes, you have," she said on a chuckle. "We all have. But if there's one thing I've learned in these forty-four summers, it's that the greatest mistake of all is not being true with the ones you love. When you trust someone, you hold nothing back. This family has known too many secrets, son."

A sinking feeling tore at Malik's gut. They stood ten feet from the runemarked door.

"You... already know, don't you?" Malik asked.

His mother lowered her voice to a whisper. "About the Valucian girl imprisoned in this temple? No." She chuckled.

Malik felt a strange mix of terror and relief. "Does Father? Does anyone else?"

"No one else. But I don't expect a foreign mage would escape your father's sense. Not even locked behind wards."

"Then, why didn't he... why didn't either of you..."

Madri clasped his shoulders and pulled him toward her. Malik sank into the embrace.

"Because your father once fought *against* this empire."

"He fought *with* the Taikans?"

"Driven by the same youthful conviction of justice that drives you now. Your father said nothing about the girl because he knew this was a passion you inherited. Your father... both of us knew you'd do what's right, given a little time to decide."

A wave of relief swept over him.

"Can Ava Rykus be trusted?" Madri asked.

Malik reached for the runemarked door, and the glyphs glowed at his touch as he spoke the words of power.

"Come decide for yourself."

Chapter 39

Wind Catcher

Ava's heart felt like it had been wrung out in her chest, so agonizing were the screams.

For a sorceress with cerebral gifts like herself, the sound was just the beginning. Ava could feel agony like it was part of her own soul. Normally, she could take measures to ward this off. But not now.

The torment in Ruan's mind was nearly overwhelming. When his screams finally faded, she felt nothing for several minutes. Ava feared he was dead, and the possibility nearly broke her.

She gripped the arms of her chair so ferociously that the ropes binding her began to cut off circulation.

The world went silent.

Then, Ava felt the pulse of unconscious peace emanating from Ruan's mind, and she crumpled in her chair in the Sacred Hall as relief swept over.

She had not let her mind dwell on Ruan the past two days. She couldn't let herself.

But now, her mind whirled. What had happened? Why was Ruan here in the temple? Why was he in such pain? The questions lingered with formless speculations that only rattled her further.

Ava was exhausted. She slumped forward, head on the shaman's desk, and drifted toward blessed oblivion, nearing slumber at last, when the door burst open. The sudden light flared in her vision.

Footsteps. Shadows.

A woman's voice. "Take this to your father."

"But..." Malik began.

"When the consul is gone, we will decide what to do with the girl. For now, I'd like a moment."

"Yes, Mother."

Ava had known this was coming. Had waited for it all day. There was no way Malik could keep the secret from his family. And she had a job to do. The knowledge filled her with strength.

The door closed, and darkness swallowed up the room.

Footsteps.

A hand at Ava's neck. The gag fell away from her mouth.

Ava licked her parched and aching lips.

"You're the shaman's wife." Ava's voice croaked.

"Clearly," the woman said.

A chair creaked as the woman took a seat. Without even the flick of flints, a small flame ignited from the woman's palm, and a lantern on the table sparked to life.

"Not bad," Ava said. She tried to sound warm, casual, but it came out stiff.

She was so tired.

The woman nodded. "Not many, even of my people, can create flames from the elements themselves."

Ava sensed a deeper meaning in the words. The woman was probing, the same as she was.

"Why are you here?" Ava asked.

"Because you've convinced my son—and by extension, my husband —that our people should leave our home. Because you and your father brought this fate upon us. And now, it falls on me to decide what to do with you."

"Are you a shaman too?"

The woman chuckled. "In truth, I thought you'd be *more* charming."

Ava shrugged, then grimaced as her bonds tightened around her wrists at the movement. "It's been a long couple of days."

The woman raised her brow. "Why are you sweating? It's quite cool in here."

Ava reached out subtly with her magic, trying to get a read on this woman. A mental wall shot up, and Ava jolted back in her seat.

"Get out of my head, girl," the mother said.

"Sorry…"

"You were friends with the Pelasius boy."

Ava nodded.

"My husband and son are both shamans. I know the look when someone else's pain becomes too much to bear."

"Is he…"

"He'll live. No thanks to your father and his… allies."

"Ruan was a good friend," Ava said.

"Not good enough, it would seem."

Ava grimaced. "It grieves me to know he was hurt."

"I've met more than one woman like you in my life."

"A Valucian?"

"A wind catcher."

"What?"

"That's what we call someone like you. A manipulator. You had that Pelasius boy wrapped around your finger. Even a casual observer could tell that at the festival alone. You used him to get where you needed. And now, you're using my son."

"Is it using someone to show them a mutually beneficial path?"

"You've proven convincing enough for Malik. But I don't see it. I think you're full of shit, Ava Rykus."

Ava tensed. Her right side throbbed, and she longed to adjust her position. "I don't want to see any harm come to your people, that is why—"

"Tell the truth."

"Madam, I—"

"My name is Madri. And I don't believe you're sorry about any of this. You sent my people's world reeling. Now, you expect us to leave our home so you can lay waste to our most sacred valley. And I don't think you give a damn about us any more than you ever cared for that Attican boy."

Ava straightened. "You know *nothing* about me!"

Madri smiled. "Enlighten me, Ava Rykus. Tell me more about your contrived condolences. Or better yet. Why don't I show you exactly what your little rebellion has done?"

Ava felt a shift in the woman's mind. She was lowering her mental walls. Letting Ava inside. "Madri, that won't be…"

"Are you afraid, girl?"

"No."

"Perhaps you should be."

Madri's walls receded at once and images flooded into Ava's vision in an onslaught.

Running through the streets of the village. People screaming. Hideous creatures darting overhead. Fear tore at her gut. Oh gods, where were her children?

A little Faltari girl cowered against a door, tears streaming. But it was not her child. And she ached with agony, wishing to help, wanting to fight, needing to find her gods-damned children.

The images changed.

A Morph swooped over the village square snatching someone into the air. Terror filled her spirit.

Gods, was that—

Ruan soared twenty feet into the air, thrashing wildly against a vicious dark-winged enemy. Then plummeted.

His head thudded on the cobblestone ground.

The vision shifted, and Ruan lay on a wooden table. Bloodshot eyes flashed open. Ruan shrieked, body jolting with spasms. Fear and pain permeated Ava's mind as though it were her own.

So much fear.

So much confusion and hurt and sorrow.

The vision faded, and Madri stood over her.

Tears streamed down Ava's face. It had been years since she'd let herself cry. All her childhood, Ava prided herself on being able to withstand anything. The ridicule of her Attican peers. The pressure of infiltrating the academy and all the bloody secrets. The tragedy that had swallowed her mother.

But the tears burst forth from some hidden spring in her soul, and Ava could not hold them back.

This was *her* fault.

It did not matter how just her cause, Ruan had been caught in the crossfire of her family's rebellion. She had done this to him.

And the walls she'd maintained for so long began to sink into the earth.

"I feel more than most," Madri said. "Perhaps you know something of what this is like."

Ava's body shook. She couldn't speak.

"In my experience, the gift manifests in one of two ways. I take on the fears and emotions of others. I can quell troubled minds, soothe anxieties, comfort grief. This serves my people well as the wife of a shaman. But you... you've learned the opposite. Learned to transcend your own feelings. To use your gifts to twist the thoughts and feelings of others. To seduce and manipulate to get your way."

The tears kept coming. Ava's body shuddered with sobs.

Madri seized her by the chin, and Ava felt all the woman's anxiety, all her anger.

"No more lies. Show me who you really are."

CHAPTER 40

FLAMEHOLM

The castle within this strange portal world was as old as the building upon the floating mountains back on the other side. Chunks of stone were missing from stark black pillars. One passage had completely collapsed. Perhaps the result of time, or some ancient conflict.

Was this place built by the Valucians or someone else? And for what purpose?

Riese was filled with questions as she followed Rykus and the Morphs down its winding passages. But she did not dare voice them now.

The interior of the fortress had been restored to some extent. The inner halls had been cleared of rubble and overgrowth, and the central courtyard was breathtakingly beautiful. Flameholm might only be a rebel hideout now, but some revolutionaries had taken care to create some beauty. The courtyard paths were lined with flowers and greenery, and an alien plant that hovered a foot off the ground.

They'd just crossed from another world through a portal set in mountains that hovered thousands of feet above the sea. Yet, something about the plants unnerved her. Riese had grown up seeing the Spires every year at the end of summer, but floating vegetation?

It was perhaps the greatest reminder that this wasn't her world, or even the Abyss. It was someplace else entirely, and the ramifications of this nagged at her gut.

But there was *hish* in this place. *Hish* emanating from the floating plants themselves, and in that, Riese found a little comfort. That and the soft reassurances brushing up against her spirit from the egg in her hands.

You are where you're meant to be.

The voice did not feel like her own. But it didn't quite feel like it belonged to the dragon either. It was somehow both and neither.

Rykus and Deven hurried across the garden courtyard, and Riese nearly had to run to keep up with them. Dozens of rebels bustled about the castle, halting activities as they passed. Most of them were Valucian or Chardonian at a glance. But not all.

A resonance of fear hung over them. Worried faces, hasty movements, hushed voices.

They crossed the courtyard and entered a wide antechamber. At the other end, tall wooden doors were guarded by a pair of Valucian soldiers with lances resting at their shoulders. Deven hurried past them, but Rykus stopped and turned to face Riese.

"You've a decision to make, Riese Torendeil. In war, there is little time for deliberation. We must move forward and make life-altering decisions in a moment."

"Like choosing to leave your daughter behind on the battlefield?" Riese asked.

Rykus's jaw tensed. He had managed incredible steadiness despite his daughter's unknown fate. Despite the destruction of his island home, and the attack on his Chardonian allies.

But at her words, Rykus displayed his fear and uncertainty for the first time since Riese had met him.

Rykus held her gaze and nodded. "The cause must always come first. My daughter and I knew that long before we ever heard of Faltara. This is a fork in your path, Riese. Everything in your life will be marked by what you choose. For all our sakes, I hope you choose right."

"And if I don't?"

Rykus sighed. "A part of you still thinks we will kill you if you don't give us what we ask for. But in truth, if you don't aid our plans, Flameholm will matter no more now than it did in the Uprising. Our revolution will die before it's begun. Our only hope is cutting off Attica's source of power."

"Cutting off?"

Chills coursed through her.

Rykus nodded. "Dragons are not native to our world. Only a few people still have this knowledge. Only a few still remember the truth about the Crossing. We did not arrive in Îrithèa across land and sea. We came from another world."

Rykus gestured out a small window, toward a purple sky rising over distant peaks.

"From here?" Riese asked.

"Not so much from here as *through* here. But this was not the only passage, as I expect you know. Our ancestors came from many lands in the wake of a great and terrible calamity."

"How could we have crossed through a gate hovering in the middle of the sea?" Riese asked.

"After the Crossing, I believe all the gates were moved. Or destroyed. Burn the ships so that all would remain committed to creating a new world. Most of the gates don't work any longer, it is said."

"How many gates are in our world?"

"There is no telling. I know of three. This one. Another in Elya. And now, one on Faltara. Which may be the most important of them all."

Riese hesitated, running her fingers over the smooth ridges of dragon scales in her hands. She could feel the spirit within, pressing against her own. It was not *hish*. Perhaps it was the power of the dragon's spirit itself. She was not quite sure, but she sensed something more. Beyond the magic she'd known all her life.

Rykus stepped closer, pulling a glowing runemarked key from his pocket. He motioned for Riese to turn around.

In a rush, as the collar was removed, she felt the breath of the gods surge back into her spirit. The resonance of the egg grew even stronger now.

"On Faltara," Riese said, "we believe that all peoples of our world came from the Abyss. From a fallen, cursed world. That is where our gate leads."

"To the... Abyss." Rykus raised a brow as he spoke the words.

"We believe we were entrusted by the All Mother and All Father, to safeguard the powers that destroyed that fallen world. But in reality, it seems we were enabling the sort of destruction that was unleashed on your island. I see that now. I can hardly close my eyes without imagining innocent people engulfed in dragon flames. My people made a terrible mistake, Captain Rykus. And I fear making another like it."

Rykus nodded. "That deliberation is how Deven and I both knew you could be trusted, Riese. Why we did not fear bringing you here."

"She's not actually your servant, is she?"

Rykus smiled. "We are all servants of the cause in Flameholm."

"She's Elyan."

Rykus nodded. "The time will come for more questions, but for now, an answer."

Riese felt at her neck where the collar had been. Felt the surge of magic coursing through her once more. The bond she felt with her dragon intensifying. She could practically hear it speaking to her. Urging her toward her destiny. Toward a new, uncertain future.

"I will tell you where the gate on Faltara is hidden," Riese said. As she spoke she felt a great weight lift from her spirit. A spark of joy burst from the egg, as though it were a child flipping and kicking in her own womb.

Rykus showed no joy. "I must ask more of you than that, I'm afraid."

"What do you mean?"

"So long as there is a way to reach the gate, your island will never be safe. It will be taken over, become a secret base for the empire. If we struck now, perhaps we could hold it for a time. That might give our revolution strength, but I fear it would ultimately bring our demise."

Riese's voice trembled as she spoke. It came out barely a whisper. "What are you asking of me, Captain Rykus?"

"I need you to take me to your Gate of the Ancients so we can destroy it."

CHAPTER 41

DREAMSMOKE

Joren inspected his work one last time. The boy Ruan was stable at last. Unconscious, having brushed up against death itself, but he would live, Joren felt confident about that, judging the strength in his spirit. And that was all that mattered.

Thick bandages were wrapped around his skull, shaggy hair sticking out at the edges, though the back was shaved. The dreamsmoke had settled in the room now, and for the first time in an hour, Joren felt only his own pain and exhaustion. The procedure had taken a spiritual toll greater than any he'd performed in years.

Urla rested her head on her son's chest. With eyes struggling to remain open, she watched Ruan's tranquil face, the cadence of his breathing.

Joren moved around the table to give them space, but Urla seized his wrist.

"Was it enough, shaman?" Her voice was barely a whisper.

She didn't know it, but Joren was certain the boy would not have survived the procedure if his mother had not been present. Which explained the level of her exhaustion. As he neared death, the boy's spirit had lashed out, as spirits often did, searching for anything to keep them tethered to the only world they knew.

Ruan's spirit latched onto his mother's. It had nearly taken her to the brink of death herself.

"Yes, Lady Consul, I believe it was enough," Joren answered. "But first, he must rest. And so must you."

Few in this world understood the true power of a parent's love. It was tangible, spiritual. Ruan had drawn on Joren's spirit too, along with the rest of his family's, throughout the operation, but only Urla Pelasius could have offered what her son required at the end.

But she too would be fine. With rest.

Joren smiled at her. For all the differences between Faltara and Attica—or Taika or Valucia, or anywhere else—they were not so different individually. This had been his greatest lesson during his Wandering. It was good to be reminded of it once more, now, of all times.

The woman looked up to him with misty eyes. "Thank you shaman. Truly."

Joren squeezed her hand. "Children bear too many of the burdens of war. Any chance the gods give me to relieve it is a chance I thank them gladly for."

Urla pondered this. "You've seen war before."

"Sadly, yes. I left Faltara for a time. It's a bit of a tradition among our most restless youths. We leave, experience some of the depravity of the southern world. Nearly all return soon enough."

"Which war was it?"

"I was... conscripted by the Taikans. Served as a healer."

"The Taikan Rebellion was my first campaign," Urla said. "And one of the fiercest I ever experienced. The Good Emperor had yet to unite the Dragon Lords. They were hoping he'd fail."

"The fighting was brutal," Joren recalled. "I tended many spirits as they passed to the World Beyond. The memories have never left me. But I saved many lives as well, and for that, I am grateful to the gods."

"I don't believe that you were only a healer, shaman. I saw the way you fought against those shapeshifters."

"No one is just a healer in war. Certainly not amongst the Taikan."

"They were more tactical than expected. The Attican generals underestimated them. I learned later that the campaign lasted a year longer than necessary because of their poor judgment at the outset.

They thought them mere barbarians. Nomads. Hunters. I've never seen a cavalry so united. And the Dragonmounts were sparse at the time without the support of the Dragon Lords. If Vitruvian hadn't led the air assaults himself, I wonder if we would have won. Attica may have fractured entirely. How different the world would be."

Urla did not detail the brutal cost of that victory. The Scorching that had ensured Taika would not rise up again.

"It was another life," Joren said, pushing back gruesome memories. "I try my best not to go back."

Urla sighed. "Would that war still disturbed me the way it did then. I've seen too much bloodshed, shaman. Even at my husband's death... I could not find tears."

"Do you regret your path, Consul?"

"No..." Her voice drifted, eyes closed.

Joren wasn't sure he believed her, but she said no more.

"You should go," Joren said. "Sleep. Your son will not wake until morning, the tinctures will make sure of that. And you've an important task ahead. And a long march."

"No, I should—"

"Your son is safe, Urla. There is nothing more you can do tonight."

Urla nodded and managed to rise with a great degree of effort. She crossed the room but paused at the door. "I meant what I said. I do not wish more harm to come to your people."

"I believe you," Joren said. "But you, more than anyone, know that war cares nothing for our wishes. I must spare who I can, which is why I must lead my people away from this place."

Urla hesitated. Joren could sense a turmoil in her spirit, though he was too weak to make sense of it just now. "Good night, Lady Consul."

She left.

Joren performed one last inspection, monitoring Ruan's breathing and pulse, as well as his spiritual resonance. It was much steadier now, despite all he'd endured. He was fully tethered to this world once more.

After burning a prayer of thanks, Joren turned to leave, only to find Malik standing in the door where Urla had been moments ago.

His son's expression was hard to read, though his spirit was unsettled.

"I know you think the Atticans are the enemy," Joren said.

"And you don't?"

Joren chuckled. "Oh, I *know* they're the enemy. I've seen the empire do far worse than anything that's occurred here."

"On your *uhmskara*."

Joren nodded.

"Why don't you ever speak of it, Father?"

"Because my experience in the outside world only further complicated my already complex understanding of the world. And you were not ready."

Malik scowled. "I came of age. I'm a bloody shaman, now. When else would I have been ready?"

"You needed to sort out your own beliefs. I did not wish to sway you. And son, you've done better than I could have dreamed."

"What?" Malik's eyes welled with tears.

Joren had been hard on his son for two long years. It had been necessary. After Derrin's death, Malik had needed to learn to be strong. It had pained Joren every moment. Each day wondering if he was failing. As a shaman, a father.

Joren strode to Malik and pulled him into an embrace.

"You had the courage to speak truth. To me. To the council. To all our people. I'm so proud of you."

Malik sobbed into his chest, and Joren held him tight.

It was some time before Malik released him. There was a tremor in his spirit.

"Father, there is one more truth I need to speak."

———

"And... you believe her?" Joren asked when Malik had finished.

In the quiet of the Sacred Hall of the temple, Joren, Malik, and Madri stood before the Valucian rebel.

A coil of rope bindings were spread on the floor, beside a leathern leg brace. Ava Rykus sat calmly in the chair, hands propped on Joren's desk.

Madri nodded to him. "The girl speaks truth. I feel it in my spirit."

Ava's eyes were heavy, cheeks flushed. She looked to have been crying, but she was even-keeled now.

"If my father can get to your gate before the Atticans, we can end their rule."

"You told her of the Gate of the Ancients?"

Malik shook his head. "She knew already. Or at least had a suspicion."

"Or she peered into your mind, son. She's skilled with cerebral magic."

"Malik is right," Madri said. "The girl has seen a gate like ours before. She showed it to me. A Valucian secret known only to a select few."

If there was another gate, then theirs could not be the only path of the Crossing, just as other nations claimed. Another gate was proof that their foundational myths were incomplete at best.

"Where?" Joren asked.

"In the Ever Sea," Ava said.

Joren shook his head. "Are there more gates than that?"

Ava shrugged. "My father says so. But I've only ever seen ours."

"You wish to destroy the gate?" Joren said. "There is a faction of our people who have proposed this same thing for years, but the proposal has always been dismissed."

"And look where that's gotten you."

Madri shot Ava a hard glare.

The girl nodded. "Sorry. Sometimes my mouth speaks before I mean to."

Joren smirked. He sensed the flash of *hish* brushing up against his spirit, knew the girl was trying to impress charm. Ava was good at it, he had to give her that. But he sensed sincerity, and if Madri—whose intuition was leagues beyond his own—felt the same, then the matter was settled.

"When will the rebels return?"

"Tomorrow."

"With an army?"

Ava's mouth twisted. "The Atticans wish you to believe that we would turn your island into a battlefield. They may even believe it. But we do not have an army. Not yet. The Valucian lords fear another Uprising, no matter their hatred of Attica. We have only a small company to carry out this mission. But if we succeed.... If we do cut off the Attican

Empire from their source of power, that could allow us the chance to raise an army."

"What of the Elyans?" asked Joren.

"We have one runeship. The same as Siga had."

"And those creatures?" Malik asked.

"Okay, not exactly the same as Siga. But they are not Elyan exactly."

Joren raised a brow. The girl was still holding things back.

"Do you want us to trust you, or don't you?" Joren asked.

"The Elyans are concerned about the growing threat that Attica poses under Athanasius's reign. My father has learned Elyan magic, taught it to me through my childhood. Taught me to enter minds. To cover up my tracks. To work my way amongst the enemy just as he's done. The Morphs are a twist of Elyan sorcery and dark blood-magic practiced by Beirusian witches. My father has gained other allies across the world. Chardonians. Valgs. Taikan. All fear Attica is on the brink of dominion over all Îrithèa. And this is what most concerns the Elyans, I expect."

"The empire has ruled Îrithèa before," Joren said. He did not believe the dismissive words he spoke, but he wanted to see how Ava reacted. "Why is this time so different?"

Ava drew a breath. "Because Emperor Athanasius is different than his predecessors. Many fear we are on the brink of another Age of Fire. We have not forgotten the devastation the Dragonmounts wreaked in Valucia."

Joren had not forgotten imperial devastation either. But he had also seen the fruitless toll of rebellion. Taika's people suffered more now than perhaps ever before.

Ava was pressing on his mind, and he did not hold back from her. He pictured the slaughter in the Taikan Rebellion. Hundreds of thousands slain. An entire city burned with dragonfire. Most rebels died. Those who survived wished they'd joined their brethren in death.

Joren could still smell the charred flesh, picture the vacuous eyes, hairless skulls, limbs stripped to the bone by flames. He could hear the screams of the dying, as he tended their wounds, knowing it was already too late.

For years, Attica declared the Scorching a necessary evil to bring peace.

And it had brought peace for a time.

Attica united. And Emperor Vitruvian became known as the Good Emperor, the Uniter. The Peacebringer.

But war always returned.

And Athanasius was undoubtedly more ambitious. It was the fear of what Joren experienced in Taika that ruled the world now, that quelled widespread rebellion, that prevented nations from banding together.

For so long, Joren had told himself that Attica was a necessary evil. Better for them to rule than for another Scorching, but he had been wrong. All of them had. He saw that now.

"What would you have us do?" Joren asked.

Chapter 42

Another Path

"You will need to remain here awhile longer," the shaman instructed Ava.

"In this secret room. By myself?"

Ava was so tired of being locked up. Tired of talking and convincing, when there was action to be done. It felt like the tale of her entire bloody existence.

"Tul Eriksein and a few others will be leading the Attican company to the Spires in a few hours," the shaman said. "I've already recused myself from the situation and must lead our people to safety as I intended."

Madri clasped her son's shoulder. "Surel will go with you. Malik and I will join the company heading to the Spires."

Malik nodded. "I'll volunteer to serve as shaman, at least until the Attican mission is complete."

"I must go too!" Ava insisted. "I'll follow in the woods or something."

Joren looked at her, eyes drifting to the leg brace in the corner.

"I've covered worse terrain in the academy trials."

"We don't doubt your ability, Ava," Madri said.

"Everyone doubts my ability," she said, trying to hold back the venom she felt. "I can keep up with a marching regiment. You saw my father fly."

"Can you fly?" asked Joren.

Her mouth twisted. "I can cover ground when I must."

The shaman shook his head. "You've entrusted the future of your rebellion to us. Now, you must trust us."

"And if something goes wrong?" Ava demanded. "I'll be trapped in this fucking safe room?"

"Only until after the Atticans march up the Soul Road," said Joren. "I'll find a way to smuggle you aboard one of our ships."

Ava hated being left out, but she had no good argument. She could only hope her father would turn up before they sailed to Valgland.

"When *will* your father return?" asked Madri.

Ava grimaced. In truth, she did not know. Perhaps he was in the woods somewhere, waiting. Perhaps something had gone terribly wrong. But she couldn't give voice to any of that.

"He will return at the right moment," Ava insisted. "Whether it is down here or up in your Spires, my father will find a way."

Joren's brow furrowed. She could sense unease in his mind. "You said this other gate is out over the Ever Sea. Even by runeship, the journey there and back must take days."

"He will be here in time," Ava insisted. "We have to be ready."

———

The rebel council consisted of Lord Rykus, Sky Captain Verina Arkhovia, and Deven lè Nir, along with two others Riese hadn't met. A Taikan woman and a Chardonian man. The woman had piercing grey eyes and raven-black hair. She wore a modest but regal gown of intricate material, embroidered with twirling shapes of flying birds. She looked like someone who had never seen the broad edge of a sword, let alone a battle. The man was Chardonian, with brown skin and flowing dark hair. His robes consisted of many colorful layers, like the feathers of a serpent.

Rykus and the Sky Captain had not changed attire since their arrival, but Deven now wore a trim white uniform with a crest of black Morph wings. Her Elyan uniform. Her dark eyes flashed, and her silver hair flowed in waves past her shoulders. Her sleeves were short, revealing strong arms etched with tattoos.

A crudely drawn map was spread across the table at the center of the council chamber.

Rykus gestured to a circular marking at the end of a long squiggle. "That's Yerida."

"This is… Faltara?" Riese asked.

It was so strange to see the forests and coastlines of her girlhood reduced to some brushes of ink on parchment. The words meant nothing to Riese.

The map spanned the entire table, though most of the island contained empty space, showing just how little was known about Faltara by the outside world. There were four other thick circles, presumably the four clan villages, and a vague mountain range along the spine.

Riese had never seen a map of the island before. Knowledge of the coastlines was necessary for the fishing folk, but for a hunter from the Jackal clan, knowledge of the forests and mountains of the heartland was all that mattered.

She traced her fingers over the patterns. No hunting tracks. No landmarks. These squiggles meant little to her, though the fjord near Yerida looked to be reasonably accurate.

"This was drawn by our navigator during the journey from the island," Rykus said. "He estimated the island is roughly fifty leagues in length, maybe twenty across at the heart. Does that sound accurate?"

Riese chuckled and shrugged. "No idea. We hunters learn the land in our minds."

The other council members grimaced, but Rykus remained cool as he went on.

"The general shape of this map we stole from a Beirusian trader. But traders only deal with the southern passage between Faltara and the uninhabited regions of Valgland. Northern Faltara is largely a mystery."

Riese nodded. "It's not well-known to most Faltari either, outside the Saber clan. The valleys are teeming with sabercats and the waters are plagued by sea dragons." She pointed to the top of the island map, which was rounded. "The fishers called this the Tip of the Spear. But that looks like little more than a nub."

"A Beirusian ship circumnavigated the island many years ago, but the trip was perilous, so I don't expect it's accurate. This interior is more detailed than any other depiction I've encountered."

Riese shook her head, surveying the lines supposedly demarcating the heart of the island she knew so well. None of it looked like the Faltara she knew.

"Which village is Starholm?" Riese asked. "The Dragyr village?"

"You can't tell?" asked the Taikan woman, whose name Riese had gathered, was Shei.

"I can't read," Riese said. "Again, little use for a hunter. I can tell you these ranges are nowhere near accurate. All the mountains and valleys look the same. Where's the Dawn Crag? The Mountain of Souls? Where's—"

"We're hoping you can assist with the details." Rykus gestured to a region of forest near the middle of the southern island. "That is Starholm."

"That's too far north," Riese said. "It should be further from Yerida. There's a whole valley that runs south along the foothills of the Narrow Peaks. There's a break in the spine of the island somewhere around here." She gestured to a point between Yerida and Starholm.

"Do you know the distance?" Rykus asked.

Riese shook her head. "A stag rider could cover it in a day during the summer. Several days in early winter. Impossible later."

"And how would a stag's pace compare with a horse?" asked the Taikan woman.

"Never seen a horse."

"We won't have horses anyway, Shei," said Rykus.

The woman huffed, crossing her arms.

The Sky Captain leaned close, studying everything with intense focus.

"And this circle?" Riese gestured to one at the edge of a river on the eastern side of the island. "I assume that's River's End?"

Rykus nodded.

"That's my village," Riese said. "Kalengal Valley should be about a day's ride, but that looks farther than Yerida."

"Look, we know this is hasty guesswork," Rykus said. "But let's try our best."

"We need to know where these Spires are located with as much accuracy as possible," Verina Arkhovia insisted.

Riese grimaced. "It is a relatively similar distance from each of the main clan villages, so knowing where you think our main villages are located on this map matters."

"There's a path out of Yerida, correct?" Rykus asked.

Riese nodded. "There's a path from all villages. We call it the Soul Road."

"How far from Yerida?" asked Verina.

Riese shrugged. "A two day journey with women and children and alkine carts."

"Alkine?" asked Mathias, the Chardonian man.

"Something between a sheep and a stag, isn't that right?" Rykus asked.

Riese chuckled. "Never seen a sheep either."

Deven smirked.

Riese peered at the map. All the mountains looked the same. These people truly had no idea where any of the major peaks or valleys were located. The entire interior of her homeland was just a mass of trees and rocks to them.

"Do you have a quill?" Riese asked. A servant fetched one and a small well of ink.

"Thought you said you couldn't read or write," Shei said.

Riese rolled her eyes. "I can draw."

She stretched toward the middle of the table and began to sweep the quill over the ill-defined mountains, trying to imagine the path from Yerida.

"There's a valley up here," Riese said. "Huge walls of unclimbable stone. Maybe half the distance from Yerida. All the village paths converge here. About halfway through that valley, there is a small... nook. Near a wide mountain that looks like a woman lying on her back."

"Lying on her..." Shei said.

"There's a section that resembles a head, nose, sharp drop, and then there's two big rounder mounds. I trust you get it. My mum says the first chieftains were men, so..."

Deven smirked again as Riese updated the map with a womanly figured mountain. "You Faltari *are* primitive."

Riese caught a flash in her eye.

"And then?" Verina asked.

"The nook passes through the mountain to another valley, then, up through a forest of snowpine. There's a final pass somewhere around here, I'd guess."

Riese marked them on the map. "It's not actually right there, because this map is terrible, but somewhere around there is a valley. The tallest peaks are on the eastern side of the range. So, you'd fly over those to reach—"

"We thought the tallest peaks on the island were further north," said Mathias.

Riese rolled her eyes. "Maybe. We rarely venture past Skarida. That's wild sabercat territory, and the terrain would be impossible to navigate with carts. Anyway, the peaks of Kalengal Valley are not the tallest in the range. It's the heart of the island because of the Mountain of Souls. "

"Right." Rykus drew back from the table.

Verina studied the map in silence for some time. "If that's so, then, we flew right over that region on our way to Yerida. But I don't recall anything resembling these Spires."

Riese shrugged. "I doubt you would have noticed them unless you knew they were there. They look like any ordinary peak unless you're in the valley."

"We were flying at night, as well," Deven said.

Verina studied Riese. "Young lady, the hope of our entire cause lies in your hands."

"Believe me, I've realized that," Riese said. "Look, you brought me here. You asked what I know and I've said it. That's where the Spires are. And that's where you'll find the gate to the Abyss. The rest is up to you."

"The girl is right," said Rykus. "Chardonia is already threatened."

Mathias grimaced but nodded. "I must leave to aid our own war effort as soon as we finish deliberations."

"Taika loathes Attica," Shei said, "but there will be no chance at raising a Taikan force without a reasonable chance of victory."

"Until this mission has succeeded," Verina clarified.

"The *akiri* are insistent," Shei said. "Taika lost everything in our last war. No one here could ever truly understand the devastation we endured. You all know only tales of a true Scorching."

Rykus nodded. "This is our only window of opportunity. We will need to use *every* resource we have to make sure we do not fail."

Deven's eyes went wide. "The Rebelmounts?"

CHAPTER 43

DEEP DOWN

Joren's spirit was light for the first time in ages. Madri and their children dozed peacefully in the main temple hall, catching a few hours of slumber before what might prove to be the most conse-quential day of all their lives.

For a long time, he simply lay there listening to their breathing, grateful to be alive, to love and be loved. Grateful to be relieved of a burden that had been weighing down his spirit more than he'd realized. Until that burden was lifted.

Yet there was no way Joren could sleep. It always seemed to happen this way before such fateful days. Before his first hunt. Before his Ascent. His first battle in Taika. The day he wed Madri. His mind simply would not still.

As the first hints of dawn drew near, he roused himself and went to check on the Pelasius boy. Ruan had not stirred, but his spirit remained firmly tethered to this world.

Dimly, Joren could sense he was not the only one unable to sleep.

After checking Ruan's bandages, he made his way to the Sacred Hall. Runes glowed at his touch, and the door eased open.

Ava Rykus looked up from her seat at his desk. She was not bound any longer, but the bedroll Madri had provided sat untouched on the floor.

"I trust I'm not disturbing you," Joren said.

"Nope."

He sensed she was still upset about being left out of the action. Ava perked up when he set her cane on the desk.

"Held onto this after the attack. Thought you might want it back."

Ava ran her fingers over the dragonhead handle and smiled. "Thank you, shaman."

"Need to pack a few things, if you don't mind."

"Sure." Ava shrugged, still slumped over the desk.

Joren stepped to her side, waiting.

"Oh, er, inside the desk, you mean?"

"Yes."

"Sorry." Ava scooted the chair back, and sat once more, watching him curiously, the cane draped over her lap.

Joren began with the drawers, removing old ledgers and journals from shamans past. There was a hollowed-out tube of southern balsam wood that contained the original spell knowledge brought over from the Dying World. Copies had been made long ago. The scroll was nearly illegible now, but it was perhaps the most sacred item in the room. That and one other scroll.

He moved to the shelf. Once again, Ava shifted out of his way. Using a stool, he reached for a small chest at the top. The runes marking the exterior glowed, and a mechanism clicked as he set the chest down on the desk.

Ava drew closer, looking over his shoulder with curiosity.

Joren opened the chest and lifted out a folded sheet of leather. Gingerly, he spread it wide on the desk, and Ava drew closer.

There were careful etchings burned into the surface. It was remarkably preserved for something so ancient. All long lines and squares.

"What is it?" Ava asked.

"I expect it is the best shot your rebellion has," Joren said, pointing to several spots marked throughout. "This is a map of the world beyond the gate. Only shamans have ever seen it, until now. Even my son doesn't know it exists."

"Isn't he a shaman too?"

"Yes, well, we've had a busy time since he came of age. This map shows the Dead City of Adria. The place my people claim to have fled centuries ago. The city is littered with nests—hundreds of them—most are now claimed by smaller dragyrs. Our best guess is that dragons took over the city after it was abandoned but slowly died off in the years that followed."

"What could kill off so many dragons?"

"Our history of the Crossing suggests a great catastrophe that changed the spiritual nature of the world. A fearsome power that infected the soul of the place. Perhaps this is the reason there are so many eggs and no living dragons. Dragyrs nest there but bring their eggs through to our world to hatch and live. The dragon nests are generally easy to find. Most of our children have taken eggs from these nests, though they are beginning to grow scarcer. But there are a few temples, shown here on this map, where troves of eggs were kept in one place."

"Dragon temples," Ava said. "So, your ancestors worshipped them?"

"The past is difficult to parse out from the histories, but I don't believe so. From what I can gather, humanity saw dragons as messengers from the gods."

"Like the Elyan cherubs?" Ava asked.

Joren smiled. "I know little of Elya, I'm afraid. But, it is relatively clear that the fate of dragons and humanity was linked in this Dying World. Hatchings stopped. Humanity fled. The dragons died off. How it played out in the end, it is impossible to be certain."

Ava's voice deepened. "Why are these temples marked by your shamans?"

"For years, I thought it was just information passed down. Like our spellbooks and histories. Gods know, we shamans love to document things. But now, whether intentionally or not, I believe it is here for this moment. So that, in a time of dire need, we could turn the empire's power against them. According to our legends, a Faltari man brought the first dragons to Attica. Rayne Seversein used this knowledge for his own gain. And now, we have the opportunity to use it to dismantle that empire."

Joren rolled up the map.

"I have seen the evils Attica has wrought. It took me longer than I am proud of to see the right way forward. But I do now, and I will do all I can to see your revolution succeed. But I hope you know that all paths of resistance are not written in blood. The wisdom to know which path to choose. That is my prayer for myself with what is to come. That is my prayer for you, Ava Rykus."

Joren held her gaze, peering deeply.

Her spirit wavered, a conflict of emotions, but she nodded to him. "I pray so too."

He stowed the map in a satchel, which he slung over his shoulders. "Madri will get this to your father."

"Thank you, shaman." The girl glanced away, a disturbance wracking her spirit.

"What's wrong?" Joren asked.

She stared at the door, her back to him. A hand drifted to cover her mouth.

"I'm sorry, but I still must insist you stay here until all this is—"

Ava Rykus turned back, tears in her eyes.

"Oh," Joren said, suddenly reminded how young she was. How young his own children were to endure all they had these past days. "I'm sure your father—"

"It's not that... it's the boy."

"Boy?"

"Ruan."

"Ah... so you *were* close, then. Truly."

"Any relationship with an Attican boy... is complicated. But yes." Ava brushed the tears away and straightened up. "Is he..."

"His injuries were grave, dear," Joren said. "But I believe he'll live."

"I'd like to see him," Ava said.

"I really can't..."

"I believe the Valucian cause is just," Ava said. "That it is worth sacrificing everything for. But knowing the toll our rebellion has taken on Ruan... I could feel him, shaman. Through the surgery last night. The fear and turmoil in his mind. The agony. Before you go. Before all this ends, I must see him one last time. Please."

"He's sleeping, Ava. And even if he were awake—"

"I wouldn't ask if he were awake. I know it would be too great a risk. But I think you, of all people, know that much can be said without words. I betrayed Ruan, nearly killed him. I need to say, I'm sorry. I need him to know. Deep down."

Joren felt the desperation in her spirit, the regret. A feeling he knew all too well. He couldn't deny the girl that.

"It will be dawn soon," he said. "But I can grant you a few moments. Nothing more."

———

Ava followed the shaman out of the Sacred Hall and a short distance down the corridor. With the aid of her brace and the return of her cane, she moved a little easier, though the ache in her leg persisted from being cooped up in that room for so long.

As she walked, she could hear snores echoing from the main hall beyond. Sensed weary spirits. Joren's family had endured much, and now, they were willing to risk even more to help her cause. She could not let herself think what else they might endure.

Ava felt guilty for manipulating the shaman.

But she could not bear the thought of lying in this damn temple, mere feet away from the boy she'd survived the academy with, the boy she cared for despite the differences of their upbringings, the boy she had betrayed.

It was true if she were to do it all again, she would change nothing. But whatever happened today, Ava doubted she would see him again. It was possible he would not even wake before all this was over.

Over the past years, Ava had impressed many truths on Ruan Pelasius. Yes, they were manipulations, but they were still truths, and he had been open to them.

Open to befriending a Valucian. Trusting a girl lower in status than he. Ava would never have ascended the way she did in the academy without him. She would never have won Campos's confidence. Would never have come to Faltara.

Now, even if he was unconscious, there was one last truth she must convey.

The shaman opened the door to the healing chamber and stepped inside. A noxious odor wafted out, and Ava paused. On a table, she could see legs jutting out of a pile of blankets.

Ava stepped into the room.

All her life, her house had sacrificed for a cause greater than their own family. In secret. While most of their people believed them blood-traitors. Her mum had sacrificed the most of all. And through it, Ava had learned not to allow herself to hold regret.

It was a useless emotion for someone like her.

Ava Lucila Rykus did what she must, that was all there was to it.

She stepped inside.

The sight of Ruan lying on the shaman's table wracked her body with tangible anguish.

Last night, she could feel Ruan's pain, but she could not see just how close to death he had been. His face and neck were a motley display of bruises, purples and yellows mixing to form a sick amalgamation, hair a greasy and matted mess jutting out from a thick bandage that covered the back of his skull and cinched under his chin.

The shaman hung back in the hall, whispering to his wife, who must have stirred when they came out.

Ava took a seat beside Ruan. The wooden chair creaked as she leaned forward, took Ruan's hand. His chest rose and fell steadily, though there was a labored wheeze to each breath.

But his spirit was still as a babe's.

Ruan was dreaming.

Ava did not often peer into dreams with her gifts. Usually, dreams were muddled and confusing, making it impossible to tell fiction from reality. One could rarely glean more than a resonance from dreams. But that was all she wanted from Ruan now.

Ava reached out with her sense, her mind brushing up against his. And she could feel Ruan's essence. Perhaps it was true, as these Faltari shamans believed, that it was his actual spirit.

Ruan's was always warm, calm, good.

He was not ruled by the jealousy and ambition of most of their peers at the academy. There was something special about him. Something truly Fjuriin—more true than any other Attican she'd met—a steadiness that balanced her own wild and bitter nature.

Now, facing that good nature filled her with pernicious regret.

It wasn't supposed to happen like this.

And gods, she hated herself for failing.

That was what she'd shown Madri. That was how she'd convinced the woman she was telling the truth. By baring the only two regrets she held in all her life. What happened to her mother with the Beirusian witch. And the betrayal of the boy she loved.

Ava had never told Ruan her truest feelings. Nor had she spoken the words, even to herself.

When he woke from this coma, his mother would fill him with lies about what Ava had done, what she'd intended. Perhaps none of this would matter.

But she reached out to his mind and tried to impress the truth. The actual truth. Which, of course, was complicated.

Was it actually love?

Ava chuckled. What did a nineteen-year-old girl know of love? She, who'd never kissed a boy she actually cared for. Who'd never bared her soul to anyone.

But deep down, Ava had longed to do both with Ruan, gods damn it. She'd longed to tell him everything about herself. Everything she longed for and dreamed for. Everything she would lay down her life for.

Slowly, Ava withdrew her magic.

Ruan twitched. She held still, but he did not wake.

Ava stood and was about to leave when she realized that the shaman and his wife were not out in the hall any longer.

She reached out with her sense, and stiffened.

There was a disturbance outside the temple.

Part Eight

Inferno

The gods move through us,
For we are their children.
From them, we were begotten.
To them, we shall return.

—"Lament of the Fallen"
a Faltari dirge

CHAPTER 44

SCHEMES

The pounding at the door jolted Malik from a dream.

"Get yer ass out 'ere, Malik!" The words were slurred. Not quite a yell, but other villagers could surely hear him.

Malik sprang from his bedroll in the main prayer hall.

"What in the Abyss is going on?" Surel demanded, sitting up in her cot.

"I don't know." Malik staggered to his feet, vision blurry as his eyes adjusted.

"Malik! Open the door."

He hurried across the room, tripping over a pair of boots on his way, cursing.

"What's going on?" Madri demanded, emerging from the hallway, his father right behind her.

"Is that..." Surel began.

Malik threw open the door. The stench of his friend's breath was potent on the air. Yuri nearly fell through the doorway, eyes wide and bloodshot.

"It's about time, yeh lyin' son of a—"

Malik grabbed the boy's arm and pulled him inside. He shot a quick glance around the empty street, relieved to see no one had been watching in the pre-dawn darkness.

Madri lit a lamp with a flare of *hish*, and Yuri shielded his eyes from the light. He staggered into the room, looking around wildly.

"What is the meaning of this, Yuri Alwensein?" Madri demanded.

Yuri's face turned, not quite remorseful, but chastened. "There been lights on here all bloody night!" Yuri said. "Why don't you tell me what the meaning is?"

"You're drunk, Yuri," Malik's mother scolded. "I can smell the mead across the room."

Yuri glowered. "Maybe I am. That mean I shouldn't believe what I see with my own eyes?"

"We've been up taking care of our people," Madri said. "And healing an injured Attican boy."

"Nah," said Yuri, gulping down a breath. "Consul left hours ago."

"God's breath," said Surel. "You've been watching the temple all night? What's wrong with you?"

Malik thought he knew, judging by the way Yuri had been acting after Aram Tulsein had come jabbering at dinner.

"Let me handle this," said Malik. He motioned toward the hall.

Surel glanced from Malik to their parents.

"Malik is right," said Joren. "Yuri has always been a friend of Malik's. This is between them."

Once they were alone, Malik turned on Yuri. "The bloody Abyss is your problem, Alwensein?"

Yuri leaned back, stunned at the force of his words. Then, he pointed, jabbing his finger at Malik's chest. He resisted the instinct to bat Yuri away, sensing the pain in his friend's spirit.

"I'm sick of being lied to."

"Yuri, I haven't been—"

"Bullshit! You know something you're not saying. And even that prick, Ulgar, is in on it. So quit lying to me."

Malik froze, horror nagging at his gut.

"I seen you two sneaking off to the shrines right after the attack. I may not've seen what you were doing, but I know it's got something to do with Riese."

Malik wasn't sure what to say. Just how much did Yuri know? His friend's mind was a wall. He could feel his anger, but no specifics. Had he seen them sneaking Ava away from the scene of the crime?

Yuri slumped onto the ground and coughed, looking like he might be sick. "Shit, you got any water?"

"Er, yeah, of course."

Malik fetched a flagon, and the boy gulped it down. He took a few breaths, eyes closed. For a moment, Malik thought Yuri might drift to sleep. His head lolled. Then, he opened his eyes.

The anger was gone, replaced by sadness. When Yuri spoke, the words came clearly.

"I'm sorry, Malik. I know you're a bloody shaman now, and we all know they've kept secrets from the rest of us. I'm just scared for her. I knew you always trusted Riese more than me. And maybe for good reason, but... that Serpent fisher oaf?"

"It had nothing to do with who's trustworthy, Yuri. Ulgar was right in the middle of the attack. He saved my life. And I needed to act fast. I trust Ulgar. That doesn't mean I don't trust you too."

Yuri sighed. "I just thought if there was a way to help Riese, you'd let me in on it. She's my friend too."

Malik didn't respond.

Yuri glanced around the room. "So, where is she, Malik?"

"You think Riese is—"

"No, I'm talking about your bloody prisoner."

Malik's breath caught. "Yuri, you're drunk. You have no idea—"

"Still lying. I shoulda known. And to think I defended you when Aram Tulsein was talking shit about you."

"Aram?" Malik's senses heightened.

He reached for Yuri's spirit, searching for some hidden malice, but finding nothing but anger and confusion.

"You shoulda heard that bastard going on at the tavern tonight. That he seen you sneaking around the woods after the battle. That you were hiding something. And I told him..."

"What did you say?" Malik demanded, a pit burrowing deep in his stomach.

"I didn't tell him anything!" Yuri said. "I said he was a prick, and of course, if you were hiding something, Aram and his father would be the last to know. And that if there was something to hide, there must be a damn good..."

Malik backed toward the window. Still dark, though morning was surely not far off. The streets remained empty, silent.

"What are you—"

"I'm seeing if you were bloody followed, Alwensein!"

Yuri went silent. He glanced out the window, met Malik's gaze, a sudden terror stirring, like a wild animal that knew it'd been spotted by a hunter.

"N-nah, I'm sure there was no one..."

Malik pulled away from the window and crossed the wide chamber toward the back hallway. He hadn't heard a sound from the rest of his family since Yuri arrived.

Yuri doubled down, reverting to anger once more. "Come on. I may be drunk, but I en't bloody stupid. Aram left the tavern long before I did. And besides, he knows where to find you anyway. Now, quit changing the subject. Is your little prisoner—"

"Oh, she's certainly here."

The voice came from the end of the hall.

Malik turned to find the Attican Lady Knight.

Vera Salyr held tight to Ava Rykus's wrist, shoving her forward. The girl grimaced, her other hand supporting herself on her cane as she walked forward.

The rest of Malik's family followed the knight into the room. Surel looked terrified. His mother angry. His father defeated.

Wielding bonespears, Aram Tulsein and his father brought up the rear, accompanied by another Attican soldier, who wielded a gladius.

The Lady Knight surveyed the main temple hall. The other soldier walked the perimeter, securing windows.

"I was informed of a disturbance at the temple where my consul's son is being tended. Lucky that Elder Eriksein came when he did. For whom should I find standing over Ruan than the very girl responsible for murdering my lady's predecessor."

The knight jerked Ava forward again. She nearly stumbled, biting back pain, as the knight ripped the cane from her grasp.

"Is this how you did it?" Salyr demanded.

A flash of *hish*. Ava answered, "I'm sure I don't know what—"

Slap!

Ava's cheek reddened. Her jaw tensed, but she showed no fear.

The knight glared. "You killed General Campos with a hidden blade. Show me. Now!"

The knight held up the cane's length, and Ava pointed to a small ring in the wood where the handle met the staff. "Twist it a quarter turn to the left. A half turn right. Then press the dragon's mouth at the end."

The dagger shot from the end of the cane, dried blood still on the blade.

Salyr's eyes grew wide with fury. In one swift movement, she cracked the cane over her knee, splitting it in half. She handed the blade end to the soldier at her side, then swung the other end around.

Ava shrieked and clutched at her neck. The splintered end left a long streak across her throat. A stream of blood trickled down, splattering on the temple floor. It was remarkable precision. If the knight had extended the attack a fraction further, Ava would be bleeding out.

The knight tossed the jagged remnant aside. Ava held her gaze, but for the first time that Malik had seen, her composure cracked. Tears welled up in Ava's eyes. Her body shuddered with stifled gasps as she fought to remain calm. The walls around her spirit weakened, and Malik felt her fear.

"Do you sense my resolve, witch?" Salyr said. "Do you sense my loathing? You're lucky you have information or you would already be dead. Try to manipulate my mind again, and I'll do worse."

More people emerged from the back hallway. All the Faltari elders. With one exception. There was no sign of the Serpent chieftain, Olma Marudeil. A third member of the Bloody Company followed after them, though Pelasius remained absent.

"Caliphus has gone to fetch reinforcements," the soldier said.

Salyr nodded. "I doubt that will be necessary. The shaman is conniving, but he's weak."

"Please leave my family out of this," Joren said.

Madri clutched Surel tight, keeping her body in front of her daughter like a shield.

Tul Eriksein shoved Malik's father forward with the butt end of his spear, like he was a stubborn alkine, and not the shaman of his own damn people.

The elder did not hide his disdain. "What were you scheming, Joren?"

"Nothing!" Malik said, before his father could answer.

All eyes fell on him.

Aram grinned.

"Malik, no," Joren said, fear in his eyes.

"My father wasn't scheming anything," Malik insisted.

"Bullshit," said Aram.

"You expect us to believe you were just holding this assassin for our own good?" Tul demanded. "Through our council, you didn't think we might benefit from hearing from one of the rebels who terrorized our festival? God's breath, I think you may very well have been in on the whole attack."

"My father didn't know Ava was here," Malik said.

"What?" The Lady Knight's piercing eyes bore into his own.

"It was me. My father knew nothing about her until a few minutes ago."

"Son, no."

"It's true," Malik said. "I hid Ava from the council. Not my father. He wasn't scheming anything."

Aram's father grinned, pulling a satchel from his shoulder. "Then, do you want to explain why your father was carrying *this*?"

The Lady Knight stepped forward and took what appeared to be a scroll out of the satchel.

"I... I don't know what that is," said Malik.

"It's a map," said Tul. "Of the dead city beyond the gate."

The knight's eyes went wide as she inspected the ancient parchment.

Malik cursed.

Yuri had slumped in a chair, holding his head in his hands.

Salyr rolled up the parchment and handed it to the soldier who had brought in the other elders. "Hurry after Caliphus. Get this to our Lady Consul now."

The woman rushed from the room. The other soldier followed with orders to guard the rear entrance. The other elders stood before the front door, while Tul and Aram blocked the way to the back hallway.

The Lady Knight turned back to Malik. "You're a liar, boy. All of you are traitors to the Dragon Throne, as far as I'm concerned. Everyone in this room will be taken to Attica to be tried. But you, Malik... only you were there when Campos died."

Salyr stepped closer, her gaze withering. Malik felt the rage emanating from her spirit like heat from a blazing fire.

"They knew nothing before the attack!" Ava said. There was no *hish*, no manipulations. "We had no scheme with the shamans, I swear it." Her eyes drifted to Aram and Tul at the hallway for a moment. "I... played them."

"Played them?" Salyr demanded.

Ava pointed to her temple as she continued the lie. "You felt my abilities. These savages think they are the only true arbiters of magic, but they have barely touched the surface. They were all too easy to manipulate. Just like you bloody Atticans. Just like Campos."

"Enough!" cried Salyr. She raised her hand to strike Ava.

A squelching sound emitted from across the room, and the Lady Knight spun.

Tul Eriksein's face distorted. The tip of a bonespear jutted out the front of his chest. The blade disappeared, and the elder fell forward.

Ulgar Fenrisein stood over the body, and the temple erupted into chaos.

Chapter 45

The Cost

Heart heavy as she left the council, Riese prayed she hadn't just made a terrible mistake. She was bringing war to the heart of Faltara.

The emperor had destroyed Rykus's island home, and now, was taking war to Chardonia. Would Faltara be laid to waste next?

Riese ventured to the courtyard while Deven and Rykus discussed more detailed plans with the others. Rebels bustled around her, most not paying her any mind. Riese held her rucksack in her lap, feeling the contours of the egg inside. The warm resonance of the dragon's spirit pressed against her own.

"What have I done?" she whispered.

Destiny.

She felt the word distinctly, unsure whether he had spoken to her, or whether it was simply an understanding between them. An impression.

And when had her dragon become so clearly a *he* in her mind? She was unsure of that also.

"Destiny, at the expense of my own kin?"

No. Destiny. Shared.

"Shared?" Riese whispered.

"Anywhere else, you'd be written off for a crazy person."

Riese glanced up to find a tall Valucian man. Strong jaw, brown hair, and sun-specked skin. He was joined by a woman with fiery windswept hair and a weathered face. Both wore dark uniforms with the emblem of a dragon with outstretched wings on their breasts.

"You're…"

"Riders?" said the woman. "Yes. I'm Rhoda."

"Desmond," said the man. "We hoped we'd find you before you left."

"It's been years since we've seen an egg." Rhoda gestured to Riese's rucksack. "May I?"

"Is it safe?"

"This is the only place where it is, my dear."

Carefully, Riese untethered the top of the sack and reached in, fingers brushing the ridged surface. The egg was warm. She hesitated.

Rhoda smiled. "It's like being asked to hand over your newborn, isn't it?"

"I imagine so," said Riese.

"Trust me, that's exactly what it's like."

Riese smiled back at the woman. She pulled the egg out and both riders gasped.

"Ash and stone," murmured Desmond.

"Oh, the gods are good," Rhoda said, a tear in her eye. "Riese, dear, you are blessed. I know this is much to ask, but would you allow me to hold it?"

To anyone else, Riese could not imagine it. But these two were the only others who understood what was happening to her, and she longed to share the experience.

Riese nodded and handed the egg to Rhoda.

The entire courtyard had gone silent. People passing slowed their pace to catch a glimpse of the shimmering crimson egg. They beamed with hopeful smiles. Even here, where two dragons soared in the sky.

"Most rebels never saw our eggs," Desmond said, leaning in over Rhoda's shoulder.

Rhoda gently turned the egg over. "This one is nearly ready for the rites if he's already speaking to you."

Riese nodded, filled with longing to meet the dragon inside.

"Can you sense our mounts?" Desmond asked, brushing his fingers over the egg's surface.

Riese thought of the stirrings she'd felt just as she arrived in this strange world. "I think so."

"Technically, it's your dragon that senses them. But the resonance is shared. Our dragons can't sense him yet unless they're quite close, but a hatchling's senses are heightened, and not yet distracted by all the other senses in the outer world."

Rhoda handed the egg back to her, and Riese was filled with relief.

"How do you know all this?" Riese asked.

Rhoda shrugged. "We Valucians have an ancient heritage. You Faltari do too."

"We do?"

"Well, the Valgs do. That's the origin of the Burned Lands, after all. And you're descended from a northern Valgish clan, so..."

Riese hesitated. She did not know what to believe about her people's history. Instead, she focused on wrapping her egg once more and stowing it within her rucksack.

Deven strode across the courtyard straight toward her, looking anxious.

"I think it's time for me to go," said Riese.

"May the winds guide you," said Desmond.

"We look forward to having you join our ranks when you return."

Riese nodded, mind racing. Again, her dragon's voice in her mind. *Destiny.*

"There you are, Riese!" said Deven. "Met the Rebelmounts, I see."

Desmond and Rhoda nodded to Deven, though without the same warmth they'd shown to Riese. Neither of the riders had been on the council, and Riese was not privy to all the power dynamics in the rebellion.

"Where's Rykus?" Deven asked.

"I thought he was with you," Riese said.

Deven shook her head. "I was conferring with the Chardonians before they left. I just checked Elora's chambers, and—"

"We saw Rykus heading toward the Stone Gardens," said Rhoda. "With Elora. I think he wanted a special goodbye before this mission."

"Goodbye?" Riese asked.

Beyond the courtyard, they followed a winding path to a fenced area outside the walls of Flameholm. The path was lined with flowers, but an enormous purple-leafed tree dominated the space, set upon a small knoll pocked with jagged stones. Its trunk was thick as a house and its branches reached out toward the heavens like many praying hands. The stones were covered in runes and two dark depressions that looked like graven eyes.

Were these the Stone Spirits the Valucians worshipped?

The skies radiated with violets and pinks as dusk settled over the fortress.

Captain Rykus stood beside a frail woman, paying them no mind as they approached. He pointed out toward the radiant sky and shifted the woman to look in that direction.

"That woman, Elora," said Riese. "Is she his mother?"

"His wife," said Deven. They paused at the base of the hill.

Rykus was speaking softly with her. Kept redirecting her attention to the sunset.

"She's been unwell for many years," said Deven.

"What happened?"

Deven shrugged. "Neither he nor his daughter speak of it. A great tragedy. Most say it happened during the Uprising."

Rykus turned, holding tight to the woman's arm, helping her walk slowly down the hill. She was so thin and small. Skin wrinkled. Eyes vacant. She looked fifty years older than Rykus, but Riese knew that couldn't be.

A pair of young women who'd been sitting peacefully on a bench along the path hurried to help Elora and the captain.

When they reached the bottom of the hill, Rykus embraced his wife. He held her for a long time, but Riese watched how her gaze drifted. She stood stiffly, as though not aware that her husband was even there, let alone hugging her before a dangerous rebel mission.

"I love you," Rykus whispered.

Then, the two women walked off with Elora Rykus.

The captain turned to them. "Riese, are you ready to go home?"

She nodded, though her face betrayed her.

"If Ava has succeeded," Rykus said, "your people will be preparing to leave the island. We will put no one in danger if we can help it."

Riese spared a glance at frail Elora as she reached the end of the gardens.

"But yes," said Rykus, "some costs cannot be helped."

Riese pictured the smoke-filled sky over the Isle of Eòreth, and she knew there was no changing her mind now. "I'm ready, sir."

"Good," said Deven. "Because we don't have any more time to delay. I've got preparations of my own, you know."

"You're not coming with us?" Riese asked.

Deven grinned. "Well... you won't get there without me."

Her hand rested on the pommel of her saber. She withdrew it in a sweeping arc and the room filled with light.

Riese's breath caught. "A godblade? But I thought only the Knights of Caadron possessed them."

It was not nearly as large as the broadsword she'd seen the Lady Knight wield during the attack on Yerida, but a brilliant emerald gem glowed in the hilt just the same.

Deven grinned. "We still have a surprise or two left before this is all said and done."

The Elyan woman swept her blade and cut a circle in the air itself, forming a misty sort of window.

Together, Riese and Rykus stepped through.

When she glanced back, Deven was gone.

The totem pillars of the Faltari shrines towered all around them, casting sharp shadows in the night. It took a moment for Riese to adjust to her new surroundings. It was a bizarre thing to be instantly flung from one world to another. From sundown in one place, to full dark in the other.

Then, she felt something.

Her heart pounded. Chills shot across her skin. She peered through the tops of the trees.

The village was still as a felled doe, but this gave Riese no comfort.

In the moment after a kill, the spirit of all things lingered for a time, brushing up against her own spirit, pleading, scared, alone. She'd felt that tension and pain more times than she could count, and it always shook her.

And Riese felt similar desperation now.

As clearly as she felt her dragon, she felt a familiar spirit in anguish.

It was Malik.

"We're too late," Riese said, fear and sorrow enveloping her.

"What do you mean?" Rykus demanded, stepping close.

"She means something is wrong. And she'd be damn right about that."

Riese and Captain Rykus both jolted at the woman's voice. Elder Olma Marudeil emerged from behind one of the totem poles.

CHAPTER 46

WHEN TO TURN BACK

Aram turned on Ulgar with rage in his eyes. With a surge of magic, the Dragyr boy flung himself like an arrow. Ulgar's spear clattered to the ground, Aram driving his knee into the boy's chest. Aram raised his spear.

Malik raced across the room as the Faltari temple descended into madness. He thrust out with a burst of *hish* as he neared.

Aram didn't see him coming. The breath of the gods struck his nemesis with righteous fury, sending the Dragyr boy reeling into a wooden pillar. Malik pulled Ulgar to his feet and spun.

His father faced off with the Lady Knight. Her godblade shimmered with threads of magic at its edge. His father hesitated. But Malik did not.

All his life, he'd been taught that *hish* was a gift from the gods, to be used to heal, not to harm. But this was a matter of survival.

Traditions be damned.

Malik released a magic attack that stopped the knight in her tracks, her blade surging to absorb the *hish*.

Joren followed up with an even mightier attack of his own, a pulse of magic that sent her careening into the temple wall with a crack. She was slow to get up.

Ava snatched her splintered cane from the ground. She got to her feet with a hitch but fought through the pain. One of the elders latched onto her cloak. Ava spun around, slashing with the cane shard, and Lysa Anadeil staggered back.

Together, Malik and Ulgar let another surge of *hish* fly. Malik's attack was weaker this time, but paired with Ulgar's magic, Elder Dannsein flew back into the statue of the All Father, sending the sacred visage toppling.

Malik felt warm energy at his back, but the force only glanced past him. His mother had deflected the attack. Madri stood at the rear of the hall, Surel behind her.

A scream.

Aram leapt across the room for Ava. She turned.

With the last bit of magic he could muster, Malik crossed the space with a *hish*-induced leap and collided with Aram, tackling him to the floor. The boy's head thudded against the hard wooden floor with a crack.

"Come on!" Ulgar shouted, racing back down the hall from which he'd come. Madri motioned for Malik to follow. Surel was already sprinting after Ulgar. Yuri, who had cowered at the edge of the action, suddenly came out of his stupor and crossed the room.

Aram lay still.

Malik helped Ava to her feet. Her right leg nearly gave out, and she pulled herself up, wrapping an arm over his shoulder. Fear and pain radiated from her spirit like a seething storm.

They crossed the room as quick as they could manage.

Malik's father wielded a force beyond anything Malik had seen that sent the Lady Knight straight through the wall onto the front deck outside. She did not stir, the blazing light of her godblade extinguished.

Lysa Anadeil fled out the front door. Brom Dannsein lay pinned beneath the fallen statue of the All Father. Unconscious. The other Attican guards had never returned from the back hall, dispatched by Ulgar when he snuck in, Malik guessed. But there would soon be more.

"Father, come on!" Malik pleaded.

But Joren shook his head. "I cannot."

He knelt at Tul Eriksein's side and began to administer a healing spell. The Dragyr elder was still breathing, though his whole chest shuddered and wheezed from the wound. The floor was covered in his blood.

Joren's gaze fell to Ava. "Get the girl to the gate, son. I love you!"

Ava pulled on his arm. "Malik!"

"Go!" Joren shouted and turned away.

The Lady Knight staggered to her feet. The sound of soldiers outside grew louder.

"Hurry, Malik!"

His mother's voice.

Malik turned away from his father.

———

Rykus drew his saber halfway from its sheath. Riese reached for *hish*.

Olma Marudeil raised her hands above her head and smiled.

"Easy now, Captain. If there's one thing I hope you learned from your wife, it's that a quick draw can lead to unwanted outcomes."

"What?" Rykus said.

"Your daughter was unplanned, right?" Olma said. "Born at the outset of an Uprising. It's a joke. Though perhaps loosed arrow would have been more apt than quick draw."

"How could you know that?" Rykus demanded.

"You knew Ava's mother?" Riese asked, bewildered.

The elder nodded. "A long time ago."

Rykus peered at her in the darkness. "How..."

"I pray there'll be plenty of time for explanations and reminiscences. But right now, whatever you've been scheming is about to be undone. If you go down to that village, your rebellion is over."

"What do you know about my rebellion?" Rykus asked.

"I knew your wife before you were wed. Before the first Valucian Uprising. I know enough to know that your cause is just and it's high time my people chose a side. Now, come, we must be swift."

Olma motioned them into the darkness of the woods.

———

Guilt raged in Joren's spirit over the damage that had been done this night. If he could prevent further harm, he knew he must. It was his sacred duty as shaman of his people, and as a decent man.

Tul Eriksein was in terrible shape, but there was a chance the

Dragyr elder would live. His wound was not quite closed over, but Joren had at least managed a solid clot.

Still, the man did not stir.

The Lady Knight brandished her magic blade and stepped back into the hall to face him. Though physically weakened, Joren's attacks had not worn down her spirit the way they could against an ordinary soldier, the way they had in the Taikan Rebellion. This woman was trained to resist spiritual attacks.

"You fight well for a peace-loving shaman."

Joren continued his healing spell longer than he should have.

Blood bubbled from Tul's lips. He coughed. Eyes squinted, and Joren breathed a sigh of relief.

"Fucking traitor!"

It was Aram who spoke.

The boy staggered to his feet nearby. He pointed a shaky spear in the shaman's direction.

Joren backed away from Tul, hands extended and empty. He bore no weapon.

Aram lowered his head and threw himself at Joren with a surge of *hish*, but like most boys, and certainly all on the Isle of Faltara, Aram had no combat experience. And Joren had more than anyone knew.

Joren side-stepped the attack. He did not bother wasting his magic. With a swift kick of his foot, Aram's entire body jolted mid-air. Joren snatched the spear and twisted hard.

Aram flopped hard to the ground.

"I'll handle this, boy," the Lady Knight said with a derisive chuckle.

Aram's eyes were wide, filled with venom. "Get away from my father, you bastard!"

Joren stood between them and the back hallway, between death and everyone he cared for in this world.

Aram sprang back to his feet, and Joren leveled the bonespear at him. The boy at least had enough sense not to hurl himself at Joren without a weapon.

The knight huffed. "That bastard is the only reason your father yet breathes, boy."

"What?"

Joren met Aram's gaze. So bitter. So blinded by passion and ego.

Always trying to prove he was worth something. Just like his father. A lifetime of generational insecurity had led to this moment.

"Get your father out of here, son."

Aram hesitated.

"Go," the knight said, stepping closer. "Death is meant for either the shaman or me. No one else."

Joren kept his concentration on Salyr. She had underestimated him at the outset, but she was just as powerful in magic. And there was the godblade. But she waited until Aram had dragged his father's bloody form out of the way.

The Lady Knight stepped forward, magic seeping from her blade.

"There's no way out, shaman. My comrades will capture your family as soon as they leave the temple."

"Why haven't they come already?" he asked.

He could sense she was wary, she knew how vital timing was in war. It was the reason she'd allowed Tul and Aram to escape. She was trying to buy more time.

Joren glanced at Elder Dannsein, pinned beneath the wooden visage of the All Father. His spirit was strong, but he remained unconscious.

"You're a good soldier," Joren said. "Surely, you wouldn't allow an innocent civilian to come to harm."

She smiled and glanced at the hall behind him. Thuds resounded as Madri and the others barricaded themselves in the back temple.

Joren had been stalling too.

Salyr leapt at him.

Joren released a surge of magic that stunned her. But she settled on her feet easily this time, a soft pulse of *hish* absorbing most of his blow.

"You've fought well, but I sense your weariness, shaman. You've only a few more attacks like that. And then, what?"

The knight shot forward, swinging the godblade.

"Now, Madri!" Joren shouted as he released one more surge of *hish*.

———

Malik's mother formed a coalescence of flame between her palms and sent it roaring down the hall. A fiery wall consumed the way to the main temple, sealing them off from Joren and the Lady Knight. The temple's back doorway was barricaded by tables and chairs and anything else they'd been able to find. The only escape was through the shaman's tunnel.

Yuri and Surel waited within the Sacred Hall, while Malik, Ulgar, and Ava hurried into the healing chambers. Smoke seeped into the room, thick and suffocating.

Malik focused *hish* on his lungs, easing his breathing as best he could.

Ruan lay upon the surgery table, unmoving, leather straps fixed to his arms and legs.

Swiftly as they could, all three of them released the straps. Ulgar took Ruan's shoulders and Malik grabbed onto the boy's boots, and together they heaved him up off the table.

At the sudden motion, Ruan stirred, arms flailing. Malik lost his grip, and all three of them fell to the ground. The boy's eyes went wide. He coughed violently.

Ava sent a calming surge of *hish*, and Ruan stilled again.

"Hurry!" Madri shouted from the hall. "I can't hold back the flames much—"

There was a crash. Flame and smoke surged as one of the rafters collapsed down the hall.

Malik and Ulgar staggered from the healing chambers and rushed for the tunnels, Ava hobbling after.

Heat pressed all around. Ava concentrated more magic on Ruan's mind, keeping him calm, though he shifted his neck as they moved.

Then, the magic ceased, and Ruan squirmed.

Another crash.

Flames raced along the roof of the hall, sending sparks.

Ava shrieked.

From the flaming debris behind them, the Lady Knight appeared, hair smoking, godblade shimmering. The woman latched onto Ava's cloak and jerked her back.

"Get Ruan out of here!" Ava shouted.

Madri remained near the entrance to the Sacred Hall, arms extended toward the wall of flames, warding them back as Malik and Ulgar staggered past. Yuri and Surel stood at the entrance, behind the now-toppled bookcase, and dragged Ruan through.

Malik hurried back to his mother's side.

Down the corridor, the knight clutched Ava before her like a shield, as flames bore down on them. Ava cried out. Flames shot up her skirt.

Unfazed, the knight shoved her forward.

Madri did not speak to Malik. She did not have to. He could feel his mother's spirit warning him, pressing against his own.

With everything he had left, Malik sent *hish* surging down the hall.

The knight staggered back at the impact, and Ava shirked her grasp, throwing herself to the ground. Madri launched herself at the Lady Knight in the same instant, and the two women disappeared in a rush of fire.

"Mother!" Malik ran forward.

The heat was sweltering. Flames filling the corridor. His skin felt like it would peel straight off his bones. And he froze.

His mother was gone. There was nothing Malik could do. His power was so drained, he knew the flames would consume him.

"Shaman! Help me!"

Malik turned.

Ulgar was dragging Ava away from the raging wall of flames, and Malik was jolted back to reality. To the mission his father had given him.

Get the girl to the gate...

Malik hurried to them. He and Ulgar pulled Ava into the Sacred Hall and shoved the door closed behind them. The runic seals glowed as they activated.

There was a thud behind the runemarked wood, and terror swept over Malik. He couldn't feel his mother's spirit.

But what if...

"Don't!" Ulgar grabbed his wrist.

"I can't leave her!" Malik shouted.

More pounding.

"No!" Ulgar shouted. "If it's the knight—"

Surel helped Ava into the tunnel, both of them coughing in the smoke-filled chamber. Malik turned back to the door, reached for the warding seals.

The door was searing to the touch. Malik couldn't feel either of his parent's resonances, and the fear was more palpable than the heat at his fingers.

What if his mother was on the other side of this gods-damned door? What if he was merely too exhausted to sense her?

"Remember the Spires, Malik!" Ulgar shouted, pulling on his arm.

Petyr Bromsein's face flashed before him, a boyish grin stretching wide. And then, the gust of wind took him to his death. Having pushed his luck a fraction too far.

Malik withdrew his hand from the door.

The runes glowed in the smoke, a haunting green. Still sealed.

Ulgar pulled him back toward the tunnel.

Screams echoed somewhere in the temple beyond, and tears streamed down Malik's cheeks as he followed Ulgar into the dark.

WHISPER

The world was searing heat and blinding fury. Salyr was gone. But she'd left her mark on Joren in the end. As flames erupted from the other side of the temple, Joren resisted the powerful Knight of Caadron one last time. It was not enough.

Salyr had dealt a devastating wound to Joren's shoulder, her godblade piercing straight through bone and sinew. His entire right side was completely useless now. Arm hanging at his side, hand dragging, he crawled across the central hall, trying to find an escape from the consuming smoke and flame.

The *hish* was nearly drained from his spirit, and Joren felt pain beyond anything he'd ever experienced.

A section of roof collapsed near the back hallway. The heart of the blaze. Distant shouts and screams drifted from somewhere beyond his clouded vision. Joren could not sense his family any longer. His spirit was fading, and his mind was numb.

Joren's eyes watered. The entire temple chamber was engulfed in flames. He thought he was near the hole in the wall where he'd launched the knight.

Distant shouts. He felt a dim sense of *hish* around him as villagers attempted to ward back the flames from outside. No one dared venture inside the temple.

Joren wished he could draw some of that breath of the gods for himself, but his spirit was too spent. Through the smoke, he finally found the edge of the room.

And realized with horror, that he'd found the wrong wall.

Flames shot up tapestries, along walls. The toppled visage of the All Father was ablaze.

Muffled screams.

God's breath! Elder Dannsein!

The man was still pinned beneath the statue. Joren did not know if either of them had any prayer of escape, but he knew he could not abandon the elder.

Joren dragged himself closer. His pain had grown distant, a mental practice cultivated across his lifetime to control his own mind's awareness. Though it would not help the damage to his body. His skin blistered in the consuming heat. Eyes stung.

Somehow, he kept moving, and that was all that mattered.

"Thank—the gods!" Dannsein coughed, tears streaking down his cheeks. The man had managed to form a ward around himself, but his spiritual strength was waning.

Joren lifted his voice as loud as he could. "When I say, withdraw your ward. Focus all your *hish* on the statue."

"But it's on fire!"

"It will burn us both, but I cannot lift it alone." Joren positioned himself, with his left boot braced against the body of the statue. His mental shield evaporated. The heat was agonizing, and he could ignore it no longer.

"Now!"

Joren heaved his left leg with all his remaining strength, and Dannsein pushed with all the magic he could muster.

The statue rolled off the elder's chest, down his legs. Dannsein screamed, still pinned. Joren repositioned himself and shoved again with his left foot.

His entire body was pain and exhaustion.

At last, Dannsein's legs slipped free. He brushed flames from his pants and scrambled to his feet. He grabbed Joren's shoulder and tried to lift him up.

"Come on, shaman!"

Joren slumped on the ground. Mind, body, spirit were utterly spent.

His vision blurred in the heat. Joren tried to roll himself over, but he could barely move. His boots were tatters. His right side was immovable.

"Get out!" Joren's voice croaked.

"You saved my life. I'm not leaving you, shaman."

Joren tried to move again with Dannsein pulling at his shoulder.

"Go, damn you!" Joren yelled.

Dannsein heaved at Joren, and his vision swam as his body lurched.

Joren rolled. Pain shot up his injured arm. Hands gripped his shoulders. Too many hands.

Joren's eyes stung, but he knew his wife's spirit anywhere. Even here, at the end.

She pulled his face to look at her. Flames glanced off her body like a shower of water, her magic warding off the conflagration. It was incredible. Beautiful.

"Don't you dare give up!" Madri shouted. "Help me, Dannsein."

Together, they took hold of his arms. Pain rippled through Joren's bones, down the right side of his body.

But they jerked Joren to his feet, and they were moving.

A crunch behind them. Sparks flying around like flecks of stars. Joren stumbled.

Dannsein's hand slipped away. The man howled.

Madri turned, and Joren's legs gave out. He slumped onto his face.

Madri rushed to ward off the flames from Dannsein's clothes. She cried out in pain, unable to draw enough *hish* to protect them all.

Through the smoke and the tears, Joren saw the gap in the wall, feet away. They were so close.

Another crash.

And Joren's head thudded against the floor. Something heavy seared his back.

Dannsein blurred past him and leapt through the opening in the wall.

Joren's vision roiled like waves in a storm.

His spirit was slipping away. He saw everything as though he were floating above his body, pinned to the floor by a fallen rafter. The heat was gone. The pain ebbed away.

A hand gripped his own, and he was back beneath the flaming beam, again. But he felt nothing. Only warmth. No pain.

His wife heaved against the beam. Her skin bubbled with burns, her magic unable to ward it off any longer.

"Get out, Madri!"

It came out so softly he was not sure he'd managed to voice the words.

His love's face twisted with horror. Madri heaved at the beam again.

"Go! Please!"

Joren brushed against her spirit. Managing one last whisper of *hish*, as he slipped into the Beyond.

There were no words.

Only love. That was all that was left of his existence in this life.

Madri released his hand, her gaze finding his one last time.

And then, she was gone, and there were only flames.

True wisdom is this:
There are many paths.
And there is only One.

—Book I, verse twenty of *The Paths of Fjuriin*

CHAPTER 48

ON THE BRINK

Urla Pelasius dreamed of fiery skies over a dark sea. Wind ripped through her braids, and she clung to her husband's waist as Voltari shot over a hillside, and the heavens opened up before them. The world stretched to the horizon, infinitely beautiful.

Her husband's shaggy dark hair whipped in the wind. The dragon dove, sending a thrill through Urla's entire body. She shrieked with joy.

Just before the incredible beast pulled up, Urla woke in her tent back in the Faltari encampment.

She was jolted from the memory-laced dream, realizing that the shriek had not been her own.

Urla bolted upright and sprang to her feet, drawing a dagger.

Shouts filled the camp.

Her tent flap shot open, and her young lieutenant Caliphus entered.

"Lady Consul, you must hurry."

"Lieutenant, what in the Abyss is going on?"

"There's a fire at the temple!"

By the time Urla reached the temple, some of the villagers had managed to douse most of the flames with a mix of water and magic. The sky was still dark. The nights were so bloody long this far north, even in early autumn.

The roof of the temple had caved in, and the main prayer hall was exposed by a massive hole in the front wall. The street was filled with smoke, and Urla coughed as she hurried over.

Several soldiers investigated, picking their way carefully amongst smoldering beams. More villagers doused the wood with buckets of water.

Urla spotted the shaman's wife, kneeling over her husband's body at the edge of the carnage.

Joren was barely recognizable, the burns were so extreme. It reminded Urla of the carnage after a Rain of Fire.

"The Lady Knight was in there," Caliphus said.

The answers were fragmentary. Ava Rykus had been found. The shamans were traitors. Salyr and the village elders had confronted them. Caliphus was sent for reinforcements. By the time he came back, the temple was ablaze.

Villagers and soldiers scrambled all around her. Two of the village elders were gravely injured, and Faltari healers were applying spells while both men groaned in pain.

An impending sense of dread hung over Urla like a storm as she neared.

A tall soldier blocked her path to the temple. She could not recall his name. He was a transfer after the Sigan campaign.

"Lady Consul, we haven't yet determined—"

She did not wait for the rest. Urla shoved past the man and walked through the hole in the temple wall.

Smoke filled her vision in the low light. All the walls were stained black. One of the supporting pillars had given out, and a section of roof was exposed above it. The far side of the entry hall was completely caved in. Parts of the floor had collapsed too, but she could see a path.

Shrieks erupted from somewhere down the hall. A crash. A section of roof collapsed deeper in the building.

Someone grabbed her from behind.

"Unhand me!" Urla commanded.

But the soldier pulled her back toward the hole in the wall.

"My son was in there. I have to—"

More screams.

Urla slipped from the soldier's grasp and stepped further into the room.

"Urla, wait!"

A shout from outside. Caliphus. Only he would be so bold as to use her first name.

She turned to find Caliphus holding onto the shaman's wife. The woman was shackled. Urla hadn't noticed that when she passed moments ago.

"Consul Pelasius," Madri said. "Your son isn't there."

"Where is he?" she demanded, rage overwhelming her.

"Please come out of there," Madri said. "And I will tell you what happened this night."

———

Ava's leg hadn't hurt this bad since her Desert trial at the academy.

They'd been slogging through the woods for nearly an hour. Ulgar led them straight up the steep sides of the fjord. The skies were dark with thick clouds, or perhaps it was smoke, but slowly, the night seeped into a pre-dawn gloom as they climbed.

For a while, Ava heard voices. Shouts echoing on the wind, coming from the village. Sometimes, they sounded close, but Ulgar insisted they were far ahead and it was just a trick of the mountains.

They pressed on. It was all Ava could do not to fall behind even while Malik and Yuri were carrying an unconscious Ruan with no stretcher. The shaman's sister remained close to her brother's side.

Ava brought up the rear. The agony in her leg was constant, even with a makeshift cane Ulgar had fashioned from a socha branch.

Everything smelled like smoke and singed hair. She had burns on her ankles and arms, but they didn't seem to be severe.

All she could do was focus on one step and the next and try to numb her mind to the discomfort.

They approached the crest of a steep embankment, and all at once, her foothold was gone and she was tumbling. Sliding.

Ava heaved, scraping her arm as she fought to remain on her front. She latched on to an exposed tree root and stopped, heart pounding.

She bit the inside of her lip to stop from screaming. The others came rushing down. A hand brushed her shoulder. Warmth spread over her leg, and then a blessed absence of pain.

"I'm sorry I'm no help with your old wounds," Malik said. "But that should ease the burns."

The shaman hadn't spoken a word to anyone since they exited the tunnel beneath the village. Ava could feel intense sadness radiating from the boy.

Surel knelt by Ava's side, her hand at her back to steady her. Gods, she hated the attention, but there was nothing for it now. Speed was the utmost necessity, and Ava was spent.

"We're nearly there," Ulgar said, motioning them up the mountain. "We must hurry."

Malik and Surel helped Ava to her feet, and they were moving again.

Her mind reeled at all that had happened. The shaman and his wife were captured, possibly dead. And their chances at stealth with this mission to the Spires were entirely lost.

The Atticans knew Ava had remained behind after the attack.

She had failed.

Ulgar stopped at the top of a ridge and peered around.

"Oh, thank the gods!"

A woman's voice. It was startling, but Ava was too tired to jump.

Ulgar relaxed his shoulders and turned. The woman embraced him.

A minute later Ava and Surel joined them.

"Olma?" Surel asked.

"It's a relief to see you," Malik said. "She's the Feathered Serpent clan elder," he added for Ava's benefit. She looked familiar. Dimly, Ava recalled her father speaking with the woman during the Festival of the Fading Sun.

They reached the nook in the mountainside. The elder pulled Surel and Malik into an embrace.

"Your parents..."

The young shaman shook his head. "My father is gone. I felt his spirit untether as we left the village. My mother..." Malik's voice trembled. "I don't know. She stayed back so we could escape. She was in great pain. But I lost her resonance. Perhaps she escaped. We couldn't risk..."

His anger and sorrow were potent. Ava's mind clouded at the intensity of his emotion, mixed with her own guilt. It was times like these, she hated her gifts. Her own feelings were enough to bear.

"The boy?" Olma asked, looking at Ruan.

Yuri and Malik had set him down near a wooden doorway cut straight into the mountainside.

"Consul Pelasius's son," Malik said.

Olma knelt down to examine him. Ruan hadn't woken again since they first brought him from the healing chamber.

"My father operated on him last night to repair injuries from the festival attack," Malik explained, gesturing at the bandages wrapped around his head. "That Lady Knight came to check on him. And all the Abyss was let loose. It was either bring him or let him die in the fire."

"You made the right choice," Olma said.

Ava could feel the shaman's uncertainty, though he did not voice it. Everything had been a matter of moments.

A tinge of shame reddened Malik's cheeks, and Ava felt a wall go up in his mind.

"And you," the elder woman said, her piercing gaze settling on Ava. "The Valucian rebel's daughter."

It was not anger in Olma's voice. Ava sensed no tell from her spirit. The woman was well-trained. Hard to read, like Malik had been the day they'd met. Olma stepped closer and peered into Ava's eyes.

"My, you look so much like her..."

"Like her... you knew..."

Olma nodded. "Elora?"

"How?" Malik asked.

The elder smiled. "Your father isn't the only person on the island who had a life-altering *uhmskara* back in their youth. Yes, I knew your mother. Your father, too, though he barely remembers me. Still, it was enough to find him when the gods demanded it."

"My fath—" Ava's voice caught in her throat. "Is he..."

Olma motioned to the door in the hillside, which seemed to belong to some sort of permanent shelter.

"Come, all of you."

Yuri and Ulgar carried Ruan through the doorway. Then, Malik and Surel. Ava entered last, alone.

Malik and Yuri rushed forward to greet Riese Torendeil, and Ava's father pushed toward her.

Ava felt his relief wash over her before he reached her. He pulled her into an embrace, and Ava broke into sobs she hadn't known she was suppressing as she collapsed into her father's arms.

"Thank the gods," he murmured, crying too.

Olma snickered. "Oh, he thanks them now. But it was all I could do to lead him away and trust that you would escape from the village to find us. But of course, Ulgar is a fine boy, and the gods are good, so I knew you were in excellent hands."

Her father shrugged. "My wife was always more devout, you may recall." He helped Ava over to a small bed in the corner of the hut and turned back to the woman.

"How did you get here?" Ava asked.

"Olma found us outside the village. Moments before the temple erupted into flames."

There was another bed beside hers, and Yuri and Ulgar laid Ruan down. Malik spent some time administering healing spells for Ruan, while Olma did the same for her.

Then, the whole group gathered around to hear the full tale.

How Ulgar had seen Aram following Yuri back to the temple and chose to tell the Serpent clan elder all he knew.

"Ulgar hurried back to help. And I kept a third eye out for outsiders. I expected Rykus would be returning before the Atticans reached the Spires, if he'd left his daughter behind. Lucky for him there was so much commotion in Yerida, or someone else might have detected him first. But my senses are keen. My mum always said I could've been a shaman if I'd been born into it. Anyway, I found Rykus and Riese. Ulgar did his part to aid the rest of you. And here we are."

The room went silent. They all glanced at one another, the same thought shared.

"What now?" asked Surel.

Olma shrugged and turned to Rykus. "Captain?"

With one hand on Ava's shoulder, he turned to the others.

"The gate at the top of your Spires must be destroyed before the empire reaches those dragon eggs. That is the mission. And we can use all the help we can get."

Malik and the others nodded, but Ava pulled away from her father's grip. "And the rest of the eggs?"

Her father shook his head. "Plans have changed. We dare not risk a venture into the Abyss."

Ava glared at him. "Without more Rebelmounts, we'll never be able to form a true resistance."

Olma scowled. "The Attican expedition to the Spires may be delayed a short while, but rest assured, they will be right behind you."

"And if we fail, our rebellion will end before it truly begins," Ava's father said. "It is the council's decision."

"The council wouldn't know a wise plan if it hit them in the nethers," Ava shot back.

Olma bit back a smirk.

Her father shook his head. "Destroying the gate is an act that could secure Elyan support. Even with a few more Rebelmounts, we stand no chance of taking on Attica without further aid. But if we can cut off the empire's entire source of power for good..."

Ava met her father's gaze. She could feel his fear. There was a greater tragedy than what had happened last night that lingered in his mind. Clouding his judgment. He pulled back, sensing her intrusion.

"What aren't you telling me?" she demanded.

"Ava, now's not the time!"

"Father, what happened while you were away? I've never known you to take the safe path. I deserve to know why you're insisting on it now."

He grimaced. "We have a mission to complete, Ava. That is all that—"

"Your island," said Riese. "It is gone."

"Gone?" said Ava, feeling a surge of pent up rage in her father's mind at the words.

"The Dragonmounts burned Eòreth to the ground," Riese continued. "In retaliation for the eggs you stole."

"The entire island?" Ava asked.

Her vision swam, picturing the rocky beaches and lush hillsides of her girlhood, engulfed in flames. Her voice was barely a whisper. "And the people?"

Her father held her gaze, eyes misty. "Every village. Every home. Every gods-damned structure, and every person within. All the people who served our house are dead. The will of the Dragon Emperor."

"Father, I—"

He cradled the side of her cheek and looked in her eyes. "We cannot afford to fail, Ava. Attica has mounted an attack on Chardonia. The Age of Fire has already come."

Ava gripped his trembling hand. She drew on no magic, but she could not shake her resolve. "Even if we destroy the source of the empire's power, they still have dozens of Dragonmounts. Do you think it will be enough for Elya to risk their own future? Their Flying Armada?"

"I don't know, dear."

"Well, I do," Ava said. "Elya will sit back and bide their time as they always have. Wait for some distant future when Attica's power has waned. Yes, we must destroy the gate, but if we don't get more eggs, our rebellion will be over."

Silence fell over the room once more.

"She's right, you know."

Ava's heart leapt at the voice.

Ruan lifted himself to sit up in his bed. He squinted as he took in his surroundings. Malik came to his side.

"You've been unconscious for two days," the shaman said. "Swelling in the brain. My father operated last night."

"Before the fire," Ruan said.

Malik nodded.

Ruan did not seem to notice. He turned his head, still squinting.

"You remember the fire?" Ava asked.

"I was in and out of things for a long time. Sometimes it was dream, sometimes reality. Sometimes something between." He turned his head. "For a while, it was hard to discern which from which. Until I figured out that it was reality that was dark."

Ava's body felt cold and hollow. "Ruan, what's wrong?"

His face was expressionless. Even after days of unconsciousness and pain and trauma, he remained composed. So Fjuriin.

"I... I think I've gone blind."

Chapter 49

Until the Bloody End

Malik did not feel guilt about what happened to Ruan. He did not even feel guilty for not feeling guilty, as he usually might, his deepest spirit chastened by his father's years of instruction. Not this time.

His father had sacrificed his life to save Ruan. If he hadn't performed that operation, the Atticans would not have cared about a disturbance at the Faltari temple.

And Malik's father might still be alive.

In his deepest spirit, Malik wished his father had never operated and the boy had been left to die. For that wish, he did feel a small amount of guilt, but it was drowned out by the other raging emotions that had overwhelmed him the minute they reached the safety of the herder's hut.

As they'd fled, Malik had suppressed the soul-crushing emptiness of his father's soul untethering from his body. Even from a distance, it had been more painful than Petyr's death. More painful than his brother's.

Malik felt more numb than he'd felt that freezing night in the Spires with Petyr and Ulgar.

There was no sorrow, only anger and hatred.

The hut had turned silent as they rested for the last time before the mission.

Ava remained close to Ruan, though neither spoke more than a few words. Olma, blessedly, had remained close to Surel, comforting her until she drifted to sleep.

Malik did feel guilty about that. He knew he needed to remain strong for his sister. But it was all he could do to keep himself from plunging into oblivion.

Though this was their last chance at sleep for likely a day or more, Malik could not switch off his mind. Trapped in a spiral. His father was dead. Gone. Just like that, and Malik was not prepared to deal with that reality.

Yuri and Ulgar had little trouble sleeping. They lay on the floor across the room, breathing heavily, chests rising and falling with an infuriating solemnity. Yuri most of all.

That dumb bastard, Malik thought.

Ava slept in fits. Ruan just sat there in silence. Eyes open, drifting but never settling.

And Malik cursed him once more.

To his credit, the Attican boy did not grumble or curse Joren, or even Rykus, whose creatures were responsible for the injuries that had led Urla Pelasius to seek shaman healing in the first place.

"Do you want to talk about it?"

He'd thought Riese was sleeping near Surel, but she plopped down beside him on the floor of the hut. Before he could answer, she pulled him into an embrace.

Amidst all the chaos, Malik hadn't realized just how relieved he was that Riese was here. That she was unharmed and believed in this rebellion too. A voice in his spirit reminded him there was hope in that. Hope to fulfill the mission Malik's father had left to him before he sacrificed himself.

Get the girl to the gate, son.

Malik pulled Riese tighter. "I'm just glad you're here. Alive."

She held him for a moment longer, then pulled back and met his gaze. "No to the talking then? Because you have the look of someone trapped in their own head."

Malik shrugged. "I just want to move. The empire won't be sitting around."

"You think imperial officers like Pelasius don't pause to plot their next moves?"

Olma and Rykus were whispering urgently back and forth, concocting some sort of plan of their own. Malik was frustrated about that too. Just left here awaiting instruction.

"We don't have time to waste. We—"

Riese grasped his forearm. "*We* don't? Or is this about you?"

Malik did not speak for a moment. Riese always knew how to cut through his bullshit.

"We can't afford to fail. I can't fail him."

"Your father?"

Tears streaked down Malik's cheeks. "There are so many things I wish I could take back since Derrin died. So many things I shouldn't have said. And should have said. My father was a better shaman than our people deserved. Than I deserved—"

All the sorrow Malik had been suppressing burst forth, and he wept.

Riese sat there, a hand at his back.

"Your father knew you loved him," she whispered. "The same way I knew, even when you withdrew from me and Yuri after Derrin died. And you're right, Joren was a better man than any of us deserved. Do you know what I remember most about your father?"

Malik shook his head.

"After your brother died, Joren never faltered in his duty. Derrin was only one of four climbers who died that year, and even though he was grieving, Joren tended to those other families and their burial rites the same way he did every year. A week after the festival, when my uncle nearly died in that tree-felling accident, your father was there within half a day. He stayed three days in Starholm to make sure my uncle survived."

"I remember. Surel and I were both angry at him for being gone so long."

"My uncle would've died if he hadn't. No other healer could've saved him."

Malik nodded, chastened by the conversation.

"Your father knew his life was about more than himself, Malik. More than his own family."

"Yes," said Olma, drawing near. She and Rykus had finished their deliberations. "Joren always kept going. To perform the duty the gods gave him, he always said."

Malik turned to her and nodded. It hurt to think of him, but the numbness and anger were not as fierce.

"Your father never wanted to be shaman, did you know that?" Olma asked, taking a seat on the floor beside them.

Malik nodded. "Not until yesterday."

Olma chuckled. "We grew up together, and god's breath, did Joren grumble about it when we were kids. He never asked for it. The way we Faltari choose our shamans is outdated, he said."

"He wasn't wrong about that."

Olma smiled. "No, perhaps not. But something changed while he was on his Wandering, as it did for me. As I expect it's done for you all now. Make no mistake about it, this is your *uhmskara* thrust upon you. As you grow older, you begin to understand how little sway you have over life. Sure, you choose small things, day to day. To eat fish or venison. To hunt this valley or another. But the big things, they are rarely within your control. Life and death. Ancestry. Wars. And you can either go your whole life raging against your lot, or you can rise to meet it. That is what your father learned during his Wandering. Joren accepted his duty —his path, as the Fjuriin would say. And he threw every part of his mind, body, and spirit into his path until the bloody end. Your father was the best man I ever knew, son."

Malik smiled, wiping away the tears.

Riese shoved Malik playfully. "See? Your father got out of his head. Maybe there's hope for you yet."

Olma patted him on the cheek and rose to her feet. "Your father was damn proud of you, boy. Now, it's time to do his memory justice."

"You have a plan?" Malik asked.

Olma nodded over at Rykus, who was waking the others. "We've got a plan. After that, it's in the hands of the gods."

"I've only one firebomb," said Rykus, holding up his rucksack.

"And blessedly, there's only one road from Yerida," said Olma. "There is a path that goes straight through a mountain about halfway up the Soul Road. Seal that off, and it may buy you enough time to reach the eggs before the Attican company."

"Except for the Dragonmounts," said Malik. "This entire plan hinges on the assumption that Athanasius doesn't send his entire winged force to the Spires. What then?"

"You will have to be impeccably swift," said Olma. "There is no denying that. But the bulk of the enemy task force will come by foot."

"How can we be certain?" asked Riese.

"Athanasius is spread on multiple fronts," said Rykus. "The emperor is at war with Chardonia as we speak. We also know he's sending an emissary to Valucia with a peace offering in the wake of the destruction of Eòreth."

"Peace offering?" asked Malik.

"My house was intended to receive a dragon egg. Athanasius has extended that offer to another Valucian lord."

"Some offer," said Ava. "Threaten them with a Rain of Fire, then talk of peace as though nothing is awry."

"At any rate," Olma continued, "the mounts are spread out on multiple missions, not just Faltara. The emperor sent a little-known company led by a woman to carry out this mission on the ground. This is a covert operation."

"How can you be sure?" Malik asked.

Rykus smiled. "We have a rebel on the council. And a few Morphs here on the island as well."

"How many dragons, then?" asked Malik.

"We don't know. A few, certainly. But most of the fleet is currently laying waste to Chardonia."

"The world will be fixated on the southern world," said Olma. "While Athanasius's most vital mission goes on here in secret."

"To extract the eggs from the Abyss," said Rykus. "That is the mission of the Bloody Company."

"So we need to beat the Atticans to the pass," said Ulgar.

"We must move quickly and with stealth," said Rykus.

"Well, I didn't choose this herder's hut for nothing," said Olma. "There are corrals on the other side of this ridge."

Ava's eyes widened. "What do you corral on a damn mountainside?"

"Stags," said Malik.

"They move quick in the foothills," said Olma. "You'll have a chance at getting ahead. Pelasius and her Bloody Company will take alkine from Yerida. Better pack animals. Better stamina. But slow and steady. And you only need to be faster for half the journey. Riese, we'll need you to lead Rykus to the Point of the Fjord."

Riese nodded. "I know a hunter's path."

"Good," Olma said. "Ulgar and Malik will join you." Olma turned to Surel. "There are provisions here, and I think you'll find decent foraging yet, maybe even—"

"No way I'm staying behind!" Surel crossed her arms over her chest, fuming.

"You're a child, dear, I don't think—"

"Surel's right," said Malik. "My father's mission is hers too, if she wants it."

"Very well. And you, Alwensein," Olma said. Yuri had kept to himself since their initial arrival. His spirit was a storm of emotions, but in truth, Malik had hardly paid him any mind. He stood when Olma addressed him. "I think it best you stay behind, Yuri."

"Madam Elder, if I may... I don't want to remain behind either."

Malik tensed.

Olma glanced Malik's direction, but she did not need to say anything to understand Malik's thoughts on the matter.

"After all that's happened, I don't think that's a good idea."

"I can't just sit around here."

"No, indeed," said Olma. "In that, I believe you're right. I'm not sure what will come of the ship Joren meant to sail to Valgland. But I suggest you find it."

Yuri looked dismayed, but Malik could not bring himself to feel sympathy, even when his old friend turned to him, pain and remorse etched across a tremulous face.

"Malik, please, I know I bloodied this up. Let me make it right."

"It's your call, shaman," Olma said.

Malik turned to the others. Ulgar shrugged. Riese masked her true feelings, but there was no doubt about Surel. Her spirit raged.

Malik shook his head. "Olma is right, Yuri. You should stay behind."

You're a damn liability. That was the unspoken truth.

Yuri hung his head and sat back on one of the beds in the corner.

"Now, Captain," said Olma, "we must consider your daughter."

"She'll be with me and the others, of course," said Rykus.

Olma pressed tentatively. "Do you think that's wise? For this mission?"

"Ava can ride. She is going to be a bloody Dragonmount for god's sake."

Ava stepped forward. "I will not be going to the Spires."

"What?" her father demanded.

"I've got a plan to buy you more time to reach the pass. And ensure there's time to retrieve those eggs." Ava glanced back at the door to the next room, where Ruan awaited their deliberations.

"Ruan?" Rykus demanded.

"I will take him down the mountain," Ava said. "Stall Pelasius's company while you prepare the explosion at the pass."

"Right into the hands of the enemy? I can't allow it!" Rykus fumed. "No, if you're not with me, you'll remain right—"

"I will *not* bloody stay behind," Ava insisted. "But I'm not going to risk slowing the rest of you down either. I know my path, Father. I can still help the mission. In my own way."

Rykus sighed, but nodded to her. "Very well."

Olma chuckled to herself. "By the gods, I believe you got more of your mother's wits than I thought. You're sure you'll be alright on your own with the prisoner?"

"Believe me, I can handle Ruan Pelasius."

CHAPTER 50

DIVERGING PATHS

They set out together, save for Olma and Yuri, who started down the fjord on foot.

Since Yuri had been seen by several in the temple last night, it was determined that he and Olma would split up further down the fjord and arrive separately. Once the Atticans left the village, he might be able to sneak aboard one of the Faltari vessels.

Ava sensed there was more to the plan that was not being shared by either her father or Elder Marudeil. But that was in their hands now.

She had her path set before her.

Ava and the others took the mountain stags and rode off together into the thick snowpine forest. Once they reached the Point of the Fjord, she would be on her own.

Ava's father brooded silently for most of the ride, staying close and constantly eying Ruan. Perhaps trying to determine if the boy was somehow faking his injury. But Ava knew it was real. She had peered into Ruan's mind. Something she had never done before.

It had not come without guilt, like most things on this damn island, but it was necessary.

All her years at the academy, Ava had resisted the temptation to probe Ruan's mind, fearing he was only using her, fearing he felt nothing, but knowing it would be a violation of the trust her mission required she keep.

She had no choice this time. Her father had insisted on proof. What she found had only made her feel worse about the way Ruan had suffered in the wake of this mission.

Ava had felt his fear. The sorrow he fought so hard to hide. The sting of her lies coursed deep in his mind.

There was nothing for it, but perhaps there was hope yet. Ruan still cared for her, and there remained a part of him that had long questioned Attica's dominion of the world, in spite of what he'd experienced on the Isle of Faltara.

But Ruan was still a student of Dawncrest Academy, and her father was right to fear him.

If she was wrong...

No, Ava could not go there, and she certainly could not tell her father the depth of the doubts she suppressed.

For some time, they remained silent.

They were still only a league from Yerida, and sound traveled from high on the fjord. Emotions were heightened, and Ava felt them all.

Malik and Surel kept close to one another, mourning their father in silence, fearing for their mother's fate.

Ulgar worried for his family back in the village, though he did not dwell on it the way the shaman and his sister did. He seemed the sort who found peace in a clear task set before him.

Riese led the group through the thick forest, seeming to know the landscape better even than Ulgar, who'd lived all his life on this part of the island. Despite the tragedies, the young huntress looked more alive than anyone else in their party. Ava felt a sense of assurance and courage that hadn't been there only days ago. And Ava suspected it had something to do with what lay within Riese's pack.

The same bond which had swiftly faded from Ava's spirit after her father took her egg from the island the night of the attack. Would she ever see that egg again?

Her heart stirred with longing. To hold her egg. To bond and train it. To soar on crimson skies as a true Rebelmount. To finally rain vengeance down upon the empire that had oppressed her people for so many centuries.

But she swiftly pushed down those longings. If she failed this mission, none of that would come to pass.

Her father waged his own inner battle, more tense than ever, and it grew worse the farther they rode. The closer they came to the juncture where he would once again have no hand in his daughter's fate.

Fear consumed his thoughts. Ava could feel it, even without delving inside.

Finally, he gave voice to the nagging question once they'd crossed the top of a steep rise and descended into the shelter of a small valley. "Why Ava? Why must *you* be the one to take the Pelasius boy?"

It was a fair question, and Ava did not have a fair answer.

"It's my path," she said.

Something that Joren had said last night lingered in her mind.

All paths of resistance are not written in blood. The wisdom to know which path to choose. That is my prayer for myself with what is to come. That is my prayer for you, Ava Rykus.

But for a man like her father, this was not an acceptable answer.

"Your mother was the Fjuriin one," he murmured, shaking his head.

"I know," said Ava. "I used to read her journals. From when she was a girl. When she met you. When I was born. When the Uprising began to turn against us. Always, she believed. In the gods. In their Path."

Her father huffed but couldn't hold back a smile. "And do you? This is the first I've heard."

Ava smiled. "Most of my life, my own path has felt like it was laid out in stone before me. Now, the way is shrouded in fog, and I think perhaps, that is the true nature of what Mother believed. None of us know how things will end. We can only choose a direction, and step forward." She met her father's gaze.

His eyes were misty. "I cannot bear to lose you."

"You always said the cause was greater than its parts. Greater than you or me. Greater than Mother's fate."

He went silent, watching Ruan riding ahead of them, a rope fixed between Ava's stag and his. His head wrap bandages were gone now, and he wore a dark woolen herder's cap.

"I've my part to play," Ava said. "And you have your own. Trust me, Father."

"Of course, I do."

"But..."

He glanced up at Ruan again. The boy kept his chin tucked against his breast, the way he always did when he was listening intently, trying to go unnoticed.

Ava smiled. "I've done all right so far, haven't I?"

"You've been brilliant, darling. Just like your mother."

"Promise me you'll do everything in your power to retrieve those eggs."

Her father reached over and gripped her hand. "On my life."

They rode deep into the woods. The towering trees were not nearly as thick as the broad-leaf forests of Valucia and Attica, but they were taller, plunging high into the skies like spears.

When Ava looked back, she could see little of the fjord behind them. She hoped it meant no one could see them from the village. Mountains loomed above them, swaths of dark grey stone rising sharply to menacing peaks lined with much sparser trees.

Riese assured them that the mountains would be their friend, in the end, offering cover and a direct path. The traditional road to the Spires wended through easier passes south of the fjord. More manageable for wagons and provisions, but a much longer route.

Ava wouldn't have minded a smoother path. The stag moved awkwardly beneath her, especially on the steeper rises, jostling her whole body as the beast picked its way over rocks and wended between sharp snowpine branches. Ava's wounds from the night before had healed thanks to Olma and Malik. But there was a dull throbbing in her leg that would not leave, and the jarring gait and brisk air didn't help.

All she could do was press on, trying to push her mind to that place where pain was distant.

It was late morning when they reached a sparse meadow, stretching before a great plain of scree. The walls of mountains shot upward on either side of them, peaks brushed with snow, and directly ahead, they faced an icy wall of pale blue.

"Gods damn," she muttered.

"That's the glacier that carved this fjord," said Malik. "So my father claimed." His voice hitched at the mention of Joren.

"This is where we part ways," said Riese. She pointed to the right, where a small path led back into the forest. Back down into the fjord and to the south. "It's a hunting track," she said, "but it connects to the Soul Road a couple miles down. It starts steep, but levels off as you get close. Keep bearing south, and you'll reach the road. We must move quickly while we're outside the cover of the forest."

They were miles from the village, but what hung unspoken between them was the knowledge of what might spot them from the skies. Dragons were coming to Faltara, if they weren't here already.

Ava's father drew his stag up close to hers and gripped her hand. "Be safe, my dear."

Ava rolled her eyes. "Don't be so cliché, Father. You didn't raise me to be a dithering fool in the face of danger."

He took a deep breath, then smiled. "No, indeed."

"This is bigger than us, don't you bloody forget it," she whispered.

Her father grimaced. It reminded her of the way he looked after he'd just taken a walk with her mother. An inevitable sadness.

"I love you, Ava." Her father squeezed her hand, then pulled away.

Malik approached. "Not being a dithering fool doesn't require ignoring the danger."

Ava smirked. "Jokes are the only way the dangers don't take hold, shaman, didn't you know?"

"Maybe I should try it sometime. If we survive I'll add it to my list of self-improvements."

Ava laughed. "A long list, I expect, shaman."

"Not if you never write it down."

She dipped her head. "I enjoy sparring, Malik. And assuming this isn't an entire shitstorm of a mission, we'll need recruits for what's ahead."

"Recruits?"

"You Faltari have magic abilities I would very much like to exploit. If we survive."

Ava pulled her reins and urged her stag forward, its hooves sinking into the scree.

With a soft jolt at the rope tethering them together, Ruan's beast followed after. Ava did not look back until they reached the cover of the forest.

By that time, the others were already halfway up the precipitous side of the glacial valley. Ava drew a long breath, pushing back against the dread that threatened her spirit.

Ruan pulled up beside her, expressionless. His bound hands gripped his reins tight, remaining impressively steady all the ride up through the fjord.

"Never knew how well you could ride a stag," Ava said.

"Before my father would let me ride with him on Voltari, he put me on the back of every land beast that could move. Even a desert razorback. This is nothing."

She had always enjoyed hearing about Ruan's upbringing. No rebellions. No childhood tragedies. Sure, his parents were bloody Attican nobles—and soldiers—but they had always struck her as different from the other academy parents. The Pelasiuses never inordinately celebrated Ruan's achievements, always pushed him to be better. Like her own father.

Ava peered down the hunting track before them. It was narrow, barely even a path at all, just a faint ribbon of trodden grass and worn terrain, winding through tight copses of trees.

"It's steep and rocky to start. You may want to hold tight."

"I don't need you to narrate the ride," said Ruan. "I've managed well enough so far. In fact, there's really no need for us to speak at all."

Ava urged her beast forward. "If you say so."

Chapter 51

Dragonmount

In silence, Ava and Ruan ventured into the thick of the Faltari forest. The path wove steeply down to a narrow canyon, and the jostling was a constant source of discomfort for Ava, especially since the Faltari did not use saddles. She did not complain, but she would have killed for one of the alchemical pain-tonics back at the academy.

The ride grew smoother as the land leveled off.

Ava could sense Ruan's irritation growing as the silence stretched. It was difficult to tell time against the overcast skies, but she thought it must be midday based on her hunger. She longed to feel the sun's warmth on her back. The morning had been crisp, and the middle of the day was not much better.

"Autumn is short here," Riese had told her during the morning ascent. "We joke how you blink and it's the dead of winter."

"How do you endure in such a place?" she'd asked.

"Mead," Riese had joked. "And dreamsmoke."

Ava smiled. She hoped the Faltari survived. She liked them an awful lot more than the Atticans she'd grown up around.

Finally, they reached a ridgeline that looked down over the treetops. The land swept down the fjord for many miles. Ava could see the faint glimmering of the sea in the distance.

Sun must be shining somewhere down there.

She could not make out the harbor or the village of Yerida from here. A narrow valley stretched long and green to the south, and to the east, mountains plunged into the clouds.

The world was utterly still. No signs of marching armies. No evidence of humanity whatsoever. Perfectly serene. Thoughts of her mother seeped in. Hazy memories of walks in the meadow outside their estate. Playing with her in the gardens as a small child. It was not until much later that she learned how rare that was for a noble's daughter. Most of her classmates had been raised by nursemaids.

The thought sent sorrow through her spirit. But they were warm memories.

"Are we close?" asked Ruan.

"We're getting there."

"Why did we stop?"

"Do you really want to know?"

Ruan grimaced.

Ava did not pry, but she sensed a wavering in Ruan's mind. One that had been festering since he woke in the hands of rebels.

"The view reminded me of my home. My girlhood. Before every part of my life revolved around advancing in the academy. Before every move became a..."

"Calculation?" Ruan offered.

"Something like that. It was not an easy time. But... you didn't want to talk, as I recall."

Ruan smirked. "Never thought I'd see the day when *that* stopped Ava Rykus from carrying on. I may not be the most talkative person in the world, but... I don't actually love silence."

"You like to listen. To learn about people. When it's silent, you're left only with a troubled mind."

"Now, more than ever."

Ava did not know what to say to that. It was a rare and uncomfortable feeling. To be unsure of the right words, the right moves. Perhaps taking Ruan was a grave mistake.

Ruan shrugged. "Well, go on, if you feel like talking, then. The view brought memories..."

"After the Valucian Uprising was ended, the healers worried I would not recover. I spent my girlhood in rehabilitation. Building up movements that had once been so gods-damned ordinary, I never knew you could take them for granted. It was exhausting. My father used to carry me on his back up the hills behind our home. On the other side, you couldn't see the villages or shipyards in disrepair. All the destruction. It was just... nature. That's what the view reminded me of."

And now, Eòreth is gone, she thought.

"I... I'm sure it must be beautiful." Ruan's face tensed.

"I'm sorry, Ruan, I..."

"Don't pity me to make yourself feel better. Accept the consequences of your actions."

"I do. Believe me, I know plenty about consequences."

"Don't act like what happened to us is the same. You chose this rebellion."

"I was fucking four, Ruan. My choice was made for me long ago. And I've lived with it all my life."

Silence stretched on again. Birds chirped. Wind rushed through the branches. Clouds began to part, and a beam of light shot over the valley below.

"Anyway, I survived the consequences. Which is more than can be said of my mother. Do you want to know how it happened?"

"Ava, you've never wanted to discuss her, so why would—"

"It was because of me."

"What?"

"It wasn't Attica that made my mother into that empty shell of a person. It was me."

"What do you mean?" he asked, softer now.

"The healers were right. I shouldn't have recovered from my injuries. I shouldn't have ever walked again. But my mother wouldn't have it. We journeyed to the Free City."

"You didn't..."

"My mother sought the help of a Beirusian witch. That sort of magic, it comes at a cost. And my mother paid it."

"Ava, I..." Ruan's voice drifted with the wind.

"Perhaps if we'd sought the help of a Faltari shaman, the price would not have been so high."

"Like my price," said Ruan. "That's what you think my blindness is? Not the shoddy work of some crazed shaman at the edge of the world?"

Ava bit back tears. "That shaman was a good man, Ruan, and you're lucky to be alive. That's what I think. I thank the gods you're alive. You've no idea what I would give to talk to my mother like this."

Ruan was silent. Emotion swelling inside him.

"Sometimes I wish she'd failed," Ava said. "I would gladly have remained a cripple if it meant my mother were still here. All our schoolmates thought me a damn cripple anyway."

Ruan chuckled. "Iriana said that behind your back the whole trip. Guess, you showed her, eh?" His voice turned dark. He was probing.

"I don't regret what happened to Iriana Thenius," Ava said. "But it doesn't mean I enjoyed watching her die. Even if she did represent everything that's wrong with Attica."

Ruan nodded. "And if it had been me Campos had chosen, and not her? If I'd have been there..."

A tear streaked down Ava's cheek. "I would not change what I've done, but if there had been a way to keep you safe, I would have. I tried..."

Ruan huffed. "You gonna tell me you're the reason Campos chose Iriana instead of me?"

"No," Ava said. "The general's plans for your house were set before we even arrived."

"My mother is Lady Consul now," Ruan said.

"Yes," said Ava. "She is."

"Campos never intended for me to bond. It was just a reason to bring my mother. To groom her to become his replacement."

Ava turned quiet. There was more beyond that. For this opportunity never would have been presented to Campos, had Ruan's father not fallen during the Sigan campaign, but she feared that was a bridge too far. She could only hope that—

Her skin pricked. Her spirit swelled as a rage overcame her senses.

Wind rushed through the trees directly overhead, sending branches flying.

The stag jolted beneath her, and Ava's stomach churned as she flew airborne. She landed on her back in an enormous thorn bush, barbs piercing her skin through her clothes and cloak.

She screamed, rolled. More pain. Blood dripping down her brow, her arms, between her fingers.

Hooves thundered as her stag raced off and disappeared into the woods.

Somehow, Ruan remained mounted. The rope tethering their two beasts had snapped. His stag bucked beneath him, but he gripped the reins with furious determination.

Ava groaned. She tried to move, but the thorns only gripped her tighter.

"Ah!" she whimpered.

"Maybe I'll never be Dragonmount," said Ruan, "but my father taught me to sense when a dragon is close."

The forest erupted with torrents of wind and a roar that made the air itself quake.

Dark masses shot over the treetops. With horror, Ava glimpsed the sharp lines of a gargantuan wing.

"Ruan!" Ava said. "No, please."

"I'm sorry." Ruan kicked his stag forward, and the beast trotted down the path, hooves thudding and fading quickly.

With a shriek of pain, Ava wrenched herself from the tangle of thorns, shredding her cloak and much of her torso in the process. She rolled onto the hard ground, eyes blurring with agonizing tears. She latched onto a sapling and pulled herself to her feet.

Ruan stopped at the clearing a hundred yards ahead. Sunlight beamed down through a crack in the clouds. He waved his arms at the sky, shouting.

Ava staggered back up the path. Wind rushed overhead, and an enormous shadow passed over her.

But she didn't stop. Couldn't stop. Not yet.

Heart racing, Ava scrambled up the hillside deeper into the forest, leaving the path to submerge herself in the thick foliage. She crossed down into a small ravine. Her foot lost purchase, and she pitched backward, sliding, rolling. She landed hard on her stomach. The woods darkened.

Wings hovered above the trees, flapping hard to hold the dragon in place. Hot sulfuric fumes engulfed the forest, making her gag.

But such a large beast could not possibly land in this foliage.

Ava pulled herself up once more, snatching up a limb of snowpine to use as a cane, steadying herself enough to scramble out of the loose scree and pine needles that had led to her fall.

Once she got out of the ravine, the going got easier again, the slope tapering off as she neared the top of a ridge.

Ava pushed past the pain, hurrying faster.

The top of the ridge was nearly in reach.

Snap!

Her stick splintered, caught between boulders, and she slipped again. Pain lanced up her leg as she dragged herself back to her feet.

Wings flapped furiously. A roar sent shivers through her body.

Ava did not move.

She had known the minute she saw the dragons that it was fruitless to try to escape. She could only hope she'd bought enough time for the others.

Somewhere to her left she heard the thud of boots, the crunch of footsteps on the forest floor. The ring of a drawn blade.

Ava turned.

A tall man strode down the slope.

The Dragonmount's black hair hung loose, flaring out from his helm. He wore black leathern riding armor with a flaming dragon emblazoned on the chest.

Slowly, he removed his helm, and Ava gasped, recognizing the man's face.

Athanasius's thin lips curled into a smile.

"There you are, Ms. Rykus," the Dragon Emperor said. "Now, where are the others?"

CHAPTER 52

DRAGONSIGHT

Riese felt the dragons before she saw them.

The mountains were silent sentinels towering above their party as they descended a narrow pass beyond the glacial wall. The autumn air cut through her cloak, nipping at the exposed skin of her neck and fingers. A valley of boulders swept before them, down to a thick copse of socha, crimson leaves blazing against their white limbs.

The world was still, save for the soft clopping of their stags, and the occasional scrape as a hoof slipped in the scree. Rays of sun streaked through the clouds above.

Then, the stillness vanished, and rage filled Riese's spirit, a shared sensation with the soul residing in the egg strapped to her back.

The unhatched dragon was screaming in her mind as clear as a babe in a neighbor's hut. A desperate, fearful warning that made her blood turn to ice.

Riese glanced around. The nearest tree cover was at the bottom of the pass, a good half-mile, and she knew they had nowhere near that much time.

"The Dragonmounts are here!"

"What? How can you tell?" asked Ulgar.

"Doesn't matter," said Malik. "We have to hide! Now!"

A sound echoed across the mountains like waves crashing in the distance. They hurried down the mountainside, stags sliding on loose rocks and dirt.

Rykus leapt into the air and flew like an arrow down the mountain. His stag reared back, and Ulgar snatched the reins.

"Where's he going?" Surel demanded, voice trembling.

"I don't—"

"Over there!" Malik pointed to a spot a few hundred yards down and to their right. Captain Rykus waved to them from an outcropping of boulders.

The rushing sound grew louder, somewhere beyond the mountain, perhaps in the clouds. The rage in Riese's spirit was a gods-damned tempest.

They rode as fast as they dared push the beasts on the loose terrain. Surel's stag slid, and she nearly slipped off as it scrambled to find purchase.

Malik pulled up beside her and steadied her, and they rode on. The ground leveled out, short alpine grass making the going easier.

Captain Rykus stood at the edge of an enormous boulder the size of a small hut. He dropped to his belly and disappeared down into a small opening beneath the base of the rock.

A sound like a wind-blown sail roared across the valley. Riese glanced up to see the breathtaking, fearsome outline of a dragon cresting a peak further down the pass. Its back was to them.

Ulgar leapt off his stag and frantically removed the reins. He sent the beast away with a whip to its rear, and it raced toward the forest below. The others followed suit. Their stags took off down the pass. Birds shot out of the treetops, screeching with terror.

Ulgar reached Rykus first and slipped into the space below the boulders.

A loud rush of wind erupted directly behind them.

Riese didn't dare look back. She gripped Surel's hand tight and urged her forward.

Rykus pulled Surel through.

A roar filled Riese's spirit.

Malik was trying to squeeze through, barely fitting with Rykus hanging half out of the space, and Riese knew it was too tight for them all.

Wind rushed overhead. A dark shadow descended.

And Riese scrambled back to a smaller boulder and leapt beneath a small overhang, pressing her body against the cold stone.

Her dragon's spirit had gone still as death now.

Shadows rushed overhead. Three Dragonmounts in total. The magnificent beasts were so much larger than any dragyr. Their wings spanned fifty feet at least, each flap echoing across the mountains.

The stags let out a distant cry somewhere below, and Riese could sense they'd caught the attention of the dragons, hopefully looking only like spooked wild beasts.

One dragon banked at the other end of the valley. The other two headed further down the pass. Terror overwhelmed her.

Faltari hunting cloaks were infused with *hish* when they were dyed, amplifying their ability to blend with their surroundings. But in broad daylight, she dared not move a muscle. A fourth shadow passed, and the entire valley resounded with the cacophonous rush of wings.

Riese held still, waiting for one of the dragons to circle back, but slowly, the sound grew faint. The dragons were moving on.

She waited until the world was silent for several minutes before she dared to move.

Then, she felt a soft whisper from the egg on her back.

Safe.

Riese emerged from the overhang and hurried to the others.

Rykus crawled out first, visibly shaken. Malik and Surel scrambled after. Riese grabbed Ulgar's hand and helped him through the narrow opening.

"We have to hurry to the tree line before they come back," said Malik.

Rykus turned to Riese. "They were searching for us."

"God's breath," Surel muttered.

"All the more reason to move!" said Malik.

They sprinted toward the forest below. Riese was glad to be off the sheer, slick surface of the mountainside. The grass and dirt of the sloped valley floor made for a much easier traverse, despite the steep descent to the forest.

Rykus remained close to Riese, though he didn't speak again until they'd reached the cover of sprawling socha trees.

"Those mounts were hunting," Rykus said.

"Could be a coincidence," said Ulgar. "They know we're out here somewhere."

But Rykus shook his head. "They knew we were close, and I fear the worst for my daughter."

"You think they found her?" asked Ulgar.

"Shit," said Surel.

"How much do you think Ruan figured out about our plan in the pass?" Malik asked.

"I don't know. Enough to be dangerous. Ava was supposed to wait to join the Attican company for several more hours. By then, it wouldn't matter."

"What do you think happened?" asked Ulgar.

"Gods damn it! I don't know!"

Silence fell over the group for a while. Birds chirped softly in the treetops.

"What now?" asked Ulgar. "They may damn-well know we're coming. And if they do, they'll be watching for us."

Rykus hesitated, tapping the hilt of the blade at his hip. Contemplating something.

"What if we don't go to the pass?" asked Surel. "If they're watching for us, maybe that will slow them down anyway."

"There *is* a more direct route to the Spires," said Riese.

"Straight over the mountains," Malik clarified. "More direct, sure. But slower. We were supposed to follow the Soul Road the rest of the way from the pass. But if we don't blow it up, they could still catch up to us, and we'll have no chance of getting those eggs."

"Don't matter if we can't *get* to the pass to blow it up," Surel countered.

"She's right," said Rykus.

"Er, I am?"

The man nodded to Surel. "In part. All of you should take this other route."

"All of us?" asked Riese. "We're splitting up?"

"I fear there is no other way. Malik is right too. The Atticans may lose a couple hours looking for us, but if there are no signs of a threat, they'll get wise quick enough."

"So, what, you're going to set off the bomb alone?" asked Ulgar.

"No. In truth, I never liked that part of the plan." Rykus removed his pack containing the firebomb and handed it to Malik. "I think I know a better way to delay them. A way that will *truly* buy us enough time to retrieve the eggs and destroy the gate."

"What way?" Riese asked.

Rykus's face had turned solemn, as though accepting an inevitable fate. "I'm going to give them a threat to find."

Chapter 53

Ilyetha

Urla marched at the head of her company. The Faltari alkine were no quicker than her own pace, and they'd felt strange beneath her legs. Unlike her husband and son, she'd always preferred her own boots to a mount. Urla had trained all her life to cross mountains and deserts on foot. She'd marched all the way from Attica to Taika in her youth.

Though that memory triggered conflicted thoughts. Of her last conversation with the shaman before he betrayed Attica. Betrayed her. Urla could not settle her mind on the matter.

She had liked Joren, even trusted him. That's what happened when you fought beside a person. It was the bond she shared with all the Bloody Company.

Now, Joren's children had run off with her rebel prisoner and left the Lady Knight dead in their wake. The shaman's family had willfully hidden the Rykus girl under her nose, and supported a rebellion that might threaten the future of the empire itself.

And yet, they had spared Ruan's life.

It was a maddening paradox.

Madri rode an alkine a short distance behind Urla in the march. The woman's hands were chained, and she was watched at all times by Sergeant Roak, along with that annoying young prick, Aram Tulsein.

The boy's father, Elder Eriksein, had remained in Yerida, and his son represented his clan in his father's stead. Elder Dannsein also remained behind, having suffered excruciating burns.

With the young shaman missing, and Joren dead, Olma Marudeil had elected to lead the company of Faltari to Valgland.

Urla had thought it a prudent decision when Joren proposed it. And she still did. At this point, the fewer Faltari on this island, the better.

She didn't trust any of them.

An operation like this could take several days. To extract a veritable treasure trove of dragon eggs from a gate at the top of a floating mountain range. And there were the rebels to deal with.

A roar erupted from the clouds, and all eyes shot skyward.

The sight of dark red dragon wings soaring over the Faltari peaks sent shivers down Urla's spine. A sharp thrill that swiftly morphed into sorrow. The magnificent, winged beast bore the same earthy, clay-red coloration as Voltari. For so many years, the sign of red wings on the horizon brought a sweeping sense of relief and excitement. Her husband was alive. The Dragonmounts had triumphed.

Now, the sight brought trepidation. Urla knew from the coloration that it belonged to the emperor's military mount. His white dragon was mainly ceremonial, though few outside the Dragonmounts knew this.

Considering the circumstances, Urla had half-expected the emperor's wrath upon his arrival, or at least outrage. The matter of the shaman's betrayal was a failure of hers and hers alone.

But Athanasius was collected and focused. Completing the mission was the only priority. But Urla knew she could not afford another lapse in judgment.

Now, his red dragon dipped its head, as it soared downward, and Urla spotted a second rider behind the emperor. Her heart raced.

Ruan... how?

She picked up her pace as the dragon soared down from overcast skies and swept out over the spearpoint tops of the snowpine trees. Great bony wings stretched wide as sails as the dragon slowed. It flapped hard at the last, pulling itself upward, and a loud rush echoed over the valley.

The thud of the landing sent tremors down the crude mountain road.

Urla resisted the urge to race forward, fearing such passion might be seen as weakness.

Athanasius dismounted first, and reached up to help Ruan slide down the dragon's side. As Ruan's feet hit the uneven ground of the Soul Road, he nearly lost his balance, but the emperor held fast to his arm, steadying him.

Considering how she'd left him, it was a remarkable sight to see him awake at all.

Urla marched forward. Ruan stood tall and proud at the emperor's side, the dragon drawing up its neck and pluming its wings. The sight stirred something in Urla. Regret? Sorrow?

Ruan's head was turned slightly away from her. He perked up as she neared, but she sensed something was wrong.

She pounded her fist against her chest in salute. Ruan returned it, but the action was delayed.

"Your son was brave, Consul Pelasius," Athanasius said. "Even with his injury, he still managed to escape the rebels and deliver one of their own in the process."

Another dragon soared over the peak, two riders once more.

Urla turned back to Ruan. "Injury?"

"The work of that shaman traitor," said the emperor.

"When I woke, all was darkness," Ruan said, no fear or sorrow in his voice.

Urla nodded, understanding the delay in his salute, the strangeness of her son's gaze.

Oh Marha...

"I assure you when we return to Attica, I will make sure my healers do all they can. But there is some fortune in the tragedy, and I believe it was no less his path. Your son brings valuable information from his time with the enemy."

While dragons searched the air for signs of rebels, Urla sent a group of her best soldiers ahead of the company to scour the region on the ground. A few scouts searched the woods on either side of the Soul Road.

It was her instinct to go with them, to be in the midst of the action, leading the search. But her role as consul demanded something different of her. She could not just go sprinting off into hostile terrain. Nevertheless, she ached for the hunt as she led the company into the depths of the island.

Urla rode one of the alkine now. Ruan rode beside her, along with their servant Pisarre, who had not left the boy's side since his return from the hands of the enemy. Ruan said little as they descended into the narrow valley, at the foot of the Sleeping Woman.

"Whatever happens, I'm grateful you're alive," she said. "Any injury is better than death."

"Not very Attican of you," Ruan murmured.

"But no less Fjuriin," said Urla. "You have only so much sway over your path. But just because—"

"I don't want to speak of it right now," Ruan said.

"Of course."

Urla glanced over at Ava Rykus, whose alkine was tethered to two other mounted soldiers. Her hands were bound, and her body jostled as the strange mountain beast ambled up the road.

Ava scowled, saying nothing, though Urla caught a glare in her son's direction. That gave her some satisfaction, at least.

The rebels are already here. How did they get to the island so quickly? Where are the others?

They had found no signs of the runeship, nor of any dark-winged creatures, but Ruan insisted the rebels were close. On foot. And Urla could not shake the memory of how the creatures had emerged during the festival.

She was on edge.

All she could do was press forward, and trust in orders she'd been tasked to carry out.

March on as normal. Give no appearance of urgency. But be ready.

The arrival of the emperor himself had only intensified the resolve of the Bloody Company. This was their chance to make their mark. If the enemy wanted to try to attack an entire company on this road in broad daylight, let them try.

They crested a ridge and a wide valley spread before them. The Kalengal Mountains plunged into the skies on either side. The wind grew sharp and crisp. Thick copses of white-limbed trees lined the foothills of the valley below, leaves blazing in shades of red.

The prominent peak at the other end was one gargantuan swath of rock. Its highest point looked like a woman lying with her head drawn back, patches of brush reminiscent of hair, sweeping down the left side of the mountain. A sharp ridge formed her neck. A long flat stretch of peak, broken by a series of small rises and dips, extended further, before rising to one last peak, looking like knees raised. And the likeness ended.

It was so human in shape, Urla might have sworn it had been fashioned so.

The shaman's wife brought her mount abreast of Urla's, flanked by Caliphus and another member of the Bloody Company.

Act normal, she reminded herself.

"Remarkable," Urla said, gazing out at the mountain. "I'm surprised she's not regarded as some sort of goddess."

"There are only the All Mother and the All Father, and they live yet," said Madri. "But according to some legends, the mountain was formed in honor of one of the greatest of their children."

"Their children being..."

"Us."

"Rather high view of yourselves, isn't it?"

"All people are their children, but we Faltari have been entrusted with special gifts and a solemn duty. Beginning with her." Madri gestured to the mountain. "My grandmother told the story of a mighty ancient woman named Ilyetha. The wife of our chieftain at the Crossing. But of course, you Atticans harbor a different tale."

"Don't we all? Go on. I'm curious."

"Ilyetha's husband died only years after the Crossing, and there was much deliberation about how to proceed. They had no children, and so there was no obvious heir. Ilyetha had a viable claim, but I suppose you can imagine how that went."

Urla nodded.

"Thousands of people had Crossed by that time, and the Great Curse that plagued the previous world still lingered in the hearts of men. There was a violent fracturing of our people. In those days, everyone possessed magic abilities, and it could be a terrifying power. In the wake of this conflict, many left the island to inhabit other lands, forming the other peoples of Îrithèa. While other clans formed and dispersed, Ilyetha remained behind, leading a small band of our ancient kin. They were not the greatest nor the most powerful, but like Ilyetha, they were wise. They understood the blessing of magic. Something to create, not destroy. It's for this reason, I believe, that magic has endured here, on Faltara, as it has. All are the children of the All Mother and All Father, but most have forgotten their identity. We Faltari forget all too often ourselves. Even a shaman may forget for a time."

"Madri, I..."

"My husband knew exactly who he was at the end. The same devotion to the gods that drove him to save your son's life also drove him to help that girl over there, and her cause."

Silence lingered for a moment.

Anger rose in Urla's chest like a flame ignited. But she tried not to let it show. Whatever was ahead, she needed the shaman's wife to think well of her. To believe she could be swayed.

"What happened?" Urla asked. "To Ilyetha? After her husband died, and she became a leader of your people."

Madri shrugged. "She stepped down from her seat as chieftain and formed a council. She remarried and bore a son, who would go on to form the four clans of Faltara. But it was her example that inspired the foundation of my people. Ilyetha did not vie for power, though she was as powerful as any of the men who fought in that great and terrible war at the beginning of Îrithèa. She played a different game. That was her strength."

Aram Tulsein rode over, shooting a glance at Madri, before meeting Urla's gaze. "We're approaching the passage, Lady Consul."

The emperor's red dragon circled the skies above, scanning the valley for threats. Another blue dragon flew further out, searching the western passes. Shimmering scales flashed in the late afternoon sun.

Urla examined the mountain ahead but saw nothing that looked like the entrance to a canyon. "Where?"

Aram pointed to a depression near the base of the Sleeping Woman.

A strand of rock rose from the foothills. It had looked like the woman's arm from a distance, but as they neared, Urla noticed enclaves in the rock.

"The passage lies there, the fingers of—"

A screech filled the skies.

The emperor's dragon banked hard as something launched from the valley floor.

With unfathomable speed, it shot into the sky.

Straight at the emperor.

———

Captain Adrius Rykus flew from his hiding place like a dead star from its home in the heavens, raining down upon the world in a streak of light.

With magic thrumming through his body, Rykus was filled with a peace he'd never before known.

No more striving. No more sorrow. No more fear and worry over his wife or daughter. Their fates rested with the gods now.

His path was set before him, and for once, Rykus understood— nothing more depended on him.

Only this last act.

This infernal distraction.

Perhaps, the emperor would die.

But Rykus knew it didn't matter. The attack alone would keep the Attican company distracted long enough that they would not dare passage until morning.

Would it be enough time for the rest of the plan? For Ava? For Deven? For his band of rebels?

It was out of his hands.

And releasing that burden seemed to send Rykus flying even faster. All the magic he could unleash, bearing him toward his target.

The air was bitter cold on his face, stinging his eyes, despite the intense warmth of magic coursing through him as he rose higher and higher. Faster than any bird. Faster, even, than a dragon.

He was an arrow.

A wing-render.

Rykus had learned to use magic to fly from his father. An ancient Valucian secret. One he'd only been able to nourish in the secluded hills of Eòreth. Beyond the sight of the empire and its many, many spies.

The Elyans called it Conjuri magic. The ability to push back against the elements of the world. But even the Elyans had not understood that there were elements in the air as well. It was a revelation that had won him an audience, and the support of a company of their Morphs.

We shall be the Flame that ignites the world. The Bringers of truth and justice.

His father had instilled this in him, as he had instilled it in Ava.

It was not just about dragons, or Valucia, or even the Attican Empire.

It was the truth of the Crossing, and the laws of magic.

The future of Îrithèa.

Ancient wisdom paired with the audacious sorcery of Elya. The world would never be the same.

It saddened Rykus, knowing he would not live to see that future.

But it would live on in his daughter, thanks to this final act.

Rykus shot through the sky. Higher.

The emperor's dragon twisted sharply. High above the Attican company. Another dragon roared from the other end of the valley.

Too far.

The emperor's dragon lurched and roared. Fire shot across the sky in a sweeping rush.

Rykus's face grew hot, but the flames swept out below his feet. He raised his blade before him. The runemarked Kirithian blade that had earned him his seat as a lord in Attica.

The emperor reared back in his saddle. He reached for his sword. Too late.

Rykus struck the emperor like a lance. Rykus's blade plunged between runemarked plates at the armpit.

Athanasius seized with pain, hands slipping from their grips on the dragon's scales. Rykus and the emperor both launched from the dragon's back together.

The emperor met his gaze. Eyes wide with the fear of an imminent death.

Dragon wings swept out above, blotting out the sky.

Rykus lost his grip on the emperor.

His magic was utterly spent, and he could not slow his fall.

His body whorled through the air.

Spiraling, plummeting.

This was his path, and Rykus was at peace.

Part Ten

Heart of the Island

At the northernmost edge of the known world of Îrithèa, lies a small island of little consequence. It is sparsely inhabited, and with good reason. Its seas are icy, mountains and coasts treacherous, and its lands are filled with all kinds of cruel beasts. What mad sort of barbarians would live in such a place?

—from the journals of Urian Fessna
a Beirusian explorer

Chapter 54

Fall

Urla's body ached with the same raw sensation that had stricken her in the midst of battle when she saw her husband's dragonfall.

Utter terror. Helpless fear.

So overwhelming, she'd nearly fallen to a Sigan barbarian's scimitar.

The entire company froze, gazing upward. Helpless. As two human bodies fell from the sky.

The emperor's dragon dove after them. Wind rushed, echoing off the mountainsides.

Cloaks of earthen green and imperial crimson rippled through the air, shooting straight down.

The dragon lurched forward, reaching for the emperor as they plunged toward the trees at the base of the mountain.

Rykus struck an outcropping of stones further up the hillside with a horrific crunch.

Urla lost sight of the emperor as his dragon curled its body around him. Branches exploded from the edge of the forest with a devastating crack.

The world went still.

Urla sprinted across the rocky terrain, a desperate prayer to the All

Mother on her lips. Soldiers swarmed around her. On foot. On alkine. The ground thundered.

The dragon did not stir as they neared.

Trees were decimated around its body as though a firebomb had exploded. The dragon lay curled against the ruined trunks of toppled trees. Blood coated the stony ground everywhere.

Urla cursed. She had seen Rykus fly during the runeship attack. But no one had considered such a threat from the ground. It was a gods-damned suicide attack. Man against dragon. So bold, so sudden, it had succeeded.

The dragon's wings were drawn tight against its body, like a child cowering from a dream terror. Its chest did not move, and Urla knew it was dead. She could not see the emperor for the wings.

"Pry them back!" Urla shouted.

Soldiers leapt in, pulling, jerking, prying the gargantuan dragon wings. They were large as a mast and sails, and locked tight in death. It took a dozen men to prize them away.

The emperor lay wrapped in the dragon's rear claws. Urla stepped closer. His face was pale, and a surge of dread filled her.

Then, Athanasius shuddered, drew a faint breath, releasing with a soft wheeze, then went still. Urla grasped his hand. No response.

A few seconds passed, and breath came again, whistling like wind over the narrow entrance of a cave.

Athanasius's nose was broken, face bloody. Lips barely parted with the breaths.

Soldiers latched on to the emperor's limbs, preparing to pull while others prepared to pry the claws apart.

"Don't move him yet! I need to examine his spine!"

A slender woman in a grey uniform slipped past the others and took charge. Cedana was the head medic of the Bloody Company, hailing from the cruel canyonlands of Southern Attica, and she knew her way around traumatic injuries. Green-cloaked imperial healers pressed around, but Cedana barked at them to stay back.

All went silent. The emperor's breaths were tepid and far apart.

"The claws," Cedana said. "They're suffocating him. He won't survive much longer. We have to loosen them, but don't bloody move the emperor until I say it's safe. Careful, careful!"

Soldiers painstakingly worked to pry back the dragon's claws, which encircled the emperor's torso, while also taking extra care not to jostle Athanasius's body in the process.

Once the claws were loosened, the emperor breathed more easily, though the whistling persisted.

Cedana knelt down and examined him. Once she had verified that the emperor's spine was not broken, the healers carefully hefted him onto a stretcher.

Cedana turned back to the caravan and cursed at the greencloaks. "What? None of you thought to erect a healer's tent?"

The greencloaks looked to Urla. "You heard her. Get on it! All of you, make camp!"

At her words, the entire company snapped out of their stupor and set to work. The sun had gone beyond the mountains, and night would come swiftly.

Urla turned to her young lieutenant, Caliphus. "We'll need scouts to scour the woods before nightfall. If there are more rebels close, we'll make them bloody pay for this. Set a perimeter. Check the canyon too. We're losing daylight."

"Of course, Lady Consul!"

"And find that rebel bastard's body!"

Caliphus barked orders, and gathered his scouts, while the rest of the company set about making camp.

Once Cedana was satisfied with the straps holding Athanasius to the stretcher, she allowed the greencloaks to move him.

Urla took one last look at the emperor's dragon. Its back was mottled with bruises from the fall. Wings tattered from the collision of the trees. The magnificent beast had offered its life that the emperor might live.

If only her husband's dragon had been able to manage such a sacrificial act.

Voltari had been pierced by a wing-render arrow, straight through the chest. Her husband was thrown from his mount.

She could still see him falling.

———

Malik and Riese managed to track two of their mountain stags in the forest shortly after Rykus left them. Malik hadn't lost all his hunter's sense during the past two years of shaman training.

They crossed the forests leading up into the mountains swiftly, riding double—Malik and Surel on one stag, Riese and Ulgar on the other. Occasionally, they glimpsed the outline of dragon wings far above, but the forest canopy offered thick cover. The last time they saw the dragons, it was nearing evenfall, and a wrenching screech echoed across the valley. There was another distant cry, somewhere beyond. Dragons calling across the island.

Riese went silent. Her brow furled, grimacing.

"What is it?" Malik asked.

She reached for the egg in her pack, fingers brushing against the coarse fabric.

"Dragonfall. They're mourning."

Shivers shot down Malik's arms. He drew his cloak tighter around his shoulders.

"You're sure," said Ulgar.

Riese nodded. "Dragons share a bond with their riders, but also with all the other mounts. A spiritual sense, perhaps. I'm learning all this as it comes. Same way my dragon sensed them back near the glacial pass. He heard them now."

"Can they sense him?" Ulgar asked.

Riese hesitated. "They share their sense freely. Not knowing he can sense it. Or that he exists. I don't think he's sharing back. But this... " She reached for the right side of her chest, where her spirit resided and Malik could sense the pain too, from his friend's sorrow.

"It was Rykus," Surel said.

Riese nodded. Tears streaked down her cheeks, and she took her satchel in her lap and held it tight as they continued through the forest.

"Took down a bloody dragon," Ulgar muttered after a long silence.

"God's breath," Surel cursed.

Riese said nothing.

"Do you... think he survived?" Ulgar asked.

Malik sighed. "I don't think he meant to. He bought us time. Now, it falls to us. And Ava. And whatever Morphs managed to infiltrate the Attican company."

They rode on in silence. Considering the circumstances, it was strangely peaceful. Malik tried to focus on the sounds around him. Birds and squirrels. The soft trodding of stag hooves. Surel's steady breathing behind him. There would be time for mourning, but right now, he had to keep moving.

The terrain began to climb again and the trees thinned. They were nearing the edge of the forest.

Malik pulled his stag closer to speak with Riese. "So... your dragon's a he, is it?"

Despite the sorrow emanating from her spirit, Riese managed a smile at this. "I think he's going to hatch soon."

"Best hope not tonight," said Ulgar. "Last thing we need is childbirth in the bloody mountains."

Riese chuckled, coming back to herself. "Not exactly the same. Dragons aren't nearly so helpless at birth."

"Yeah? How do you know?"

"I... just do." She smiled. "But anyway, hatchings require special rituals. Performed by other riders."

"So after all this."

Riese nodded solemnly.

If we survive, Malik thought.

It was near dark when they reached the tree line partway up a mountain. No signs of dragons above.

A sweeping climb of loose scree led up to a treacherous peak of enormous boulders above them. They left the stags behind and set out on foot.

Twilight came, but the fading light did not slow their progress. Enhanced with the occasional use of *hish* focused on their eyes, all four of them were able to aid their ascent through the treacherous passes leading to Kalengal Valley.

Malik urged them to use it sparingly. Gods knew, they'd need all the spiritual strength they could muster to survive a second Ascent and a return to the Abyss.

Not to mention the dragons hunting them, and the imperial company marching for the same destination.

But they were descendants of the gods, gifted with the power of their breath, and they had a mission that could determine the future of all Îrithèa.

A mission that Joren and Captain Rykus had given their lives for.

And now, it would demand everything from them.

First, though, they must brave the night.

CHAPTER 55

BARGAINING CHIP

Ava Rykus mourned her father's death in silence. Once the emperor was taken to the healer's tent, parties of soldiers were sent to scour the woods.

Despite her sorrow, this made Ava glad. The Atticans seemed to have no idea how many rebels they were dealing with. A point she'd exploited when she was first interrogated after her capture. Ruan seemed to have determined less than she'd feared about their true plans, and the Atticans had lost hours of precious time.

Because of her father.

Now, Ava could only wait, and pray it would be enough for the others.

Stakes were driven into the ground in the center of camp, and Ava and Madri were tied with their backs to the wooden poles, hands behind their backs. The angle made Ava's arms ache.

Once they were secured, the Atticans barely paid them any mind, they were so distracted by the dragonfall.

But Aram Tulsein kept close. Silent and brooding, until a group of soldiers came near, bearing a stretcher. The Faltari boy sprinted over to them and motioned over to the prisoners.

Ava's spirit splintered. The stretcher carried a body, covered in a dark cloth, and her entire body wracked with an uncontrollable sob. Her breaths were desperate, empty gasps, wrists numbing as she strained against her bonds. The soldiers set the stretcher down in front of her. Aram began to draw back the death shroud, and Ava closed her eyes. Tears streamed down her cheeks, dripping from her chin to the cold hard ground.

Aram seized her face, jerking her neck to the side. Pain shot down her neck and back.

"This is for my father, you bitch. Now, look!"

Ava opened her eyes. Her father's face was caved in, unrecognizable. Skin purple and yellow. More like a heap of bloody flesh and shattered bones than a human man. Her stomach churned. She tried to turn away.

Aram's fingers tightened on her jaw. "This is what your little rebellion has wrought. Don't tell me you're too weak to face what you've—"

Thud!

Ava jerked her head as Aram's fingers were wrenched free of her. The blur of a man came from somewhere behind her, barreling into Aram.

The man threw the boy to the ground and leapt on top of him. Aram struggled to free himself, reaching for magic, but nothing happened. The man had placed something around the boy's neck in the scuffle.

He punched Aram in the stomach, and the boy curled up on the ground, clutching at the strange runemarked collar.

"Resist again and you die, heathen!"

Aram froze.

Ava knew that commanding voice.

Ruan Pelasius stepped into her vision, and Ava realized who the attacker was. The head servant of House Pelasius.

"You have no authority over these prisoners, boy," Ruan said, towering over him. "Or the body of this fallen rebel. Or anyone else. The empire has everything under control. Do you understand?"

Aram grimaced. "I was just—"

One more punch to the ribs shut him up.

"Guards," Ruan addressed the men who had brought Captain Rykus in the first place, "take the rebel's body to Consul Pelasius, as you were bloody ordered. Then, help finish preparing the camp."

They nodded and took the body away.

"W-what is this?" Aram demanded, reaching at the collar around his neck. The servant raised his fist and Aram held still.

"It's not meant for you," said Ruan. He held up a second collar. "But it will be, if you come near these prisoners again. Understood?"

Aram glared impotently as the servant lifted the runemarked collar off his neck.

"You're here to help guide the way to these Spires," Ruan said. "Nothing more. You're not here to guard our prisoners. You're not here to fight our battles. You're here to point left or fucking right. You got that?"

Aram nodded, blood pouring from his lips.

"If I catch you here again, you'd better be ready to join them."

The Pelasius servant shoved him, and Aram scampered away, cursing and muttering to himself.

Ava looked up. Ruan's empty eyes stared off. His face was unreadable.

"Finish this up, Pisarre," Ruan said. "We've other matters to see to."

Pisarre walked over to Ava and Madri and placed one collar on each of their necks.

A bloody Attican invention, if ever there was one.

The servant watched them carefully for a few moments. He whispered something to Ruan. Without another word, Ruan and his servant left.

Numbness settled over her. Ava had not realized how much of her body's warmth had been subtle hints of her magic. In minutes, she was shivering, and her hip ached worse than it had in ages.

The camp bustled all around as evening set in.

Ava hung her head, tired body drooping. She pushed away the image of her broken father from her mind.

Instead, she pictured him streaking across the sky, more free than he'd ever been. Her father had spent so many years, tied to Eòreth, tied to the ruse that he was a blood-traitor to his own people, tied to tending to her mother, tied to a dream of resistance that never quite materialized.

All her life, he had wished to use his gifts in battle. For there to be no question of his honor in Valucia.

A gods-damned dragonfall. Ava smiled. *Oh, the songs that will be written about you, Father.*

If they survived this ordeal, it was the sort of act that could rally more rebels in Valucia, whatever their king's cowardice.

So long as the story was told. And it would be. Ava would make it so.

Madri had said little since she arrived, and Ava understood why. Captain Rykus wasn't the only one to sacrifice for this mission. Madri's family had given much, and more might be taken by the end.

We will make their deaths worth it, Ava thought.

———

Night descended. Ava's stomach ached with hunger, but no soldiers came to offer them sustenance. The Attican company milled about erecting tents, tending fires, musing nervously about what would happen as this mission unfolded. About the faceless enemy they were up against. About the dragonfall.

Even without her sense, Ava could feel the tension like a physical presence infiltrating the camp.

Dragonmounts circled cloudy skies, scouring the forest and mountains, as well as the Soul Road ahead.

Unease lingered in everyone's minds in the wake of the attack, but their emperor's survival sustained them. There was an arrogance about Atticans, no matter what came their way. Far as Ava could tell from the murmurings of passing soldiers, no one feared failure. They were angry and eager to fight.

See how ready you bastards are when the time comes, Ava thought.

"How far are the Spires from here?" Ava whispered.

Madri was weary. Her head hung low, chin resting on her chest. Her shoulders shuddered, but she roused at the words. "Half a day's journey. They hoped to march through the night before this. Your father bought some time. Don't worry, milady, your vengeance won't wait much longer."

Ava jolted at the words. She'd never heard a Faltari speak that way. "Milady?"

Madri smiled. Her eyes flashed, pupils narrowing.

Ava's heart leapt as she understood. "When did you make the switch?"

The woman tilted her head. "Your father bought us more than time. He gave us the distraction we needed to prepare for what's to come. Now, quiet. Someone's coming."

Finally, a servant came with water and salted venison. The young man did not speak to them, but Ava noted the Pelasius crest on his cloak.

The night stretched on, but Ava could not sleep. Her heart was racing, wondering what was coming and when.

At last, a commotion rose across the camp. Soldiers rushing.

Madri stirred. "Do you think it's the—"

Footsteps behind her.

Urla Pelasius stepped from beyond the nearest tent, accompanied by several soldiers.

She did not spare Ava a glance. Consul Pelasius strode straight to Madri, knelt in front of her.

"You spared my son, though he was your enemy. You claim duty towards humanity itself, but how far does that extend?"

"What do you mean?"

"The emperor is near death."

Ava's spirit soared. Could it be?

"Our healers can do little for him. The dragon eggs are one thing. They are military pieces on a board. But an outright assassination? That is an evil that could upend our world."

Yes, Ava thought.

"You could help him," said Urla.

Madri lifted her head and looked directly in the woman's eyes. "Why would I do that?"

"This dragonfall gives the rebels a fighting chance, but it by no means guarantees victory, whether the emperor lives or not. What follows, and each individual's actions, those will not be forgotten. Should your son fail in his rebellion..."

"Are you threatening my son?" Madri asked.

"I'm offering you a bargaining chip, should this turn out poorly for you."

Ava's heart soared. This was it. Their chance to finish what her father started. But she knew she should not appear happy.

"Madri, don't be a fool!" Ava said bitterly.

"Be quiet, girl," Urla said. She peered into Madri's eyes.

"Very well," Madri said, "take me to your emperor."

Chapter 56

The Price of Life

Urla led the shaman's wife through camp, trying not to let her mind wander about all the things that could go wrong.

As they walked, Madri inquired about the nature of the emperor's wounds.

Head trauma. Sword wound. Possibly a crushed lung.

"I'll need instruments," said Madri. "Magic alone is rarely enough for such injuries."

"I'm certain the instruments of imperial healers will do just fine."

"Let us hope. Of course, I'll need these shackles removed. And the collar."

"Once we reach the patient."

Guards were stationed on every side of the emperor's tent. Caliphus motioned them through and followed behind.

Urla could smell the coppery tang of blood before they entered.

Madri gasped at the sight of death in the room.

A woman lay upon the floor of the tent, dressed in the green robes of the imperial healers, but she was no Attican. She had silver hair and porcelain skin, and she was very much dead. Lying at the foot of the emperor's bed in a pool of blood.

Madri looked from the body to the bed. "But where is—"

Swords rang as guards entered the room behind them. Athanasius followed. He did not walk quickly, but he wore a fresh uniform. His face was bruised, and he looked utterly exhausted, but he was very much alive.

Madri's expression betrayed confusion.

Urla kept her hand on the hilt of her blade, but as she suspected, the woman did not blow her cover immediately.

"Y-Your Grace!" Madri stammered. "Gods above, I'm relieved to see you're awake. I was told you were…"

"Dying?" asked Athanasius, smiling weakly. "Little help from *this* healer, I will tell you that."

"I thank the gods."

"Do you?"

Madri stiffened, back straightening, body tense. "Of course, Your Grace. That is why I've come."

"You were not needed," Athanasius said. "And it is a good thing too. What would it have been? Not a poisoned tonic again, surely. Perhaps something more barbaric? A scalpel through the eye, perhaps?"

"Gods above, never!"

"God's breath," said Urla. "That's the proper curse here on the island, is it not?"

"Er, yes," said Madri. "But like most believers in the All Mother and All Father, we swear in many ways."

"You wear many faces," said Athanasius. "There is no denying—"

Madri threw herself forward, raising her shackles to strike Athanasius.

Urla was ready. Before the woman reached the emperor, Urla drove her gladius through the assassin's back. The woman shrieked as she slumped at Athanasius's feet, blood bubbling from her lips.

She did not die instantly. The woman lay on the ground, muttering unintelligible words as her breaths faded. She gasped.

And then, it was done.

The assassin lay motionless, face up, eyes wide, blood pooling.

As the color faded from her cheeks, something shifted. Her brown hair turning raven black, skin turning from pale to a soft olive shade.

"Bloody Taikan!" Athanasius spat on the woman's body.

"I didn't realize these things could take on different human forms," Caliphus said, kneeling for a closer look.

The emperor nodded and stepped back. "The Elyans call them Morphs, and they use a form of blood magic, the arcanists tell me. Likely the reason the collar didn't expose her. But she would have needed the real Faltari woman's blood to take on her likeness."

"Then where is the real shaman's wife?" asked Caliphus.

Soldiers scrambled about the camp, but Ava could not gather what had happened. The Atticans seemed to be preparing for something, but to Ava's chagrin, they did not possess the fear and urgency of an assassinated emperor.

Ava appeared to have been forgotten about. Entirely unimportant in the wake of whatever was going on. Squadrons of soldiers marched past, bearing large packs, armed with bows and lances. None of them even looked her way.

Despair crept into her thoughts. Already her vision of the Morphs rising in the camp seemed a child's delusion.

Footsteps thudded on the ground behind her. Ava looked up.

"Madri?" Ava asked, shocked.

The shaman's wife had returned, led by a pair of new soldiers, one a tall woman, the other a young and hefty man.

Madri hung her head as she stopped beside the pole, hood of her cloak pulled up. She did not kneel back down.

A hand gripped Ava's shackles from behind.

"What in the Abyss is going on?" she demanded.

"Don't make me gag you, little Rykus." The woman's voice sounded familiar.

"What?"

Keys jangled softly and a lock clicked.

The woman helped her stand. Ava turned and gasped, hope surging in her chest. For a brief moment, the guard let her true face show through the guise.

It was the leader of her father's band of Morphs.

"Deven!"

Her face shifted once more. Looking like an Attican guard again. "Only the best for the heir of the rebellion."

And the stocky man. Ava recognized him as well.

"Yuri? I thought you were leaving the island."

"I was never good at obeying orders," he said.

"And Madri," she asked, nodding to the shaman's wife. "You're the real....."

Madri nodded. "It's me."

"Then that means..."

"The assassinations have failed." Deven began to fix Ava's shackles in front of her. "And we must hurry. The camp is distracted for now, but someone is going to come looking for you soon."

"Where did you get the keys?" asked Ava.

"No time," said Deven. She jerked Ava to her feet.

"What about..."

"Quiet, rebel swine!" Deven shoved her forward and began marching her away.

Yuri led Madri a short distance behind. Soldiers hurried around, but no one spared them a glance in the sparse torchlight.

They weaved through the encampment and soon reached a tent near the outskirts. As they approached, a man emerged, tent flapping open.

Ava's breath caught.

It was Ruan's servant. The same one who had put Aram Tulsein in his place. Pisarre's eyes widened at the sight of them.

Ava's heart raced.

But Deven did not hesitate. She shoved Ava forward. Into the tent.

There was shouting in the camp outside. Soldiers running.

Ruan stood alone in the sparse room within. His eyes drifted. Never settling. But he turned his head toward the entrance. Toward her.

He kept still. All of them did. But the sounds of shouting soldiers faded.

"Thank you, Yuri, Deven," Ruan said, as Deven unshackled both prisoners.

"What in the Abyss is going on?" Ava demanded.

Yuri dipped his head. "We got the keys from him. He helped us."

Ruan took a step closer.

"Helped? You turned me in, Ruan!"

He nodded. "I'm sorry about your fall, Ava. When I sensed the dragons were near, I feared the others would be caught. Unless we gave the mounts a distraction. And you were planning to turn yourself in anyway. I thought I could do the most good if it looked like I'd bested you. And if you thought so too. And well... I believe it worked."

Ava didn't know what to think. What to believe. "I don't understand."

"I always knew you were up to something," Ruan said. "Knew you were using me to get close to Campos. That you harbored some... rebellious tendencies. I never told you that I felt the same way."

"Same way... why didn't you tell me?"

Ruan shrugged. "Same reason you never told me, I suppose. Even though you knew I questioned the goodness of the Attican Empire. And when I woke up in that herder's hut, no one would have believed me. And... well I needed to know who you really were. What this rebellion was truly about. You and I were always playing games."

"Ruan I..."

Ruan reached his hand out, and Ava closed the space between them.

"You weren't the only one hiding your true self," he said.

"Why are you helping me, Ruan?" she asked, still unable to believe this was real. "This could ruin you. Ruin your house. Your future. Your life."

"Let me show you."

Gently, Ruan removed the collar from her neck and cast it aside. Her blood rushed as magic returned to her body.

Ruan closed his hands over both of hers and lowered his head. Ava filled with warmth. There was no hesitation, no facade. For the first time, Ruan Pelasius revealed everything. He opened his soul to her, and Ava could feel the truths that he'd always hidden. The doubts and unease he'd harbored about Attica, even before they'd met.

Back in the herder's hut, she'd hoped. She'd always known he was different than the other Atticans. When she thought he'd betrayed her in those woods, all those hopes were dashed. But now...

Ava reached up and brushed Ruan's cheek, and he smiled, sinking into her touch. He pulled her in, wrapping his arms around her.

"I believe in your cause, Ava Rykus," Ruan said. "I believe it is just. And that is worth risking everything for in this world. It is greater than house or family. Greater even than love."

"Love?" Ava demanded.

Ava stood on her toes, slid her hands up and cupped Ruan's chin with both her palms, and she kissed him. Ruan's lips froze for the briefest of moments, taken by surprise, but quickly they parted, welcoming her.

His lips were full, soft, warm. For years, she had longed for this. Ava had been so fearful of being wrong, about compromising the rebellion, she had not let herself be vulnerable to true love. All the boys at the academy had been distractions, tools, manipulations.

But Ruan...

Ruan loved her, and Ava loved him.

She knew now that she had for quite some time. But always, she had held back. Unable to believe that any future was truly possible with an Attican man. But now, all the secrets that they had hidden from one another during their years at the academy, all of them evaporated.

Ava smiled as she kissed him again, and again, his warmth radiating over her, through her, all around. The world had never felt so full and—

Yuri cleared his throat.

Both of them parted, blushing.

Deven and Pisarre were standing watch at the door. "Things are growing quiet again," Deven whispered.

"I'm going to get you out of here," Ruan said. "All of you."

Yuri rolled his eyes. "Right now... tomorrow... next week?"

Madri brushed his arm in a matronly fashion. "Are you telling me there was no prolonged and impassioned departure of your own before this mission?"

"That was different."

"Departure?" Ava asked. "Ruan, you're coming with us..."

Ruan shook his head. "There's more good I can do back here. And besides, if I go sneaking off, people might get suspicious before—"

"Oh, they're suspicious already."

Ava's entire body tensed at the malicious voice of Aram Tulsein.

Chapter 57

Night's Bane

Aram brandished his bonespear, face contorted with loathing.

Ava tensed, instinctively placing herself between the Faltari brute and Ruan, despite the fact she bore no weapon. Pisarre stood beside her, hand on the hilt of a dagger at his belt. Deven and Yuri both drew blades at the other side of the room. If it came to a fight, the boy would lose, but the commotion might be their downfall.

"Don't do anything foolish, son," said Madri, stepping to meet him.

The boy glared. "Which Madri is saying that?"

The shaman's wife remained calm, expressionless. "The woman who has known your family her entire life, Aram. Who mourns what happened to your father last night."

"Don't you dare play me with your bullshit sympathy!"

"Whatever you may believe about me or the Valucian rebellion, your father would not want you to throw your life away."

"You had no problem throwing my father's life away."

"He lives, Aram. And so do you. And we are called to do something good with this life."

"Those are the words of a woman who knows she's on the losing side."

"Aram, please listen to—"

"It's funny," the boy interrupted. "The only reason I knew to follow you was that shapeshifting trick. First, I see one Madri heading to see the emperor with the consul. Then I see you coming from the other end of camp. A heathen trick."

"And what are the Atticans, if not heathens?" Madri asked.

"They are the future," said Aram. "Our future. Our ancestors saw this. My father does too. And I will make it so."

Madri offered a sympathetic look. The boy was distracted by the exchange, by his own self-righteousness and anger and insecurity.

Ava could feel the emotions washing over her as if they were her own.

"I'm not convinced you believe all that, Aram," Madri said. "Your father certainly doesn't see the empire that way anymore."

"And what do you know?"

"The council's decision about this mission has changed, Aram. It is time to close the Gate of the Ancients as the Feathered Serpent clan has long proposed. Our partnership with the empire is over."

Aram peered into the woman's eyes. He hesitated, searching for words.

Ava glanced at Yuri, then Pisarre, pleading for someone to make a move.

"You'll find out soon enough," said Madri. "Turn me in, if you must." She held out her fists to him, as though prepared for shackles.

Aram seized her wrist.

And Madri opened her palm.

A cloud of powder shot up into Aram's face. He cursed, staggered back. Coughing, spluttering.

Ava leapt forward to attack, but Madri caught her and threw her back, hand closing over Ava's mouth. They hit the ground hard, and Madri dragged her further away from the boy.

Aram dropped to the ground, clutching at his throat, and then went still. All in the span of moments.

Madri released a held breath and let go of Ava's mouth. Ava gasped. The others kept their distance.

The dust faded from the air, and Aram did not so much as shudder. He lay perfectly still.

"Gods," said Ava. "Is he... dead?"

Madri shook her head. "No."

Yuri took a couple steps closer and coughed, swiftly retreating again. "God's breath, that stuff packs a punch."

"I want some of that," Deven said with a sly grin, keeping close to the door, blade at the ready.

Madri revealed the small clay vessel she'd hidden in her palm. A crude alchemical vial. Maybe an inch tall with a tiny cork stopper, which she replaced.

"One direct whiff of night's bane can knock a grown man out for several hours," Madri said.

"Probably all night for him, eh?" Yuri smirked.

Madri shook her head. "Don't count on it."

"Was it true what you said?" Ava asked. "About the council?"

Madri shrugged. "The council, yes. Though no thanks to Aram's father, I'm afraid. Same boar's ass he's always been. But my people have chosen to help you, Ms. Rykus. We have chosen rebellion."

Ava's father had held hope at unlikely alliances. A hope her mother had instilled long ago. Ava had always held her doubts. A shaman's family, perhaps. But all the Faltari people?

"How?" she asked.

"We Faltari may be set in our ways. But the revelation of our ancestors' bargain with Attica was unsettling to most of our kinsmen. They just... needed an extra nudge in the right direction."

"Your husband," Ava whispered, clasping the woman's hand.

A tear traced her cheek. Madri nodded, smiling. "It is always one. Before it can be many."

Deven cleared her throat. "We've a long night ahead. Tomorrow, we fight. And we all have parts to play."

"How many of you are there?" Ava asked. "Where's the runeship?"

"We have until tomorrow at midday to prepare the way."

"You're not coming with us," Ava said.

Deven flashed a smile, holding up a scroll she'd stowed in her cloak. Ava recognized it from the Sacred Hall in the temple. "I've got my orders."

"Joren's map?" Ava asked. "I thought the Atticans took it back in Yerida."

"They did," said Madri. "And it was given to Consul Pelasius."

Ava looked to Pisarre and Ruan, who both grinned.

"I thought it might come in handy," Ruan said.

"My mission is to the Abyss," Deven said, stowing the map once more. "Your mission is to aid the Faltari and slow the empire." Deven offered a salute. "For your father."

Ava saluted back, Valucian style, hand to her forehead, palm facing outward.

With that, Deven left them.

Yuri took over guarding the entrance while the rest of them prepared for their flight from the camp.

Pisarre disappeared into another room of the tent and returned with a leather trunk. The servant dropped it in their midst.

Inside were uniforms of the Bloody Company, dark grey trousers and jacket, with gold and crimson threads, the emblem of House Pelasius on the breast.

"It's dark enough, you should be able to slip out before anyone realizes you're not an Attican patrol," Ruan said. "Talk to no one. And pray to whichever gods you serve."

Ava's uniform was long in the arms and bunched beneath her armpits, but in the dark, she hoped it was subtle.

She whispered a Valucian bedtime prayer that her father had taught her as a child.

Eirè un galàthas. Cì reôn al fèren.

Into the night. With you, never alone.

Ava reached for Ruan's hand, while the others gathered near the entrance. "I've never hated a goodbye more," she said.

"If we survive tomorrow, I'll find you again. I promise."

Ava pushed away the implications of that ominous word.

If...

Pisarre opened the back entrance to the tent, and they hurried for the edge of camp.

———

"What do you mean she's gone?" Urla demanded.

Caliphus's jaw trembled before he answered.

"We are about to march, Lieutenant. What the bloody Abyss happened to our prisoner?"

"Th-that Faltari boy. Tulsein. We found him near the prisoner's stakes. Behind a tent. Out cold. Some alchemical substance."

"Aram Tulsein was ordered not to go near them again! No one saw anything?"

"There are men who saw soldiers leading the prisoners away, but no one knows where—"

"Both prisoners?" Urla shouted.

"In the chaos of the dragonfall and the preparations for the night march, the men couldn't be expected to—"

"Don't you dare make excuses, Lieutenant!"

"Yes, Lady Consul. You're right, it was my oversight. I think it must have been more of those—"

"Of course it was the Morphs, gods damn you!"

How many are in our bloody midst?

Urla paced the lane between tents, shuddering at the thought of facing the emperor with this news.

So much had happened at once. In that, Caliphus was right.

One squadron had already ventured up the pass. And the next was nearly ready to set out. Passing soldiers likely thought that the other squadron had been ordered to move the prisoners.

But it didn't matter now. The girl was gone. The emperor had gone ahead, despite his frail condition. And now, she knew why. Athanasius had already known what she'd been unwilling to accept. Her company was completely compromised.

Caliphus straightened up. "I've sent soldiers to scour the—"

"That's a waste of time. Our mission is at the end of this road. And our camp has already been infiltrated by bloody Morphs."

"Perhaps you could gain some information from the Faltari boy," Caliphus said.

"He's alive? I thought you said he was poisoned!" Urla shouted.

"Drugged. He denied everything, of course, but—"

"Lead with that information, next time, Lieutenant. Mother above!"

CHAPTER 58

OF THE FLAME

Urla left her investigation with the weight of all Îrithèa seeming to press on her mind.

Caliphus fell in stride, and they hurried across the camp for her own tent.

"Guilty, right?" said Caliphus. "He must—"

"Leave Aram Tulsein shackled and collared. He can wander down the mountain or off a cliff for all I care. Prepare to march."

"Of course, Lady Consul. Er, did he tell you the same fool story?"

"You mean, did he have the balls to accuse my son of treachery to my face? The very one who brought the prisoner to us in the first place? Yes, he was so bold."

"The alchemists detected night's bane before he woke. I spoke with them while you were interrogating him."

Urla grimaced. "Native to the island?"

"A Valucian concoction, Lady Consul."

"The Rykus girl was searched on arrival, yes?"

Caliphus's face shifted. "Certainly. But with these creatures in our midst..."

"Perhaps," Urla murmured.

All this was taking too long, and Caliphus would have known the urgency of this matter. He would have immediately told her about Aram.

She slowed her pace and looked him in the eyes. "I'm sorry, Lieutenant. You're right. Those Morphs could be anyone, that's the unnerving thing, isn't it?"

Caliphus hesitated, uncomfortable under her gaze. "Certainly unnerving. Do you suppose there's a way to know?"

In the corner of her eye, she saw the man's hand shift from his side toward the hilt of his dagger.

Caliphus never wore daggers.

Urla stepped back.

The man lunged for her. Missed. Momentum carrying him past her.

Urla drew her gladius and drove it through the man's side.

Soldiers came running from across the corridor between tents.

Urla stamped her foot on the man's wrist, and he dropped the dagger. His mouth bled like the foam of a babbling brook, spilling over teeth rather than stones.

"F-f..."

Urla withdrew the gladius sharply, pulling it down and out, leaving a chasm in his side. Blood erupted from his mouth. A waterfall. His eyes stilled.

Blades drew around her, but they did not attack.

Blood pooling, the man's features began to change. Hair lengthening, turning Elyan silver, body slimming.

"Gods! That's not Caliphus!" One of the soldiers shouted.

Urla turned to them. "We march now!"

The soldiers left her, and Urla strode away, eyes watching every corner, every shadow.

She reached her tent, looking for Ruan. And immediately sensed something awry.

———

Ava struggled to keep up with Yuri and Madri.

Shadows danced in the menacing limbs of the forest. Obstacles, masked by darkness and fallen leaves, reached out with phantom hands and sent her reeling more than once.

There was no going quietly for Ava, and it amazed her how Yuri and Madri managed to tread so lightly.

She envied the ease with which the Faltari used magic. She'd always been so stifled by the secrecy required of her at the academy. If she survived this night, she vowed she would learn.

But to survive, she had to keep moving. Each footfall seemed to scream from the ground, thudding hard, her leathern brace creaking in the cold.

They did not know if they were being pursued. But there were soldiers in the woods behind them. Somewhere.

They began to climb. Ava was vaguely aware which direction they ran in the darkness, but Yuri and Madri knew the way.

Madri reached the top of a ridge and slowed. Ava's lungs were strong, but her leg was throbbing.

The woman held up a finger to her lips, as Ava and Yuri caught up. Ava stilled her breath and listened.

Branches swaying. A drizzle of rain on fallen leaves. The dampness had helped soften their footfalls, at least.

"I think we are clear now," Madri whispered. "I hear marching."

"The scouts were called off?" asked Yuri with a deep exhalation.

"I think so, yes. Which means we must hurry."

"Great," said Ava.

Madri smiled. "You're doing fine, Ava."

"Don't patronize me."

"You've impressive endurance."

Yuri was huffing. "Glad someone does. God's breath! All the way from Yerida in one bloody day."

"And we've more to go," said Madri, moving forward. "But we can go a bit slower for a while."

Yuri looked at Ava enviously as he fell in stride with her. "Seriously, where'd you build this kind of endurance? Even with... you know..."

Ava shrugged. "Dawncrest Academy. How does a guy like you move so quietly?"

Yuri smirked. "Uh, excuse me. What do you mean, guy like me?"

Madri smiled back at them, shaking her head. "I think it's more than endurance learned at the Attican academy, Ava. As is true of Yuri's stealth. You move with constant pain, but do not tire, and I expect you're able to dull your pain as well."

Ava nodded. "I thought I was just powering through."

Madri smiled. "I could sense the *hish*, even if you couldn't. Whatever you've been told all your life, Ava, you are strong. And you've honed your spiritual strength all on your own. It's quite impressive."

"Not all on my own. My father taught me some when I was a child."

"But you can't..." Yuri ventured.

"Fly?" Ava finished for him. "Afraid practicing that would have been a pretty obvious risk at the academy."

"You focused on other, more subtle skills," Madri said, pointing to her temple.

"They've carried me this far, I guess. But I'm not sure how much farther I can go tonight and still be of use."

"Don't be so sure about that," Madri said.

A branch snapped. Ava's heart leapt. She turned to find Olma Marudeil emerging from the trees atop a mountain stag.

The forest stirred with half a hundred rustlings at once.

Dozens of stags appeared from the darkness. Faltari bearing bows and bonespears over their backs, dressed in thick fur-lined cloaks, faces painted with dark streaks.

They'd been all around, and she hadn't seen or heard a thing.

Olma drew near, a grin stretching wide. "Didn't think I'd send that oaf Yuri alone, did you?" Olma asked, stepping down. She pulled Ava into an embrace.

A tear streaked down Ava's cheek. Madri had said the Faltari had chosen rebellion. She hadn't fully realized what that meant.

"My people had a choice. For centuries, we've hidden from the problems of the world. Even benefitted, while the Atticans grew in strength. While they persecuted and subjugated our world." Olma's gaze drifted to Madri. "Our shaman reminded us of our true calling."

Ava looked around in awe as more people emerged. There must have been a hundred Faltari, maybe more.

A war party.

"We cannot stand by or flee while Athanasius has his way with the world," Olma said. "I intend to make sure your rebellion gets the dragons it needs. And then, we will close that gate for good."

"You know what the emperor did to my homeland," Ava said. "Athanasius will retaliate, whatever comes of this mission."

"We may not call this island home much longer," Olma said, louder, for all to hear. "But if we die, it will not be for a bit of land. It will be heeding the call given us by the gods."

Olma turned to the others. "Sons and daughters of the Flame, may the world be brighter for our burning!"

CHAPTER 59

BACK TO THE SURFACE

The first hints of dawn had just begun to creep over the edges of the horizon, when Riese neared the crest of the last peak into Kalengal Valley.

The climb had been long and cold. In the deep night, it began to rain. Wind whipped icy sea air up the mountainside, cutting through to her bones. Riese had expected the rain to turn to snow. She hoped it would, for then it would not pelt her in the same unrelenting way. But the All Father was rarely so accommodating.

Hish helped, but Riese feared depleting herself before her second Ascent. And besides, she could endure cold. She'd spent what seemed half her lifetime in the sparse peaks of the island. Hunts often lasted days. One winter when crops had been low and game was scarce near River's End, Riese had spent an entire week hunting in the deep snows and glaciers of northern Faltara. Every night she slept in a snow cave and shivered beside her father.

Riese regretted never saying goodbye to her parents. Regretted not being able to see them before this mission. Did they have any idea what fate had taken her?

No, she couldn't let her mind dwell on such things. Olma would tell them. And the mission lay before her. She pressed on, the summit in sight.

Most of the climb, her body produced sufficient warmth from the effort. But she wished for her fur-lined boots and woolen gloves. Helpful as Olma had been at the herder's hut, she had not packed them nearly enough layers for the Kalengal Mountains this time of year. The Feathered Serpents did not know the interior of the island nearly so well as her own clan. Coastal folk always underestimated how short the autumn was in the peaks. How swiftly the weather could turn.

Now, as they reached the last summit, the wind stilled, and the clouds parted.

Riese, Surel, Malik, and Ulgar looked down upon the sacred valley of their ancestors as the sun approached the horizon, somewhere far beyond the mountains.

Faint light spread across the inky sky. The masses of the Spires loomed in the distance, hovering near the center of the valley, where the sweeping Mountain of Souls dominated the landscape.

Grey light pushed against the darkness, slowly permeating like dye in a barrel.

Riese met Malik's gaze. He was troubled, fearful. Usually he fought to hide such emotions, but the death of his father haunted him, and Riese wished she could do something. But there was nothing to say. This mission was the answer.

Surel was doing better, or at least she was not in visible despair. The tragedy seemed to have matured her overnight, and her mother's strength and determination had risen to the surface.

Ulgar was harder to read. Pensive. Sarcastic. Impatient. If it had been up to him, they would have run most of the night and likely drained their magic entirely. Begrudgingly, he'd listened to reason. But clearly, slow and steady was not his general way of doing things, and exactly what had got him into trouble on his first Ascent.

As they surveyed the valley, cloaked in shadows, they rested for the first time in hours. A sense of relief washed over the entire group, but it was soon replaced by sighs and shuffling feet.

"It's cold not moving," Surel muttered.

Riese nodded, pointing down the mountain. "We'll want to reach the tree line before the sun hits this ridge. Those dragons will be here before the rest of the Attican company."

"The journey down will be easier," said Malik. "I think we can spare more *hish* to warm ourselves now that we're close to the source."

Ulgar grinned, jaw shuddering as he spoke. "What? You guys c-cold?"

They chuckled, the warm laughter rattling Riese's bones.

Riese focused on her spirit. She *could* sense the difference, like taking a step closer to a fire. The power at the heart of the Mountain of Souls. The only reason any of them could manage a climb up the Spires.

Carefully, she drew threads of magic from the world around, into her spirit, then, into her heart, and let the pulse of her blood carry that strength through her body. The same way she knew this island without a map, Riese knew the paths within her body, like creeks and rivers, waterfalls and lakes formed from the melting of glacial ice.

The chill faded, and as they continued down the steep mountainside, her body warmed, and Riese began to think the gods might be on their side after all.

A voice within affirmed it, though she knew the source of that voice resided in the pack on her shoulders, wrapped in cloth and nestled tight in a thick scaly shell. She reached back, brushing her hand over the side of the rucksack.

Antari's mind was growing clearer every day, stronger. The name had come to her in the night as she climbed and shivered, and she did not know where it came from. It had taken her some time to realize it was the dragon's thoughts, not her own.

He had a name.

Riese could feel *hish* emanating from Antari's spirit. The magic she'd known all her life, but there was something else as well. Something wilder and more powerful. And she could sense that other power in her own spirit too.

The one she'd felt in the dead world when she'd first found her dragon. It was here too, in her own world. And it was growing.

———

Cloaks and boots were drenched, and the path of sparse stones and trampled mountain grass grew soft and muddy, slowing the Bloody Company down as the night wore into a pre-dawn gloom.

Urla remained close to her son throughout the ride. Pisarre rode beside Ruan, offering soft instructions as they went, though for the most part, his mount guided him just fine.

In hindsight, Urla realized that her son likely felt a greater kinship with their head servant than either of his parents over the past few years. Though Urla had prided herself at balancing her duties, this balance had been much easier to maintain in Ruan's childhood, during the Good Emperor's reign.

Ruan had grown up largely in times of peace, and Urla had been more present early on, more aware of his budding thoughts and ideas. But her son had come of age in a time of persistent conflict.

Glorious times. A period of expansion. And any Golden Age could not be won without such times of duty and valor.

But Urla had missed most of her son's adolescence at war, and she had never considered the potential cost. Never entertained the possibility that her son might become disillusioned with the very empire his parents fought and died for.

Was that why Ruan had done it? Keivan's dragonfall?

No matter how she tried, Urla could not deny what she had seen with her own eyes after she'd sent Pisarre to help Ruan prepare for this final march to the heart of the island.

Traces of powder on the floor of her tent.

Night's bane.

She'd not needed an alchemist to confirm it.

That bastard Aram Tulsein had been right. Urla knew it in her heart.

Her own son, student of the esteemed Dawncrest Academy, destined for the Path of Crimson Skies all his life.

A blood-traitor.

Does Pisarre know? she wondered. *He must.*

Urla hadn't seen them apart since Ruan had returned from the hands of the enemy.

How much did they know? What had Ruan and Pisarre ascertained about the emperor's true scheme during the march?

And what was she to do about it?

———

Colors seeped from the clouds on the horizon beyond the Spires, casting them in a soft glow. Oranges and yellows shifting towards fiery reds. It was one of the most stunning dawns Malik had ever witnessed. He should have been filled with awe. The warmth of the morning should have thawed his body and stirred his soul.

But Malik felt nothing.

Body, mind, and spirit were dulled. He'd drawn little *hish* to warm himself all night. Surel had been shivering so hard that Malik had used up magic he couldn't spare to keep her from slowing them down. Now, his sister walked with a determination Malik could no longer muster.

He lagged behind as Riese and Ulgar paused at a ledge above a sweeping drop off a short distance from the tree line. Fog hovered in the dark recesses of the valley like wights emerging from the stonework of the dragon temple.

And like the ethereal monstrosities, Malik felt like he too was removed from his body. He could see the dread and sorrow enveloping him, but he didn't have the strength to ward it away any longer.

Riese motioned him over and pointed into the fog. He peered into the shifting greyness and noticed wispy pirouettes rising from the valley.

"Smoke," he whispered.

"Cookfires," said Riese.

"The Dragonmounts?" asked Ulgar.

Malik thought Riese would have sensed them like she did before. That's what they'd been counting on.

"Look closer," said Riese.

Malik peered into the shadows. It would be at least an hour before the sun crested the peaks, but Malik directed *hish* to his eyes, enhancing his vision, and spotted several dark angular shapes on the valley floor. Not wings.

"Tents," he whispered.

"At least a dozen of them," Surel said.

"No way that company beat us here," said Ulgar. "Not with that bloody dragonfall."

"You're right," said Riese.

"Then how did an entire company of soldiers get here before us?" Ulgar demanded.

"The same way Pelasius's company got to the island after the attack," Malik said, mind clawing its way back to the surface. To the mission before him.

This changed everything.

Riese cursed. "They've been here this whole time. One of those mounts must be a Knight of Caadron."

"God's breath," muttered Ulgar, "the entire march up the Soul Road was a distraction."

Chapter 60

Mysteries Beneath

The fog thinned as they descended into Kalengal Valley. The heart of the island.

Malik's body and mind were growing stronger again, though he was not sure what good it would do. If the Atticans were already here, how were they going to reach those eggs?

Riese stood still, raising a hand to stop.

A mighty rush echoed from the Attican encampment. Sharp wings cut through the fog above the tents.

"Dragons," said Ulgar. "You mean you didn't..."

"They must've been sleeping," Riese muttered. "I... I don't know. Antari didn't sense them."

A dragon, the deep green of a distant forest, rose over the hills at the edge of the camp. Gargantuan wings flapped furiously, sending near-visible ripples through the air, as the beast took off.

Magic aids their flight, Malik realized.

It was not so noticeable as they soared, but for such an incredible creature to launch itself from the ground, it now seemed obvious.

A red dragon followed, clawing its way up and up. Then, a third appeared, scales shimmering as golden as the sun.

The Faltari youths crouched low, drawing their *hish*-infused hunting cloaks tight.

The dragons soared higher, dark wings silhouetted against a bleeding dawn. They were flying away, toward the eastern end of the valley.

"Hurry!" Riese led the way toward the tree line, hunter's feet gliding near-silently despite the loose terrain.

Blessedly, the foothills shielded them from the camp. And the dragon sentinels were still climbing, up near the Spires.

They hurried faster and soon slipped into the cover of the forest. Malik could still hear distant flapping, but the dragons had flown beyond his vision.

Riese stopped at a small outcropping of boulders jutting out from the copse of snowpine. It was a narrow opening, but Malik could see pyramidal tents rising from the base of the valley to his left, and the distant outlines of dragons ahead, circling the valley now.

"They're watching the horizon," said Malik.

"Watching for that runeship, you mean," Ulgar said.

"Rykus said they would arrive by midday," said Riese. "It's our job to make sure we've got cargo for them."

"Well, what are we waiting for then?" Surel demanded.

Malik held up a hand. "We can see everything from here. Just wait a moment."

Riese nodded, patting Surel on the back. "A good hunter takes stock of the terrain before diving in with her spear."

They remained still, waiting to see what the Dragonmounts would do. Five total circled the valley, and the sight of them sent chills through Malik's body. The incredible beasts flew above the Spires, but Malik could still sense their magic.

The resonances were strange to him. Far less like any sacred beast he'd ever encountered. Malik sensed them much the way he could his own kinsmen. He wondered if this had to do with the bond shared with their human riders.

A couple of the dragons flew beyond the ridge line and out of sight, but three remained, circling the skies while the camp awakened.

"Why don't they fly up to the gate?" Ulgar asked.

Malik shook his head. "I don't sense anyone up there."

"You sure your sense is that strong?" Surel said.

Malik bristled at his sister's words. For so long, he hadn't wanted this training, and now, he resented Surel for doubting his shamanic ability. "Father could sense every climber during the Ascent."

"And you just came of age."

Malik sighed. "I don't know if my sense is that strong. But I can sense the dragons and their riders. I can sense the resonances of soldiers and one strong magic resonance in the camp below. But on the Spires, there's nothing."

"That makes no sense," Ulgar said.

"Well," said Surel, "let's get ahead of them then. This is our chance to—Malik, what are you doing?"

Malik stepped closer to the edge of the rock for a better view. None of this added up. The Atticans snuck ahead, and then, didn't send anyone up the Spires?

He could make out the distant blurs of soldiers readying themselves in the haze below. He peered closer, reaching out with his spiritual sense.

"Malik!" Surel hissed. "What in the Abyss are you—"

He turned back. "They're not going to the Spires."

"What?" Ulgar demanded.

Malik pointed across the valley to the base of the Mountain of Souls. A figure wearing all black strode up the foothills of the mountain, where only days ago, Malik and Riese had cast their dragon eggs into the pyre, where Malik had mourned Petyr Bromsein and the other fallen youths. Where Malik had become a shaman of his people.

The dark figure moved slowly, weakly, flanked by a pair of guards, whose runemarked armor glowed, even from such a distance. Behind them, a small company of browncloaks marched after them.

"Imperial arcanists," Malik said. "And I think..."

"That's the emperor," said Riese.

Malik nodded. "And he's the source of that strong magic resonance I've felt. I... I think he's the Knight of Caadron who brought this company here."

His stomach sank, thinking of something his father had taught him long ago.

There are mysteries beneath the mountain. Mysteries about the gate and the Spires and the Crossing. Mysteries about the very nature of magic. Inscribed in the walls. Buried with our dead. Mysteries we've only begun to unravel.

"Athanasius isn't here for the eggs," Malik said. "He's heading for the crypts beneath the Mountain of Souls."

"The crypts?" Ulgar demanded. "What for?"

Malik paced near the edge of the outcropping of stone, seeing little, mind racing. "My father believed the magic in the Mountain of Souls contained the true source of power that holds the Spires in the sky. The same power that works the Gate of the Ancients."

Riese had gone pale. "Rykus said there were more gates. Most just don't work any longer."

Malik cursed. "Athanasius doesn't care about our gate, because he doesn't need it. He just needs to know how it works. And if he's heading down—"

"Malik!"

He turned at his sister's sharp whisper. Surel pointed to the sky behind him. The others ducked back into the cover of the forest.

Slowly, Malik turned back. A dragon dove from the Spires and soared over the valley, flying toward them.

He froze.

A great fearsome resonance swept over his spirit. That same unnerving feeling that was both human and beast, both the creative power of *hish*... and something else.

Chaos. Fury.

The spiritual darkness both enthralled him and chilled him to the bone, just as that power had swept over him in the dragon temple in the Abyss.

That power resides in dragons too!

The dragon dipped lower, flying straight at Malik.

———

Surel hissed her brother's name again, desperate to rouse him from his trance. Terror shot through Riese.

The dragon soared closer. Her own dragon's spirit tensed, desperate to remain a secret from the fearsome beast.

Riese seized Surel's wrist, holding her back. They ducked down, barely daring to breathe, but a cautionary voice spoke clearer than it ever had.

Don't move. It can't see us.

Malik's shoulders shifted, about to turn.

"Stay still!" Riese hissed.

The dragon flew straight at them, dipping lower into the valley. Dark grey wings formed a stark outline against the dawn sky.

It flapped its wings hard and veered sharply upward. Riese held her breath, as it soared over their heads and disappeared beyond the forest.

When it was gone, Malik slipped back into the cover of the trees.

Surel punched her brother in the arm. "Don't scare me like that, Malik! God's breath!"

"I... I'm sorry," he whispered, standing stiff.

Surel began to tear up. "I-I can't lose you too."

Malik pulled his sister into an embrace, and Surel shuddered against him with silent sobs.

"What were you doing?" asked Ulgar when they split apart.

Malik sighed. "Trying to understand." He turned to Riese. "The power in the Abyss..."

"It lives in them," said Riese. "You sense it too."

"Along with *hish*," said Malik. "I think that's why the dragons can only hatch here in our world. And I think that's why you were the one to form a bond."

Malik studied her carefully.

Understanding came like an ember, slowly smoldering, and then roaring to life, as Malik spoke.

"You kept your head in that temple. With the stone faces. I think the power of the Abyss lives in you, Riese. Maybe in all riders."

Yes, it is true, Antari whispered in her mind.

"Our ancestors used to speak of the Great Curse lingering in this world," Riese said. "They weren't just talking about dragons. But magic."

Malik nodded. "The Attican Empire has only brushed up against the potential for magic. But there is more than even we understand. There are answers beneath the mountain. Answers about the gates, and the Crossing, maybe even the Curse. And I need to keep them from the emperor."

"How?" said Surel.

Malik gestured to the pack Rykus had given him.

"The firebomb? But what about the gate?"

"If my father was right, destroying the heart of the mountain will destroy the Spires, and the gate along with them."

"Shit," Ulgar muttered.

"But the rebellion will die without those dragon eggs," said Riese.

Malik nodded. "I will give you as much time as I can."

A cry rang out across the valley.

The first soldiers of the Bloody Company emerged at the eastern end, marching along the Soul Road toward the emperor's camp.

———

Their goodbyes were swift, never acknowledging the fact they might be permanent.

Malik had already lost his father. His mother... he did not know what had happened to her.

And now, he watched the rest of his world race away into the woods.

He feared that it was for the last time.

Part Eleven

Children of the Gods

Sons and daughters of the Flame,
May the world be brighter for our burning...

—a passage from *The Crossing**

Annotation by Joren Adensein: "We cast dragon eggs into the flame. We choose to live at the edge of the world. Are we really making anything brighter? I fear we've lost the true meaning our ancestors intended. Or perhaps, it's time we formed a new meaning all our own.

Chapter 61

Mountain of Souls

The Bloody Company marched across the valley in a long orderly line.

Malik remained at the outcropping of rock for some time after the others left. He surveyed the valley in much the same way his father did during the Ascents.

The emperor had gone underground through the main entrance to the Mountain of Souls. Malik was tempted to race after him. Take the shaman's entrance in the forest that led more swiftly to the heart of the island. But wisdom told him to wait.

The crypts were a maze beneath the mountain, like veins weaving through its cavernous body. If Malik ventured too quickly, Riese and the others would have no time to retrieve the eggs.

So Malik watched and waited.

For the past two years, Joren had taught Malik a second sight, a spiritual sight. All that time, Malik had resented the training, but he understood now what his father had always tried to instill in him. Everything had prepared him for his path ahead. Every trial and tragedy, his hunter's past, and his shaman's future. The storm during his Ascent. Derrin's death. His father's sacrifice.

And now, this mission to finally set right what their ancestors had gotten wrong.

All these years, their people had abstained from the temptations and power games of the world beyond. The stains that lingered from that dead world they had fled.

It was not dragons their ancestors feared, but cruel and terrible power.

Somewhere along the way, their ancestors lost sight of that. And handed the empire the key to their power, so that this island, this valley, would be preserved. So that Faltara would remain clean while the entire world was stained in blood.

But the Faltari were not clean.

Not yet.

Reaching out with *hish*, Malik felt resonances across Kalengal Valley. A subtle undertone of fear and unrest permeated the Attican company. It felt like the all-encompassing sense of dread that overcame River's End as a storm bore down from the icy northern peaks of the island.

Malik remained still, watching the legions from the Soul Road as they marched. Soldiers from the emperor's camp bore loads of freshly-cut lumber and coils of rope, which they left near the Faltari ceremonial hill.

Three dragons patrolled the sky now. The other two had ventured beyond sight. The remaining sentinels kept to the jagged rim of peaks surrounding the valley. At times, one would soar near the Spires, but never too close.

Malik could sense a sharp wariness in the beasts each time they drew close.

The dragons feared the Gate of the Ancients, their spirits tense and irritable each time their riders brought them within a few hundred yards. Resonances flared like fanned flames.

He felt the opposite from the resonances of his sister and his friends as they ascended the Mountain of Souls. Their determination and courage were growing, Peace filled their spirits the higher they climbed.

Slowly, something more emerged in his shaman's sense. Something that had not occurred to the Atticans to prepare for.

The legions were ready for Valucians and a flying galleon. They even suspected enemies in their very midst. But they did not know of the other band of rebels converging on the sacred valley of Faltara. The Atticans thought Malik's people had fled the island in fear.

But many remained.

Folk who knew these mountains like their own children. People who breathed magic like air, bodies hardened by sorcery honed across centuries, practiced freely, in a way no one in Attica could ever understand.

They were cloaked in incantations. Malik felt their spirits on all sides of this valley.

Drawing closer.

Malik hadn't felt them until after his companions left. His spirit had been so weary from the long night, but the Faltari had been close behind. Traveling in small parties, filtering in through the shadowy forests at the other end of the valley, spreading like termites through rotten wood.

The Faltari had come to fulfill their forsaken destiny.

Shivers raced down Malik's spine as he watched without seeing, listened without hearing. Sensing all that converged on this valley.

He opened his eyes.

The Bloody Company came to a stop at the top of the hill where Malik had cast his egg into the flames.

He felt a surge in his spirit, the most recognizable pulse of magic raging, as the emperor formed a portal with a sorcerous blade and emerged from the depths of the mountain in an instant to greet Consul Pelasius.

Malik stood.

It was time for him to go.

———

The emperor's wrath was as swift and sudden as Urla's own rise to power. Before her entire company, she was brought low. Her head throbbed from the blow. Blood pooled in her mouth, and she spat.

One more kick to her ribs, and Urla did not resist her ruler. She dipped her head in deference, laid out on all fours on the ground.

Athanasius backed away, chest heaving, and began to pace by the charred remains of Faltari ceremonial pyres. His footsteps were slow and weak.

"You *and* your company will not fail me again. Now, get up, Lady Captain."

Captain, not consul...

Urla raised herself from the ground. One knee, then an elbow to that knee, remaining upright but kneeling in submission.

She wiped the blood from her chin. It likely looked worse than it was, but it was enough to make her flush with shame.

"Yes, Lord. As you command," she said.

Athanasius showed little emotion as he beat her before her company. His voice was icy and even. "You will lead your troops up the floating mountains, even without the shaman's map. You will bring back as many eggs as they can carry. I don't care how you manage to get them there. You will find a way."

Urla's initial protest had led to this whole display. A vain attempt not to punish all the Bloody Company for the loss of the map, for the Morphs that had infiltrated their ranks, and the loss of the rebel prisoner. To punish her.

All of it covering up for the other failure that Athanasius himself had not prepared for.

The dragons would not go near the Gate of the Ancients.

Athanasius was weak from the dragonfall. He could not form a portal to the gate without climbing the Spires himself. And the emperor seemed most concerned with whatever lay beneath the Spires. He did not tell her why. He did not trust her any longer.

He was exhausted, fearful, unhinged.

And he's sending me to my death along with the Bloody Company.

Athanasius walked away, trailed by his entourage of arcanists and personal guards. The rest of his battalion had returned to the camp before they arrived.

Urla, to her own surprise, felt weary, more than anything else. Her soldiers shuffled around awkwardly, refusing to meet their captain's gaze. This hurt more than anything the emperor could do or say.

Pisarre knelt and attempted to help her rise. "Lady, please ..."

Urla shrugged him off and stood of her own volition.

Athanasius might be the most powerful man in the world, but in his current state, he punched like a student fresh from the bloody academies.

Caliphus drew up beside her. The real Caliphus had been found before the night march, drugged to sleep while that damned Morph had run around in his form.

The academy boy, of anyone, had any right to be fearful now. But a bitter resolve had come over him when he'd woken from that forced slumber.

"You heard the emperor," Caliphus said. "We march for the Spires."

Urla nodded. "The Dragyr chieftain's son informed us of a way up the mountain, and a bridge to the first spire. That is our path."

"Lady Captain," said Roak. "How?"

All of the Bloody Company sensed the emperor's fear, and it shook them more than any battle they'd faced.

Roak gazed upward and pointed at the floating hulks of stone looming above the mountain.

It was a fearsome sight, as though they might plummet and crush them all at any moment.

"There are large spans between these Spires. And we have but wood and rope."

"The Faltari climb with sorcery," cried another. "This is a doomed mission."

After all they'd been through together, what stung was the fact that they deserved better. Better than her. Or Athanasius. They were good men and women, all of them. Brave and loyal and true.

Caliphus met her gaze, a fire behind his eyes. He looked to Urla out of respect. Both of them knew her time as leader was coming to an end. She nodded for her second-in-command to address them.

"You're right," Caliphus said. "This is a near impossible task. But you forget, we are the Bloody Company, led by the infamous *Kraal ni Mira*. We march before dragons. We trample nations beneath our feet and go to the ends of the world to preserve Attica's power. And if our emperor demands we conquer the skies as well, then that is what we will damn-well do!"

The Bloody Company pounded fists against their chests and roared.

"When we bleed, we bleed for Attica!" Urla shouted. "And if we die, then let it be for glory! Now, get a move on!"

The words came with more conviction than Urla felt, but they roused her company. Their expressions turned from dismay to defiance and determination.

Caliphus nodded and saluted, a note of pride etched in his battle-hardened face. "You heard her! Let's move!"

They prepared to march, gathering lumber and building supplies that had been left for their doomed mission by the emperor's battalion before they arrived.

This mission was for the Bloody Company, and only the Bloody Company.

The emperor's soldiers remained in the valley below. Two hundred strong stood ready to defend the valley against... what exactly?

Athanasius hoped to cull Morphs from Urla's ranks by sending them up the Spires. But had they infiltrated his troops as well?

Gods, every legion soldier might very well die on this island.

And for what?

She turned to Pisarre. "I need to speak with my son one last time."

———

The top of the Mountain of Souls came easily for a hunter like Riese, even climbing through the wild terrain on the back side, so as to go unnoticed from the legions below.

Her senses were heightened as they reached the bridge to the first spire.

Riese, Surel, and Ulgar paused, surveying the long span of rope and sparsely tethered boards of snowpine, stretching from the side of the mountain's peak to a ledge near the base of the first island of stone hovering above.

Riese gazed up through the winding canyons that formed between the Spires. Dark dragyr wings flashed near the upper masses, and her heart raced.

Her dragon's spirit thrummed a warning that sent shivers shooting through her body.

I'm afraid, Antari whispered in her mind, more clearly than ever. Like it was her own thought.

Riese grimaced. There was no point in trying to hide anything from her dragon. She knew Antari felt it all, even before their bond was complete.

We're all afraid, she whispered to him. *But there is no other way.*

She took the first step across the bridge.

Chapter 62

The Bloody Mother

The Bloody Company became a dark thread, weaving its way up the Mountain of Souls. Caliphus led at the front. Urla and Ruan brought up the rear, while Pisarre rode a short distance ahead of them. When she felt certain her words would go unheard, Urla spoke to her son.

"Where did I go wrong?"

Ruan remained stoic as ever, always so bloody composed. "Mother, I'm not sure what you—"

"Don't!" Urla snapped, though still maintaining a sharp whisper. "You betrayed your house, your nation, and your mother. For a low-blood Valucian girl. I've already sorted it, so don't bother denying it. And I expect this may be our last conversation, so at least do your mother the honor of telling her why you did it."

Ruan nodded. "How did you know?"

"Night's bane. There were traces of it in the dirt of our tent. Though I suppose I knew the first time I saw you with Ava Rykus."

Ruan scowled. "You think I did what I did for love?"

Urla sighed. "Then, for what?"

"I suppose I studied too hard at the academy." Ruan chuckled.

"What do you mean?"

"You know I never fit in, Mother. Son of a Dragonmount, sure. But a middle lord married to a woman determined to fight her way past her own modest upbringing."

"Ruan, I—"

"I don't blame you for that, Mother. If anything, I admired you more for it. But surely you can see, it's not exactly the path of many noble mothers. I found myself in a strange no man's land. The highborn didn't respect me for my birth, and the lesser nobles were jealous of my house's dragon. But I was determined to prove my own worth, in my own way. I didn't make easy friends at Dawncrest, and I knew my battle future lay in the skies, not swords and spears."

"Sparring was never your natural affinity," Urla said, smiling despite herself.

"So, I studied. History. Geography. The mathematics of flight. Military tactics. Like the Dragonmounts of old."

"Campos said you were top of the class."

"Though the old riders of the Golden Age may have been brilliant, scholarship was... not celebrated by most of my peers in the way I might have expected. Perhaps that left me open to other ideas. And yes, I suppose Ava had her own influence. But so did Pisarre. His ancestors were conquered too, did you know that?"

"I thought he was Attican."

"His people were grafted in before the Golden Age. The Kracians, a nearly forgotten kingdom now, at least in the empire's eyes. The ancient emperors once enticed them, much like the Good Emperor attempted to do to Valucian lords like Rykus. But like I said, it was not love for a Valucian girl that convinced me. It was our own troubled history. All the ways we've glossed over the constant war and upheaval and bloodshed that has plagued Îrithèa. And for what? Do you know it's been half a millennia since Attica Proper has even been attacked? Our own borders have been safe for centuries, and yet we have the gall to call our enemies rebels and insurrectionists? Defending land we stole long ago?"

"It is never so simple," Urla said. "Any good student of history would know that."

Urla had seen the conditions rebels lived in. The ways in which their resistance and poor leadership only brought more devastation on the common folk.

"Perhaps..." Ruan mused. "By the time I met Ava Rykus, my mind was open. I wanted to understand more about her people, the Uprising. I grew to suspect she was not the blood-traitor we believed her to be. I had no proof. Just a feeling. Like a truth festering. Perhaps you've experienced something similar with me."

Urla grimaced, but offered no response.

"In the end," Ruan continued, "when I was thrown into the heart of this conflict, I knew it was my path. And I made my choice. Just like the shaman's family did."

They rode up the mountain in silence. Ruan spoke treason. Heresy.

"What now?" Urla whispered eventually.

"That is for you to decide, Mother."

"I am a shield maiden of Attica. What do you expect me to do?"

Ruan nodded, head jostling with the movements of his alkine as they neared the steep crest of the mountain.

"You served Attica all your life. Father sacrificed his own. And still, the emperor let you take the fall for his own misjudgments. He was the one who sent Rykus to the festival. It was his own arrogance that led to his dragonfall. Now, Lieutenant Caliphus leads the Bloody Company from the front. And you're back here. Even if you survive, what future do you think you have?"

Urla fumed, despite the truth in her son's words. She did not have the luxury of choice like Joren did. Or even like her son.

"This is not about the future, Ruan. It is about duty. Honor."

Ruan pulled back on his reins and came to a stop. "Then why haven't you turned me in? A blood-traitor in your midst. I think you know your path has changed. I think you've known it for some time, deep down."

A shout rang out ahead, soldiers running back down the trail.

Urla raced up the final stretch, feeling as though every step of this damn campaign had been one doomed move after another. Her stomach felt as though it were eating her from the inside out. Dread and inevitability wracked her body like the aches of an illness.

Her son remained at the back of the company with Pisarre, while soldiers crowded near the summit of the Mountain of Souls.

An expanse of at least two hundred feet lay between them and the first spire. The bridge that Aram had described had been cut. From the other side.

Already at Caliphus's orders, soldiers were hastily erecting an immense ladder of tethered beams, like the siege ladders used to take enemy walls. Except this would not send a man up a wall, but over a deadly chasm.

Perhaps it would work with a few attempts. With a few necessary sacrifices.

And then, there would be the next spire, and the next. And all the exposure and danger on the climbs themselves. Above, she could see an expanse of vines stretching several hundred yards between upper spires.

How many sacrifices would it take to reach that gate? And what lay on the other side?

The shaman's map was gone, and the rebels had already beaten them there.

The Faltari lost youths every year to the climb, and they were bloody sorcerers. They grew up in these mountains, anticipating their eventual Ascents all their lives.

The emperor didn't care about the risks. His hope lay beneath this mountain. This mission was but one last attempt to bleed this island dry, no matter the cost.

Ruan's words echoed in her mind: *Your path has changed.*

Soldiers carried the first siege ladder toward the expanse to test it. Long and cumbersome, one of the shoddiest ones she'd ever seen. The lumber in this valley was thin, trees stunted from growing at such heights. The logs were strung together, looking like the flimsy project of a child.

Urla raised her fist and shouted. "Hold!"

All eyes fell to her.

"Lady Captain?" Caliphus asked, eyes cold. "We have our orders."

The Bloody Company fell silent.

Urla did not know what to say to these brave soldiers she had served alongside for so long. She could not bear to send them to their deaths. She was their *Kraal ni Mira.*

The Bloody Mother. And yet...

"We bleed for Attica," said Caliphus, eying her. "You said that."

Urla nodded. "Yes, like all of you, those words have been instilled in me, even before the legion training camps. Even before my days at Dawncrest Academy, the will to bleed for my country was instilled. But this is not a sacrifice. It is suicide."

"And what would you have us do? Betray our emperor?"

"I would have you live, Lieutenant. All of you. The choice is up to you. But I am still your captain, and I will not order you to jump off a cliff."

Caliphus stepped forward, bearing a pair of runemarked shackles. The act pained him, and he did not hide it from the rest of the Bloody Company.

"Then... it is my sworn duty to relieve you of your post, Lady Captain."

Urla did not resist her young second-in-command. She held out both her hands, and let the man perform his duty. The cold steel stung her bare skin as the shackles closed around her wrists.

"I'm sorry," Caliphus said.

"Never apologize for doing your duty." Urla stepped back, and a pair of soldiers seized her arms and held her still.

"Now," Caliphus said, turning to the others. "We will ascend these bloody Spires, or we will—"

"Wait!" shouted Roak, running up the trail from the rear.

Caliphus turned, glaring. "Don't anyone else go chickenshit on us now."

"Down below," said Roak. "Don't you hear it?"

The company quietened.

Cries rose from the valley floor.

Urla turned, gazing down from the peak at the valley below. Through the tips of snowpines, she could just see the edge of the emperor's camp.

Soldiers scrambled, fell.

"We're under attack!"

———

They were halfway up the second spire when the cries erupted down below. It wasn't until they'd reached the top that Riese was able to see what chaos had taken over the Attican camp.

Arrows flew from across the valley. Volleys like she'd heard of only in tales from traders during the Festival of the Fading Sun.

War had come to Faltara.

Hope surged in Riese's spirit anew. They might win this day, after all.

"Rebels?" asked Ulgar. "From where?"

"Those volleys are coming from the forest, along the mountainsides," said Riese.

"It's us," said Surel, grinning.

"How can you tell?" Ulgar asked.

Surel rolled her eyes. "I'm a shaman's daughter. Malik isn't the only one who learned a thing or two from my father."

"Our people..." Ulgar marveled, gazing down. Another volley erupted from the trees. Dark streaks bearing down, soldiers falling between tents. "Going to war. I never would've predicted that in a thousand years."

"Our people fought before the Crossing," Surel said.

"Not as comforting as you might think," Ulgar said on a laugh.

"They're giving us a shot," Riese said. "Drawing away the Atticans."

"And the dragons too," said Surel.

Dark wings soared from the other end of the valley. With a roar, an explosion of fire ignited the trees.

Riese whispered a prayer. Were her parents out there? Her uncle and cousins?

"Well, shaman's daughter," said Ulgar, "anything we need to know about *this* crossing?" He pointed to the massive expanse of vines that stretched between them and the next spire. Wisps of fog hung in the expanse, lingering around the lengths of vine like ghostly fingers.

Surel nodded. "Yeah, don't fall and bust your leg like you did the last time you were up here."

"That stings," said Ulgar, as he stepped up to the first vine. "I'll have you know that—"

Riese felt a sudden raging in her spirit. A warning. She grabbed Ulgar's wrist and jerked him back onto the ledge.

A jackal bounded along the vines and leapt, a snarl echoing across the chasm.

Riese ducked.

Claws scraped her shoulder. She staggered back, foot slipping on the ledge. Surel seized her cloak and pulled her to safety.

Riese spun, reaching for the spear on her back, but the creature was gone.

It had leapt off the spire.

Webbed skin stretched wide as the winged jackal drifted downward.

"Shit, there's more of them," Ulgar said.

Riese followed his pointed finger. Two more dark blurs leapt from the other side of the vine bridge.

Further up, dragyrs swarmed around the uppermost spires, screeching like ravens.

"Come on!" Riese said, stepping back out on the vine.

Chapter 63

For Our Burning

Fire raged. Smoke surged through the forest of Kalengal Valley like an angry serpent, writhing and unrelenting. It was nothing like her father's tales at all. Dragonfire was pure horror.

Shrieking, a pair of Faltari archers plummeted from nearby trees, bodies incinerated in the direct line of fire. In one great flood, flames ripped through a stretch of forest at least one hundred yards in length, and quickly the flames spread.

Ava could hear the roar of other attacks. Three Dragonmounts lay waste to the valley. Wherever the other two dragons were, she feared they would be here soon.

During her years at the Dawncrest Academy, Ava had heard it said countless times that none could withstand the wrath of dragons.

Ava had scoffed.

She believed her father. Believed Valucia could resist, if only they were given their chance. But Ava had not seen a real battle. She had never witnessed a Rain of Fire.

But the Faltari elders had prepared for this onslaught, staggering their kin at varying depths throughout the valley, so no single attack could take out more than a few at one time, making it seem as though their numbers were greater, spread across the valley. And as smoke seethed from the trees, it would be even harder to gauge.

Ava kept close to the shaman's wife. A horn blew, and she and Madri, along with Faltari posted across the valley, released another volley of arrows. They had no way of knowing if their attack hit its mark. It was a shot and a prayer from vantage points all around the valley.

The ground shook as another swath of forest was consumed in flames behind them.

Ava could feel the heat from front and back, though the nearest flames were one hundred yards or more from her.

Another horn blew.

She released another arrow. In the meadow beyond, she heard the cries of Attican soldiers.

The Faltari had attacked near the edge of the valley, but the dragons had sent flames rushing up from the tree line, attempting to push them back out of range of the camp.

Madri gripped her wrist, pointing into the thick of the smoke. Toward the valley again.

"They'll drown us out here!" Madri shouted. "We have to keep moving forward!"

"Into the flames?" Ava demanded.

Madri trudged into the thick smoke. Ava could barely see. She coughed as she drew a breath.

"Use your magic!" Madri said, gripping her shoulder. "Push back against the poison in the air."

Ava focused magic on her airways. Her years at the academy had long strengthened her lungs. She could function well on short breaths and strained conditions. And if she could use magic to ward off physical pain. Why not this?

She concentrated her awareness on her breath as she took it in through the cradle of her arm, letting her magic serve as a sort of filter before it entered her lungs. She coughed again, expelling the waste.

"Good," Madri said. "Now, hurry!"

The shaman's wife led Ava over fallen limbs and crackling branches. Somewhere, a tree crashed and sparks flew.

Flames parted before them as they reached the heart of the blaze. A surge of magic issued ahead as they went. And the heat began to abate under Madri's power.

Dragonfire burned hot, but to Ava's amazement, much of the

destruction was muted by the damp environment from the rains of the previous night. The areas directly hit burned hot but soon smoldered and died as the flames spread themselves too thin beyond the nexus of the attack.

Madri's magic amplified this effect. The fact she was able to do this, while optimizing her breaths through the smoke was something Ava envied. But Madri was not the only Faltari with such extraordinary ability.

More joined them at the edge of a long black scar in the forest. The smoke thinned, and the flames had all but burned out around them.

Ava felt heat through the thick soles of her boots so close to the freshly charred ground.

Another volley of arrows launched from behind them, but Madri shook her head when Ava reached for an arrow of her own.

A dragon swooped low and let a burst of flame rip through the trees further back toward the mountains. A couple minutes later, another group of Faltari joined them.

"They think we're retreating," Ava said.

Madri nodded.

Another burst of arrows from further up the mountain.

"Some of us are," she said.

The trees writhed with smoke. More Faltari emerged. A couple dozen now. And Ava expected there were more in other parts of the valley, shrouded by their enchanted hunting cloaks and plumes of smoke.

"You planned this," said Ava.

"They rely on terror," said Madri. "They want us to fear them lighting up this valley."

"Don't you?"

Madri smiled. "Not while the emperor is still here. They are pushing their flames away from the valley. Playing it safe. And the closer we get, the more timid those dragons will be."

The shaman's wife raised a hand to the others.

They marched forward, going faster with each step toward the open valley, and the Attican camp on the other side of the trees.

———

The world was raging madness. The roar of flames in the distance. Smoke spilling through the forest. Screams of the dying on the air.

But Malik did not falter.

He sprinted through the trees at the edge of the encampment as his people descended on the imperial force. Hope stirred in his spirit more than ever before.

The last time Malik was here, he was ashamed of his people. Confused and angry and desperate to flee.

Nothing but pride filled his spirit now as he made his way toward the shaman's entrance to the Mountain of Souls. It diverged from the path leading up to the summit early on.

He kept his bonespear before him as he crept through the undergrowth. Soldiers sprinted down the mountain. Dark creatures took flight. More screaming. It was a terrible, awesome sight as the rebel Morphs attacked the Atticans from within.

Malik crouched low, slowing his pace. The swarm of resonances was overwhelming, and he'd been forced to dull his sense, so he could focus on the task at hand.

The undergrowth was thick at the base of the mountain, and the track was difficult to spot, even from the main path. Malik hurried along the edge.

A sharp rustle.

Malik spun.

Dodging a swinging gladius, he reached for *hish* and sent the Attican soldier slamming into a tree. The man crumpled to the ground and went still. Unconscious.

Malik could see a clear line to the main path.

Another Attican turned and met his gaze. The man stalked toward him, brandishing a war bow.

Malik froze.

The man was young, wearing the blue tower sigil of House Pelasius. Malik recognized the Bloody Company officer from Yerida. Urla's second-in-command, Caliphus. He was covered in blood.

The officer glanced at the soldier slumped against the tree, and his eyes blazed as they met Malik's. His nocked arrow was leveled right at him.

"Where are you going, shaman?" Caliphus demanded.

"I'm fighting with my kin," Malik said, reaching for *hish*.

"Don't! You'll be dead before you attack, magic or no."

"Your comrade's not dead," Malik said.

"What's it matter?" the officer asked. "He will be soon enough. Those bloody Morphs turned half our company against one another."

Caliphus stepped from the path.

"Your friends already reached the Spires. Cut down the bridge. Don't reckon you fell behind, though, did you? Where's this path lead?"

Malik focused his sense. He'd never tried to manipulate the world at the speed of a flying arrow before. But there was always a first time.

"It's just a hunting track," Malik said.

Caliphus smiled. "Let's find out together!"

The arrow flew. Malik sent a surge of *hish* out in front of him and dove. The arrow whipped past him, sending fur from his cloak flying. A sharp pain filled his shoulder.

The arrow thudded into a tree behind him.

He looked up.

Caliphus lay crumpled at the edge of the track, crying out as a man pulled a spear from his back. The man whipped the butt end of the spear around, knocking Caliphus out cold.

The man grabbed Caliphus by the shoulders and shoved the unconscious man upright against a tree.

"Pisarre?"

A voice from the undergrowth.

The man hurried over and helped a young man onto the hunting track.

Malik tensed.

It was Ruan Pelasius and his servant.

But why had they saved him?

Malik backed further down the path. Ruan and his servant strode toward him. The servant whispered something.

"Please, shaman," said Ruan. "We helped your mother escape last night. Let me help you now."

Malik could feel the truth in the boy's spirit. He shifted his pack on his shoulders. "I am going under the mountain to close the gate for good. This mission is mine alone."

"Close the gate," Ruan said. "Under the mountain?"

"Get yourself to safety. As far from here as you can." Malik turned away from them.

But Ruan called after. "We know where more firebombs are."

CHAPTER 64

Collision

Hands shackled in front of her, Urla staggered down the mountain path. Bodies were strewn upon the ground as she neared the bottom. Soldiers she'd led and served with for years, chasms ripped through their stomachs and chests. Entrails spilled. Blooding seeping into the earth.

She'd seen countless soldiers die all her life, and the Bloody Company had known hundreds of fallen over the years. It had always pained her, but it was part of the life of a soldier. It was the necessary price of honor and glory.

This was different. Because part of her had welcomed this. Had sided against the emperor.

More bodies littered the path, though there was no sign of enemy troops anywhere.

How many Morphs had infiltrated her troops? They had rooted out a few more after the attempt on the emperor's life, like the one impersonating Caliphus. But they had feared there were more, walking around in the likeness of their comrades. Bodies left somewhere along the Soul Road. Maybe even back in Yerida.

Urla spotted a fallen soldier, lying in a pool of blood, staining long silver hair.

An Elyan, just like the Morph that had attacked her last night.

There was no sign of Ruan or Pisarre.

But Urla did find Caliphus near the base of the mountain. Her devoted lieutenant was slumped against a tree near the edge of the valley. Through the undergrowth, Urla could make out the fire and smoke and violence of battle in the camp beyond.

She knelt next to Caliphus's unmoving body, a pang of grief rising unbidden in her gut. The keys to her shackles hung from his belt.

As she reached, a hand clasped her own.

Caliphus's eyes opened. Blood gurgled from his lips. "The Bloody Mother here to collect her due, heh... g-guess I never thought it'd be true for me."

"Caliphus, I—"

His grip tightened. "Don't... don't you dare fucking apologize." He released her. She took the keys, and quickly undid her shackles.

Caliphus had closed his eyes again. Urla peeled back his uniform and grimaced at the ugly wound.

"Did you know all along?" Caliphus whispered. "Were you in on it?"

"On what?"

"This slaughter... y-your servant did this," Caliphus said. He coughed up blood.

"Pisarre? Was Ruan with him?"

Caliphus's head rested back against the tree. His eyes were closed, but he spoke one last time, his voice softer with each word. "Went... after... shaman..."

"Shaman? Where?"

But Caliphus had faded.

Urla grabbed a gladius from another fallen soldier and hurried to the battlefield.

———

From a ledge near the top of the final spire, Riese could finally see everything. The midday sun shone bright this high, though the valley was cloaked in smoke and flame.

The Attican camp was embroiled in battle. Dragons lay waste to the forest all around.

Dark wings approached on the horizon. Glints of white sails emerged from billowing clouds in the eastern skies.

The rebels!

Hope surged within her. Riese reached up and found purchase on the jagged face of the last spire with her right hand. Then her right foot. Her hand nearly slipped on a loose hold.

Dirt and scree cascaded behind her. She tried again, reaching higher. But the hold held firm. After that, it was a string of a few more moves, and she pulled herself up to stand at the top of the world for the second time in a matter of days.

Dragyrs swarmed around the gate ahead, circling, swooping toward the platform of stone, but they did not fly through. Nor seemed to pay Riese any mind. Still, she kept watch in the corner of her eye as she turned to help the others.

"Watch that loose spot," she called back.

"Oh, don't worry, we saw it," said Ulgar.

"Shit fell right on our heads," Surel added.

"Sorry!"

Malik's sister poked her head above the peak, and Riese pulled her to safety. Ulgar followed.

"Well, they're worked up worse than last time," said Ulgar, watching the dragyrs pensively.

"Think it's the battle?" Riese asked.

"Seems like they're fixated on the gate," said Surel.

"Well, let's hope they stay fixated a bit longer."

Riese led the way toward the narrow spine of rock they called the Blade.

"I'm not taking any chances this time," Riese said, and stooped down and positioned herself to shimmy across, straddling the rock just like Yuri had during their Ascent.

It felt slightly safer, in the event a dragyr swooped near, but it also kept her on the exposed lip of rock for longer than she liked. It took all her focus to keep her eyes fixed on the other side as she inched her body across the twenty foot span.

Soon enough, she was across, Surel and Ulgar right behind her.

Seven dragyrs circled the gate, and a few more soared higher up, near the smaller distant spires that rose beyond. The beasts shrieked but never came close enough to pose a real threat, even as they approached the Gate of the Ancients.

"They were riled on our Ascent," Ulgar said. "But they were peaceful until me and Aram arrived. This is different."

"I mostly dealt with them on the other side," said Riese, gripping her bonespear tight. "These ones are staying back."

They're afraid, Antari whispered across their link.

"If they were already like this before we got here," said Surel. "Then, that must mean..."

Ulgar nodded. "I don't think we're the first ones up here."

———

Ava remained near the edge of the battlefield, firing arrows from the tree line while the Faltari engaged the Attican company in the meadow beyond.

Fires smoldered up the hillsides, a couple still blazing hot farther up the mountainsides.

More dragons neared, coming from opposite sides of the valley, flying through the thick smoke.

A manic screech filled the sky.

Ava could hardly believe it. Since the failed Uprising, the Valucian dragons had remained hidden back in Flameholm.

No more.

Wings whorled as the Attican red that had been laying waste to the forests reared back. An icy blue dragon shot down from the smoke shrouding the valley. Taking the Dragonmount completely by surprise.

The two dragons collided.

Spun through the air, claws scraping. The Attican rider went flying from his mount, and the Valucian blue latched on to the throat of the red and wrenched.

The red dragon's neck went limp, and it plummeted.

Chapter 65

Paths of the Dead

Urla knew a lost battle when she saw one.

The moment the Rebelmount attacked, she knew. The imperial riders were too accustomed to owning the skies. They were not prepared to defend them.

Flashes of her husband's dragonfall flashed through her mind. On the Sigan plains, Urla had gone into a battle frenzy. Becoming the famed Bloody Mother that had brought her so far in her life as a soldier. Urla ended that battle bathed in the deaths of her enemies.

But now...

Urla did not fight.

She no longer knew which side ought to prevail. But there was one thing she did know without question.

Her son had gone after the young shaman and she had to find him.

Madness overwhelmed the Attican camp. A Faltari rebel came at her. A young man with the over-confidence of a first battle that he was winning. The man leapt with super-human strength, shooting toward her, bonespear extended.

But he was not trained for combat. Despite the speed, a slight shift of her body sent him blazing past her, and she kept right on running.

Dragonfire split the sky. Urla could not tell if it was Attican or Valucian through the smoke. Urla pushed toward the edge of camp.

And spotted her house's sigil on the back of a cloak. All her soldiers wore the white crest on black. But the blue tower was reserved only for officers, and the lords and ladies of House Pelasius.

Holding tight to Pisarre's wrist, Ruan followed after a young man in a Faltari cloak, fleeing from one of the emperor's provision tents.

Urla ran harder, dodging the exchange of blows between two Faltari women and an imperial soldier.

Ruan and Pisarre disappeared beyond the tents. Urla ran harder.

And then, her feet flew out from under her.

Urla crashed to the ground. Someone on top of her. She twisted, reached for her gladius, turned.

To find a bonespear in her face.

"Madri!"

"Drop your weapon, Consul." The woman's furious eyes held hers, and Urla knew the woman would kill her if she did not obey.

Urla dropped her gladius on the ground. She raised her hands in surrender. "I saw your son. He was with Ruan."

———

Beyond the gate, the Abyss felt... different.

Riese could not put her finger on it at first. Of course, there was the absence of *hish* in this place. She'd felt that the last time.

As she strode up the canyon path from the gate, toward the ruined city of the Ancients, Riese realized what it was.

Her thoughts were no longer shared. Antari's spirit had become faint. No longer warning or encouraging her. All at once, her dragon had gone dormant again.

The Attican dragons wouldn't come near this place, Riese thought. Because they cannot survive here.

Despite the distinct feeling that they were not alone, there were no signs of anyone else. There were not even dragyrs in the grey skies this time.

"I don't like this," said Riese.

Ulgar and Surel said nothing, but seemed to withdraw inward, much like her dragon, in the absence of their magic, the emptiness of this dead world pressing on them. They gripped their bonespears tight and pressed forward.

But Riese did not feel the same weight.

There was power in this place, and her spirit drew it in like breath. She did not feel as strong as she did in her own world.

But Malik was right. Another magic lived in her too.

She did not feel empty in the Abyss. And this scared her nearly as much as the silence.

The three crested the final rise and looked out at the scattered remains of a once-mighty city. The toll of the past day seemed to come over Ulgar and Surel. Both walked slower, and Riese had to consciously adjust her pace.

Their boots crunched on fragments of dark gravel that littered the streets. But as they continued on, it grew louder.

No, it was another sound. Distant thuds and a louder crunch. As they reached the long expanse of the main thoroughfare, unintelligible voices carried across rooftops.

Who was here?

Riese hurried from the center of the wide lane, and led the way, following the edge of the road, toward the temple where she'd gotten her own egg.

They passed the street where she'd fought off the dragyr that attacked Petyr Bromsein. The pounding grew louder, followed by something horrific she couldn't explain. Something spiritual, but darker, more chaotic. Surging with finality after several loud pounds. Screaming filled her mind. Sending waves of pain coursing through her spirit.

Then, it happened again. And again.

Surel gripped her arm. "What's wrong?"

Riese had stopped, just before they reached the next street, her back pressed against the ruined wall, eyes closed, hands pressed against her temples. She hadn't realized she'd stopped.

"I... I..."

She shook her head.

It was the feeling she'd felt with the dragonfall. A dragon's spirit being cast out into the great chaos.

Riese had felt it one other time. When the Ascendant threw their eggs into the fire. Each soul screaming in her mind.

"Someone… is destroying the eggs."

Riese felt sick, unable to fathom how or why someone would do such a thing, even though she had cast her own dragon into the fire only days before.

But hers had lived, thanks to their potential to bond.

She pressed on and stopped at the edge of the torn street. What she saw sent shivers shooting through her. Dozens of soldiers in white uniforms. Riese had seen that uniform before. Deven lè Nir had worn it to the rebel council.

Riese felt sick.

The Elyans had fooled them all. Used the notion of rebellion to reach the source of their enemy's power. Not so it could be used to aid the rebellion. So they could destroy the very power that could free the oppressed nations of Îrithèa.

The soldiers swung glowing runemarked war hammers down upon an egg in the streets. Blow upon blow, until there was a great shudder. A pulse of chaotic energy exploded up the street as the precious scaled egg cracked open. More soldiers emerged from an ornate doorway, bearing more eggs in their arms.

Riese turned and froze.

Ulgar and Surel both stood still. Enormous, white-uniformed soldiers held them, hands covering their mouths.

A familiar face stepped from behind them.

"Deven," Riese said. "God's breath! What are you doing?"

The woman's thin lips pursed, then shifted into a smile. "I must thank you, Riese. We never would have reached this place without you."

"Where did all these soldiers come from?"

Deven smiled, hand resting on the hilt of the godblade at her belt. She motioned to her soldiers. and they eased their grip on Ulgar and Surel, though they took their bonespears.

"Rykus did a fine job keeping the Atticans distracted last night. A gods-damned dragonfall against the emperor. Morphs in their very midst. It gave me the chance to move on the Spires in the night unnoticed. After that, it was simply a matter of forming a portal outside the gate to bring soldiers from Elya."

"You used him," Riese said. "You let Rykus die so you could reach the eggs yourself."

"Rykus sacrificed himself for the mission. To destroy the source of the empire's power. That was the order of the council. We always had the same goal."

"This is not what Rykus wanted."

Another burst of magic pierced Riese's spirit as another dragon expired.

"No," said Deven. "Rykus thought too small. Too fixated on Valucia, and this little corner of the world. So long as there are dragon eggs, and other gates with the potential to reach their source, the Attican Empire will always be a threat. We can't just close the Faltari gate. We must destroy the source of power itself."

Riese's body ached as soldiers down the road continued their slaughter.

"If Attica loses their dragons," Deven said, "their power will diminish. Perhaps not as fast as Rykus would have hoped, but their power will fade, nonetheless."

"And Valucia? Chardonia? The other nations who've struggled here in the West for centuries? You never had any intention of helping them, did you?"

Deven lè Nir eyed Riese. She clasped her on the shoulder. "I admire your passion, Riese. But you and Rykus both were not thinking long term. It is that sort of short-sightedness that has plagued the West ever since the Crossing. Do you know how many rebellions and insurrections have transpired over the ages?"

Riese shook her head.

"No," Deven went on. "Of course you don't. Because you Faltari have lived with your heads up your own asses all this time. And now that you decide to give a damn, you think you have all the answers?"

Riese hesitated.

"You're right," Deven said. "Rykus's rebellion will fail. Gods, he didn't even have the support of the other Valucian lords. And Chardonia, his greatest ally, they will fall in a few months. But without any future dragons, Valucia *will* find its freedom, one day, and so will other nations."

"And Elyans won't have to spare a drop of sweat or blood," Riese said.

"You've no idea what Elya has sacrificed. This is your first hint at war. I'm twenty-three, and I've already fought in two wars in the East. Nearly a dozen campaigns. A good captain does not lead her troops into a needless war, Riese Torendeil." Deven gestured at the crumbling walls around them. "This world was destroyed by dragonfire and needless wars. If I can spare our world the same, I will do whatever it takes."

Riese did not know what to say. What to think.

"I like you, Riese," Deven said, holding her gaze. "And I admired Rykus. I see the spark he saw in you. Now, it is your turn to do what it takes."

"What could I possibly do?"

Deven held up a map of the dead city and spread it open for them all to see. Several sites on the map had already been checked off with large Xs. "Most of these sites have no more than a handful of eggs remaining. It seems the Attican supply is not so large as we feared. But as I understand it, you found a larger store."

Riese made up her mind at what she must do. She drew a long breath, then nodded. "Deeper in the city. I... I don't think it's marked on this map."

"Very good" said Deven. "Lead the way, Torendeil!"

———

Beyond the chaos of battle, Madri motioned toward a path through the woods, and Urla followed.

She had not seen Ruan after he disappeared from the camp tents. But she knew that Madri and her family shared a connection beyond any Urla could fully comprehend.

All she could do was trust as they wound through the smoke-filled woods, eventually leaving the path entirely, and following the base of the Mountain of Souls.

They came to an opening that looked like little more than a hole in the ground.

"The original entrance to the caverns," Madri said. "Before my people turned them into crypts."

Urla barely fit through the opening.

Inside, the cavern swiftly expanded, though still, Urla had to stoop in many places. The stone was creased with a curious source of light, like emerald veins branching between the cracks.

"What is this place?" Urla whispered.

"The heart of the island," said Madri, "whose mysteries your emperor is trying to unravel."

CHAPTER 66

SECRET OF VALUCIA

The caverns branched in a dozen different directions. Even Malik did not know where all of them led. Many were still being explored as his people lay more of their ancestors to rest.

It was easy to get lost. One time when she was nine, Surel wandered off for a couple of hours, while their father prepared a resting place for a member of the Feathered Serpents clan. Derrin found her outside the runemarked door of the Spirit Realm.

The strange tendrils of magic that threaded all through these caverns gathered there, pulsing, seeming to lead wanderers down, the same way they led spirits to the next life. And as he had expected, this was the same place he found the emperor.

Malik watched from a side passage. He'd taken the more direct route from the shaman's entrance in the forest. The front entrance was ceremonial and close to the burial crypts. But Malik guessed the emperor had wasted much time wandering the paths of the dead before finding his way here.

The emperor's resonance was weary, spirit plagued by anger and frustration and fear. Body on the verge of complete exhaustion.

The resonances of Riese, Surel, and Ulgar had gone dark before Malik entered the crypts. The runeship had reached the valley and dark-winged Morphs joined the dragons in the skies. Faltari charged from the forests.

All the while, the emperor and his brown-cloaked arcanists attempted to decipher the sorcery sealing the door to the Faltari's most sacred chamber.

But they did not know it was bound by spirits and oaths.

There was so little Malik understood about magic. He knew that now more than ever, but these Atticans knew far less.

While the arcanists worked, a guard ventured back and his blade drew with a sharp ring as he spotted Malik.

"Drop your weapon!"

Malik's heart pounded in his chest as he set down his bonespear. Despite the certainty in his path, he was walking defenseless into the hands of the greatest enemy in the world. Once Malik dropped his weapon, the soldier pulled him from the shadows.

The emperor turned from the chamber door.

"Lord, found this rat scurrying in the dark!"

The soldier shoved Malik forward, pricked his back with the point of his sword. A warm trickle of blood dampened his shirt.

Athanasius strode forward, smiling. "Well, you must be the young Faltari shaman." The emperor's voice was smooth, silky. Though he looked like he'd been dragged to death and back.

The guard pressed his blade against his back, ready to drive it through should Malik dare make a false move.

Athanasius waved the man off. "Come now, Sergeant. This is a man of prayer." His smile was strangely inviting. It was no wonder he'd won over the courts of Attica, not to mention, becoming the non-hereditary heir of their Good Emperor.

Malik nodded. "You have brought war to my island, Lord. But I come in peace."

Athanasius flashed that smile again, teeth a strange amalgamation of the emerald light of the mountain's magic, mixed with the flickering fires of torches.

Another guard returned, holding Malik's sack.

"Found this further up the passage," the guard said.

Malik cursed as the man dug in and pulled out Rykus's firebomb.

The emperor raised a querulous brow. "Come in peace, indeed. It would seem we've stumbled upon the right place, after all. And found the *precise* person to get us there."

———

The halls of the dragon temple were silent. Even their footsteps seemed muffled.

Riese led the way through the crumbling outer halls, and then, through a statue-lined entrance to the worship chamber within.

Deven gasped at the brilliant sight of the ceremonial basin upon the dais, casting fragmentary prisms of light all around the enormous room.

"Gods!" Deven said, gazing around the intricately carved vaults in the ceiling, and the windows in the dome that looked down on the dais.

"Do you think dragons came in here?" asked one of the soldiers.

Deven shook her head. "Windows aren't big enough."

"They must be thirty feet across!"

"You clearly haven't seen a full-grown dragon," said Deven with a grin. "No, I wager the ancient dragons would just poke their heads through during ceremonies or the like. If we climbed onto the roof of this place, I bet we'd find some sort of landing stations. Who knows? Maybe that was even the inspiration for the landing pads first built for our runeships. Some ancestral memory."

"How long you think it's been since we inhabited this place?"

"Millennia," said Deven. "At least."

Riese said little. Ulgar and Surel kept looking to her, trying to determine what her play was. Or if she had one.

All Riese could do was hope they followed her lead when it came to it.

She let the Elyans carry on with their awe-struck praise of the Abyss, searching for more connections to their renditions of the Crossing.

People always searched for the answers they hoped to find. Riese knew that truth too well.

All the hints she'd offered her parents about her romantic inclinations had always, somehow, found a way to give them the opposite impression. The one they wanted to see, where she produced offspring and kept her feet firmly planted in the mountains of Faltara, becoming a cabin wife, with a fine hunter of a husband, like Vinder Perinsein.

Her people's views of this dead world had always supported their history, their version of the age of the world. Their reasons for hiding away on this island. Their beliefs.

And these Elyans would do the same.

Riese wondered if anyone could know the truth about the past—even if they were to comb over the Abyss for years looking for clues—maybe everything was too tainted by their own minds. Their own delusions.

Of course, that was what she was counting on.

Riese led Deven and the others down one of the main aisles, partitioning vast rows of benches, where ancient worshippers once sat.

They were empty, now, but Deven speculated what it must have looked like when thousands filled these halls and uttered prayers.

With each step, they were being lured deeper into this temple. Riese could feel that other power growing even now.

They reached the dais at the center of the hall, and Deven went straight up the steps to examine the trove of dragon eggs, eyes never wavering to the pillars that loomed over the spot.

No faces there yet.

———

Ava's heart soared.

The best kept secret in Valucia had been unleashed at last, and the Atticans were not prepared.

Ava had spent all her childhood listening to her father speculate, dream about the moment the Atticans first realized the sky no longer belonged to them.

The other imperial mounts were split across the valley, both converging on the Valucian blue, when the second Rebelmount emerged from the smoke. Emerald wings pulled in tight, it dove, while the blue faced the Atticans head-on.

A cacophonous boom erupted from the other end of the valley, drawing the attention of the indigo dragon.

White sails loomed as the runeship emerged from the clouds beyond the Spires, and dark-winged Metamorphi took flight, streams of black, like bats pouring from a cave. The indigo let loose a stream of fire at the ship, but another boom sent it diving to evade the attack.

An Elyan cannon, armed with firebombs launched from a rune-marked barrel.

The Valucian dragons both converged on the Attican grey. It was not as breathtaking as the surprise dive of the first attack. Flames lanced across the sky as the grey tried to fly out of the thick smoke that hung over the valley.

But it was no match against two Rebelmounts.

Twin bursts of dragonfire shot across the grey's back as it fought to rise, and its rider fell, engulfed in the flames.

Cheers erupted from the battlefield as the second Attican dragon fell, wings shredded by the Valucian beasts.

We only get one chance to reveal our hand, Ava's father had always said.

She just wished he could have lived long enough to witness it.

At the sight of the runeship and the second dragonfall, the indigo dragon fled, disappearing beyond the valley.

The other two Attican dragons had still not returned, and Ava suspected they never would.

She was so transfixed by the sky battle, she didn't realize the battle in the valley had ceased. All across the fields, Atticans dropped their blades and spears, and fell to their knees in surrender.

———

"Lord Emperor!" the Attican guard said between frantic breaths. "The rebels are here!"

Athanasius nodded, showing no emotion.

"They've slain two of our—"

"Enough," the emperor said. "Quit quibbling. Either the rest of our dragons survive the raid, or they do not. There is nothing I can do now, and it is of little consequence."

"Lord, little—"

"We are on the doorstep of the greatest secret in all our world. The origins of the Crossing itself." Athanasius turned to Malik. "Alright, shaman."

Malik stepped up to the runemarked door, praying he wasn't making a grave mistake. But he felt in his spirit that this was his path.

Just like the door to the sanctum back in the Temple of Yerida, this door was meant to be opened by shamans alone.

Malik spoke the dead language— *"Melana esso tanai"* —and pressed his palm to the runemarked stone that lined the doorway.

Glyphs illuminated with a golden light at his touch, responding to the words and the oaths that bound them.

The stone door shifted with a jolt, and Malik pressed it inward. Light exploded from the opening, and Malik led the emperor inside the Spirit Realm.

———

Urla felt as though the vast weight of the entire mountain were pressing down upon her the deeper they went. Menacing stone walls grew so tight in places, she had to walk sideways or even crawl.

She'd always hated confined spaces, as any warrior would. The idea of stumbling upon an enemy in this close, dark space—with nothing but the faint light of the veins of magic weaving through the stone—made her skin crawl.

But for the barely perceptible tracks left in rare soft places in the cavern floor, they wandered alone. Despite only occasional evidence, Madri always seemed sure of her way.

Each of Urla's breaths seemed impossibly loud, echoing off the caverns, or else the walls of her own mind. She couldn't tell.

Madri held up a hand, and Urla froze. Listening, breaths held.

Indiscernible voices echoed faintly up the corridor.

"Malik," Madri whispered.

"And?"

"I don't know. My husband and son are better trained at sensing spirit resonances than I. There are others with him, and one possesses an incredible magic power. I think it must be..."

The voices faded, and the halls went silent once more.

Madri's expression shifted.

"What's wrong?" Urla asked.

"I've lost my son's resonance," Madri said.

"Do you mean he's dead?"

"No. A rush of resonances, all at once. He's gone with the emperor into the Spirit Realm."

"But if your son intends to destroy the gate, why would he—"

"Because Malik's not the one who will destroy it," said a voice from the darkness.

Urla reached for her dagger. Stones scraped behind them.

"No sudden moves!"

Urla knew that voice. She made to turn but felt a sharp prick in her back. "Pisarre, you've served me faithfully your whole—ah!"

"I said, *no sudden moves*," Pisarre hissed, pressing the spear with uncanny precision. Close enough for her to know he meant it, but soft enough not to wound her.

Urla remained still, breaths even, calculated. "I'm not here to stop you, Pisarre. Where is my son?"

"I'm here," said Ruan from somewhere behind Pisarre. Relief rushed within her.

"Thank the Mother," she whispered.

"Why are you here?" Ruan demanded.

"Urla spotted you," Madri said. "Following my son through the shaman's passage."

"We thought you were together," said Urla.

Ruan whispered something to Pisarre. The servant protested, but after a brief exchange, he relinquished the end of his spear.

"You may turn around," Pisarre muttered.

Urla moved slowly, like the prisoner Pisarre saw her as. She kept her hands raised above her head.

Pisarre addressed Madri. "You're here freely? She did not force you?"

Madri nodded, remaining close beside Urla.

"Move apart," Pisarre ordered.

Madri stepped forward. "We came for you. And for Malik. To help..."

Ruan clapped the servant on the shoulder and whispered one last order, and Pisarre stepped back. Ruan drew closer to Urla.

"Why are you here, Mother?"

Urla smiled. "You were right, son. My path has changed. You helped me see that. And... well, I've made my choice."

His expression softened, his lip trembled, and he stepped closer. "I believe you."

Urla pulled her son into an embrace. There were so many things she did not know. But she knew this was her path.

Ruan stepped back.

"Malik has taken the emperor out of our way. We must go."

"Your way to where?" Urla asked.

CHAPTER 67

SOURCE

Riese, Ulgar, and Surel remained at the base of the dais, while Deven and a pair of Elyan guards began to remove eggs from the basin.

"Shit! There must be a hundred of them!" Deven marveled. "We should have brought everyone. I'm going to need you too, Kesler!"

A pair of soldiers kept spear points trained on the prisoners' backs.

"But Captain," said the guard named Kesler. "We can't just leave the prisoners un—"

"We'll need their help too," said Deven. "This is the motherlode."

Ulgar and Surel looked to Riese. She hesitated.

"The Abyss with that," said Ulgar. "We en't gonna—"

"You will if you want to get out of this place," said Deven. She set an egg on the dais, and one of the soldiers swung his war hammer with a hollow ring as the runemarked weapon struck home.

One more swing, and the egg cracked. A surge of dark energy erupted from it. Inside, there was nothing but an empty shell shattered on the temple floor.

But Riese felt the loss in her spirit.

Sorrow swept over her, the same way she felt at the Festival of the Ascension.

It was true, many of these eggs might never have been bound. Might never have hatched. But it did little to quell the sinking feeling in her heart.

Whatever their reasons, what these Elyans were doing was a bloody tragedy. A genocide.

But Riese had a part to play for a while longer. She did not know how much Malik had told Ulgar or Surel about their first experience in this place. After the storm and the night spent on the Spires, the strange encounter in this temple had been overshadowed by all that followed. Riese, Yuri, and Malik had escaped unscathed. Whatever spirits were trapped here had not followed them. Perhaps they could not leave this room at all.

Riese turned to Ulgar. Kesler was waving his spear at his face, while Ulgar crossed his arms and backed away from the dais.

"Stop!" Riese said. "We'll help."

Ulgar glowered at her, but Riese closed in on him, praying he saw what she was trying to do.

"What do you want me to do?" Riese asked. "These bastards will kill you. And they're going to do this, one way or another."

"Maybe," said Ulgar. "But I think they won't have enough time, unless they're willing to stay here in this world for good."

"What do you mean?" demanded Kesler.

"What I said, boar's ass," Ulgar shot back. "The gate will be destroyed soon. And I think you should know your captain has no intention of leaving this place in time."

"Quiet, boy," said Deven.

"Or what? You'll kill me? We're all dead already."

Deven snatched Kesler's spear and swung the end around, clocking Ulgar across the jaw. He dropped to the ground at the base of the bowl of dragon eggs.

Surel ran to him, knelt by his side, glaring fire at Deven.

But the Morph captain turned to Kesler, whose tone had turned to ice.

"This is a bloody suicide mission?"

"Enough!" Deven shouted.

Her words echoed. All fell silent, glancing around the expansive chamber.

"Is this true?" asked another soldier.

"We entered through the gate, not with your godblade," Kesler said. "It doesn't work here, does it?"

Deven sighed. "No, I cannot form a portal in this place."

"You bitch!" Kesler muttered.

Deven rolled her eyes. "There are other bloody gates here, you fools! Just as in our world."

Kesler chuckled. "And you know where they are? How to open them?"

"I have intel."

"On a gods-forsaken dead world? Has the Scholerat been sending scouting parties? Oh, wait! Of course not, else we'd have just gone through that way in the first place!"

"Our mission is to destroy the Attican threat!" Deven said. "The entire threat. And we will stay here until our mission is complete!"

Riese glanced at Ulgar and nodded. He'd played his part well. So well, she'd nearly believed him.

While the Elyans argued, Riese handed Surel her pack.

She stepped toward one of the pillars, and whispered, "Don't look them in the eyes."

The Spirit Realm swarmed with resonances, dancing around the room like flits of light. The magic presence stopped the emperor and his royal guards in their tracks. Mouths gaping, eyes wide. Bodies tense, despite the beauty of this place.

It was a spiritual presence beyond anything they had experienced in this world.

Athanasius strode toward the center of the cavern, where the veins of power converged, like a thousand phantom tributaries in the same spiritual bay. Mists lilted from a small pool, drifting high to the roof of the twenty foot chamber, and settled there, glowing.

"The Source," said Athanasius.

Arcanists in brown robes swarmed around the room, kneeling down to investigate the sorcerous veins further.

Athanasius turned to Malik. "That is what it is?"

Malik nodded. "The heart of the island, though it is filled with many mysteries. My father believed the gate was merely a channel, just like the runes marking the entrance to this place. Like the armor your Attican officers wear."

"But the gates bear no runic markings, do they? At least, they didn't seem to from the air."

Malik nodded, still trying to gauge how much the emperor knew. Had he visited other gates?

"No," Malik said.

"Incantations?"

Malik hesitated. He felt certain the emperor would sense if he lied. "My people have few legends about the origins of the gate itself."

"Hmm."

"We believe it was here before the Crossing. Likely built by our common ancestors as they spread to this new world. But my father always said that the Gate of the Ancients was a vessel."

"Not a source of power."

A short bald arcanist remained close to the emperor's side. Two guards kept spears fixed on Malik while the emperor was near.

Athanasius gestured to the pool. "And this?"

"Our connection to our ancestors," said Malik, "and the Source of our magic."

"Your people are curious," said Athanasius to Malik. "To wield magic so freely. Even in Elya, magic is ordered and regimented. Their sorcerers are trained in only one aspect of magic."

"Most of my people have strengths in only certain aspects. Perhaps there is wisdom in such focus."

"Your people hold all possibilities, nonetheless. And you shamans... you possess an even greater power. This Source is the reason."

"We are baptized in this pool," Malik lied. Quick and subtle. One untruth in a stream of verity. "We spend our lives honing our gifts and using them to aid our people. All Faltari live close to the Source. We spend our lives practicing magic, but even most—"

"I would be baptized," Athanasius insisted.

"Lord, you're not Faltari. You're not trained to withstand the expansion of your spirit."

"Come now," Athanasius said, gripping Malik's jaw in a fierce hold. "We share a common ancestry, right? These gates are proof enough of that. What is Faltara, or Attica, or Valucia? Even Elya? Names. Places. And you've no idea my experience with magic."

Malik feigned hesitation. The emperor's lust for power was more than political. In Attica, few were allowed to wield magic. Yet Athanasius, a middling lord, had managed to rise to the highest station in all Îrithèa. He ordered Dragonmounts and Knights of Caadron, and all the other Attican schools of magic. Even so, Athanasius wielded a godblade himself. Rode dragons into battle.

Such a person stood no chance against the temptation of an even greater power.

"It would be unwise," said Malik.

Athanasius loosened his grip on Malik, offering a smile. "You must do what is in the best interest of your people, shaman. Just like your father did all these years. And all the shamans before. Yes, you may have chosen resistance, and maybe the Valucians will pull off a miracle on this island and fly away with a few dragon eggs. But your people? What happens to them after the rebels flee, and my Dragonmounts burn this island to cinders? I could spare them, Malik, if you give me what I seek."

Malik did not answer at once. He paused, feigning contemplation. "Alright."

Athanasius led the way, mists swelling. As they neared, the pool of magic glowed brighter.

"Step in," Malik said, holding out his hand.

The bald arcanist and the guards both glanced warily from Malik to Athanasius. But the emperor waved them off.

He stepped in.

The pool was shallow. Mists rushed around him, surging from veins lining the Mountain of Souls.

Malik gripped the emperor's hand tight. Athanasius tensed, but did not let go, as the spirits of the dead greeted him.

———

The stone pillar slowly transformed and the stunning likeness of a beautiful woman began to emerge. Her face was long and thin and elegant. The skin of her face shifted from corpse grey to a light bronze. Dark flowing hair. She looked incredibly Attican.

The Elyans argued, paying Riese no mind. She held the stone woman's gaze longer.

In the corner of her vision, she sensed more movement above and below as more faces appeared, but Riese did not look away from the woman. A ruddy color seeped in, and the eyes spread wide. Full, dark beautiful brown eyes that drew her in.

Riese stepped closer, ignoring all the warnings erupting in her mind.

Magic surged. So strong, she could feel the vibrations. Not *hish*, but that other, opposing power. If the power she'd known all her life were like the air she breathed, this one was the sea.

A raging maelstrom.

The power grew, and Riese felt it in her own spirit. A twin power to *hish* that lived in her.

Not just here, but in her own world as well. It was the reason she could bond with her dragon. For dragons fed on both powers. She could feel Antari's fury, though his spirit was dim, having been cut off from *hish*. And in this place, where only that rushing spiritual force of chaos resided, it was the reason Riese was not transfixed by the statues.

It must have been the reason Petyr Bromsein had been able to escape this place so easily, too. His egg had held the potential for bond, and so must he.

Malik and Yuri would have been overcome by the dark spirits in these halls, if not for Riese.

Dark threads of shadow began to weave up the sides of the pillars like vines, spreading, knotting, climbing. Power surged all around her.

"Gods ab—" the soldier's curse was cut off. The arguing had ceased.

Riese whispered. "Ulgar? Surel?"

"What's happening?" Ulgar asked.

"The Elyans?"

"They looked," said Surel.

"I need you to remain calm," Riese said. "Gather as many eggs as you can into our packs. Don't look up."

There was no answer, but she heard the rustle of clothing and boots as they worked.

Threads of magic coalesced above the pillars, shadows glowing with a haunting luminescence.

The power grew.

Riese did not know what would happen. She could only trust. The stone woman's lips were full of life now. When she breathed, the dark power reached for Riese.

This was her path. Riese knew it deep in her spirit, where the forces of both aspects of magic resided.

"God's breath!" Ulgar murmured.

The woman's face began to disinter from the stone face in the pillar, drifting ghost-like, and yet full of life, smiling.

Riese withdrew her gaze and turned to where Ulgar and Surel cowered, eyes on the glowing floor, as dark energy brushed past them.

"Run!" Riese shouted.

———

Urla followed Ruan into the depths of the mountain. The walls closed in around them, and still they went on. The caverns wound deeper. The threads of magic surged, casting wild flickering light all down the tunnel.

Madri took a long breath.

"What's wrong?" asked Urla.

"We're nearly out of time," said Pisarre.

They entered a vast chamber. The walls climbed to thirty feet or more, by Urla's reckoning. Several giant pillars plunged into the ceiling. Every surface was covered with runes.

"What is this place?" Urla asked.

"The Hall of the Ancients," said Madri.

"All these runes..."

"They tell the story of the Crossing," said Madri. "Written down by our ancestors. And transcribed to our sacred texts. Warnings about the past, instructions for the future. The role of magic for our people. Our sacred duty, given to us by the gods."

Urla could barely breathe, as though caught between that old world and the present.

Pisarre investigated one of the pillars, and began to remove the ruck-sack from his shoulders. He took the other from Ruan.

"This is it," said Pisarre. "This is the place the shaman described."

"This hall is directly below the Spirit Realm," Madri said.

Ruan removed a large satchel from his pack and handed it to Pisarre. The smell was pungent.

Firebombs...

Urla's servant placed the bombs beneath two pillars on opposing sides of the chamber and strung together a thick cord of fuse between them.

"Where's the rest?" Urla asked. "We'll need to run cord back out the corridor with us."

Pisarre shook his head. "We could not find enough. There was no time. It must be lit here. And now, I must ask that you take Ruan to safety."

"Pisarre, no, there must be—"

"There is no other way. Take Ruan back the way you came. I will do what must be done."

"But—"

"I've made my choice," said Pisarre. "Now, go!"

———

Eyes on the ground, Ulgar and Surel raced down the dais steps. Riese grabbed her pack off the ground.

A hand seized hers.

"What have you done?" Deven demanded. She did not look up from the ground. She must have realized something was off before it was too late. Maybe the Elyans knew more about the Abyss than she'd thought.

"I did what I had to do," said Riese. "Now, you can either come with us or stay. Your choice."

"Not without my men," Deven said.

Writhing shadows had formed a thick pillared mass above them. Power radiating into the dome above the dais.

"Gods damn it!" Riese muttered. She stepped back and pulled them, one by one, from their trance.

"Run," Riese ordered as Kesler came to. He seemed to have been stirred from a dream.

"Now, Kesler!" Deven commanded.

The Morph captain waited to leave until all four of her soldiers woke and ran ahead of her.

Riese's heart pounded. The power in the room had nearly reached its crescendo. Shadows swarmed all around the temple, spreading out from the pillar at the center.

Ulgar and Surel lingered near the exit.

"Get out of here!" Riese screamed.

She barely heard her own voice.

She and Deven brought up the rear. Deven drew her godblade, though here, it did not glow.

The soldiers rushed ahead of them. Riese sensed movement in the rows of seats on either side of the aisle.

"Holy shit!" shouted one of the soldiers. He turned and froze.

Riese dared a glance and saw the dark ruined skin of a corpse walking straight down the row toward the man.

"Nyvel!" Deven shouted.

But they were too far away. More corpses rose from their seats and walked toward him, pulsing with black threads of magic.

One appeared beside the aisle and pulled him in. Nyvel followed, and the corpses fell upon him like wolves.

"Gods above!" Deven cried.

"Don't look them in the eyes!" Riese ordered.

Ulgar and Surel had fled the chamber for the outer halls, and the other Elyans sprinted after them. Kesler tripped. Turned. And froze.

Rushes of shadow pulsed from the center of the room. And more corpses rose from their seats in the temple. Not quite body. Not quite spirit. Some ethereal between.

Deven raced ahead and swung her blade. It cleaved a head clean off as the walking corpse reached for the man. Deven kept her eyes down but managed to take down one more. Her blade thrummed with the energy.

Riese grabbed Kesler up from the floor.

"Get him out!" Deven shouted.

Riese urged the man along, running faster than she'd ever run in her life as the walls danced with shadows.

She glanced back one last time.

Deven fought off one more creature and then sprinted after.

"Go, go, go!"

Chapter 68

Crescendo

Resonances flitted around Malik, like sparks from a raging fire that consumed the Dragon Emperor.

Athanasius all but disappeared in the glowing mist.

Soldiers pressed closer. Blades drew.

Malik held up his hand.

Athanasius's grip tightened on Malik's other hand. He began to tremble, and Malik jerked him from the pool.

The emperor collapsed onto the cavern floor.

Arcanists rushed forward, knelt at his side. A pair of Attican palace guards helped him sit up, but he pushed them away.

The emperor panted heavily, as though he'd been running for his life. Slowly, he calmed, focusing, steadying his breathing.

He's been spiritually trained, Malik thought. *To some extent, at least.*

"Lord, are you okay?" the bald arcanist asked.

Athanasius nodded.

"What do you feel?"

The emperor looked shaken. Malik wondered what he'd seen. What spirits had come to him?

"Did you find what you sought?"

Athanasius turned from the arcanist to Malik, smiling strangely.

"Lord?" Malik asked.

"You lied, shaman."

Malik did not answer.

"You hoped I'd be visited by some phantasm, did you? Hoped some nightmare of my past might overwhelm me?"

Malik knew it was useless to lie. "No one can know what one will see in the pool. We see what is required. What the gods deem fit."

"You think me your enemy, shaman. But what does it say about your gods if they showed me exactly what I desired?"

"Lord, what did you see?" asked the bald man.

"I saw the truth," said Athanasius. "Of magic. Of the Crossing. The gates. The world we fled. All our bloody myths. None of them were entirely wrong or right. They were reflections. This place is a mirror."

Dread twisted in Malik's gut. He had made a terrible mistake. Whatever might be said of the young conqueror, Athanasius was no liar. Truth poured from his spirit. The emperor's body was spent, but his spirit was a blazing fire.

And Malik feared him more than any person he'd ever encountered in all his life.

"Lord!"

The voice came from the door.

The emperor turned, along with every man and woman in the room.

Malik kept his eyes on the floor. He reached out with his spiritual sense, searching for his sister's resonance. For Riese and Ulgar.

Still nothing. They needed more time.

"The battle is over! Our dragons are—"

"It doesn't matter," Athanasius interrupted. "I've found what I require. It's time for us to leave."

The emperor reached for his godblade.

And Malik lunged at him.

———

Riese ran from the inner sanctum of the temple, weaving through the outer chambers. A chill came over her like plunging into an icy river.

Ulgar had shut the chamber door behind Deven, but with horror, Riese realized it had not been the same door they'd entered by.

She glanced down the hall. Shadows poured from the inner temple like writhing flames. Shooting down the corridor toward them.

"God's breath!" Surel said.

Riese grabbed her wrist. "Don't look, damn it!"

They ran harder. The strange flat light of the Abyss marked the temple exit. Kesler reached it first. Then, the other soldiers.

Deven pulled Surel through the narrowly opened stone door. Ulgar and Riese followed, and they shoved the outer doors closed.

They sprinted down the steps. The grey sky was empty. No dragyrs in sight. On they ran toward the city gates.

Shadows began to spread into the sky, transforming the grey light to an ever-darkening hue.

As they passed through the outer entrance of the city and made for the pass to the Gate of the Ancients, Riese dared one last look back.

Tendrils of shadow shot from the heart of the city, shrouding the skies in a blanket of darkness, permeating the streets, wrapping themselves round the crumbling towers like dead fingers. The shadow kept expanding.

If it reached them, Riese feared they would die and join the horde of ancient spirits that haunted this place.

As they descended the pass, Riese found herself overtaking the others. The absence of *hish* took a greater toll on them, the longer they remained in this dead world.

The pass opened, and Riese caught the first glimpse of the Gate of the Ancients.

Behind them, shadows shot down the pass like a flood of darkness.

———

Malik rolled on the cavern floor, tangled with the emperor. An elbow jabbed his ribs. Malik held tight to the emperor's wrist, preventing him from reaching his godblade.

Malik and Athanasius moved so quickly, no one dared attack for fear of wounding their ruler. A hand latched on to Malik's shoulder from behind. Another seized his arm.

Malik focused all his *hish* and sent a pulse of magic that exploded from his body, sending both men flying backward.

Athanasius twisted. Malik shoved him down, tried to pin him, but the slender man squirmed. His knee connected with Malik's thigh, sending pain shooting up his leg.

Malik loosened his grip, and the emperor wrenched himself free, tumbling to the side as Malik lunged after him.

His leg gave out with blazing pain.

Guards seized Malik from behind, pinning his arms behind his back in a cruel hold that strained his shoulders. He shifted his leg. The muscles ached, but nothing serious. It had been a skilled move, triggering a vulnerable pressure point at just the perfect moment.

Athanasius did not reach for his blade. He smiled at Malik.

"A lot of fight for a man of the gods," said the emperor. "I'll give you that."

Malik seethed. "You know nothing of the ways of the gods."

Athanasius chuckled. "Perhaps not. Perhaps I should learn, hmm?"

Malik eyed him.

"After this island is destroyed, of course."

Malik's voice wavered. "N-no! You can't!"

"You failed, shaman. Failed your people. Failed your rebellion. But I think I shall find some use for you yet."

Malik grimaced, but his mind was only barely present. His spirit trained on the gate.

His sister's resonance blazed to life, somewhere above.

It was time.

With all the *hish* that Malik had left in his spirit, he focused. Reaching for the spirit who would finish this mission.

The guards tightened their grips. Thin, coarse ropes wrapped taut around his wrists from behind, cutting, burning. Something clasped around his neck, and his body chilled as *hish* seemed to evaporate from him.

The emperor drew his godblade with a sharp ring and swept it through the air. The shard of gemstone in its hilt flashed, the blade slicing through the essence of existence itself.

Opening a door across the world.

Malik feared it was too late. Feared Pisarre and Ruan had been captured. Feared something had surely gone wrong.

The guards shoved him toward the portal. It was like looking through a pool of water. Clear but distorted. A blurry hall towered on the other side. Pillars of painted stone. The high back of an enormous throne with pluming dragon wings. Colors shone, torches burned.

Welcoming him.

Ava searched the camp for any sign of Ruan. The Faltari used *hish* to press back against the flames that encroached on the camp. Plumes of smoke began to thin to a haze that made Ava cough. But she remembered what Madri had taught her and focused magic on her lungs, on the air entering them, and pushed out the toxins from the smoke. She still coughed, but her breaths were filled with life. If only she could aid her vision at the same time. Between her breathing and her effort to dull the pain in her hip, she could manage nothing more. It was something she was determined to master.

Ava realized she'd quit imagining if, but when.

When they left this island. When the rebellion took flight. When she was reunited with Ruan, with Malik and Riese. When the rest of the Faltari joined their cause.

Most of the rebels were dealing with the surrendered Atticans or helping the Faltari with the blaze. Some made to enter the crypts beneath the Mountain of Souls to search for the emperor, but Olma ordered them away. Ordered everyone to make for the other end of the valley, away from the destruction.

Ava followed the flow, eyes searching for Ruan.

Morphs darted through the skies. Far above the Spires, she could see a swarm of dark wings and faint screeches. The runeship settled in an open field near the edge of camp. It landed at the base of a hill, and the bow jutted into the skies at a bizarre angle.

"Ava!"

She turned at the voice. Her heart leapt as the ugly faerie darted over to her.

"Lir'ghe!" she said, shaking her head.

"You are looking like... how do you say... sheet."

The Kroqala hovered about a foot from her face, arms crossed over his tiny chest. She smiled.

"I feel like sheet," she said.

Ava supported herself with the butt end of a spear and strode toward the ship. She spotted some familiar faces. Though because of her training at the academy, she did not know many of the rebels by name.

There was no sign of Deven. Ava hoped the Morph captain had caught up to Riese and the others.

Ava climbed the gangway of the runeship. Its wing-sails still stretched wide, ready to fly.

She crossed the deck swiftly, other Kroqala darting all around. She glanced up at the Spires. It was hard to tell anything in the haze.

Verina Arkhovia stood at the helm, sharp black skirts fluttering with the breeze. "Glad to see you made it through, girl. I promised your father I'd see you become a Dragonmount. And I hate breaking promises."

A surge of sorrow wracked her at once. She choked down a sob and nodded and then glanced around the valley, marveling. They'd defeated Attican dragons. The entire Bloody Company had surrendered, along with the emperor's secret battalion. And soon the rebellion would have the eggs they needed.

Ava glanced up again.

"The Morphs will let us know the minute there's any sign of—"

The Sky Captain's words were cut off. The ground shook violently. Rumbling. Grinding. As though all the mountains were being churned beneath them.

Smoke and dust erupted from the ceremonial entrance to the Mountain of Souls.

Ava seized Verina's wrist. "You have to fly now!"

The fierce woman did not protest. The ground shook beneath. The mountains quaked. The ship rattled and groaned. Verina shouted an order.

Lir'ghe darted off, and swarms of glowing blurs shot all around.

The ship lifted into the sky.

Shadows poured from the mountainside. The distant skies had turned dark in the Abyss and flashed violet and crimson like some hellish lightning. Riese sprinted toward the end of the valley.

The Gate of the Ancients loomed ahead. A stark arch of shimmering stone, like the moon, against an ever-darkening world. Surel leapt through. Then, Kesler.

The other two Elyan soldiers lagged at the rear, and Deven urged them on. There were voices on the air, growing louder. At first, Riese had thought them peals of thunder. But there was a cadence to them. Ancient words.

Words she recognized from her own world.

Elesa volonai. Menassa elonai.

Utlesa sheshonash. Alesa renonash.

Riese sprinted harder.

Ulgar leapt through the opening, and Riese reached the gate right behind him, heart raging in her chest.

Screams.

Riese turned.

The wall of shadows was close behind her. One of the Elyan soldiers was gone. Swallowed by the darkness.

The other had stumbled. Deven pulled on his arm. There were faces in the swarm of shadows. Dark hands reached for Deven and the soldier.

Wights.

Deven drew her blade and swung as the first reached her.

A dark shadowy blade formed in the creature's hand to meet hers. The soldier tried to pull himself forward, collapsed.

Riese looked back at the gate. She was steps away. Ulgar waved her through.

But Riese thought of Petyr, during her Ascent, fighting off the dragyr. Thought of Malik, who had nearly died to save him and Ulgar during the storm, and how she wished she could have been there to help them.

She turned from the gate and sprinted back toward the wall of darkness.

Deven swung her godblade, parrying back and forth. Another creature shot toward them. Flying without wings. Deven drove her blade into the first wight's empty face, and it vanished. Shadows lancing up the length of the godblade.

Riese's boots skidded on the loose gravel beneath her feet. She hit the ground hard as she reached the soldier. Tendrils of shadow wrapped around his legs, pulling him into the dark.

Riese grabbed the man's arm and pulled him to his feet. She reached for the power in her spirit. The chaotic fury that radiated from this storm of shadow, from these phantom creatures that were consumed by it. And she pressed back against it.

Deven slew another wight, but more shot from the wall of darkness.

"I've got him!" Riese shouted. "Go!"

Deven turned and sprinted for the gate.

The shadows reached Riese, and she went utterly cold. But she did not let go of the soldier. She braced her shoulder beneath his arm and heaved him to his feet.

The cold enveloped her.

Riese moved through the darkness, dragging the man on. Faces swirled around.

With all the strength in her spirit, she pressed back against the wights, warding them off with the furious magic of this dead world.

The soldier hobbled forward, unable to put weight on one of his feet. Riese pushed on.

The voices were a cacophony all around.

Elesa volonai. Menassa elonai.

Utlesa sheshonash. Alesa renonash.

Riese thought she heard shouts, trumpets. Crimson shadows streaked through the darkness.

But there was light ahead. The silver glow of *hish* blazing in an arc.

The gate!

Riese heaved the man forward, and together they tumbled through into the bright day of their own world.

Ulgar and Surel helped Riese to her feet, and Deven and Kesler tended to their wounded comrade.

All at once, Riese felt her dragon's spirit, rushing to meet her own.

A warning.

And the gate exploded with light.

CHAPTER 69

FALLING SKIES

Somewhere in the caverns beneath the Mountain of Souls, Urla and Madri held tight to Ruan, and they ran.

Stumbled. Fell. Ran again.

The ground roiled beneath them. They were near the shaman's entrance when the blast came. Rocks ground with a sickening crunch. Dust shot from the depths of the mountain.

Urla swore she heard screams somewhere behind them.

The world stilled.

All the magic that wove through this place winked out at once, plunging them into darkness.

———

The Spires shuddered beneath Riese's feet. To her knowledge, in all the years her people had climbed these floating hulks of rock, they had never wavered. Not one had ever fallen in all Faltari history.

Her dragon's spirit roared. The initial jolt of *hish* from below had sent the uppermost spire tilting.

Riese grabbed hold of a rock to steady herself. Surel began to slide on the slick stone platform that surrounded the blazing Gate of the Ancients, but Riese managed to hold her. Ulgar crawled toward them.

Blinding skies swirled in her vision.

Antari's voice spoke into her mind. *We have to get off! Now!*

The ground shuddered, then steadied.

Riese pointed to the edge of the spire. A glowing sail jutted through the clouds.

"The runeship!" Deven shouted.

The Elyans transformed into their dark-winged forms and took flight, Deven and Kesler holding tight to their injured comrade's arms as they flew toward the oncoming ship.

Riese, Ulgar, and Surel clung together as the spire shifted again.

Another pulse of *hish* surged from beneath them.

Riese grabbed on to Surel's hand. "We've got to—"

The clouds began to shrink. They were falling. The spire leaned to the side, thundering as it collided with the spire below them.

The world spun. And Riese knew there was only one chance.

"Jump!"

All three sprinted to the edge of the platform as it teetered downward. Riese kept her eyes fixed on the sails.

With all the *hish* she could muster, she launched herself from the edge.

Wind rushed through her hair, whipping her face, as she fell.

Shadows flashed around her, darkening the brilliant skies. For a second, she thought she'd somehow fallen back through the portal.

Talons grabbed onto her, tearing her skin.

She cried out. Still falling.

And then, Riese was swept upward, the talons holding tight. The pain was excruciating, and Riese had no *hish* left with which to ease the pain. She'd lost it all from her journey to the Abyss.

The Morph grinned.

"Now, we're even!"

It was Deven.

She had flown back for them.

Riese glanced to the side and spotted Surel, in the arms of another Morph from the runeship. It took two more to handle Ulgar.

But all of them soared toward a golden glow. Riese's vision blurred as they descended toward the deck.

The strange demon faeries rushed all around. Riese felt the warmth of their magic washing over her. The pain abated.

Deven drew up sharply for a landing.

And Riese collapsed onto the runemarked ship.

———

Urla had never experienced complete darkness before. She'd thought she had a handful of times. During her trials at the academy. During an embroiled city campaign when the Bloody Company was trapped in the remains of a ruined tower.

But always, her eyes could adjust. Small slivers of light would provide her some small anchor for reality.

Here in the depths of the Mountains of Souls, the dust had settled. Rumblings had ceased.

But no light came. The magic that had bound this place had been destroyed in the explosion in the Hall of the Ancients, and the collapse of the heart of the island.

Now, there was nothing. Nothing but the stone beneath her hands. The cold that made her bones ache.

Ruan remained stalwart. Madri was knocked unconscious in the blast, and the two of them ventured on, dragging the shaman's wife after them.

Urla feared the worst. That somehow, they'd been turned around, or ventured down a different corridor by accident. But Ruan insisted this was the right path, and Urla had no choice but to believe him.

After the initial explosions, the true quakes began.

The destruction of the Spires, Ruan speculated.

They held tight to one another and waited as booming quake after booming quake shook the Mountain of Souls to its core. The cavern seemed to turn on its end, and Urla feared the entire world might collapse upon them.

But the mountain held.

And now, they wandered on through the darkness.

When they reached a fork, they were forced to stop. Urla gently tried to wake the shaman's wife, but Madri was out cold.

Urla sat in the dark beside her son and thanked Marha he'd been spared.

"What do you think will come after this?" Ruan mused.

"Now that I'm a blood-traitor same as you?" Urla asked with a huff of dark laughter. "Death?"

"Not funny," said Ruan. "I'm serious, Mother. What will you do?"

"I'm still working that out," Urla said.

"Maybe it's good we're stuck here then."

Urla gripped his hand. "What will you do, son?"

Ruan thought in silence before he spoke. "Before Ava knew I was a rebel sympathizer, I imagined being a Rebelmount. Both of us. I had no idea about Faltara or the gate. I was naive, I suppose. A kid secretly in love with a girl and a romanticized idea of what rebellion might be. I'd never left the academy."

"That is how we all are in our youth."

"I have a hard time believing that."

Urla smiled thinking back to it. "When I graduated from Dawncrest, I was in love with your father, though he didn't know it yet. I was in love with the idea of what it meant to be an Attican soldier. Of being a woman with promise in a man's world. I had a romanticized view of the empire and the Good Emperor and the notion of a new Golden Age to come, which had just begun to take root in people's minds."

"And now?" asked Ruan.

"I still love Attica," Urla said. "It is in my blood. In my bones. But you and the Faltari, and yes, even Ava Rykus, have helped me see that Attica is deeply flawed. That there is a world beyond it. That there must be. I just don't know what that looks like yet."

"According to our myths of the Crossing, Attica restored order to a vengeful, chaotic world. Have you ever heard the Valucian tale?"

"No," said Urla.

"Ava shared this with me. Looking back, she must have sensed there was something trustworthy about me even then. But it paints a different picture of the world before Attica."

"How so?"

"For a short time, after the Crossing, the world was at peace. Small kingdoms formed out of the peoples that ventured to this new world. They were fearful of the war and destruction that they fled, and they vowed to live in harmony. The first Dragonmounts of Îrithèa were a force of peace in the world, unbound by the ties of nations. This was a thousand years before the supposed Attican Golden Age. No empires. But nations did not war. They conducted free trade. They explored the seas and new lands of this world. And they lived in peace. According to Valucian lore, it was Attica that sowed discord in the First Age."

Urla was silent for a long time. "How can anyone know what is true so long ago?"

"I don't know..."

"Well, what I know is..." Madri's voice cracked.

"You're awake!" said Urla.

Urla and Ruan both helped her sit up.

"Thank the Mother," Urla said, squeezing the woman's hand. Her skin was clammy, but Madri squeezed back.

"How do you feel?" Ruan asked.

"Like a mountain fell on my head."

They chuckled.

"How long were you awake?" Urla asked.

"Long enough to tell you that this Valucian tale sounds quite self-indulgent... I suppose, much like my own people's version of the Crossing, in that way."

"Then, what do we believe?" Ruan asked.

There was a flash.

Urla guarded her eyes.

Madri had formed a flame with her magic. Slowly, Urla's eyes adjusted to the new light.

Little more than a candle, the flame hovered in her palm.

Madri's face was covered in dust, as was Ruan's. They looked like they were wearing some comical mask from one of the drama performances beloved in Attican theaters.

"My husband agonized over these tales," Madri went on. "Spent his life studying the ancient teachings. Every year, Joren would spend hours in these caverns, in that chamber we fled, investigating the inscriptions from our ancestors. And yet, all that time, he continued to deliver the dragon eggs our children suffered and died to retrieve, and he handed them over to a cruel empire. He kept it secret, just like his father, and his father before him. I always wondered what nagged at his spirit, but

Joren did not let me see until the very end. If there's one thing I begrudge him, it is that. He sought truth while he lied. He agonized over what was right, while delivering power to evil."

"But your husband did what was right in the end," said Ruan.

"He did," Madri said. "He did, indeed. Let's pray we learn the proper lesson from his sacrifice."

"What lesson?" asked Urla.

Madri slowly raised herself to stand. "We do not live in the past. We do not reside in tales about ancient utopias and Crossings and fallen worlds. There may be truths we must unravel about our past, but what matters is how it moves us now. We are writing the history of our world in this moment. That is why my husband gave his life. That is why my people aided this rebellion. And now, Urla Pelasius, it is your turn to decide what you will do in the days ahead."

She motioned down the left corridor. Her flame flickered off the dark cavern walls. "We're nearly out. Come."

WHAT FOLLOWS

Gargantuan boulders were scattered across the ruined terrain of Kalengal Valley. The Spires had cracked on the sides of the Mountain of Souls, tumbled and shattered, as they carved crevasses into the mountainside.

Shards of stone had rained all over the valley, and there were many dead to be mourned. Both from the battle and the destruction of the heart of the island.

After the runeship landed and the dust of the explosion settled, Ava resumed her search for Ruan Pelasius.

She longed for her dragonhead cane again. The splintered remnant of a spear helped some, but it was not the same. She hadn't realized how much security she'd found in the familiar feel of that black cane until it was lost. Until she was alone. Without her father. Without the boy she loved. Without even her gods-damned cane.

Ava walked the camp in despair, despite the victory.

Riese and the others had rescued eight dragon eggs from the Abyss. Ava knew they would not all be able to be hatched, but along with the three her father had stolen at the Festival of the Fading Sun, and the two fully-grown dragons they'd kept secret all these years, they had the makings of a true squadron of Rebelmounts to be reckoned with.

Verina Arkhovia assured her this was a glorious victory. Everyone assured her as such.

But why didn't it feel like it?

The Attican companies were stripped of their weapons and bound with ropes and their own runemarked shackles, gathered in the meadows beside a shard of spire that jutted out of a hillside like the broken head of a spear.

What story might someone conjure up about what happened if they stumbled upon this place a thousand years from now?

There was no sign of the emperor. No sign of Ruan or Malik, or their mothers.

Yuri and Ulgar ventured into the caverns with a small company through the main entrance but returned a half hour later.

The crypts had caved in during the explosion, and there was no way back.

Riese and Surel mourned with their friends, fearing the worst for Malik, and despite the fact that she had barely cried a day in all her bloody life, tears streamed down Ava's face with them.

Tears for the shaman's son. For her father. For the Isle of Eòreth consumed in flames.

For the cruel cost of war that Ava now understood was universal, regardless of its merit. She had never known battle or rebellion.

She had not known anything.

And no matter how many people tried to assure her this was a victory, she didn't fucking feel it.

Night approached, and Ava was pacing near the edge of camp when Riese Torendeil found her.

"Olma said someone spotted Ruan during the battle. With his servant."

"Pisarre?"

Riese shrugged. "I don't know his name. They were headed into the forest. Coming from the munitions tent with large sacks over their shoulders."

"Munitions... Firebombs?"

Riese nodded.

"Then, that means they were in there too..."

"I don't know," said Riese. "Olma and the Morphs and that Sky Captain, Verina, all of them agree, we have to leave as soon as possible."

"Leave?"

"Leave the island," said Riese. "Deven the Morph, she's got that godblade. But she can only transport small groups at a time."

Ava could sense the turmoil in the girl's spirit. Over the shaman, over her experience in the Abyss. All of it.

"I came to tell you, there is another entrance to the crypts. In those woods where Ruan was headed."

Ava perked up at this. "Really?"

"An ancient entrance. We're going to check. Me and Ulgar and Yuri. See how far back we can get before we all have to leave. Thought maybe you'd want to come."

That was all Ava needed to hear.

———

They ventured into the woods at the base of the mountain. There was no true path, it was barely a deer track, but Riese was a huntress, and despite the disintegrated trees that littered the forest and the scars that had been rent by fallen spires, Riese was able to lead them down the faint path well enough.

Ava struggled to keep up. Riese moved slow enough at the front, though, that if Ava hurried, she could keep the others in sight. Impatient, Ulgar and Yuri tried to blaze ahead, only to come back, unsure of the path.

Surel kept close to Riese.

And Ava followed, trying not to think about more than putting each foot in front of the other, using her spear to ease the pressure on her bad leg.

She could practically hear her father's admonition.

It's your leg! There's nothing bad or wrong about it. It's just yours.

It was easy for him to say, but Ava had never argued. She knew her father was only trying to help her feel better and telling the story he needed to believe about what happened.

Her leg's current state was the mercy of a witch's healing that had cost her mother's sanity. But it could never be bad, not in her father's eyes.

It is your path. Nothing more.

Her mother's faith in her father's words.

And now, he was dead. And the rebellion that both her parents had sacrificed for lay stretched before her, as uncertain as the track they followed through the woods now. But she was alive to walk it. Ava had to remember that.

"Gods, you're bloody serious."

Ava looked up.

It was Surel, waiting for her. Riese and the others had gone on ahead around a fresh-carved fragment of spire.

Ava forced a smile. "Thanks for waiting."

"You hate it," said Surel.

"You're perceptive."

"Mother's daughter, right? Never tire of hearing that."

"I like you," Ava said. "Sarcasm is my favorite coping mechanism too."

"Well, let's hope we don't match too hard. We already lost our fathers. I'd just as soon let the similarities end there."

"I hope so too," Ava said. "You're strong, you know."

"Damn right," said Surel. Her face twisted, and Ava could feel the tumult of emotions that emanated from her spirit. Fear for her mother and brother. But the girl pushed it all down and saved face. "You, too."

Shouts rang out ahead, and both of them felt nothing but the horrific toggle between dread and hope.

They passed through a massive scar in the trees from a fallen boulder. Ava carefully picked her way over tree trunks cleaved straight through in some places, reduced to kindling in others.

They reached the edge of the mountain, and Ava saw him.

Ruan Pelasius, standing at the base of the mountain, near a small hole, barely larger than the head of a barrel. Anyone passing might have thought it nothing but a wolf's den.

He stood beside Urla and the shaman's wife. At the sight of Madri, Surel raced forward.

Ava hurried after and pulled Ruan Pelasius into a fierce embrace.

He nearly toppled over, and she with him, but Ruan steadied himself and pulled her tight against his chest.

"Told you we'd find each other," he said, a smile teasing his lips.

Ava looked up into those dark brown eyes, and brushed dust from his face. "I'd kiss you, but you look like shit."

He grinned. "I can't say for certain, but I expect I'm not the only—"

She kissed him anyway. Dust and soot and grime and whatever else, be damned.

———

Grief and fear and doubt welled up in Riese's heart, and she did not push the feelings away. She had been holding everything back, but now that the mission was over and her best friend was still nowhere to be found, she couldn't contain it any longer.

Riese wept, and Madri pulled her into an embrace and cried too. Surel stood back, biting her lip, trying to hold back silent sobs.

Ava and Ruan both cried and laughed as they held one another. Ulgar crossed his arms and slumped against a tree, exhaustion overwhelming him. Yuri just stood there, turning away, his hand on his brow, but Riese suspected he was crying too.

Silence fell, and the sky darkened.

Riese stared at the small cavern opening.

But Madri shook her head. "We won't find him in there."

"We have to look."

"Malik was with the emperor," Madri said. "Right until the end. But I don't sense his resonance any longer."

"Athanasius had a godblade," said Ruan.

"Which means the emperor almost certainly escaped the blast," said Madri. "I am not sure what happened after. This mountain was home to many souls. Without the source of magic that housed them, I do not know what became of them. But I can tell you that when my first son died two years ago—even in the Abyss—I felt the loss in my spirit. I feel my husband's loss too. But Malik... no...he's alive. Of that, I am certain. But he is not here in the crypts. Nor on Faltara."

"Then where?" asked Riese.

The distress in Madri's expression was answer enough.

By the time they reached the edge of the forest, night had descended. Cookfires were lit. Soon, a ceremonial pyre would be ignited at the top of the hill, where all Faltari ceremonies were held in this valley.

It would be the last.

The air turned frigid, and Riese pulled her hunter's cloak tight around her shoulders. Riese could feel the turn from autumn to winter coming fast on the air. If a storm came, she was certain it would bring snow.

Valucian rebels and Elyan Morphs bustled about the runeship. One of the side wings had taken some minor damage from dragonfire. There was one large, singed section missing near the tip of the wing, and the hull had been damaged from exploding shards of the Spires.

But the rebels had come prepared with extra material. Runemarked lumber glowed at the edge of camp, turning from a soft luminescence to a fiery brilliance, while the curious demon faeries buzzed about the ship.

Riese wondered at all the ancient events that must have led to this moment. The worlds and histories that had collided here in Kalengal Valley.

She knew little about Elya. The Valucians had kept their secrets in the midst of Attica's occupation, and Faltara... what would become of her people now?

What would become of the rebellion?

Riese had said nothing about Deven's true orders in the Abyss. Nor had Deven spoken of Riese's defiance while they were there.

It had been a harrowing flight. Elyan soldiers were lost. But they'd brought eggs to aid the rebellion, as planned. It was a story none of the survivors had had time to agree to. And yet, it was the one they all shared.

The Gate of the Ancients was gone, lost somewhere in the heaps of rubble. The Spires were reduced to a boulder field that spread across the once open valley. Forever changed. Even in the dim firelight, the absence in the skies was haunting.

After supper, Olma Marudeil was set to address the survivors.

Riese ate supper with her father. Her mother and little cousins had remained back in Yerida. Along with many other Faltari. Mothers, children, the elderly.

As the evening wore on, Deven began to ferry them from Yerida. It was an intermittent process, as Deven had to replenish her *hish* between passages.

Ulgar ate with his family, and lingered after, chatting with his parents and playing with his younger brothers when they arrived through the portal.

Surel remained with Madri for a time, until a pair of her friends arrived, desperate for the tale of her Ascent, which she recounted eagerly. With all too much laughter, in Riese's opinion. But that was just jealousy. Surel was still a girl at heart. Even after her Ascent.

But Riese... she would never be the same.

After supper, she took out the dragon egg to show her father.

"Can I..."

Riese smiled and handed it to him. Ulrik turned it over, marveling.

"Is it just me, or is it glowing?"

She nodded. "Antari wants to hatch. And soon. But it will require a ceremony, so the Rebelmounts tell me."

Her father shook his head, turning it over. "It's been over twenty years since I last held an egg," he said. There was sadness. "I... I never told anyone this at the time, but it took everything I had to cast my own into the pyre. I felt like I was tearing out my own heart."

Riese held his gaze. A tear trickled down his cheek. "Maybe you were meant to be a rider too."

He sighed. Another tear came as he turned the egg over. Riese felt a surge of emotion, from her own spirit, from that of her dragon's.

She glanced down. When she looked up, her father's eyes were misty, but he held her gaze. He handed back the egg and his hand rested on hers.

"Losing my egg was nothing compared to the night you were taken. I didn't care that you'd lied. That you'd planned to run off on *uhmskara*. I just wanted to know you were alright."

Riese nodded. "I left because of this," she whispered. "Mostly."

His jaw tightened. "I want you to know, no matter what path you choose. Now. Or fifty years from now. You'll always be my daughter."

Now, it was Riese with misty eyes.

Her family was never one for spilling emotions, but Riese scooted closer and her father wrapped his arm around her shoulders, and they sat in silence, admiring her egg, and gazing into the cookfire, while others milled around them.

Then, her mother arrived and smothered her with hugs and kisses and prayers of thanks to the All Mother.

For a while, the sorrow melted away, and Riese basked in the love and comfort of her parents. Her cousins came, pushing and shoving. And her aunts and uncles recounted the events of the past days, and Riese listened.

It was not long before they wandered off. People were starting to make their way toward the hill, nervous and eager for what Olma had to say. And Riese sat alone a while longer.

She already had a pretty good idea what was coming, and she needed to sit with it all. Her eyes wandered from the darting flames of the fire to her egg again. And then, she gazed up and watched the smoke slither into the heavens.

Riese could make out the ridge line of the mountains that surrounded this valley. All her life, she'd found the sight beautiful. But now, gazing up at the open skies where the Spires should be, she just wanted to leave.

But what followed… that was yet another thing shrouded in mystery.

War. Rebellion. Her dragon.

The two Rebelmounts, Desmond and Rhoda, had visited earlier. Assuring her that they would see to her hatching ceremony as soon as they returned to the Valucian hideout.

"You holding up?" Yuri plopped down by her side and clapped her on the back in a brotherly fashion.

"Just tired," Riese said on a sigh.

Tired, yes. And fearful.

This rebellion had not even begun, and it had taken everything from her. She feared she was not up for the task ahead, though the voice of reassurance in her spirit helped some.

"You want me to leave you alone?" Yuri asked.

Riese shook her head and scooted closer.

"Where's your betrothed?" she asked.

"Back in Yerida... but, I'm not sure that's gonna work out so well with Elda, if you want to know the truth."

"How come?"

"See, before I left, I assured her this would be a one-time mission. She's more of the settling down and popping littles type... but after all this..."

Riese turned to him and punched him in the shoulder. "You're a gods-damned rebel now." She laughed.

"Ha, yeah, that's about how that conversation will go, I expect. Can't say I'm looking forward to it. She's taking the ship to Valgland."

"After all this, I don't think they'll be taking any ship," Riese said. "You heard what the emperor did to the Rykus kingdom. Athanasius will make Faltara pay. No ship moves fast enough to beat Dragonmounts."

"Then, how... oh, that Morph with the godblade, huh?"

Riese nodded.

"She's cute, huh?" Yuri winked and punched Riese in the shoulder playfully.

"Quit."

But Yuri could never resist. "Assuming you're no longer matched with Vinder Perinsein, of course."

She groaned. "I think me running off on *uhmskara* right after our match may have given him second thoughts. No time for that, right now, anyway. No more than you."

"Yeah," Yuri said, "but that Morph *is* cute though. You know, when she's not one of those dark and ugly creatures."

Riese shook her head and smirked.

Streams of people had begun to move toward the meadow.

"Come on," said Riese. "It's about to start."

CHAPTER 71

FATE OF THE FAITHFUL

Olma Marudeil stood at the top of a hill, before the last pyre that would ever be lit on the Isle of Faltara. Those who had fallen during the battle were wrapped in shrouds, and their bodies were carried before the others.

They sang the song that was reserved for those who fell during the Ascension. The same words that had echoed in the darkness back in the Abyss.

"Elesa volonai. Menassa elonai..."

"Utlesa sheshonash. Alesa renonash..."

The gods move through us. For we are their children.

From them, we were begotten. To them, we shall return.

Why had the words of the Faltari lament come to Riese in that world? Was it her own mind playing tricks? Or something more?

But the lament was fitting, all things considered.

Riese stood near the back of the crowd, remaining close to Yuri. As Olma began to speak, she felt a strong hand brush her shoulder briefly as her father joined her. And they watched as, one by one, dozens of rebel and Faltari dead were cast into the flames.

Urla Pelasius came to join Olma, and the same respect was given to the Attican fallen.

Riese gathered that there had been some drama among the clans over this decision, but it seemed right to her.

The soldiers hadn't chosen this war.

The Atticans stood on the right side of the crowd, in chains. They dipped their heads as Urla Pelasius spoke an Attican prayer over their fallen comrades, and then, the imperial dead were also cast into the flames.

Over one hundred people died in total.

Riese could not help but think how few that number must be compared with the cost of a true war.

All the people of Faltara were brought to the valley for the ceremony, thanks to Deven's godblade.

The Morph captain stood near the back of the gathering. She looked utterly spent, cheeks drawn tight over her bones. Eyes heavy. Thoughtful.

"Friends," said Olma, raising her hands to quiet the crowd after the last body was incinerated. "It has been a fateful day. A solemn day. And a choice stands before us all. After conferring with the elders—as well as those who fought, and those who remained back in Yerida—one thing is clear. Our time on this island is over."

Soft murmurings filled the crowd, but they were not in protest. It was a truth they'd all known.

"First, the matter of the Atticans. We were preparing ships to leave the island while the Atticans carried out their mission here. But we will not be leaving the island by that means any longer. You Atticans fought bravely and have acted honorably as our prisoners. We would have you take the ships, wherever your path may go from here."

Urla nodded and saluted her, and then, joined the rest of the imperial soldiers.

"As for us," Olma continued. "We stand at a crossroads. Some of us chose to stand against Attica. To aid this budding rebellion. And cut off the emperor's supply of dragons. Some of you did not agree with this path. Some may feel that your time of war is done. And some may feel a duty to aid the rebellion further going forward. You've every right to choose what you will. I've been asked by the other elders to step down as elder of the Feathered Serpent clan, and rather, to serve as shaman, at least temporarily. Joren used to joke when we were younger that I was better suited than he, so I suppose it's fitting. I expect he was wrong about that, but nonetheless, it is an honor that I do not take lightly.

"We have always been a people of peace, and at the moment, we do not have a home. Escorting our people to safety will be the first duty and priority for myself and the other elders. With the help of the Elyan sorceress, we will travel from here tomorrow by means of her godblade. Those of you who wish to join the Uprising will journey another way."

Ava Rykus and Madri stepped forward.

Ava was the first to speak.

"People of Faltara. I..." her voice cracked, but Ava managed to maintain her composure. "I cannot begin to thank you. For centuries, my people have dreamed in secret of freedom. And all their lives, in secret, my parents dreamed the same. We uttered ancient prayers. We shared ancient tales. Of a nation united by our Dragonmounts. Free of tyranny. Free of occupation. The sort of freedom known in few corners of the world, except right here in Faltara.

"Now, that freedom is in more peril than ever. It is not lost on me how much you sacrificed so that others might have a chance at building a life for themselves. In truth, I can ask no more of any of you. Many gave their lives already. And if you choose to leave this island, and begin a new life somewhere, perhaps even far beyond the reach of the Attican Empire, I would go to my grave grateful."

Madri stepped forward, wrapping an arm around Ava briefly, and then, she spoke.

"But it is not our land or our freedom that makes our people," Madri said. "We Faltari share a power few can claim in Îrithèa. A connection to the magic powers of this world beyond most others. Our shamans have taught us that this was a special gift from the gods. That we were chosen to be different. They believed our gifts gave us a sacred duty. And it was that belief that drove Joren to sacrifice his life, and my son to risk his own."

Madri pinched the bridge of her nose to ward off tears and continued. "And that belief is one I've come to share. We Faltari have never gone to war. We have never risked the safety of our own land. Until now. A great task lays ahead for this rebellion. Rallying the Valucian kingdoms. Raising dragons. Training rebel warriors. And I believe it is *my* duty to see that task through. I will be forming a company of mages.

Faltari, who will train in the arts of war and magic. Sons and daughters of the Flame. Perhaps this is what our ancestors always intended. Or perhaps, this shall be a new path."

Riese turned, but Yuri was gone. He was already making his way to the front of the gathering. Ulgar met him at the base of the hill, and so did Surel.

Riese's father turned to her.

"I hold no delusions of being a Dragonmount," Ulrik said. "But I will fight beside my daughter."

Riese and her father strode to the front of the gathering, along with dozens of others. Faltari of all ages, of all clans. Fishermen and hunters. Bakers and carpenters and more.

And their people gazed up at them proudly. All could not go to war. Some would raise children. Some would build a life to come back to.

But some would fight.

"We shall be the Watchers at the edge of the world," Madri shouted. "Dutybound to fight against evil, against that darkness we fled in our Crossing. All those years ago, our ancestors were tasked to make a better world. And we will hide from that task no longer! May we become that Flame. And may the world be brighter..."

Riese lifted her fist and shouted. One voice amongst many others.

"For our burning!"

————

Urla could not sleep that night. She could not shake everything that had happened on this gods-forsaken island.

In the tattered remnants of a tent, she lay huddled under blankets. Alone.

Ruan had hardly left Ava's side since they escaped the crypts.

After tossing and turning for hours, Urla left her tent, and wandered. Normally, when she could not sleep, she walked the camp, checking on her company.

But the Bloody Company was not hers any longer. She had forsaken them. And she had put them in a damned precarious position. Her company had failed their mission from the emperor. And she feared there was no future left for the Attican survivors if they returned.

Most of the Faltari slept beneath the stars, huddled under furs. They left the tents to the Atticans. Somewhere, Urla expected, her son was lying beside Ava Rykus, basking in the light of the stars and of first love.

This brought a smile to her lips, followed swiftly by sadness.

Her own love was gone. Her son had chosen his path. And she could not bring herself to commit to her own.

Urla found herself near a shoddy shelter, little more than a sheet draped from the edge of a shard of one of the Spires. Groans uttered from within the medic tent.

There were no guards. All Attican weapons had been destroyed in the pyre that evening, and the imperial soldiers were bound for the night. All but her.

She ventured into the tent. Nine wounded soldiers lay there.

A young Faltari woman sat up as Urla entered.

"Sorry, Lady Consul, I thought you were..."

"A threat?" Urla asked.

The young woman shrugged.

"No threat, and no longer a consul. No longer a soldier, I expect. But even so, I must thank you for what you've done for my comrades."

"We've healed them as best we can under the circumstances. They'll live."

"I'm grateful. Do you mind if I check on them?"

The young woman nodded. "Of course not."

Urla walked among the injured. It pained her how many had fallen. That was always true, but it was different this time.

"What are *you* doing here?"

Urla started at the familiar voice across the tent. She walked closer.

"Caliphus?"

"Thought I died?" he asked. She nodded. "I was close. Thought I did die, in fact. Blacked out after you ran off during the battle. And then, I woke. Some Faltari dragging me away from the mountain in a mad flight. I passed out, and when I woke, the Spires were gone. Suppose those Faltari saved my life, didn't they?"

"I expect so, Lieutenant."

"Dumb bastards," Caliphus said, shaking his head. "You don't save your enemy."

"Perhaps..."

Silence stretched between them. Caliphus stared off into the darkness. He was young, but he didn't look it any longer.

"You're the highest-ranking officer left now," Urla said. "Reckon the Bloody Company falls to you."

"That's right," said Caliphus.

"You can't go back to Attica, Caliphus. You know that, don't—"

"That's for me to decide, Urla."

"The emperor will make an example out of each one of you. Surely—"

"Yeah, I know. We'll have a long march and a long voyage to figure things out."

"There are free companies in Beirus. Mercenaries."

"We don't need you to look after us any longer."

"Old habits don't die, right?" Urla asked.

"You never answered my question... what are you doing here?"

"I... I don't know."

"Never thought I'd see the day that the *Kraal ni Mira* was searching for answers. Course, I never thought I'd see her turn blood-traitor either."

"Caliphus, I..."

"Look," he said. "If you're gonna be a traitor, be a gods-damned traitor. Far as I'm concerned, you made your decision already. You chose the enemy. I can think what I want about it, but it is what it is. You make a call. You stick by it. That's the officer's way. So go on."

"What?"

"Go on," Caliphus said. "That's why you did what you did, right? You believe in their cause."

"I defied the emperor because he was sending my company to their deaths, Lieutenant."

"And..."

"And because I don't believe in the Attica of my youth anymore."

Caliphus huffed and shook his head. "There you have it. At least be woman enough to admit it."

Urla nodded. "I should go."

"You've got a revolution to begin. And I've a nation-less band of mercenaries to lead away from this gods-forsaken island."

"Tomorrow," Urla said. "Tonight, you rest."

"Yes, tomorrow."

One last time, Urla saluted her lieutenant with a fist across her chest. Caliphus nodded in return.

"The company is in good hands," Urla said.

"That they are, Lady Captain. That they are. Suppose the rebellion is, too."

Caliphus slumped back on his bedroll, and Urla left. When she returned to her tent, she fell right to sleep.

CHAPTER 72

IKÀRYA

Riese Torendeil led the way across the gangway of the runeship. On either side, the skies of the Eyrie stretched out to infinity beneath her. The others followed.

She led the way through the ancient remains of the structure atop the floating mountain.

The journey from Faltara had gone without event.

The Atticans were first to leave Kalengal Valley. Once the imperial soldiers disappeared down the Soul Road, Deven lè Nir formed portals so that the Faltari clans could journey to a new land. It would take several passages for them all.

Riese had underestimated the Morph captain. Despite Deven's orders in the Abyss, she remained true to aiding those who had fought against the Attican Empire.

The Faltari who chose to join the rebellion all journeyed on the runeship.

And now, Riese led them down to the Valucian gate to a secret realm, where they would begin to build their rebellion.

Ulgar, Yuri, and Surel followed after her, and then, the others, including Urla Pelasius.

Riese was wary of bringing the Attican warrior, but Ava Rykus was insistent that her loyalties were true. Madri insisted the same. They were far more perceptive than she, and Riese had to admit, they would need a true warrior if they had any hopes of training an army.

They stood at the edge of the vast hole in the skies in the heart of the floating mountain, which formed this second Gate of the Ancients.

Several voices of doubt echoed off the walls.

Riese chuckled. "What? Just because this gate opens into the skies, it's different than ours?"

"Uh, well, yeah," said Yuri. "This is way bloody scarier."

Laughing, Riese jumped.

———

On the other side of the portal, the rebels made their way to the ancient fortress of Flameholm.

Antari's spirit soared from his place on Riese's back, perhaps sensing that they might soon be able to complete their bond.

Ava Rykus walked beside Riese, grinning. She strode down the hill with one hand on a wooden staff, the other clutching Ruan Pelasius's hand.

"This place... Ruan, I would give anything for you to see it."

"Well, paint me a picture."

Ava did. She described the strange violet skies, and the crystal clear lake at the bottom of the valley. Brilliant colors. The plumes of mist that gushed at the base of the waterfall. The towering overgrown walls of the ancient fortress beside it. But she spent the most time describing the Rebelmounts.

The Valucian dragons had flown ahead of the runeship, scouting the way from the Isle of Faltara to the floating mountains above the Ever Sea.

The dragons entered from the skies beneath the Valucian portal, shortly before Riese led the others through the human entrance.

Now, the two beasts danced across the sky in this bizarre realm at the edge of the world. Riese marveled as she watched the dragons dive and twirl through the air, in tandem. Antari spoke in her mind, more clearly than ever, and with an attitude.

Don't just stand around gaping. We've a bond to form.

Riese chuckled. *You see them, don't you? Through my eyes.*

Through the eyes of my rider, Antari said through their bond.

During the sky journey, Riese had held the egg in her hands as often as she was able. His shell glowed brighter than ever, sharp beams of crimson light radiating from the ridges between scales.

I nearly lost you in the Abyss, Antari said in her mind. *I feared I was slipping into slumber once more. This partial bond is not meant to last this long. We must complete it, or the window of opportunity will forever be lost. No more waiting.*

———

In the same chamber where Riese had met with the rebel leaders, her egg was set upon a pedestal at the center.

The two Valucian dragon riders placed their hands on the egg. Rhoda grinned at Riese.

Antari's shell glowed so brightly, it was nearly blinding. Like trying to stare past the sun.

Everyone else in the room looked down at the floor. Ava and Ruan were there. Riese's father. Yuri. Even Deven.

In the days and months to come, there would be more ceremonies.

Once reunited with the eggs that Rykus had stolen during the Festival of the Fading Sun, Ava and Ruan had both formed their own partial bonds.

And there were more riders to be found.

Five of the eggs from the Abyss had passed the Proving. Far more than a normal Ascent. Riese expected it had something to do with that temple. The way it was preserved. After all, her own egg—and one of the other original three—had come from the same source.

The remaining eggs would pass amongst rebels to see if there were more who held the potential to bond.

Riese prayed that her father would be among them.

Antari told her to have faith.

And with that spirit affirming her own, she did.

The bond was so mysterious, and it was the most beautiful thing she'd ever encountered. Over the past several days, she felt as though she'd slowly awakened to her fullest self.

No, not quite full.

Rhoda and Desmond smiled at her, unfazed by the brilliant light. They whispered words in an ancient tongue, and strangely, Riese understood their meaning.

Îriatha, dur en mìdi èsse. Dur en mìdi ròthea. Dur en mìdi èffe. Îriatha, essère.

Awaken, spirit of my spirit. Blood of my blood. Flame of my flame. Awaken with me.

Fire blazed at Riese's fingertips. Her entire body was wreathed in flames. They were part of her. And she reached for the egg.

The light was so blind everyone in the room shielded their eyes. But Riese held the egg as radiant beams of light exploded all around the chamber.

Tiny red claws appeared in the cracks between scales. They pried, and the body inside pressed against the stone-like casing. The cracks grew brighter. And then, a nose broke through.

Riese was tempted to help it, but she understood that this was vital for Antari to bring himself into the world.

Hish and that chaotic other power rushed inside her. It was said that *hish* was so named because it was breath, the essence of creation.

If one power was breath, Riese thought, the other was flame.

No, not flame exactly.

A word came to her she had never heard in all her life, and she knew it was the same tongue as the sacred incantation of the bond. *Ikàrya.*

Wrath and fury.

That power surged in Riese's spirit, and that of her dragon. Wings spread wide, and the shards of egg scales shattered on the floor of the chamber.

Antari's crimson wings spread wide. For a moment, their eyes met. Hers a brilliant blue, and she saw them as though peering into a pool of water.

He was looking at her.

And she was looking at him. And for a moment, their sight blurred and became one.

Narrow slits and fiery irises, briefly morphed with her own. The spirit of her dragon rushed over her, through her, and Riese could not tell where she began, and where he did.

She blinked, and she saw Antari more clearly again, her body orienting to the heightened state of shared consciousness.

Antari arched his back, gazing out beyond the ruined chamber, and power surged from the depths of his being.

Fire exploded into the sky.

EPILOGUE

The darkness was utter and complete. But Malik could hear thunderous cheers somewhere above. Down here, it was a dull drone. But their spirit resonances emanated with exuberance, triumph. Victory.

He did not know why. Not exactly. But he sensed enough, and Athanasius must have wanted it this way.

Malik was somewhere beneath the capital city of Attica, he knew that much.

When they first crossed through Athanasius's portal from the crypts, Malik had found himself in the imperial throne room. A vast chamber with towering pillars and wall-spanning canvases depicting ancient victories of dragon battles. Statues so life-like, Malik had to look more than once to believe they were not real ten-foot tall soldiers.

The runemarked collar had dimmed his shaman's sense to a faint hum. Not quite as entire as the true absence of *hish* in the Abyss, but enough to keep him subdued. Not that Malik would have had a prayer of fighting his way free in an imperial palace swarming with guards. Even with magic.

Malik had gone down into the crypts beneath the Mountain of Souls, believing he was walking to his death. He had succeeded in his mission of destroying the Gate of the Ancients. He was sure enough of that.

In his weakened state, Athanasius's final portal was nearly the death of him. Between transporting troops to Kalengal Valley in secret, and the ordeal of his dragonfall—not to mention all that had happened in the Spirit Realm—the magic toll was nearly too great. Athanasius had collapsed in a heap back in the palace.

The Knights of Caadron were off fighting a war in Chardonia. And by the time the emperor was strong enough to return to Faltara, everyone was gone. A ghost island.

Some of this had been relayed to him by the emperor. The rest, Malik had pieced together from guards who slid food through a small opening beneath the cell door each morning and evening.

Days passed.

And Malik waited. The emperor needed him for something. Needed him strong and healthy.

The flow of *hish* was weaker in the world beyond Faltara, and with the collar, Malik could only draw spider silk-like threads to his spirit. It was not enough to form any significant magic, but given enough time, perhaps...

Malik was determined to be ready when his opportunity came. Whatever it required.

His cell was formed of runemarked stone. Strong and durable. Malik doubted even a mighty sorcerer could break it.

That was not how he would escape.

So, he waited.

Somewhere far beyond thick layers of stone, a magnificent swarm of resonances celebrated. Even with only traces of *hish*, he could sense that.

There had been an Attican victory. Was it against Chardonia?

What had become of all the others? His family? His friends?

He would give anything to know what was really going on in the world.

———

Malik did not know how long it had been—weeks, certainly, maybe months—before the door to his cell opened.

The bald arcanist from the crypts approached, and an enormous guard followed. The man must have stood seven feet tall. His arms were thick as tree trunks, and he brandished a glowing sword.

They left the cell and wended their way through a maze of corridors formed of a sandy-colored stone. The passage was well-lit. Small oil lamps staggered every few steps.

Malik was struck by just how bright and ornate even these prison walls were.

"H-how..."

"How long has it been?" asked the arcanist coyly. "Three months." *God's breath.*

They reached a wide stairway that circled downward and began to descend. There was a chasm to the side of the steps. One massive yawning hole the width of a village, at least, and they were winding their way down along the sides of it.

Down and down.

Remarkably, the walls glowed brighter the further they went. Their path left the chasm behind, and they followed a wide corridor. Somewhere deep underground.

Much like the Hall of the Ancients beneath the Mountain of Souls, glyphs covered the walls in all directions. Etched in characters utterly foreign to Malik, all straight lines and sharp-angled shapes.

The chamber opened up into a vast hall that shone with bright golden light.

Dressed in exquisite black robes and a blood-red cloak, Athanasius strode down a staircase at the center of the room, descending from a platform made of pale white rock.

Upon the platform stretched a crude archway of stone.

The guard drew his godblade and stepped behind Malik as the Dragon Emperor neared.

Athanasius smiled. "Shaman."

"A Gate of the Ancients." Malik could not take his gaze away from the archway.

"Right here beneath the city," said Athanasius. "It's been quite the undertaking to excavate this chamber, and it cost a good many lives. But all progress requires sacrifice, doesn't it?"

Malik's stomach churned. To the side of the arch, he noted a section of upturned earth, the ornate stone floor of the chamber completely ripped open.

They weren't done digging.

Athanasius turned his back to Malik and admired the arch. "My ancestors didn't require Faltara's gate until after the Golden Age. Some-time centuries ago, this gate failed, and they were forced to look else-where in order to obtain dragon eggs. But no longer."

"This is what you saw in the Spirit Realm," Malik realized with dread.

"Soon, even the Far East, even Elya will be bent low by the might of Attica. And you will have aided me in this, Malik Jorensein. Someday, scribes will write my name in the histories. Athanasius the World Breaker. Bards will pen songs of wonder and horror, of crimson skies..."

Malik's body went weak. Raw aches of terror wracked him.

Athanasius turned his back and admired the arch.

"Now, we just have to make this gate work, and we will usher in the greatest Age of Fire this world has ever seen."

END OF BOOK ONE

Acknowledgments

This book is dedicated to my parents for numerous reasons. They taught me to read and write, for one thing, and have been some of the biggest cheerleaders of my work. They've demonstrated what it means to care for others and to be dedicated and disciplined. They instilled in me a sense of justice that has guided me throughout my life, though we may not agree on all things. And my parents fostered in me a love of good stories from an early age. I have many memories of my father reading to me as a child before bed. My mother's positive feedback on my first short story gave me the courage to write more. I truly would not be who I am without them.

Becoming a father myself has drastically impacted my own perspective on life. So, I suppose it is no great surprise that this tale came to be told from the perspectives of both parents and their children. Parents were primarily absent or dead in my previous works, as they are in many stories, and a family unit was a dynamic I really wanted to explore in this series. Even if death does not escape them all.

Here, there are families who are flawed, who challenge one another, who butt heads, but through it all, love each other deeply. I know I am fortunate to come from such a family.

This book was also loosely inspired by tales of heroism during WWII, both of citizens and soldiers. The initial story spark came while reading about an historical account of an island that caused a great deal of trouble for the Axis powers when the local people resisted occupation. No part of this story is meant to connect to real events in any literal way, but that spirit of heroism in the face of great darkness was one I strove to capture in this book. It is a spirit that has always inspired me. I'm grateful for those who have sacrificed in order to shape our world and make it better. There is more work to do, and I hope we all can face our own moment with such valor.

A huge thanks to my editor, Sarah Chorn, who understood the vision for this book, and helped make it infinitely better. Tim Campbell gave the book a whole new life in audio form. He captured the spirit of these characters perfectly.

Joe Requeza created a cover illustration that depicted Kalengal Valley in breathtaking detail, and managed to capture the essence of this book in one brilliant image. Rachel St. Clair created a cover design that somehow made it even better.

The interior illustrations were completed by some absolutely incredible artists: Sutthiwat Dechakamphu, 21, and Anderson Magalães. I'm honored to work with you all!

Thanks always to Kaitlin and our two boys, Logan and Parker, who put up with a father and a husband who is often lost in other worlds. And thanks to my siblings, for love and encouragement, adventures and plenty of sarcasm.

Lastly, I am filled with gratitude for all the phenomenal people who funded this book on Kickstarter. None of this could have come together without all 699 of you, who took a chance on a book you hadn't yet read. Thank you, thank you!

In alphabetical order those people are:

A - C

Toria Abbott | Emma Adams | Brett Adams | John Adams | Julia Adamson | Oluwadarasimi Adebayo | Krista Adrick | Codey Aker | ALB | Aldchad | Alejandra | Alex | Andrew Alford | Ryan Alford | Jason Allison | Walter E. Alvarez Jr | Angelica Alves | Gregory Amato | Ria Angell | Anja | Antoinetta Aquila | Alyssa Arce | Deborah Ardila | Kaitlyn Armstrong-Jackson | Arty | Nikki Auberkett | Dave B. | C. B. | Jan B. | Nathan B. | Stedman B. | Jack Baer | Barry Bain | Ronan Baker | William Bakley | Helena Balogová | Callum Barber | Derek Barrios | Peter "Tonour" Basak | Sarah Bazan | Polina Bazlova | Chris Behrsin | Jacob Benedict | Timothy Bertagnoli | Spencer Biddle | Avinash Biersack | Jack Bilton | Katie Bird | Odge Blaker | Brett Blakley | William Blevins | Jacob Blevins | David Bobbitt | Roseann Boehm | Carissa

Boehmer | Jesse@BooksatDawn | Jay Bower | Michael Box | Shane Boyce - @boycereads | Anne-Mette Brandt | Stephanie Breis | Janelle Breson | Kaleah Brewster | Noah Brody | Jules Broussard | Alexander Brower | Ian Brown | Quinton Brown | Jason Bruening | Logan Bryant | Dakota Burton | Amanda C. | Bridget C. | Candice C. | Eileen C. | Allegra Calderaro | Dan Calderman | Marena Callahan | Gabrielle Camassar | Shawn Campbell | Franchesca Caram | Evett Cardwell | Tyler Carlos | Meredith Carstens | Zack Cassada-Ward | Eleanor Casson | Randy Castillo | Rafael Castillo | Alex Chamberlain | Paul Chamberlain | A. Chan | Chandler | Tyler Cheek | Allen Cheesman | Scott Chisholm | Dennis Choi | Gianna Christopher | Vivian Cicero | Erik Cieslewicz | Gianni Claudio | Rosetta Clinton | Jaci Clouse | Mieke Coetzee | Shawn Cole | Jacob Conrad | Hailey Contreras | Bernhard Conz | Heather Cooper | Alexandra Corrsin | Nick Cota | Covington | Nathan Covington | Tim Cross | Brittany Crowder | Valentin Crz | Gail Cu | Lindsay Cundiff | Faelyn Curtis

D - F

Jarret D. | Lena D.W. System | Habble Dabble | Anna Darelli-Anderson | Graham Dauncey | Dyfan Davies | Starr Z. Davies | Andrew Deans | Jessica Deen Norris | Kenny DeGroff | Monica Dempsey | Fred Dery-Gareau | John Devlin | Aaron DeWaard | Zack Dewell | Joe Diamond | Brooke Dixon | Nadina Doce | Nikolas Dodson | Greg Donnell | Shantel Doss | Angelo Drakontaidis | Drosfix | Ryan Drost | Julie Drucker | Dave Dufour | Alex Dummer | J. Durborow | D. Easterlin | Vernon Edejer | Ben Edwards | Ben Edwards | Edrie Elen | Ellie | LN Emmert | Elisha Eshoo | Andy F. | Emily F. | Fallenzap | Amber Ferguson | Christina Fernandez | Irinel Finco | First first | Conall Fisher | Gabriel Fisher | Emma Flaws | Chuck Fleet | Kimberly Florendo | Florentina | Devin Ford | Josefine Fouarge | Heather Fox | Chris Frank | Kaia Frieling | Caleb Friesen | Bria Friestad

G - J

Izabella G. | Jonas G. | Morgan G. | Joseph Gaglio | Rick Gagne | Erick Garcia | Kimberly Gaylord | Talon George | Luka Gerovac | Fillie

Gibson | Quinn Giguiere | Katrina Gilles | Amanda Godbey | Matt Godec | Alex Godinez | Aaron Goodman | Elizabeth Gorman | Derek Gorny | Eric Gossett | Charlie Gottlieb | Melissa Graham | Thomas Gralapp | Sean Gray | Jeffery Greathouse | Alisha Green | Vance Green | Danielle Green | Adam Greenhow | Michael Grovenburg | Ben H. | Brittany H. | Ryan H. | Patrick Hagan | Ben Haggblade | Brandon Hall | Nathan Hall | Dominik Halper | Michael Haney | Alex Hanold | Matias Hansen | Nick Hapshe | Kevin (Peage) Harper | Aubrey Harper | Alex and Kathryn Hastings | Levar Hayman | Aaron Heart | Jeffery Heileson | Krista Herberger | Kent Herbst | Annalee Hernandez | Billye Herndon | Dilyana Hezhaz | Evan Hill | Alicia Hintzen | Sibylle Hobi | Emma Hobson | Michael Hoddersen | Grace Hoffman | Kelly Hogue | Cole Hokkanen | Justin Holland | Luke Holmes | Zachary Holohan | David Holzborn | Devon Hood | Gigi Bear Horton | Noah Hovan | Emily Howard | Huezo | Anne Hulin | Brady Hunsaker | Justin Huntress | John Idlor | Geddy Israel | Scott Jackson | Rufolio Jackson | Tom Jackson! | Pemry Janes | Lord Nikolas Jeffery | Per M. Jensen | Drew Jenson | Jezza | Magnus Sang Min Johannessen | Ashley Johnson | Michael Johnson | Steve Johnson | Ben Jones | Cordell Jones | Jaki & Daniel Jones | Kate Jones | Robert Jones | Eddie Joo | Jacob Joseph | Jacob Joyner | Iris Juylyenne | Abigail Jyrkila

K - M

Barry K. | Jordan Kachinsky | Robert Karban | Jimmie Karlsson | Simon Karlsson | Jennifer Katsch | Eric Kayla | Charles Keller | Boe Kelley | John Kern | Tanvir Khan | Tim Kimball | Brittnay King | Thomas Kjelsen | Callie Klopfenstein | Susie Klopfenstein | Heather Koch | Kodiak | Peter Korman | Eric Kovacs | Karina Krogh | R. M. Krogman | Lord William Krueger | Kupo | Kurt! | Jennifer Kurz | Samantha Kushmier | Ethan L. | Megan Lagarde | V. Lambert | Samantha Landström | C. T. Larson | Dan Lawrence | Claire Lee | Rebecca LeGrand | David Leighton | Lauren Lennon | Katherine Leslie | Kyle Leubka | Catherine Levinson | Alex Lewis | Anna Liang | Joey Linzey | Jerrett Little | Nicolas Lobotsky | Casey Loehrke | Lyan Lopez | Kenneth Lucarelli | lulu | George Lundie | Joyce Lynn | M. | Caity M. | Brad Mabie | Johnny MacIsaac | Brittany Mack | Jason

Mackay | Ben Madeley | Madeleine Magsano | Naomi Mahala | Rachel Maifret | Megan Malicoat | Felix Maranzino III | Gianluca Marcheselli | Stephen Markling | Jennifer Markowski | In loving memory of Basil Martin | Wendy Martinez | Matthew Mason | Craig Mayne | Jacqueline McCarthy | Austin McClain | Gerald McDaniel | Jacob McDaniel | Shannara McDunn | Baron Zack McFarland | Jack McGahan | James McGinnis | Kate McGovern | Sean McKnight | Michael McLendon | Jonathan McNutt | Rachel Mekus | Sancho Melis | Pedro Mendes | Menno | Jessica Meuth | Stormey Miles | Angela Miles | Sean Mills | J. Mills | Angela Mitchell | Michael Mitchell | Alberto Mohammed-Dawson | Lisa Mohr | Benjamin Enrique Molina Cañas | Ricardo Monascal | Cristiana Monteiro | Mike and Eileen Moore | Tina Moore | Zack Moore | Frances Morey | Nathan Morgan | LaToya Moritis | Jasmine Mosley | Joshua Motter | Natalie Munford | munzer

N - R

Avery N. | E. Nabeta | L. Nabeta | Niki Nalam | Nalamba | Brandon Neal | Nekoyang | Korbyn Nelson | Bev Nelson | Benjamin Newton | Niels | Danielle Niven | Adam Nooney | Azfar Noor | Alice North | Charles Norton | Maira O. | Tim O'Brien | Tegan O'Connell | Matthew O'Hagan | Odette | John Orefice | Jennifer Osterman | Victoria P. | Rafael Pacheco | Padonfane | Panchito | Michael Panzarino | Brendan Papz | Jeffrey Parker | parv | Yash Patel | Nicholas Paynter | Brian Pedroza | Jeff Pena | Paul Perez | Lukas Peschel | Ben Petitt | Justin Phelan | Neil Phillipa | Matthew Phillips | Niamh Phillips | Sam Pickerel | Lydia Pierce | Ellen Pilcher | Karine Pilon | Katie Pirowski | S. Cu'Anam Policar | Viktor Polívka | Chelsea Porter | Jackson Pugh | Jesse Pummel | Qavee | Cal Quinlan | Alexis R. | Curtis R. | Rhianne R. | K. Raine | Marcos Ramirez | Cayden Rasmussen | Jenna Raven | Asia Reads | Bob Ream | Connor Reese | rg9400 | Annie Richer | Leah Rick | Brandon Riggs | Diego Riley | Jessica Rippley | Douglas Rist | Jessica Ritchey | Joe Rixman | Bradley Roar | Todd Roark | SaraBeth Roberson | Adam Robinson | Gina Rochester | Sarah Rogers | Michael Roloff | Daniel Roop | J.D.L. Rosell | Caitlin Rowoldt | Cheryl Ruckel | Raevyn Rumley | Tomas Rydland

S - T

Adriano S. | Brianna S. | Bryce S. | Nathaniel S. | SafePondDemon | Jennifer Saldana | David Sanders | Ken Sanders | Erik Sapp | Richard Sawyer | John Schafstall | Domien Schelstraete | Jared Schmitzer | Armin Schopfer | Kim Schwarz | David Scoggind | Kevin Scott | Baird Searle | Blake Severson | Kristen Shafer | Sharlona | Michael Sheehan | Allen Shipley | Shawna Shulde | Tiya Simon | Aayush Singh | Evert Jan Smit | Christopher Smith | Erin Smith | Ethan Smith | Heather Smith | Kent M. Smith | Kyle Smith | Ryan L. Snay | Alex Sogn | Edward Somers | Melissa St-Pierre | Shannara M. Stanchly | M. Stanley | Arie Starry | Sarah Steenbergen | Kelsey Stenberg | Nicholas Stephenson | Alex Steuber | Natasha Stevenson | Steven Stewart | Dallin Stgelais | Melissa Stordahl | Rhesa Storms | Gordon Sturgeon | Ellen Sullivan | Kyle Sullivan | Michelle and Perry Swenson | Matt Swinnerton | Johnathon Szaefer | D. T. | Rebecca Tesauro | Andy Thompson | Maleesha Thompson | Kiefer Tonkin-Caudery | Traci | Chloe Treacy | Cheyenne Trujillo | Arild Tvedt

U - Z

Cierra Uy | Marianne S. v.d.Z. | Alycia Vaillancourt | Rodney van Valburg | Kristy Van Wyhe | Mike Vance | Matthew Varley | Javier Vega | Annalena Vera | Freya Vevette | Nikhil Vohra | Garrett Voorhees | Hannah W. | Max W. | Barrett Walters | Tamara Warren | Mikayla Watkins | Luke A. Watkins | Madge Watson | James Webb | Leslie Webb-Tinsley | Dustin Weddle | Hunter Welborn | Bryanna Welch | Brenden Wells | Kenyon Wensing | Julie Wenzel | Hunter Whitfield | Abbey Wigen | Duncan Wilcox | Annarose Willhite | Breck Williams | Joshua Williams | Denise Williams | Neil Williams | Quan Williams | Arthur Wilson | Cheyenne Wilson | Ren Wilson | Tim Wilson | Trevor Wilson | Aidan Wingerberg | Timbre Wolf | Kyree Wolfe | David Wolfson | Alan Wood | Spencer Wright | Abe Xero | Philip Xyret | Susan Yamamoto | Nancy Yee | Jasmine Young | Zeth | G. Zweck

About the Author

S.A. Klopfenstein is an epic fantasy author from the American West. His love for fantastic stories began as a child with *Narnia* and *Lord of the Rings*, before being swept up by many modern epic works as he grew older. His influences include those classics, as well as Martin and Sanderson, and more recently, John Gwynne, M.L. Wang, and Pierce Brown. It is the joy of his life to be able to spin his own tales now. He is the author of the Shadow Watch Saga and the Rogue System trilogy. *Children of the Gods* is his eighth novel.

He lives with his wife Kaitlin, their two boys, and their dog, Iorek Byrnison. When not writing, he prefers to be in the mountains or spending time with his family.

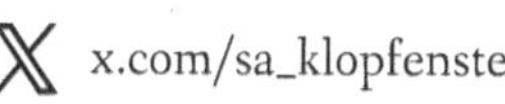 x.com/sa_klopfenstein

 instagram.com/saklopfensteinauthor

tiktok.com/@authorsaklopfenstein